The Norwayman

THE MACMILLAN COMPANY
NEW YORK · BOSTON · CHICAGO
DALLAS · ATLANTA · SAN FRANCISCO

MACMILLAN AND CO., LIMITED
LONDON · BOMBAY · CALCUTTA
MADRAS · MELBOURNE

THE MACMILLAN COMPANY
OF CANADA, LIMITED
TORONTO

JOSEPH O'CONNOR

The Norwayman

_____

THE MACMILLAN COMPANY · NEW YORK

1949

PRINTED IN THE UNITED STATES OF AMERICA
BY THE VAIL-BALLOU PRESS, INC., BINGHAMTON, N. Y.

ANNE

You cajoled and cosseted this tale into being.
Now see what you have done.

Foreword

The Bay of this story is any one of the hundred salients the Atlantic has thrust into the land between Shannon and Fastnet. It is so like the others that the reader who knows that austerely beautiful coast has a wide choice of background for the tale.

The people of Manistir are any one of the separate communities walled off from each other by the coastal mountains, who still use Gaelic and its modes of thought and tolerate the ills they endure in this life for the rewards they will reap in the next. Mike and Maire (Maura), Thade and Joany and the rest have lived so intimately with me for the past half year that I shrink from denouncing them for the figments they really are. But I can say this of them—they are composite of the friends of my youth, whose lives covered the end of an old world and the beginning of a new. *Beannact De le h-anaman na gcarad.*

Contents

The Norwayman

CHAPTER 1 · *The Island Home*

THE BAY opens its wide round maw to the southwest and ten thousand miles of salt water. Seawards it ends in two stark triangular peaks, five miles apart—the Fang to the south'ard and Black Head to the nor'ard. Midway between the two lies the Shark, the loneliest gobbet of land in the West, dropped carelessly from a giant mouth into the sea.

The island looks more like a whale than a shark, an anchored whale swimming hard but making no headway in spite of the bow wave of white foam the breakers make on its bluff head. It looks still more whalelike when the smoke rises on calm mornings, straight and white, from the chimney of the only house on the island—a blowing whale.

The house is hard to see. Its grey walls and weathered thatch are lost to sight against the neutral heather of the hill that shields it from the ocean gales. The first sturdy pair, who found in their young hearts the courage to live their lives together and alone on the Shark, chose the site for the house cunningly. It faces in towards the land across the Bay and overlooks the one level expanse of loam in the island, and the only sandy cove. As soon as the house was built, they laid with their hands a boat slip of smooth rocks which they pried from the cliff and rolled laboriously on the looms of oars into position. They were a pair of stouthearts who asked nought of life but what they could make or take. Before the first son came to claim his share of his mother's strength, they had fenced in the fields from the hill and had ferried a heifer and a pair of ewes out from the mainland. The long line of Macks of the island was firmly established in their lean, isolate patrimony.

When Mike, the third in succession, had married off his sister on the mainland and had seen his brothers well settled, he brought out the indomitable Mary Horgan to the Shark—Maire Mack, as she came to be known within the Bay and without, wherever her shock of tawny hair was seen blowing in a stiff sou'wester in the bow of Mike's pollack boat. He brought her across the Bay from inside the Fang the day after they were married, Maire pulling the bow oar with a will and keeping an eye on the three new fish boxes, that contained all her personal belongings, in the stern. When the black boat grounded on the sand at the slip, Maire cocked the blade of her heavy oar regattawise and yelled, "Up the Macks and who'll say boo to a Horgan!" Mike's answering yell joined hers and woke the gulls to whirl and scream over their heads.

He jumped overside into the shallows and pulled Maire onto his broad shoulders and waded ashore, bowed under the lively load. With a swing of the hips he dumped her on the powdery sand and shouted, "Boo for the Horgans! Boo!" Maire grabbed at his arms and pulled herself to her feet. She drew him powerfully towards her and tipped him over her hunched shoulder on the flat of his long back. "Up the Horgans! Hurrah!"

Mike was on his feet like a cat, his arms outstretched to catch the exultant Maire and spank her presumptuous bottom for her. As eager as he for a showdown, she dug her feet in the sand. Stooping under the long arms, she took the shock of his charge on the round of her strong white neck and got her own arms firmly around his waist. The impact winded them and they stood motionless, straining for breath, locked in each other's arms.

The appalling thought flashed through Mike's mind that if he failed to trounce this fighting lady, well and truly, here and now, h was doomed to a life of disputed authority to the end of their days. To escape such a fate he must forget that she was a woman, a dear and precious girl, who had come full of promise to share his days and nights, his weals and woes, till death did them part on this lonely island. He would make it an all-in fight.

Maire had her head tucked low and her arms in a tight grip around his middle. Bending forward to throw his weight on her back, he locked his hands under her breasts and threw his heels high in the air. The suddenness of the move, which went with her own steady pull, brought her back on her heels and beyond. While she tottered backwards, Mike wheeled in mid-air and came down plump on top of her. Giving her no time to fight back, he threw his arms and legs around her and started to roll down the slope to the sea. Maire's struggles only increased the speed of the dizzy progress. Mike's determined silence and reckless drive broke down her last reserve of courage and she screamed the scream of a beaten woman:

"Save me, Mike, save me!"

Mike ground his teeth and swung her faster to the brink to plunge sidelong into the water and go under. He sat up and pulled Maire's head just clear and looked straight into her streaming eyes.

"You're a grand girl, Maire, the full of any man's heart, and I love every inch of you, but there's no room for anyone but a Mack on this small biteen of an island."

A ninth wave, bigger than usual sluiced over their heads as they sat. When it receded, Maire threw back her yellow mane, lifted her face to Mike's and skirled, "Up the Macks—*every time!*" The battle was won; precedence was fixed under one banner; nothing was left to mar their happiness but extramural affairs.

They stood up and waded ashore, wet to the pelt, Maire's clinging blouse concealing none of her ripe development. She laughed at Mike's, "What'll we do now?"

"What'll we do but strip to the skin and dry ourselves? We may as well get used to each other; we'll have many an eyeful from now on. Come on, Mike *a chree*; sure, I know already you have hair on your chest."

She pulled the skimpy blouse over her head and stepped out of the skirt, heavy with salt water, spreading them and her stockings to dry in the sun. She did falter at slipping down the pink knickers and turned her back to Mike to do it. When she turned round and found him shirking at the pants, she ran around him and pulled them down from behind.

"Come, get out of them, sir, if you don't want to catch your death of cold. I won't eat you."

She took his clothes and laid them among her own and completed the fusion of their lives.

Despite the shock her feminine realism had given to his male niceness, Mike suspected the tone of authority she was assuming, however gaily she spoke, and walked down to the boat.

"We may as well pull her up above high water while we're drying."

"You're the boss, Mike."

His heart sang at the beauty of her, bending to the heavy lag of the boat as it left the water.

"Heave—heave—heave," he chanted to time the pulls: "Fine and tough—fine and tough."

Mike snugged the boat on an even keel, stowed the oars beneath the thwarts, and lugged the fish boxes out on the gravel.

"We'll carry these 'suitcases' between us up to the house; the duds will be dry enough by the time we're back," said Mike.

"Oh! Oh! Look, Mike; look at the cow," Maire squealed and got Mike between her and the cow which had appeared on the bank over the landing cove.

"What's all the excitement? Sure, you weren't expecting reindeers on the Shark?"

"She's a milch cow. Who milked her while you were away? And you let me think there was no one here but our own two selves. Gi' me that box, the one my clothes are in."

She ripped the lid off and threw all sorts out on the stones till she got a gingham overall to clothe her nakedness. She flung an apron to Mike, saying, "You take that and tie it round you before we are shamed."

As Mike fumbled with the strings of the unaccustomed garment, Maire snapped them from his fingers and had them pulled tight in a trice.

"Tell me," she asked in an urgent whisper, "tell me, who did you leave to milk that cow? Can he see us from the house?"

"He has been looking at us for the past five minutes," said Mike. " 'Twas his curiosity brought Drummin along to see what he was admiring. Don't you see him peeping through that furze bush at you? The calf I mean." He hailed the calf. "Hallo, Sucky; see the nice new missis I have brought home to you! You can say good-bye to free milk from now on, me boyo."

Maire stooped and grabbed a fistful of gravel to fling at the calf, but he cocked his tail and wheeled off out of sight. Being a thrifty young woman and her disgust still unrecorded, she let Mike have the gravel in the small of the back.

"Aisy, me daisy," said Mike, "or I'll make you kiss the part to make it well."

"Tell me, Mike Mack, before I stir out of this: is there anyone but us on the island?"

"Devil a one but you and me and the stock."

"Then what's keeping us standing here like two statues without a stitch o' the clothes on us?"

She shook her head in the direction the black calf had taken.

"And you, my bucko; I'll see if skidder and skim will cure your eyesight for you."

The suggestion of ownership in the cattle and of responsibility for feeding them for the future filled Mike's heart with affection for this high-spirited partner of his. He drew her roughly to his eager arms and kissed her passionately. She clutched him to her breast and wept with joy; tears alone could relieve the fulness of her heart.

The house was hidden in a hollow where the hill met the lowland, a hundred yards from the boat slip. When they reached the near rim of the hollow, Maire stood and lowered her end of the box slowly to the ground. Mike watched her anxiously as she surveyed the cluster of low buildings, one by one, and started to tell her what each one was, but she stopped him with a wave of her free hand. Her eyes rested long on the dwelling-house before they went the round of the outhouses and the redstone walls that enclosed it all and came back to the house again.

"What a snug, warm home we're going to have all to our two selves, Mike *a chree!* God bless the hands that built it and the dear souls that lived in it and left it so trim and tidy after them."

"Amen," said Mike, and because fears for her approval had gone deep into him, he reverted to the Gaelic he always used when deeply moved, "*Beannacht dilis De le h-anam ar ghaibh roinn.*"

"*Ar dheis De go rabhaid anocht,*" said Maire in response, and both bowed their heads and blessed themselves.

The door was on the latch, the floor swept clean, and the fire set with dry turf around a heart of furze kindlings. Mike had seen to that before he left for the mainland. He turned round in the doorway, holding out a polite hand:

"Welcome home, Mrs. Mack; top of the morning to you, ma'am, and what a fine dress you're wearing. Come in and take off your coat, ma'am."

Maire darted in under his arm. Eluding his attempts to catch her, she seized a broom and bade him conduct himself until she'd have the kettle boiling.

"You can bring up the rest of the things from the boat, and you might make yourself fit to enter a respectable house if your clothes are dry."

As soon as he was gone, she slipped on her working clothes and pried into all the presses and cupboards to get her bearings. She located the matches and the groceries easily but could find neither a well nor a water barrel, inside or out. She lit the fire and had another hunt for water. She bit her lip and grinned at having to ask Mike where it was; she was not given to asking for guidance of anyone. But there it was: she couldn't make tea without water. Taking the kitchen bucket on her arm, she shrugged her shoulders and went down the path to the cove. Mike laughed when he saw the bucket.

"Oh, Maire, forgive me; I didn't show you the well; but there's no harm done. Come and I'll show you now."

He led her along a paved path just above high water to a rock that barred the way to further progress and jutted out into the tide. He pointed to a cross cut deeply into the smooth face of the rock a foot or so higher than the seaweed level.

"The well is there, under two feet of salt water, my dear."

"Michael Mack, if you want your tea, you'll stop your play-acting and show me where to get the water for it."

"Amn't I after showing it to you? All you have to do is wait for the fall of the tide and you'll get lashings of the finest spring water in Erin."

Tears of disappointment filled her eyes; her lovely home without water! The sight of her wet eyes drove the mischievous glint out of Mike's. He chuckled and slipped the bucket off her arm.

"Go back to the house, dear, and I'll have the full of this on the hearthstone for you in no time."

Wondering at the undersea well, Maire returned to the house and soon lost herself in the adventure of finding the wherewithal for a meal worthy of the first evening in her extraordinary new home. Yellow-fat bacon hung from the rafters; a barrel of salt herring stood behind the door; the huge wooden bin held "two-way" flour in one compartment and fine meal in the other, and on top of the bin she found a stoneware basin of sour milk, just the thing for baking light bread. When Mike brought in the pail of water, the kitchen was rich with the smell of sizzling bacon and new-made bread, the table was laid, and at the head of it stood the big sugan chair with Maire's apron spread over the back rail to keep the heat of the fire off his own back. For the third time that day a lump filled his throat to suffocation for love of this wonderful girl.

Bent over the hot turf embers, she cut off his urge to romance by saying over her shoulder.

"Leave the water here near me, Mike, and go out and see if that inquisitive calf left us enough milk for the tea. I'll have his life if he stripped his mummy dry."

Drummin, thrifty lady that she was, had the needed "stripping" held over for the calf's night ration, but she yielded it to Mike with bovine impartiality. The meal was a complete success.

An hour after, replete and happy, Maire disengaged herself from

Mike's arms and asked him was he joking about the well. Water is too important an item in a woman's economy for uncertainty, let alone joking about it. Would he set her mind at rest? Mike looked at the double-weighted clock, which Maire had wound up while he was out.

"The tide is about right. Come on while the light lasts and you'll see the whole mystery."

In the creeping dusk they walked, arm in arm, down the path, each with a pail in the free hand till they reached the Well Rock. It stood high and dry in the wet sand from which the tide had receded, and from its seaward side a spout of clear water poured in a set curve out on the sand. A shelf had been cut into the rock under it and on the shelf Mike placed Maire's pail to fill first, then his own. He placed them, brimful, at Maire's feet, saying:

"Seeing is believing. Taste it and test it, the sweetest water in Erin's isle."

He raised a pail to her lip.

"Drink our health Maire; our health and happiness for the days that lie before us."

She took the pail in her hands and looked into Mike's eyes over the rim,

"I doubted your word, Mike, but it is the last time ever. I will believe your lightest word from now on, joking or earnest."

Crinkling her nose at him before tilting the pail to drink, she added in a mincing accent:

"Your Lordship's humble servant wishes your Lordship your Lordship's very good health."

" 'Tis your Ladyship is in her picky this evening. As you won't wish us a right good health . . ."

"Poor old Honest-to-God. Very well then, I'll give the toast you want and I want, too. God be good to Mike Mack all his days and leave Mary Horgan, that was, the health to serve him and love him always as she does this night, amen."

The night had fallen in earnest by then, so that Mike had to lead the way home. Maire pondered over the problem she'd have, to keep the house in fresh water. How did the old people manage? Was there no other well in the place? How did the cattle get water? She'd ask Mike, though she'd prefer to find out for herself, and, anyhow, she'd do something to improve the Well Rock. They were dead-tired when they entered the kitchen; it had been long day since they left the mainland, and they went to bed.

CHAPTER 2 · *Settling Down*

THEY lay abed late the next morning, late for them, and Maire got Mike to talk of the island and its ways. He told her of the busy house they had before the family scattered, of the heavy hauls of herring and mackerel the brothers caught while enough of them were still at home to man the seine boat and the "follower"; of the fun they had had dickering with the fish buyers, and the fine wads of notes they brought home to the wise old man, their father. Mike's mind ran to the sea too much for Maire's liking and she had to lead him back to island affairs by guileful queries. Yes, there was another well but that was away at the far end, near the Cealluragh, the old monks' cells, half a mile at least from here.

"Wait till after the breakfast and I'll show you the whole properly from Carrigard, up on the hill," said Mike.

The window showed faintly pale in the dark room and Mike slipped out on the floor.

"Follow me and you'll see the day, our first day, breaking the ring of mountains to the east."

She was out at his heels and through the kitchen to the front door where she stood beside him looking eastwards over the black waters of the Bay. The chilly air struck hard and fresh on her body, still bed-warm, as she moved to shelter under Mike's lee.

"Look, Maire, there it is, the dawn on the hills of Erin."

She saw a sudden turning on of all the lights in the world, radiating broad bands of flaming colour up from a monstrous lamp hidden be-

10

hind the distant hills: yellows, reds, and golds blinding the lower sky, and gilding the hilltops with liquid fire. The speed of the changing lights and the dominant force of the sun rushing up from behind the distant hills thrilled her innermost being. His final leap, clear into the sky, to drown the Bay with quivering light and embrace her and Mike and all in one instantaneous breath of ambient warmth, stilled her soul. She stared motionless until Mike touched her arm.

"Oh, my dear!" was all she could say, and then again: "It was so silent! Not a sound; not a sound in the whole wide world, and it on fire."

"We'll make a day of it," said Mike after breakfast, "and go up to Carrigard where you can get a good view of the Shark from its own back. Wait till I find the long glass; we'll want it when we go up to the Lookout on top of the hill."

The hill began to rise from the levels about fifty yards behind the house, where the heather took over from the green grass. A brown track rippled from the back gate across the field and wound deviously up to the right towards a great splinter of grey rock that protruded from the hillside like a broken rib.

"That's Carrigard," said Mike. "There's a grand view of the Bay and the mainland from it."

They were both barefoot. No one wore boots on the island where neither whitethorn nor blackthorn grew and furze died in the smothering heather. After crossing the grass, side by side, Mike led her into the narrow path through the stone fence that cut off the mountain from the plain.

"Women and children first, sir," she cried and pulled him back by the jersey to pass him by.

Maire shied at the picture of herself plodding at Mike's heels like a tinker's slut, slinking along at the heels of her swaggering bucko. Maire, God bless her, had "the big feel." She broke her own trails and, like Murphy's mare, did best at the head of the funeral. Mike, unused yet to her ways and unaware of the mannerly practices of mainlanders, laughed good-humouredly at her whimsey and told her to follow her nose if she preferred it that way. They were soon at Carrigard where they sat down with their backs to the great rock and their competent bare feet bunched together on a thick tussock of soft green moss.

"There you are, ma'am; the map of the Shark coloured green and bounded on all sides by a deep blue. The green is dry, the blue is wet, so fill your eyes with what you get."

Maire smiled at the rhyme while her eyes roved wide over the Bay and the circling hills and came back to the island and the house. They always came back to the house. Mike broke into her silence with a pedagogue's drawl.

"Now, children, comes the geography lesson. Where will it begin?"

"At the cove, sir, please. Then follow the coast line all round."

He pointed out the beauty of the little harbour. Like a bite taken out of a cake, it showed in the narrow plain that skirted the hill.

"Those two black dots on it are the seine boat and the follower. The two smaller ones out from the slip are the storeboxes for keeping the lobsters alive till the buyers come. Straight east from the cove, out in the Bay, where you see the seagulls wheeling, is the Bay Rock, the best spot in the world for whiting and red gurnet."

"Mike Mack, will you please stay on dry land? You're as mad for salt water as the gulls over our heads. Spread out your toes, sir, till I see are they webbed."

She pointed to a huddle of weathered stones lying low under the northern end of the hill in the distance and asked what it was.

"That's the Cealluragh, where the monks lived hundreds of years ago when the Shark was tied to the mainland. Those are the beehive cells they lived in, poor men. That's the Sound beyond it—"

"At sea, again, sir? We'll give the geography lesson a rest," and she snuggled closer to Mike, closing her eyes.

Satisfied with mere proximity, they sat silent and relaxed for a long time. Maire's mind was the first to slip into gear again. She looked through squeezed eyelids to the south where her old home ought to be in a fold of the hills across the Bay. Mike handed her the glass, already focused.

"Here, try this; you'll never find it with your bare peepers." Mike knew she couldn't see the Horgans's house. He had, in his lovesick hours, searched for it with the glass many a time and searched in vain. But it would please her to try. In his own wise way he wished her to learn that the old home was out of sight. Out of sight, out of mind, he thought. She'll settle down here all the sooner now.

She handed him the glass with a thin smile, saying, "That's that," and stood up expectantly.

" 'Tis too soon to go down home yet. Let us make a job of the exploring and see the rest of the Shark from the Lookout," she suggested.

"The rest?" said Mike. "There's no rest. The Shark is only half an island. Long ago it was split from snout to tail like a herring, and one half thrown away. That's the Shark and 'tis all there under your eyes."

He faced up the hill to the Lookout, fifty yards above them, and with a sweep of the hand waved her into the lead:

"Ahem! Ladies first."

Maire bowed graciously in condescension and gave him a clout on the ear as she passed by way of bounty. Her white legs flashed as she sped upwards but Mike, stung by the unexpected assault, sped faster, and passing her halfway to the top, slowed down to a crawl and said, as if to a setter pup in training.

"Heel up, there! Heel up."

Like the setter pup, Maire felt that she was being trained too. This was her second lesson in wifehood, in the reality of the promise she had given only yesterday to obey Mike till death did them part. She was learning that she was no match for him in physical strength, strong as she was. He had punished her first challenge by an ignominious ducking in salt water. She must now traipse submissively at his heels to pay for that box on the ear. Well, things could be worse. Mike didn't lose his temper and he always laughed after winning. He was a great big boy it would be a sin to sour. She wondered what he was thinking of her last impertinence as he climbed the path in silence.

"Mike."

"Well?"

"I'm sorry."

"For what?"

"For that slap."

"Ha! Ha!"

"Honest and true, Mike?"

"You're sure you wouldn't like to be up here in the lead?"

"Quite sure."

They had reached the base of the cairn of boulders that crowned the Lookout before Maire knew it. Mike held out a hand to her.

"Take a good grip of this and keep your eyes closed till I tell you."

The warm feel of his fingers lacing themselves in hers dispelled the fear that she had tried his temper too much and made her draw the forgiving arm about her. In an access of obedience she covered her closed eyes with the other hand as Mike guided her up and into the ring of boulders.

"Now, have a dekko."

She gasped and clutched Mike wildly. The solid massive mountain was gone, vanished! An abyss, an empty abyss, fell from her feet dizzily down to a distant boil of lazy water that seemed to wait for her. She sat down and pulled Mike down with her to the security of the hard stones of the cairn. He patted her shoulder and roughed the yellow hair and cuddled the trembling girl to restore her shocked senses.

"I had no call to frighten my girleen the way I did. I should have remembered the fright I got the first time I saw it myself. Turn your back to it and we'll steal away home."

Maire shook her head. She had been taken unaware and had shown Mike the very feminine failing she detested most—collapse in the face of immediate corporal danger. Any woman will face the terror she is prepared for; she will even attack it. Maire thought she had trained herself to meet unexpected shocks too, but here she was, shaking as cravenly as the giddiest ninnyhammer in the world. And before Mike, of all men! She pushed him from her and drew a deep breath. She'd show him and herself that she was no cringing faint-heart, afraid of cliffs and deep water. As she rose to her feet, Mike held her down.

"Easy, girl: do it the way I did it when my heart was up in my mouth with fright. We will crawl on our tummies to the brow, side by side, and look out at the far horizon first. You won't feel anything out there but level water. When you draw your eyes in along the face of the sea to the foot of the cliffs, you won't notice the drop from here. Come on and show me you are as fast on your belly as you are on your feet."

They left the cairn by the landward side and went prone on the ground, facing the rise of the cliff. Maire, wriggling forward by Mike's flank and keeping her head well down, waited for the crucial moment in complete confidence. She knew now what to expect and what to do and, more reassuring still, she had a body grip of mother earth that soothed her. Mike stopped and put an arm about her.

"Remember; look straight out to sea," and he tipped up her chin to make sure she would.

A limitless expanse of pearl-grey quietude spread, out and away, under a faint film of still cloud, into a distance as remote as forgotten time. It gleamed in the midmorning light like cutler's steel, lying level everywhere. The eye felt, rather than saw, the distant rim swollen to a curve by the fulness of the waters. The peace of it entered Maire's heart, waking within her the first beginnings of that love for the sea which grew with the years until it surpassed the more prosaic, practical love Mike bore it. She rose up on her elbows to be free to range with her eyes the hundred-mile sweep of horizon that stretched from the dimly seen headland in the south to the faint smudge of blue-grey cliff that barred it to the north. She felt no inward quakings as she followed the shore line back, past the capes and inlets and islands and cluttered rocks, to the foot of the precipice, down which she could now look with calm considering eyes.

"There's Mike Mack's farm before your eyes, Maire," said the quiet voice, "and do you wonder now why I am always thinking of it? I know it better than I know the face of the island. The acres of sandy bottom out there where the two puffins are diving, that's a great feeding ground for the plaice and white sole. A bit west of that is the Leac, a long, low street of smooth flat rocks crowded with whiting during the warm summer days and with hardy red gurnet when the water cools in the autumn. I know the 'rough ground' and the narrow winding lanes of mud that run through it as well as you know the borheens at home on the mainland. I'll show you the clear grounds my father showed me and the ones we found out and marked for ourselves, myself and the brothers."

"But how can you mark out a patch of sea, Mike?"

"I'll show you when we try the Bay Rock some evening. I warrant you'll get to know the bearings of the good grounds and the bad ones before the year is out, Maire, and to find the one you want in the dark of the night too."

Maire drew back from the edge and rose to her feet. Housewifely qualms were stirring in her. As she turned reluctantly from the sea that fascinated her, she saw a bunch of flat corks swaying lazily in the swirl that played around the rocks below her. Mike followed her questioning stare downwards and chuckled as at a great joke.

"That's where the fisherman beats the farmer. Your father, now, boasts that the grass is always growing to him, even in the night. While he is sleeping, the grass is working for him. But three fathoms below that float of cork there's a little man of mine, working away the round of the clock. He traps big blue lobsters for me, and keeps them alive and kicking till I come to pick them up. And he's not alone. I have a gang of them. Look! Count 'em, bobbing their heads to the swell along the shore, working for the two of us now, every man jack of 'em."

"My head is addled by you Mike, telling me too many things, when all I want is to take them in as they come."

Tearing herself away from the sights she would stay with if she could, Maire wheeled about and sped down the path for home.

"Find a job that'll keep you busy till I have the house in some trim and a bite of dinner ready for your Lordship."

CHAPTER 3 · *Unpleasant Discoveries*

WISHFUL as she was to do the rounds of the lobster pots with Mike, Maire had to stay at home for a full fortnight putting the house and offices in order. When she stood at the front door, with a pair of "kingbows" on her, wondering whether she should begin outside or in, her heart fell. The yard was one clutter of flotsam: oar looms, anchor chains, pulley blocks, and sheaves thrown anyhow on scattered fish boxes and curing barrels. It was plain to be seen that Mike had no ideas on order or system and that she would have to see about it. It would be horse-work to shift them. Though the heaviest of them might be light to her strong practiced arms, she thought it only right that the man that made the mess ought to clear it up, under her instructions, of course. Mike could do that while she put his house in order.

If the house was in disorder, why not? Mike had lived alone since the youngest sister got married, and men are no good about a house; the odd one that is spoils it by getting too nosy. No fear Mike will get in her way inside the four walls of a house, thank God. Well, there was no good in complaining; sour looks won't sweeten the job, so here goes in the name of God.

When Saturday came, Maire's wealth of energy was nearly spent. Alone she had shifted every stick of furniture out to the yard for sand-scrubbing and back to the new positions she had chosen for them. Pots and pans, delf and turnery, stood in their appointed places, like new replacements of their old selves. The whole house smelled clean.

17

She was very tired but very satisfied as she stood on the kitchen hearth and admired her handiwork.

As she ran her eyes over her rejuvenated chattels, she seemed to take an inventory, and a speculative look grew on her face as she made her count. Two things emerged to puzzle her. She had not come across as much paper, plain or printed, as would light a pipe in the whole house. She would talk to Mike about that; tactfully, of course, lest she might shame him if he could not read. That was a matter she and Mike would settle for themselves. The second was a more serious problem. If she mishandled it, she might wreck their happiness before it was safely launched. But the fact remained that some one had depleted the house of its stock of equipment. There was only two of everything in a house that was overcrowded until Nora left it to set up for herself at Trabeg. Nora was the last woman in the Shark and Nora must be made to restore the purloined goods, without creating a scandal, of course.

Mike spent a long time bestowing his tackle tidily in the open shed before he came into the kitchen that evening. Maire saw him, through the window, pausing in the act of soaping his face as if thinking out some unpleasant problem, which he would keep to himself if she let him. He was cooperating fully in her schemes to keep everything shipshape and prevent even the smell of fish reaching the house. The washing up he was lingering over so long was part of the campaign. She decided to postpone any reference to Nora and the missing furnishings to some evening when Mike was easier in his mind.

When he did come in at last, feigning a great good humour and wide-eyed approval of the wonders she had worked on the whole premises, she followed his lead. Whirling her skirts like a ballet dancer, she pirouetted from dresser to table and cupboard and press and finished the dumbshow of her achievements in a flourishing curtsey at his feet.

"How does your Lordship like the work of his handmaiden?"

"Grand!"

He attempted an awkward imitation of her posturing, but his heart was not in it and he soon subsided and sat down.

The supper was eaten quickly because neither was disposed to linger at the table. As soon as Maire had lit the big hanging lamp which swung from a rafter over the hearthstone, each took up the present urgent chore: hers to finish the heavy woollen fishing socks Mike would soon be needing for the winter nights, and his to repair a seine which dogfish had cut through. Mike made his own needles out of the blades of broken ash oars, smooth double-tongued ones, which he used as slickly as Maire plied her wire knitting needles. She looked across the fire at the slim loose-shackled length of him and the tousle of black hair hiding his thin sallow features, and wondered what was troubling his usually calm mind. A heavy lop on the whiting ground, perhaps, or a run of dogs raiding the pollack lines.

"Was it the spillers you were working today, Mike?" she asked.

"No, then, it wasn't." He bent lower over the net that spread from his knees out on the floor and said no more, for a good five minutes. "I tried the pots to the north along Foil Craorach."

"Any good?"

"Not much."

"Wrong bait, perhaps?" she suggested.

"No . . . but there was something wrong *about* the bait. It was gone and whatever took it was gone too. First time I ever heard of lobsters getting out of a sound pot."

"Surely no one would rob the pots and row three miles to do it. There is a mile and a half of open water between Foil Craorach and Black Head, and, of course, it would have to be done in the dark. Tell me, who could find the floats under the cliffs in the night?"

"That's what I am asking myself and finding but one answer, the answer I don't want to admit."

"Nora's man, Conny Shuckrue?"

"The very man. He spent all his time here when he was courting Nora and got the run of the island. I wouldn't put it past him."

Maire thrilled at the luck which opened the way to her design to compel Nora Mack to bring back the stolen household goods. She was certain that Nora was the guilty one and that she was party to the raid on the lobsters, if she wasn't actually in the boat with Conny.

"Did you give Conny all Nora's fortune? Do you owe them anything?" Maire asked to make sure of her ground.

"Catch Conny Shuckrue marrying on tick," said Mike with a show of his teeth. "That eel had to get the last farthing before he'd name the day for the wedding. No, Maire, they haven't a penny against me, thank God, and I hadn't to touch your nest egg to do it, either."

"Was Nora willed the blankets and sheets and knives and forks, or were they part of her fortune along with the money, Mike?"

"Not at all, girl. You'll find all those things packed away in the room presses. But sure, you have found them long ago, haven't you?"

"All the blankets in this house are down on the two of us at night. I am wondering what we'll do for a change when I have to wash those two. Where are your eyes, Mike, that you can't see how empty the dresser is and the back kitchen and the dairy?"

Mike threw the net off his knees and went the round of the rooms, opening cupboards and drawers and presses, while Maire sat knitting by the fire till he finished. He was boiling with suppressed rage at his own simplicity and the guile of the sister who played on it for her own ends. Nothing but immediate and crushing action would relieve his red mood. Maire preferred delayed, but considered, action. She must create a diversion, something on which to expend himself and gain time for herself to work out a plan to wring retribution from Nora. She jumped to her feet, stimulating a hot resentment, and called for action.

"Get the storm lamp lighting, Mike, while I am putting some warm things on. You'll need your waders and the oilskins. Get a move on."

This sudden diversion damped Mike's overwhelming anger like salt on a blazing fire. He fumed; the headlong stream of vengeful thoughts eddied and halted and slowed down as he fumbled at the wick of the lamp. Maire watched him as she pulled one of his blue jerseys over her head, but said nothing. Her ruse was working. Maire was never so happy as when watching her plans working, except perhaps, when divising a two-, or three-stage scheme for securing a worthwhile end. This little trick of appearing to feed Mike's rage, while she was really switching it off, amused her, it was so easy. Wait till she planned her campaign against the Shuckrues. It would be a water-tight plan, but she needed a day or two to piece it together. She slipped into an oilskin coat and took the storm lamp from Mike with a great show of determination. Mike restrained her by holding on to the lamp and gripping a sleeve of her oilskin.

"Go brea bog, a stor! Tog go brea bog e. Take it easy, Maire girl. What can we do at this hour of the night? Sit down and we'll talk it over."

"And let slimy Conny spend the night laughing at us? What does he think we are? A pair of rabbits?"

She flashed her eyes and spread her nostrils as if she meant it. Indeed, her acting was becoming real even to herself. If Mike took fire again and joined in this mad midnight foray across the Sound to chastise the Shuckrues, her self-bred tantrum might prove earnest enough to commit her to it. Fortunately he did not. He was his own calm, cool self again, drawing her to him with the easy assured strength against which her own considerable vigour, she had learned, was useless. She surrendered the lamp with reluctance and allowed Mike to pull off the oilskins while he led her to the hearth.

"Well, well, well," he laughed, "wouldn't Nora give one of those sweet pussy-cat grins of hers if she saw Thahailen in a temper. She used to stamp her foot at me and tell me I was as tough as the woodbine, the thahailen, when she failed in rushing me."

He palmed his needle again and went on with remeshing the net. Maire resumed her knitting and said nothing. Her eyes closed, though her fingers sped busily on, keeping time with the busy mind that was planning Nora's defeat. It was bedtime when she opened them again and tapped Mike's shin with her toe.

"Thahailen, a chroi, that's a great name for you. You're tough and you're strong and you sweeten the air around you."

But in her own mind she added: You need a support to grow on, my dear, and with God's help, I'll be that support as long as you need me.

When he embraced her in the dark of their room, she whispered in his ear, "Dear old Thahailen."

CHAPTER 4 · *Father John Cleans Up*

FATHER JOHN MILES stood with his short sturdy legs firmly planted on the cut stone threshold of the presbytery door and surveyed the wide expanse of mountain and moor, brown bog and green pasture that lay within his parochial jurisdiction. Father John always did that after breakfast. It was the surest way of arranging the day's activities, for he could see all the little whitewashed houses of his flock, in clusters of twos and threes where the land was good, and spread apart where it reached up into the heathery hills. All but the houses of the Coombe, which lay to the north, hidden from his view by the upper mass of the hill on which the presbytery stood. No wonder the Coombe got out of hand occasionally.

Father John was young, as parish priests go. An old man had preceded him and allowed the young people too much latitude, so that the bishop worried while he waited till Providence took the matter in hand, and called the kindly old soul to his eternal reward. His Lordship, the bishop, had a twinge of doubt as he looked at the iron jaw and felt the dynamic possibilities of the curate he was proposing to send as parish priest in succession to an effete old saint. Father Miles might rush his fences, he feared, and antagonize the young backsliders. This forceful priest, he remembered, had spent three years on the Pacific coast, helping in the organization of a new diocese in a mining district. The forthright methods of new countries are too crude for motherlands. As if he guessed the bishop's thoughts, Father John's eyes risked a twinkle which lit up his face and softened the set firmness of his lips. His Lordship's eyes twinkled in reply: two friendly ships dipping flags to each other. He stood up to indicate that the talk was ended, poised the episcopal ring for osculation, and saw the new parish priest to the door. "*Suaviter in modo sed fortiter in re*, Father," floated down the steps after the parting guest.

Father John came into an empty presbytery after the auction that disposed of the old man's scanty effects. He bought only a bed, a table, and a chair for his immediate needs, and had to pile his own things, a cartload of books and an armful of clothes, on the bedroom floor. Before attempting to furnish the bare, echoing rooms, he would take stock of the parish. To do that he had to call the parish clerk into council. The old saint's records of parochial affairs had petered out long before his death, all except the record of births, deaths, and marriages. These he had written with scrupulous pen into the faded folios of the book he kept among the vestments in the sacristy.

There was no other scrap of paper to tell the new incumbent what revenue in the form of dues, stipends, and fees he might expect from the flock whose impassive faces he had seen for the first time at the "Ite missa est" of his first public Mass in the parish of Manistir.

He went down the resounding flagged corridor to the back yard, and called "Thade! Thade Carey! Are you there, Thade?" Out from a dilapidated cowhouse came a hardy, withered little man in loose, over-size black clothes, fussing with a heavy yard brush. His sharp Roman nose and undershot jaw stuck out so pugnaciously that they belied the good will that shone in his bright, deep-set eyes.

"Is it me you want, Father? I was doing a bit of a clean-up after the auction."

"The clean-up can wait, Thade. Come inside, I want to talk to you."

It was dark before their long conference was finished. It was interrupted by only one short stop to brew black tea, which they prepared themselves and drank while they continued the census of the parish. When it was ended, Father John had learned that his ecclesiastical jurisdiction ran over fifty-three townlands, which he would enter in alphabetical order in a suitable ledger in due course, and two

inhabited islands. He had learned the names, and, where it was necessary for purposes of discrimination, the nicknames of the heads of the
three hundred and eighty-one houses within his borders. And he had
written into his notebook, for visitation, a list of the bedridden and
the infirm. They would be his special charges. It was a great day's
work, and they badly needed a walk to stretch their weary bones.

"The fresh air will do us good, Thade; a walk and a smoke. You do
smoke, of course, don't you?"

"Limerick twist, Father, black Limerick twist."

When Thade had unravelled some twist in the heel of his fist and
stuffed it into his pipe, he lit up with loud smacks of his lips to kindle
the reluctant tobacco. Father John preferred the readier cigarette. They
paced the path up and down once or twice before the young priest
spoke.

"I want your advice, Thade. If you care to give it, I shall keep it as
closely *sub sigillo* as if it were given in the confessional. If you do not,
I shall be sorry, of course, but I shall not hold it against you."

Thade had served a long succession of parish priests, and had heard
this opening to a searching inquiry into the private lives of "his" people
more than once. He had been expecting it, and was ready with his
blandest manner and a voluble eulogy of all the outstanding church-
goers and benefactors.

"No, no, Thade. It isn't the beatitudes nor the litany of saints proper
to the parish of Manistir I want. Comminations and a litany of native
rogues would fit better into my mood and the privacy of this quiet
garden."

Thade puffed his pipe and pondered on this direct assault on his
prepared defences.

"H'm, now, Father Miles, h'm—I can't say that I understand you
rightly. Comminations, now; what might they be? Are they a part of
that New Code that's addling old codgers like me, Father?"

Father John smiled into the dark. He understood Thade's prevari-
cating tactics and made a more direct attack.

"Tell me what you know of the gang of roughs who are running riot in the Coombe. Who is the ringleader? That is, if you are not too terrified of him to whisper his name in the dark." He guessed that Thade's bright eye and stiff jaw would resent such a dare.

"Me, Thade Carey, terrified of that scum? Up to his dirty puss I read his seed, breed, and generation, when he and his scallywags tried to rob the Holy Souls' box for drink. Me, terrified of that scum of Satan!" He spat fiercely into the night air and snorted through the resonant Roman nose. "That lowborn whelp!"

"But my good man, you haven't whispered his name to me yet. Who is this terror by night?"

"Sure the world knows him. Brohul Sweeny, the rowdy who ran off to Glasgow to avoid a month's hard labour for robbery and stole back again with the new divilry he picked up there. Before going he worked alone, but now he runs a gang, if you please, like the one he joined in Glasgow."

"Oh! A Glasgow gangster, Thade. He fights with razor blade so?"

"Oh, no, Father, he's not a cutthroat, out and out. The knuckle-duster is bad enough. He floors you with that and kicks your brains out with his boots when you're down, but he doesn't cut your throat. Oh, no; he isn't that bad, Father!"

"I must call on this Brohul of yours, Thade. But 'tis time to let you off home. Good night, and thanks for the whisper."

Early next morning the presbytery Ford climbed over Maum Pass into the Coombe and sped down the winding road till it reached the borheen which led to Brohul's home far up on the hill. He lived there with his sister, Deb, who had barricaded the little cottage against him when he returned from Scotland and withstood a two-day siege until he broke through the thatched roof. She gave him reluctant service under duress, while she prayed for deliverance.

Father John parked the Ford in the entrance to the borheen, blocking it in the proprietary way of presbytery cars, and crossed the fields to the cottage. His sturdy frame exuded vitality and purpose as he topped the fences and strode up to the half door. Embarrassed by the unheralded appearance of a priest, of all persons, at Brohul's door,

Deb stood speechless before him, forgetting the traditional courtesies.

"Is your brother in, young woman?"

"He is, Father," and drawing the half door inwards, added, "Won't you come in, Father?"

Father John walked to the yawning fireplace and wheeled round. "Where is he?" She pointed with outstretched arm to a closed door but uttered no word. The priest crossed the kitchen and knocked peremptorily on the door.

"Are you there, Sweeny?"

A bed creaked heavily as Brohul's boots struck the earthen floor. "Who the hell are you?" he snarled from inside the door.

Father John pushed it open with his foot, and got his first view of the outlaw he was determined to break. It was evident from the matted hair and wrinkled clothes that Brohul had been sleeping fully dressed after a night on the prowl, and that he was in a sour temper. His froglike face was pursed threateningly as he crouched forward, with his left hand thrusting deep into his pocket.

"I'm your parish priest."

The gangster shot a fierce look towards his sister and snarled, "Was it you sent for him, you bitch of blazes?"

Deb answered never a word. She stood leaning on the knuckles of her right hand against the table, on which her cup still stood, half full of tea.

"I need no invitation to enter any house in this parish, nor do I leave before I have done my best for that house."

Brohul breathed in snores, as a bulldog growls to foment his own rage and to intimidate his opponent. Hunching his shoulders, he hissed: "Say your say and get to hell out o' here, Mr. Inquisitive."

Staring straight into the grinning face, Father John folded his arms and spoke in a quiet voice, which, by sheer contrast with the hoarse mouthing of the other, clothed his words with grave authority.

"It is your practice to break into gatherings of peaceful people at the head of a band of youths, whom you have misguided into riot and ruin. Your heart is evil, but it is a cowardly heart which needs the backing you wring from these foolish boys."

Brohul bellowed: "Blast you! You liar," and spat filthily at his tormentor. The priest glanced at the spittle which fouled his coat and continued:

"I am holding a concert in the parish hall next Thursday for a worthy purpose. I came here to warn you not to dare to break into the hall by yourself or in company, nor to try to enter it on any pretext, even by paying the shilling at the door. I warn you again: if you attempt to break in, you'll be sorry, very sorry."

He turned to the outer door, ignoring Brohul by presenting his back to him. Losing all discretion, the gangster leaped after the overconfident priest and raised the hidden knuckle-duster to strike. Quicker than he, Deb seized the teacup and flung it into her brother's face, blinding him with the bitter tea. While Brohul groped for her with wheeling arms, Father John swung her out the door, which he closed by the latch grip.

"Thank you, my girl. I'm afraid I have brought trouble upon you by my visit. You can't stay with that madman now, so you had better come with me. I'll see that you are looked after."

Deb shook her head, "No, Father. You needn't worry about me. That madman is not as mad as you think. He knows he can't do without me, and won't lay a wet finger on me. All he'll do is bellow like a bull. Let him bellow."

Brohul was trying to drag the door open from inside and shouting wild threats at those outside. Father John slacked his grip just enough to let his prisoner get a firmer hold of the door and pull with all his strength. Then he let go suddenly and Brohul crashed backwards on the kitchen floor. It was no part of the priest's plans for crushing the rowdy young rams of his flock to try fisticuffs with their leader. He was arranging his own time and place for a showdown. Just now he must lure the ram to the slaughter by a pretence of fear, by running away. And off with him, before Brohul could get on his feet, to shout a string of curses across the fields after him. As he reached the Ford he saw, outlined against the clouded summit of the hill, the menacing figure still shouting. He smiled inwardly when he heard the threat he had angled for.

"Watch out for me on Thursday, me bucko," cried Brohul. "I'll be there, and I'll blow your bloody singsong to blazes."

Father John swung the car to the right after recrossing the pass out of the Coombe and drove to Kilduff school. He spent half an hour in the senior room on an informal lesson in civics, which he spoiled, as most brilliant scholars do, by excessive elision. When the pupils trooped out to lunch, he held the teacher back and closed the class-room door. Jim Brehony and he looked each other in the eye; they had not met before. Father John liked the fine-drawn face and the lithe frame of the schoolmaster, though, he thought, he might have kept his shock of fair hair under better control. He had a habit of throwing it back off his eyes as a colt throws back its forelock. Brehony, the priest thought, is a dependable fellow, and he is captain of the football team which Thade Carey praises so much. Yes, Father John would take him into his confidence.

They retired to the rostrum, where Jim heard his pastor's extraordinary scheme, first with astonishment, then with growing approval, and finally with a hearty laugh. As he saw Father John to the car, he held out his hand, saying, "You can rely on me and the boys, Father, and I shall be up at the presbytery this evening without fail. Good-bye, and good luck to the concert."

That evening and Wednesday evening the young schoolmaster and the young priest spent two hours upstairs in a large empty room with the door locked. Their conclaves must have been strenuous, because they came downstairs, flushed and winded, to the very plain tea Thade, the clerk, had ready for them. "Well, Jim," queried Father John, as he walked to the gate with his fellow conspirator, "How's the morale for tomorrow night?"

"Never better, Father. I'm as full of tricks as a fox's cub."

They laughed in enjoyment of their secret joke as they shook hands and parted.

The parish hall was full by seven o'clock on Thursday night; all the long forms and loaned chairs being packed except the front row. Those bore large cardboard notices marked "Engaged" in red letters. Father John was master of ceremonies and sat on a chair at one side of the improvised platform, announcing the items and keeping an eye on the crowd around the door. Jim Brehony and his footballers, who had acted as ushers until the house filled, occupied the seats behind the row of "engaged" ones and sat very still.

The applause for Mary Kate Kelly's tremulous rendering of "I'll Walk Beside You" was at its peak when loud turbulent shouts and rough jostling at the door cut it short. Brohul and his huskies had arrived. Up through the centre passage he led them, swaggering and yelling, to the vacant front seats, sent the cardboard squares spinning high over the silenced audience, and planted the gang in the chairs. Sticking his thumbs into the armholes of his waistcoat and tilting back his chair, he grinned up towards the master of ceremonies.

"Next item," he commanded. "Get a move on. Blast yer eyes, don't ye see us waiting?"

Father John came to the centre of the stage and surveyed the hall calmly with unruffled face. His eye came to rest on Jim Brehony, blinking a query. Jim nodded in reply.

"The next item is No. 3 on this program," he announced, as if reading from the paper he held in his hand. "It is an all-in wrestling match for the championship of the Coombe, between James Brehony of Kilduff and—" he paused and stared down at Brohul, "John Sweeny of the Coombe."

A gasp of amazement swept through the hall as all eyes left the announcer to centre on Brohul. The impudence of the challenge and its publicity stunned him stiff, so that he glared motionless at the bantering smile with which Father John provoked him. A surge of blinding rage seized him. Rushing from his place, he charged up onto the stage to rend the lone figure asunder, unaware of the speed with which Jim Brehony followed at his heels, and blocked his escape. The audience cheered the seeming eagerness of the contestants and woke Brohul to a sense of isolation, up there under the lights. He stalled, as if to return to the gang, and stood weighing his chance of rushing Brehony when Father John's voice intervened.

"The bout will be the best two out of three falls, free style and all-in. The prize, which goes to the loser, is a free passage out of this parish to parts unknown. I shall referee the bout and present the prize."

Jim Brehony had slipped off his coat while the announcement was being made, and looked very slight in slacks and bare torso. Brohul began to see a quick, easy win for himself. One kick in the fork, and another on the skull when he falls will settle that dandy's hash, he thought, and he proceeded to remove his upper clothing. His boots thumped heavily as he took his crouching stance.

Father John raised his biretta high, saying, "Get ready," and bringing it down in a wide sweep, snapped out—"Go." Jim rose to the balls of his feet and, swaying from the waist to follow Brohul's bearlike feints, held his arms slightly forward and watched the scheming eyes. They flashed warning of the treacherous kick in time to sidestep, seize the boot at the top of its swing with both hands, and twist the ankle cruelly outwards. Jim threw himself on Brohul as he crashed, gripped the left wrist while he planted his heel in the armpit, and screwed the locked arm clockwise. Brohul screamed in agony and lay prostrate.

"First fall to Brehony," called Father John in the high monotone of ringside announcers. "Get set for the second."

Jim rose and moved lightly to his position while Brohul struggled to his feet. His left arm hung limp as if the deltoid muscle had been torn loose, but the right arm worked wickedly still, and the eyes glared vengeance.

As Father John raised his biretta to start the second fall, Brohul saw his chance to maim this upstart priest, the author of this staged trap, the coward who ran away across the fields in fear. Lowering his bull head, he charged. And missed. And found himself crushed, face down to the boards, with Brehony on his back, twisting and forcing his right elbow up to the nape of his neck. Something ripped in a sear of pain, and Brohul fainted. Father John readjusted his stock, which had slipped over his vest in the encounter, and asked the audience to sit down quietly.

"Our program is not finished yet. The concluding item begins when this discredited warrior comes to his senses." Turning towards Jim Brehony he added, "Get the marshals and the band in their places, James. I'll nurse this fellow while you're away."

In ten minutes Jim was back to say that all was set outdoors. Brohul was conscious again, but unable to rise on his dislocated arms. His craven eyes searched the priest's face, wondering what part *he* had in "the concluding item," crippled as he was. He soon learned. Father John beckoned to his lieutenant and, between them, they raised the broken man to his feet.

Turning to the people, he said: "Go out quietly and take the stations the marshals assign you. I want you all to see the loser get his prize."

It was dark as pitch when Brohul was led out to take his place at the head of the eerie procession. He glimpsed the band in front and heard the priest and the schoolmaster fall in behind him. When four marshals appeared with flaring turfs held high on pikes to lead the band, Father John raised his hand and the drummers rub-a-dub-dubbed the time of "Brian Boru's March."

Accordians and fifes took it up, and the rogue's march to the Old Quay began. The red flares cast their crimson glow on Brohul's bowed head and stained his lifeless arms a gory hue as he walked alone and hopeless at the head of the procession which tramped to the rhythm of the march, in ominous silence, down to the quay, where the crowd halted and the band switched to the "Dead March" in *Saul* while he was shepherded across a gangplank into Pats Kelly's smack. When the priest and the schoolmaster had followed him, Pats pushed back the plank, slipped the mooring ropes and started the Kelvin into a roar which smothered the band and sent the smack speeding into the night. No one spoke until they had cleared Black Head and felt the boat surge to the ocean swell, rolling heavily past them in the gloom. Father John faced the south'ard and quietly said, "There she is." Brohul raised his head and saw a pinpoint of red light appear and disappear far off to leeward; he wondered what it boded for him.

Twenty minutes later they were nearing a drab, untidy steam trawler, coming dead slow to meet them, and as they drew alongside its skipper hailed them. "Ahoy there. Come around to our port side and tie up."

Father John climbed aboard, had a ten-minute chat with the bluff skipper, which ended in the transfer of half the takings at the hall to the skipper's keeping, and slid down a rope to the smack again. He turned to Brohul.

"Don't attempt to come back. Your gang is already broken up and dispersed. Your shoulders will be attended to, and you will be fit to work your passage in a fortnight. If you have sense, you'll do what you're told and remember this night of grace."

A stubby crane swung overside, letting a rope fall into the smack. Pats tied a bight under Brohul's arms and shouted, "Heave away." The donkey engine clattered noisily and slung him up like a sack of meal to drop him on the deck, a very chastened, a very sorry man. As the smack turned for the run home through the dark, the trawler blew three hoarse blasts of her foghorn in farewell and beat out to sea.

"That's the end of Brohul, Father," said Jim to the figure crouched beside him in the bow of the smack.

"Let's hope so, Jim."

The smack chugged along sturdily, sliding easily to the swell, and Pats intoned an endless air till they rounded the Head. Out of a reverie Father John spoke to Jim.

"One never knows. Little I thought, when I enrolled in Kitsumu's gymnasium in 'Frisco, that jujitsu would prove more efficacious in certain parochial cases than pastoral theology."

When he got into bed just before dawn, he remembered that he should write to the bishop to report progress. Sleepily he shaped his letter:

"And, my Lord, despite any rumours to the contrary that may reach your ears, I can assure you that I acted in this matter *suaviter in modo et fortiter in re*. . . ."

CHAPTER 5 · *Retribution*

SUNDAY morning broke fine and calm, and the Bay lay peaceful in the warm haze of settled weather. Out on the Shark it promised to be a lazy day, unfit even for playing at fishing from a drifting boat, and neither Mike nor Maire could laze.

"We haven't been to Mass for a month, Mike, what with fog and bad weather. Get yourself shaved while I'm finding our shoes and putting a shine on them," said Maire.

"Righto," said Mike, "and you'd better put the dues for the priest in your purse. Ten bob is our Chistmas due, and the same at Easter."

It was ten o'clock by the time they made the Old Quay and put on their shoes for the walk to the chapel. The road was dotted with Mass-goers, in twos and threes, moving unhurriedly eastwards full of talk. The chapel yard filled slowly, the men crowding about the walls in groups, discussing common things ponderously in Gaelic or guffawing behind their hands at crude innuendoes; the women filing along the path to the main door with frequent halts for whispering gossip. Maire and Mike had gone their separate ways, too; Maire having to submit to the cheek kisses and sly raillery with which newly wed women from outside are welcomed to the parish. There was a great rush of men into the chapel, when Thade Carey, in green-black soutane and crumpled surplice, came and rang the altar bell at the church door.

After the Communion, Father John slipped off the maniple and entered the pulpit to deliver a short Gaelic sermon on the gospel for the day. Then he turned to domestic matters.

"It is my intention, with the assent of the diocesan trustees, to erect a memorial in this House of God to your late lamented pastor. As many of you are only too well aware, he was childlike in his disregard for money; so much so that many of you traded on his simplicity and withheld his dues over a period of years.

"Now I know, my dear brethren, that the mere mention of this project wakes fear of a special levy in your minds. But be of good cheer. I have no such intention in mind. I propose to devote the unpaid dues to this worthy project and I am determined to collect them without fear or favour. Not in full, except in cases of perverse obstinacy. In general, I shall accept a year's dues for every two years of arrears—to be paid in addition to the current dues. In some cases I may arrange to receive the arrears by instalments, and, my dear brethren, I wish to assure you all, and particularly those to whom this assurance applies, that my ears and my heart will be open to cases of real hardship. These need have no fear. God bless you all. In the name of the Father, the Son, and the Holy Ghost, amen."

The backsliders looked up at the strong face as he turned to leave the pulpit and, remembering the ruthless punishment of Brohul, decided to compound with him to escape his certain chastisement. Maire knew that Mike's parochial account was clear and could face the interview which she was to have with this dominant priest, free from doubts about dues. She was not so sure of herself, however, in regard to the proposal she was to put to him. He was sure to examine it minutely and reject it if it struck him as being too presumptuous. She shrugged her shoulders and brought her thoughts back to her prayers, the prayers after Mass which the congregation were reciting aloud with the heartiness that children display at the end of the school day.

Allowing the priest time to unvest and to say his own *preces post missam* undisturbed, she knocked at the sacristy door. Thade the clerk stared at her as he let her in.

"Who might you be? I can't say that I know you and I thought I knew every sinner's soul in the parish."

"Hard to blame you for not knowing me: I'm Mrs. Mack of Shark Island."

Father John cut short Thade's inquisition and took his visitor by the hand. The hand shocked him; it felt so hard to his own softer palm and so unexpected in a girl whose skin showed freshly smooth and whose eyes shone clear and untroubled into his own. "This girl isn't afraid of work," he thought, and noting the firm contour of her face, he added, "and she has a mind of her own." He waited for her to say what she had to say, standing, because there were no chairs in the sacristy.

"I have the Easter dues with me, Father. Mike, my husband I mean, told me to bring them for him." She smiled demurely and continued: "Perhaps he wanted you to see what sort of a wife he married. He told me, too, that the island dues are paid up to date except these." She handed over a 10-shilling note which the priest took and recorded in his notebook.

When he reached for his biretta to go, Maire held him with her eye.

"I beg your pardon, Father, but there is something I'd like to put before you in private," she said, looking pointedly at Thade, who was stowing the vestments away.

Father John had had experience in California of women with strange sex complexes, who inveigled unsuspecting young priests into compromising situations. He had had one narrow escape himself; perhaps this damsel might have notions, too. He studied her face again, the short nose, the steady, wide-set grey eyes, and the decided firmness of the mouth, and recognised a spirit akin to his own in its sane strength. Still, better be sure than sorry; he would hear her tale *coram publico*, in the light of day.

"Very well, Mrs. Mack," he replied, pointing to the door. "We can have our little talk on our way to the presbytery."

When they were clear of the groups lingering in the chapel yard to gossip, he spoke to Maire in the comforting voice of a confessor.

"Now, my child, what's worrying you?"

"Nothing, Father. I'm not worrying; it is Mike's sister, Mrs. Shuckrue, who may come to you, Father, to worry you about me. In fact, I'm sure she will run to you, weeping her eyes out, when I shock her into making restitution to her own brother."

Father John frowned at her with searching eyes that appraised her strong body. Maire shook her head at his unspoken suspicion.

"Oh, no, Father John, I have no notion to tear her hair," she assured him with a smile. "Skull-dragging I leave to scolds and children."

"But, my girl, aren't you telling your story backwards? Why not start at the beginning?"

Maire made short work of her tale—of her discovery of the empty drawers that should have been full and of Mike's list of the missing goods.

"And what do you want me to do?" asked the priest.

"I am hoping, Father, that you will do nothing. That, when Nora comes to you, you will satisfy yourself that she has these articles and that she took them away secretly. I don't like to say outright that she stole them."

"And, pray, my good wom—girl, what action do you intend to take?"

Maire walked a few strides in silence before she answered him. When she did reply, her deliberate mature way of giving it cleansed her words of any trace of impertinence.

"May we leave it to Mrs. Shuckrue to tell you, when I have done it, Father? If I tell you now, you will immediately take steps to prevent it. I'm sure you will, even though I promise you that no harm will come to anyone."

"Nor any scandal?"

"Nor any scandal, Father. Not even a breath of scandal."

Father John stood still and faced Maire. "Very well," he said. "You have walked far enough, Mrs. Mack. You may wish to call on Mrs. Shuckrue before you go down to the boat," he added with a wry smile.

"Perhaps I will, Father John."

Mike and his brothers, Con and Dan, with their wives, were waiting for Maire when she left the priest, and the family party proceeded down the Quay Road towards the post office. The men could have a drink while the women collected their letters, if there were any, and bought the week's groceries. Maire got three letters, all in formal official envelopes, which she stuck in her purse, and made her purchases, one of which drew a salacious wink from the shopkeeper. It was a baby's bottle with a spare nipple and a small packet of fuller's earth. Seeing Conny Shuckrue in the bar with the other men, she slipped out the back door, after leaving word with the lewd man behind the counter to tell Mike she'd be back soon.

A byroad went from there to Trabeg where Nora lived, a few hundred yards down towards the sea. While Conny was engaged, the coast would be clear for a sisterly chat with the wily Nora and a look at the lie of the land.

Nora received her with open arms.

"Take off your coat, my dear, and sit here out of the draught of that old back door. I'm tired of telling Conny to put up a back kitchen to kill that draught."

"Sorry, Nora, but I can't stay long this time. . . . Oh! what a darling, dear little baby," she exclaimed, running to the wooden cradle on the hearth, and stooping to coo to the plump little occupant. "Isn't he a dote? Or is it a nice 'ickle girlie?"

"That's young Conny, Maire dear," Nora proudly informed her.

"Isn't he the image of his father?"

With much clucking and playful tickling they established young Conny's lawful paternity in the approved manner and allowed the nondescript, undistinguished mite to relapse into his happy coma.

Deceived by Maire's girlish gush into thinking that this dreaded first meeting was over without any of the coldness which her conscience had feared, Nora grew radiant with sisterly affection.

"What's your hurry? Keep an eye on Conny Beg while I get a drop of cream for a cup of tea out of our hands. Do, like a good girl."

Nora ran off to the dairy and gave Maire the precious minute she needed. Darting into the rooms, she drew out drawers, opened boxes and trunks, and closed them quietly after running her fingers through the contents. Long before Nora was back, she was seated by the cradle, adding to her inventory of soft goods a list of the ware and cutlery she had found in the kitchen. Her inference of Nora's guilt was proved to the hilt. Nora was a thief and, better still, she was a fool. Pity she looked so like Mike, with her dark colouring and her wealth of glossy black hair; it would feel like hitting dear old Thahailen to punish Nora.

They drank the rich tea and talked of the island and parted with a great effusion of good will at the door.

"Don't fail to send for me when your own time comes," Nora called in a laughing skirl after Maire. "I'm a great midwife now."

CHAPTER 6 · *Tim's Will*

THE ebb of the tide was with them when the Macks made their two-mile run back to the cove and a late dinner. Towards four o'clock they thriftily changed into workaday clothes and put away their unaccustomed shoes for the gratifying ease of bare feet. Maire discouraged Mike's proposal to have "a nice cuddle and snooze for the evening and to hell with the world outside." She had those letters to read to Mike and they might require discussion before answering them. And letters provided the best material on which to improve his very slight acquaintance with the written word. He was a slow pupil of the genus that works to please the teacher.

"We'll go up to the Lookout, Lazybones, and read in comfort."

Hand in hand they climbed the familiar path and settled themselves snugly on the cairn, facing out to sea. Three English trawlers, moving dead slow to the heavy drag of the trawls and well inside territorial water, were the only vessels in sight on the ocean.

"The bloody robbers!" said Mike with a bitterness born of many fruitless attempts to warn the trespassers off.

Maire ignored his explosion and arranged the letters on her lap. Handing the first to Mike, she asked him in a precise schoolma'am voice to read the address:

Mr. M. McGillicuddy,
Shark Island

He spelled it correctly and guessed the words rightly because he had got similar letters before. But when she opened the envelope, he balked, after the strain of construing the first line, and gave the letter to Maire.

"Ah! read it yourself. Sunday's no day for unnecessary servile work." She rose to her feet and bowed deeply to him.

"I'm happy to make your acquaintance, Mr. McGillicuddy, and how is Mrs. McGillicuddy and all the McGillicuddys?"

Mike made a grab at her, which she eluded, and told her to have sense and get on with the letters. She sat down in the crook of his arm, so that he might follow the words as she read.

"This is a 'Demand Note from the County Council for £1 2s. 6d., rates payable on 225 acres, 2 roods, 25 perches at Shark Island.' What do we do about this, Mike?"

"Burn it, Mrs. McGillicuddy," said Mike promptly. "We never pay rates. Why should we? We have no roads, no waterworks, no nothing."

"But the sheriff will come and distrain, if we don't," said Maire.

"Divil a fear he will," he assured her. "The sheriff that tried that on my grandfather was sorry he did. The old man made off with their boat and left him and the bailiffs marooned till they came to their senses. Oh, no! This sheriff won't bother us."

Maire nodded her appreciation of Mike's pithy statement of the case and opened the second long envelope, which bore a Dublin postmark.

"Shall we burn this, too? The Land Commission give us *six days*, in red print, to pay eighteen and ninepence, the half-year annuity. Do the Macks pay up or defy them?"

Mike laughed. "The old grandfather tried the same game with the Land Commission, but it was himself that regretted it. The government sent an army of policemen in a patrol boat and they lugged the poor misguided old man to the county jail till he cooled off and paid up. We'll pay up too."

"Very well," said Maire, "I'll send them their eighteen and ninepence. But I'm thinking we'll do what my father did with his annuity. He bought it out for a lump sum. My father was nobody's fool."

"Like father, like daughter, *a haisge*," said Mike, squeezing her closer to him. "You are the business manager of the firm of McGillicuddy and Mack. Do as you think fit, dear."

Maire kissed his ear to ratify the appointment, and slit the last envelope with a hairpin, after observing that it had a Boston postmark, and wondering who knew Mike there. She ran a quick eye over the contents and drew a whistling breath. It was her turn to squeeze poor Thahailen, on whom a crushing blow was falling out of a clear sky.

"Bad news, my dear; very bad. About your brother, Tim."

Mike sat up out of her mothering embrace and took the letter as if to see for himself what it said and handed it back at once.

"Here, put me out of my pain."

Maire patted his arm as she read.

THE COMMONWEALTH OF MASSACHUSETTS
Suffolk County
Probate Court and Court of Insolvency
Boston

ELMER KEEFFE, *Register*
Mr. M. McGillicuddy
Shark Island
Eire

Re: *Timothy McGillicuddy (decd.)—Case 2758*

DEAR SIR:

The Will and Testament of Timothy McGillicuddy, who deceased on March 17 of this year in the City Hospital, Boston, was presented in this Court on April 1 by Desmond L. O'Donnell, Jr., 38 Fremont St., Boston, Mass., attorney for the deceased, and was issued, approved, and certified of the Court, April 13.

The said Will and Testament names his brother, Michael McGillicuddy, of Shark Island, Eire, as sole legatee in respect of the estate, real and personal, of the deceased, which has been certified at $2873.36, for the purpose of probate.

Any communication you may desire to make with this Court should be made through an attorney duly empowered by you.

Yours very truly,
ELMER KEEFFE, *Register*

"My God! My God! My God!" Mike groaned in an agony of grief.

Maire put her arms about him and uttered no word of sympathy but let him empty his heart of its smothering sorrow. She hoped he would break into tears, though a man's weeping is a terrible sight at any time, or even give vent to loud curses if they did him good. Anything but the silent struggling suppression of both tears and moans. At last he heaved a long deep breath and looked into her eyes through a pale thin smile.

"Would you read it again for me?" he asked, and when she was finished, he said: "How long it took them to let us know. He's gone four months unknown to us, without a prayer that would help him to his reward—Tim that would pour out his heart's blood for you. Maire, girl," he said, "it was Tim taught me all I know: to feather an oar, to splice a rope and make a clove hitch on it. 'Twas Tim showed me the foul grounds and the clear, out there where those bloody Englishmen are tearing the bottom of their gear for want of knowing. Many's the wild night we weathered together, and now he's gone alone, without Mike."

The blessed tears came at last, welling up in his eyes as he stared out over the waters, and beyond, to where Tim lay among strangers. Maire broke in on his repining and, running her fingers slowly through his hair, said in a warm, bosomy voice:

"We can do a lot for him yet, Mike dear. We can get Father Miles to say a novena of Masses in the chapel and another here on the island on the anniversary of his death. We can . . ." She was going to say what the brothers, Con and Dan, and sister Nora would do, too, but her design against Nora threw its shadow across her thoughts. That would have to be postponed; she dared not stage a family row of major importance during a period of family mourning.

"We won't forget Tim; be sure of that," she assured him.

Mike rolled over on his stomach and cupped his chin in his hands to look meditatively eastwards across the Bay. It was evident that he was recovering from the shock and would soon be his own questing self again.

"I'm dying for a nice cup of tea," said Maire. "You wait here and I'll run down to the house. I'll call you when it's ready."

She knew that Mike would be ravenously hungry. Nervous excitement is always followed by physical exhaustion which only food or drink will satisfy. She also knew that the Boston letter was going to transform life on the island, and she wanted time to think things out by herself, undisturbed by Mike's presence. A full hour passed before she stood at the back door and called:

"Heigh-eigh-eigh, Mike! Heigh-eigh!"

CHAPTER 7 · *The Derelict*

"Do you know, Mike," said Maire, as she raked the ashes over the turf coals to keep them alive until morning, "I have been thinking for a long time that we badly need someone to help us and to keep an eye on the place when we aren't around ourselves. What do you think?"

"I'm glad it was yourself mentioned it first, but I have been feeling the want of a second man in the boat to leave you free for the house-work. Old Johnus would suit fine." And he added with a roguish wink, "A younger fellow might find too many small jobs around the kitchen."

This manifestation of the unexpected interpretation which a second mind often reads into our own considered statements put Maire out of her stride, but only for a moment.

"U'm! Yes. But perhaps a woman would suit us better. An oldish one, of course, who wouldn't be getting too much in *your* way, like a young one." She punctuated that riposte to his jibe about the younger man with a flick of her tongue and a mocking grin.

"And perhaps you're right," Mike replied with a knowing look, guessing that she was preparing for a natural event taking shape. Maire blushed at his random hit.

"Although what you have in your mind, Mr. McGillicuddy, is not in mine—just yet, it might come true, and wouldn't you and Johnus be a great help to me then."

"Right again, Mrs. Mack. Neither of us is a trained rabbit catcher, and Johnus, poor man, is too old to learn."

Ignoring Mike's inept joking, Maire seized on his premature hopes

44

of paternity—or were they premature, she wondered?—to push her advantage.

"I was thinking we'd take a run home—home to my mother, I mean—tomorrow. Mammy could persuade Joany Cronin to come out here and live with us. Joany is a great worker and has a heart of gold. With her husband dead so long and the children scattered to the four quarters of the globe, she'd hop at the chance, I'm sure."

"Very well, so. I'll go down to the slip and tidy up the two-oar boat for an early start with the morning's tide. I won't delay."

But before they fell asleep, Mike raised the matter she had deliberately evaded all the evening—the consequences of the American letter. She felt she had sound reasons for withholding the news for a week at least: to encompass Nora's downfall being the strongest and most immediate.

"You know, Maire," said Mike, "we'll have to see Father John about the Masses and tell my brother Con and the others that poor Tim is no more. Wouldn't it be better to put off the run home till we have done that?"

"Thahailen, *a stor*, you are too straight and too innocent for this wicked world. You can't see how crooked and selfish others can be when their own interests cross yours. There's one word in that letter which is sure to raise a storm. Wait till I show you."

She drew the letter out from under the pillow.

"Listen to this: 'The said Will and Testament names his brother, Michael . . . as sole legatee.' What would me bould Nora do when you told her that? And what will Con and Dan do? Too well you know that they'll hire separate motorcars to rush them posthaste to town and hire separate solicitors to make ribbons of Tim's will, if they can't get their own claws in it."

"But we must make no delay about the Masses. I couldn't rest the nights, thinking of Tim waiting for them to relieve him, Maire."

"Let me arrange with Father Miles, Mike, and I shall go straight to him as soon as Joany Cronin is here to mind the house."

"Very well, so," said Mike, rolling over on his side to sleep.

As Maire had anticipated, Joany Cronin jumped at the offer of a secure home with a girl she knew and loved, though she dreaded the run out to the island in such a small open boat. Mike took at once to the hardy woman whose bright little eyes gave him one keen look of appraisal as she stepped into the boat and then twinkled her good will. Her happy chattering shortened the row home and boded well for the future.

"We would be giving ourselves away if we went to the presbytery on a weekday," Maire said the morning after Joany was brought to the island. "Why not wait till Sunday, when no notice will be taken of a chat with the priest in the sacristy after Mass. And I haven't had a day's spillering with you for ages. What about it?"

"I suppose a few days more won't be too much for Tim to wait, on top of the four months' delay since he died, though I don't like it. Get your tackle and we'll try the Wild Bank for hake."

The Wild Bank lies out at the extreme limit of line fishing in a rowing boat, and Maire felt half surprised and half elated at Mike's treating her as a reliable hand for such a man's job. There was a breeze from the sou'west, lively and refreshing, which would take it out of her on the steady pull out to the Bank, but which would be on their stern quarter, a "sodjer's breeze," for the homeward reach. Mike had the boat afloat off the slip when she came down, laden with two-way bread, some strong, hand-churned butter, a quart bottle of thin skim milk, and half of the sow's tongue her mother gave her. Mike loved meat because he seldom got it; this tasty bit would be a pleasant surprise for him out on the Wild Bank.

Mike had a pleasant surprise for her too. He had stepped a light mast for'ard of the bow thwart to carry a small lug and had shipped a weighty flagstone for ballast. He intended to sail the boat to the distant fishing ground and spare Maire the labor of the oar. It would entail tacking a long reach to the south'ard, but it would save time and a heartbreaking slog against the head wind.

Her heart sprouted wings when the boat cleared the shelter of the Shark and came alive, heeling gracefully to the light sailing breeze and rising daintily to the lift of the ocean swell. It promised to be a memorable day. It was already cleansing her busy mind of its perplexities. By the time they were off the Fang she had forgotten Nora and the will and everything—everything but Mike there in the stern, relaxed and confident, the white trailing clouds over head and the myriads of dazzling ripples that broke the long curves of the rollers. The short leg from the Fang to the Bank took but a scant twenty minutes, and by ten o'clock Mike was seeking out the bearings which located the famous but fickle Wild Bank.

He found them and showed them to Maire after he had dropped the mooring stone over the bow and paid out the fifty-foot rope after it. With a sweep of his arm he took in the surrounding waters and pointed downwards to the depths beneath them.

"Four fathom below us it lies; a level mountain of sand and fat mud —acres and acres of it. It feeds crowds of fish that do be jostling and fighting to snap the grub out of each other's gobs."

Even as he unrolled the picture of the submerged paradise for hungry fish to Maire, Mike was baiting the hooks with slices of mackerel belly, white and greasy, and testing the lead sinkers.

"Give me a dab of that butter, Maire, and I'll show you how rich the bank is."

Daubing one of the sinkers with butter, he dropped it overside and let the line run till he sounded bottom. Jogging the lead a few times, he hauled it up and showed Maire the minute shellfish and crawling things that had stuck to the butter.

"That's what delights the palate of hake and cod and ling, and the ground fish, like turbot and brill, and the darling black sole. The place is alive with them."

Maire smiled her understanding of his enthusiasm and egged him on.

"Why call it the Wild Bank if it is the wonderful place you say?"

"Ah! You wouldn't ask that if you were here in a ground swell. When the heavy ocean rollers, which grow big in deep water, strike this mountain of mud, that has only a bare four fathom to cover it, they break asunder in a boil of mad confusion. Even the fish scoot down the side of the bank into deep water for safety."

All the hooks were baited within the half hour, Mike in the bow in charge of four lines and Maire tending two in the stern, and a busy silence fell on the boat. The fish were feeding freely. When Maire had caught a dozen or so of hake and a beautiful turbot, which made her shout with delight, her sharp ears picked up a faint, high-pitched hail coming over the water. Shading her eyes with her hand, she discovered four black spots, looking piteously small in the waste of heaving water, and asked Mike if they were boats.

"Sure," he replied. "That near one is Conny Shuckrue and the Gow; Nedeen Barry and Sean Og are in the green boat between us and the Fang. I'm not sure of that eastern boat, but Johnus and his nephew are in the one to the north of us. You can see how big the Bank is now. We are all along the outer verge of it."

Maire's eyes roved the horizon, looking for other boats and seeing none. She and Mike were the furthest out. But Mike's practiced eye was keener and kept swinging to the sou'west every now and then. Long before Maire could be certain that the speck she imagined she saw blurring the horizon was really there, Mike told her in an urgent undertone to pull in her lines and be ready to take the bow oar as soon as he lifted the moorings.

"What's up, Mike?"

"Watch that snake, Conny. He knows what's up. I'll tell you as we go."

As quick as they were, Shuckrue and the Gow were already under way and putting their backs into their oars before Mike and Maire got going. By the time Mike had the boat headed for the black object floating low in the water to the south and had taken a bearing over the stern, Conny was almost abreast of them.

"Don't let him hustle us," Mike whispered. "We'll take it fine and steady. You have a good half hour's plugging ahead of you, girleen; no need to spend yourself in the first five minutes. Follow my stroke —bog-brea: bog-brea: bog-brea."

"Bog-brea: bog-brea: bog-brea." Maire echoed his timing with voice and oar until she felt their boat gain speed and settle into a steady rhythmic pace. Then she thought it time to learn the cause of this sudden change from fishing to racing.

"What's all the rush?" she asked of Mike's poll as she reached out forward—a short question to save breath.

"Not sure yet." Mike was equally economical of breath. "A ship's boat." After a few strokes he added, "Adrift." He rowed steadily on. "If there's no one aboard, she's ours," and he nodded towards the boat straining to pass them, "or Conny's, if he gets to her before us."

It was a dingdong, dead-level struggle for what seemed miles to the girl in the bow, who began to foresee a terrible fight for possession if both boats reached the wreck together. Mike rowed doggedly on but asked from time to time, "How's it going, Maire, girl?"

"Fine" always came back to him, clear and strong, so that Conny might hear, too. He wasn't more than an oar's length away to leeward. He watched her slyly, biding his time to play a mean trick on her that would end the indecisive race to his own advantage.

"Come on, Gow. We'll rattle up a dozen," he shouted over his shoulder to his bowman.

"One—two—three—four." Their tough oars bent to the powerful heaves and their boat drew up to bring Conny level with Maire and his oar closer to hers. With a yell to startle her, he thrust the blade of his oar under the loom of hers and yanked it out of the tholepins into her stomach. Winded and shaken, she lost her grip of the oar, which went rolling over the gunwale, and drifted astern.

The race was over. Shuckrue and the Gow paddled away with whoops of derisive laughter towards the drifting boat, now not more than a quarter of a mile away. Maire sat up on the thwart from which she had fallen backwards and glared after them, too baffled for speech. Mike, with hunched shoulders and bowed head, followed with unseeing eyes the oar floating uselessly just out of reach. He seethed with rage.

"Oh! the shame of being bested by such a pair and in such a raw, mean way! Damn and blast their souls to blazes."

But Maire never cried over spilled milk. She shrugged her shoulders in her characteristic way of saying, "That's that," and dismissing an unpleasant incident.

"We may as well try to fish for that oar if we mean to go home to-day," she suggested.

Mike shook himself together and turned a discomfited smile towards her.

"You're the boss," he said, picking up the remaining oar to use as a stern scull and work the boat to where the other was floating. He soon retrieved it and handed it to her.

"With Mr. Shuckrue's compliments."

Over her shoulder he saw Conny and the Gow boarding the black boat and moving about like two hounds on the scent. His intent gaze sent hers in the same direction to wonder with him at the strange inaction that came upon the boarding party. The two figures, silhouetted black against the distant sky, stood relaxed a while and then, scrambling into their own boat, rowed back to the Bank like two tired men. They did not cast a glance at the pair who watched them pass in silence.

"That's queer," Mike observed to himself, "damned queer." And turning his head towards Maire, he said, "We'll go and see what let all the steam out of the buckoes."

They soon reached the mysterious boat and climbed into her. She was badly broken up, as if a heavy spar had fallen athwart the gunwales and crushed them. She was useless as she lay and would cost a lot to repair. As treasure trove she was a liability, unless her lockers proved fruitful. Mike poked around, unmindful of Maire's interest in a torn sail lumped in the bow until she tapped his arm.

"There's someone under that sail, Mike. I'd swear it moved."

He eased himself past her and raised a corner of the sail. Sure enough, a man lay huddled under it; a man little older than himself but as blonde as Maire, in beard and hair. The mouth gaped wide, showing the dark tongue that filled it, and the eyes were closed and withdrawn into their sockets. Mike dropped the sail back on the face as he would cover a corpse, respectfully but with a finality.

"But he's alive, Mike, I assure you. I saw the sail stir," Maire urged.

Mike removed the sail again and straightened the huddled figure on the floor of the boat. They had no water to pour upon the swollen tongue, and tried drops of the thin skim milk instead. Though there were no immediate results, Maire still believed the man had moved and was not dead. They finally decided to lash the boats together while they transferred him to their own, and then sail home to the Shark instead of rowing. Maire was thus left free to rekindle the faint spark of life which she divined rather than felt in their inanimate load, while Mike steered the boat on the long run back.

Out of a long silence he laughed his contempt for the avaricious pair who abandoned the seaman when they found his boat was a dud.

"What can you expect from swine but dirt?"

The cow was bellowing to be milked, it was so late in the day when they rounded the entrance to the cove and called Joany to help carry the strange man to the house.

Joany was "in her element" with the sick and disabled. Her dear departed husband was so long adying that Joany knew all about resuscitation and the invalid dietary which could be concocted on a mountainy farm. When they deposited the unconscious man on the kitchen table, she took complete charge. After a serious discussion with Maire, who was not accustomed to being superseded, she issued her orders to the others while she herself was busy preparing a bed of fresh straw stuffed into flour sacks. She laid it as near the fire as was safe, and had four bottles of hot water, encased in her Sunday stockings, ready to place around the patient. While Mike and Maire were stripping him and wrapping him in a warm blanket, Joany slipped into her own room and returned with a very small flask of whisky.

"Ye never suspected I was a secret drunkard, did ye?" she asked with a twinkle of her left eye.

Through the evening she and Maire worked incessantly, massaging the man's limbs between regular stops for feeding him with sweetened warm water and drops of diluted whisky. They were exhausted when their reward came. The patient's brow twitched and his tongue drew back into his mouth with a sighing breath.

"Thanks be to God and His Blessed Mother," cried Joany. "He'll be talking by dawn and hungry for a drink by breakfast time. Go away to your bed, a stor: I can manage alone till midnight and you can finish the night with him. Off with you out of my sight."

CHAPTER 8 · *The Missing Belt*

THE long spell of calm weather broke next morning into the worst gale that had struck the Shark since Maire came to live there. It began with stiff blustering squalls from the southeast which slanted into the cove and made Mike run down to the slip to see that everything was secured and battened down. The wind backed as the morning wore on and by mid-day it was driving sheets of rain and spume in from the sou'west with a deep booming roar. Although the house was sheltered by the Lookout hill against winds that had any westering in them, the rain kept the Macks indoors, with little to do but nurse the patient. The women had transferred him to a bedroom which had a fireplace, after bathing him in the kitchen, and were sitting by the fire, knitting and waiting for him to wake into consciousness.

Mike was with them when the man opened his eyes, which were as blue as Maire's and looked bluer in the pallor of the surrounding skin. Mike sat at the foot of the bed and smiled into them.

"Hallo, old stock! How's tricks?" he said in a friendly voice.

The eyes looked up into his, travelled slowly to Maire and Joany and back to Mike.

"Fine," breathed the stranger, like a ventriloquist, without moving a lip.

Before night fell on the household marooned by the gale, the patient was talking freely and telling his story. He was Knut Ollsen, ship's carpenter on the tramp steamer *Bernadotte*, out of Trondhjem with a cargo of Swedish iron and salt fish for Bilbao in Spain. It would be a long story to tell how he came to be adrift, all alone, in the dinghy. He was not too clear in his own mind about it yet, but it would come back to him, bit by bit.

Mike told him how they found him and brought him to the island and why they had abandoned the boat. Ollsen went silent at the end of the exchange of narratives, as if there were something on his mind which was hard to put into words. He seemed to be looking a question.

"What is it you want to say?" Maire asked him. "Don't hesitate to ask us for anything we have." She smiled as she continued. "You can guess by looking around that this place is no hotel. But anything—"

"No. Your house is beautiful to me and will always be beautiful. But . . . before you left the boat, did you see . . . my belt?"

"No," replied Maire. "We found no belt in the boat nor on yourself when we took your clothes off."

"I always wore it next to my skin. I never went without it." He looked at Mike and said, "I kept my money in it—all I had."

Mike's eyes met Maire's and their brows rose inquiringly. The stranger misread the silent query, thinking they doubted his story of the belt, and hastened to amplify it.

"It was a black leather one with three pockets on each side and K. O. stamped on it." He smiled rather disconsolately as he went on, "I have been K.O.ed all right. It had a brand-new £10 Bank of England note in each pocket.

Mike pursed his lips tightly and shook his head to discourage any inclination Maire might have to hazard an opinion on the fate of Ollsen's belt. She, more astute than he, had no notion of giving voice to her certainty about what happened to it, or even of revealing her certainty in headshakes or mouthings as Mike had done. She looked Ollsen calmly in the eye as she commiserated with him.

"That's awful, Mr. Ollsen. Sixty pounds is an awful lot of money to lose in one slap."

"Worse than the loss, ma'am, is the great debt I owe you and Mr. Mack, which I can't pay now. But I shall find some way to clear it, before I leave you."

"Who's talking of debt and leaving? Sure you're hardly here yet to talk of leaving, and it will be time enough to talk of paying a debt when you draw one on you."

Joany closed the argument by declaring it time for the poor addled man to get a rest and a wink of sleep. Maire followed Mike up to the kitchen to discuss this further evidence of his brother-in-law's turpitude and to use it as a lever to force him to assist her in the operation against Nora, the plan for which was now clearly plotted in her mind.

"We must put a full stop to Master Conny's wholesale robberies before he disgraces Nora and the whole of us. If the Civic Guards get wind of them, we will be in the mouths of the people, disgraced for ever. But, Mike, if you are guided by me, we can teach him a lesson he'll never forget and no one but ourselves be a tittle the wiser."

Mike reached his decisions with a slow deliberation which used to goad Maire into fizzing impatience. His exasperating processes of thought outraged her own speedy intuitive judgement, but she had learned how to expedite them by handing the premises of her argument in logical order to her dear deliberate spouse.

"Conny Shuckrue has committed three barefaced robberies under our very eyes. First, our household goods, then our lobsters, and now this poor stray's hard-earned money. We'll take first things first, as Father Miles advises when we are addled about where to begin to clear up the messes we run ourselves into. Conny stole the house things first, and they are the first things he'll have to cough up."

"That is right and fair," Mike replied judicially. "You have a way of forcing him to do it, you say. Let us hear it, then. The sooner the better."

"Yes," said Maire, "the sooner the better. As soon as this gale blows off, we'll pay Mistress Nora a visit, yourself and myself, and bring her to her senses. That is, if you back me to the limit, no matter what I do."

"I'll back you, Maire, *a haisge*, in anything short of bloody murder."

The gale held for two days, but the heavy seas rolled in multitudinous procession from the west long after the wind had died down. There was no hope of launching a boat even in the lee of the Shark until the swell subsided, so that the four on the island were still marooned,

though not house-bound. The women concentrated all their attention on their patient, while Mike spent most of his time on the Lookout searching the water for the wreckage which always came in after
heavy weather. Heavy seas broke up the ships sunk in the Kaiser's war
and floated the imprisoned cargo, especially if the cargo was buoyant,
like timber and barrels containing rum and schnapps and molasses. A
man could take his time in picking up timber, but he had to take risks
in salvaging barrels. Barrels crack like eggs on the first rocks and they
are very tricky to handle off a small boat in deep water. It isn't every
man can salvage barrels.

Mike located a scatter of timber baulks—mahogany by the colour of
them—thrashing about in the turmoil of surf below him along the
rocks. They could wait for a calm day; he would tow them around to
the cove where he had a fine pile of baulks stored up for future use.
Of course, the black boat, Ollsen's boat, was smashed to smithereens
long ago. It was useless to be looking for her now, but there might be
some other flotsam out there, drifting through the Sound.

He left the Lookout and followed the cliff top towards the southern tip of the Shark, squaring the water with his eyes for the dark permanent spot which meant a morsel of wreckage. Yes! There was one,
a hundred yards out, floating sluggishly in the waves that sped on faster
than its reluctant drift. Would it clear the point of the island? What
was it? And whatever it was, was it worth the risk of trying to pick it
out of the rough water at the point? Ach! He would have a shot at it,
but he must not let Maire stick her nose in the business.

He took advantage of the ground to hide his stealthy way to the cove
and had the boat pushed out when he heard Maire's voice, more im-
perative than inquisitive, asking:

"Where do you think you're going, Mike Mack, in that cockleshell
of a boat? Is it tired of life you are to attempt facing out into that mad
sea in her, and alone into the bargain?"

Now, although Mike deferred to her rulings in most things, he could
not tolerate her interference in his own special province—the sea. The
note of command in her voice spurred him to obstinacy and, without
deigning to reply, he jumped into the boat and rowed away. She

watched him as the boat turned round to the south'ard, bitterly regretting her hasty words, and stood stock-still, biting her lip in thought. He must have seen something approaching the south point and was gone to get it. She would go to the point too, overland, and be there to lend a hand if she could. She would need a rope and, perhaps, the small buoy. With the light line coiled over her shoulder and the buoy in one hand, she sped to the point which she reached before the boat.

Looking to windward, she saw the object of Mike's daring attempt nearing the cauldron of foam that smothered the reef in which the point ended. It drifted on as leisurely as a grazing cow, on a course which would clear the rocks by a bare rope's length. Maire crawled out along the serrated reef to the shelter of a splintered fang from which she could see the bit of flotsam to windward and Mike to leeward. She called between cupped hands to attract his attention and saw his head nod in reply. The boat was just nosing out of the shelter of the land and would need all his skill to keep her from swamping when the ocean rollers lifted her up on their careering backs.

Maire called again and pointed with outstretched arm to where the prize was soberly rising and subsiding as it passed outside the furthermost reach of the breakers. Mike dipped the handles of the oars to show that he understood and had sighted the wreckage over his shoulder. It was but thirty yards out in the race. If he could make a dash, grab the thing, and jibe back into the shelter before the boat was swamped, the trick was done. Maire knew what he had decided to do and the risk he was taking and she started to forestall part of that risk. Signalling to Mike her intention by holding up the buoy with the line attached for him to see, she flung it out beyond the surf, trusting the breeze to carry it towards the boat. Mike divined her plan and, edging to meet the buoy in its lively bobbing course, caught the line with his boat hook, and made it fast to a stern cleat. Maire paid out the line sparingly lest the slack foul on a rock, and watched Mike make his dash for the black object as it slid down the slope of a monstrous wave. Tying the line with a fisherman's bend to a spline of rock and passing a bight over her shoulder, she planted her feet firmly and prepared to take the strain when Mike stopped rowing to make his grab.

He shipped his oar quickly before he made it, leaned out over the gunwale and seized the cord with which the wooden object was bound. Maire screamed in dismay. A huge comber lifted the boat while she was listing under Mike's weight and threw him overboard into the trough as it passed majestically on. Mike came up gasping but still gripping the parcel in his right hand and clinging to the gunwale with the left. Maire stiffened her body against the line—straight and taut now—and began to haul it in, but the water made it slip through her hands. Winding another turn about her body, she summoned the aid of her powerful legs and in a dour tug of war heeled her way, inch by inch, backwards from the sea. Mike had managed to lift his body onto the boat and was already breast-high on the gunwale in his struggle to clamber aboard. Maire maintained her dragging retreat inland until she saw the boat well into the shelter and Mike at the oars again. When he signalled the all clear and cast off the line, she quietly fell backwards on the plateau of rocks which she had so painfully won, and fainted. But when he came, in sodden slacks, running to help her, he found her sitting up, rubbing her buttock ruefully.

"I'm wondering, Mike, which of us is the biggest fool. You who hasn't the gumption to keep out of harm's way, or me, that hasn't the sense to leave you stuck in it."

She waved him away when he moved to help her to her feet and got up by herself, shook the dirt and bracken off her skirt, and threw him the rope to coil and bring home.

"And for the Lord's sake, don't let Joany and Ollsen know what cracked pots you and I can be."

She hadn't forgotten the cause of their perilous experience. Straight back to the cove she went, just ahead of Mike, and down to the boat where he had left it half drawn up, with the wooden case still on the stern sheets. She took it up, shook it near her ear, and handed it to Mike to open.

"It feels light, whatever is in it," he observed as he cut the whipcord binding and prised off the lid with his jackknife.

Their heads were close together in eager expectancy when they removed the cotton-wool packing to disclose the contents.

"*Eggs!*" they both exclaimed incredulously. "*Eggs!*"

Mike took one of them in his hand, weighing it with an up-and-down motion.

"And to cap it all," he laughed with disgust, "they're empty. We ran the risk of our lives for a dozen eggshells!"

He raised the box to fling it back into the sea, but Maire restrained him.

"People do not pack ordinary shells in a mahogany box for fun. We'll hold on to them till we know what '*Throchilus colubris*' and '*Gallus bankiva*' mean."

CHAPTER 9 · *Detection*

THE weather is of prime importance on the Shark. It postpones
settled engagements and originates impromptu ones, so that Mike
never made cut-and-dried plans to do a specific job on a specific day,
but was always ready to avail of a favourable slant in the weather to
carry out a notion which he kept at the back of his mind for just
such a happy chance. Maire, too, was ruled by the moods of sea and
air and was as weather-conscious as Mike and almost as weather-wise.
She did not name any particular day for disciplining Nora Shuckrue,
because she wanted reasonably fair weather for it and the certainty
that Conny would not be at home in Trabeg to obstruct her plan. But
she did hint to Mike that the September sheep fair in Cahirsally presented the most likely chance of Conny's absence for at least twelve
hours. The fair was only two days off—Wednesday to be exact.

"But, Maire, *a stor*, you know as well as I do that Shuckrue has no
sheep nor ever had," Mike interposed with a quizzical look in his
eye. "So, what business could he have at the sheep fair?"

"Don't pretend to be simpler than you are, Mike. What better
chance could he get for breaking a £10 note on the sly than a busy
fair day when the town is full of strangers? And I know by the glint
in your eye that you have guessed what Conny has in his mind, too."

"Sure, let us hope for fair weather for the fair day. I'll have the punt
ready tomorrow night for an early start on Wednesday morning."

It was still dark when Mike stuck his head out the bedroom window
and informed Maire that the sky was clear of cloud and that the

59

wind was light and from a good point—the southeast. Joany had heard them talking and had the fire going and breakfast ready before the dawn broke. Ollsen called "Good morning, good folks," to them from his bedroom to let Joany know he was ready for his morning cup of tea and that they need not whisper while they ate, lest they wake him.

The boat reached the strand under Trabeg about six o'clock, the usual time for people who intended to travel to Cahirsally. The lorry always left the shop at seven. No one would be surprised to see the Macks ashore so early on a fair morning, least of all the Shuckrues, but there would be some surprise if they dawdled around too long. Accordingly, they reviewed the parts each was to take in the family drama, as they made the punt fast to one of Conny's boats. Mike was to slip across the field to the shop and back again to tell Maire when Conny reached it, and so on. There was no fear of error, it was all so simple.

Mike did not go the whole way to the shop, because he saw his man leave the house and step out briskly up the lane. Giving him time to reach the shop, Mike returned to Maire and walked with her to Nora's door, where he left her to operate on that unsuspecting lady. He himself went on his way as if he, too, were going to the fair, and had business in the shop. The bar was fairly crowded when he entered, the men taking tots of neat whisky "to kill the raw morning" and the women sitting on crates by the wall, stolid as Oriental statues in their great woollen shawls. He ran his eye over the faces and spotted Conny in close discussion with the Gow at the end of the counter, both dressed for town. A roar and rumble, which ended in a coarse race of the asthmatic engine, announced the arrival of the lorry outside, even if Bill Hannen had not chanted his hackneyed phrase:

"Time for one more quick one, gentlemen."

Bill was postmaster, publican, lorry man, banker, mortgagor, money-lender, and legal confessor to Father John's parishioners in sickness and in health, in business and in sport, waking or sleeping, alive or dead. In the realm of the spirit, Father John was supreme; in the domain of the flesh, Bill reigned with unlimited powers.

Mike followed the departing customers to the lorry and found the man he was hoping to meet seated comfortably in the cab beside the driver. John Joe Barrett was catlike in his love for comfort and in his self-centred assumption of his right to the tidbits of life. He was very neat, too, in his ways, and very observant. Nothing escaped his girlish, long-lashed eyes, nor was any ruseful move misconstrued by the subtle brain behind them. Mike beckoned him out of the cab.

"Will you do me a favour in town, John Joe?"

"Of course I will, Mike. What is it?" he flashed the all-seeing eyes once and bent them to his boots again as he imitated Mike's whisper.

"Would you keep an eye on Conny Shuckrue for the first hour in town and tell me what shops he goes into or what strangers he has a deal with."

John Joe was too canny to ask crudely what was behind the unusual request; he would have no difficulty in finding out for himself. Nor did Mike ask him to keep the matter secret. John Joe never talked an idle word.

"Righto," he said as he stepped up into the cab again. "I'll be seeing you tonight when we get back from the fair."

"No hurry," said Mike as the lorry started up. "Sunday will do."

He kept out of view of Conny's house as he went back and launched the boat to wait until Maire and Nora appeared according to plan.

Although Nora's welcome was very effusive, Maire sensed an abstraction, as if her mind were continuing a distressing train of thought in its depths while it maintained a limping sequence of talk from its outer rim. Her eyes showed that she had been weeping all the morning and that she would start again at a touch.

"Sit down, Nora, and tell me all about it," said Maire giving "the touch" and watching her sister-in-law relax into a chair, throw her apron over her head and release her pent-up feelings in unrestrained cries. As she watched the bitter agony, her heart changed to sympathy for the distraught woman and with the change of heart came a change of mind. She would help rather than humiliate an already humiliated soul, and the kindest thing she could do now was to let Nora cry herself to a standstill without intervention. When the paroxysm died down, she took Conny Beg from his cradle, placed him on his mother's lap and went out, closing the door after her.

"Mike," she said when she had reached the strand and called him ashore, "all my plans are blown sky-high. Nora is in trouble and we have got to do something about it."

He eyed her in wonderment at the sudden switch from war to peace and suspended judgement, waiting to hear the morning's new developments before he committed himself.

"I believe she has discovered the full depth of her husband's depravity at last," Maire continued in a suasive voice, "and is ripe for her own conversion to her natural decency. Come on up to the house and help me to comfort her."

Nora remained seated in the chair when they entered the kitchen and directed a sisterly sort of smile at her brother. He drew a chair close to hers and, taking one of her hands in his, assured her in the kindliest way that nothing was as bad as it looked if you only confided it to a friend.

" 'Tis all about Conny, isn't it?" he added. She nodded in assent.

"The Gow was here with Conny last night?"

She started in surprise at Mike's knowing of the Gow's surreptitious visit. She had assumed that her brother was concerned only with a domestic row between her and Conny which he wished to compose.

"What do you know about that thieving vagabond?" she asked.

"I know everything. In fact, I know more than you do, and it was to protect you and the good name of the Macks of the Shark that Maire and me are here now."

"You know about . . . the strange money?" she asked in lingering doubt as she searched their quiet steady eyes for assurance.

"Yes, and about the raid on the lobsters, and—I don't want to salt your sorrow, Nora, *a haisge*, but I have to say it—I know all things you and that man of yours removed by night from our house while I was away getting married. And Maire knows it too."

Nora's wifely defences crumbled and tears filled her tired eyes again.

Clasping Conny Beg to her bosom as if to protect him from the consequences of his father's delinquencies, she told her tale.

"Conny sent me to bed early on Monday night and stayed up by the fire mounting hooks on the long lines, and I dozed off when the child fell asleep. Voices I heard through my sleep woke me and I cocked my ear to listen. I wish I didn't, for it was then I heard the truth of the story Conny gave me about finding a belt on the Old Quay after some tourists had dropped it from their car and gone off the Lord knows where. It was empty, he told me, but it would be useful, empty or full, to keep up his oil-pants. I believed him till the Gow gave the game away, claiming his share of the money. When that rogue stole away in the dark, as he came, I tackled Conny and begged him on my bended knees to hand the belt and the money to Father John to do the right thing with them, but he only laughed at me and went off to bed, leaving me crying on the cold hearth till morning. And on the same hearth I am ever since, disgraced and heartbroken."

"You are neither disgraced nor heartbroken yet, Nora. Nobody but Maire and myself have an inkling of the story and, with God's help, we'll keep it within the four walls of this house. . . ."

For the first time Maire intervened, gently but firmly, to remind them that Father John would have to be consulted, as to the redemption of Conny if for no other purpose.

"We can settle the matter of the lobsters, the household things, and even the belt, among ourselves, but Nora's pot of troubles would still be boiling if Conny weren't made to amend his ways, and nobody under heaven can bring him to his senses but the priest."

"But who will tell the priest?" asked Nora. "I could never face him."

"I will," said Maire.

"He'll be very hard on us, I suppose?" Nora hazarded, looking for reassurance into their faces.

"If 'the ill-gotten goods are restored,' the catechism says, 'the gravamen of theft is largely remitted,' " Maire quoted to comfort her sister-in-law and, mindful of her own interest, to ensure the voluntary return of the property she had plotted to recapture by guile.

Mike, in a gush of the old brotherly love, broke in with further comfort for his sister.

"We'll forget about the old lobsters; you can count them out: Maire need not mention them to Father John at all."

Not to be outdone in good deeds, Maire suggested that Nora should retain some of the quilts and a blanket or two, perhaps, and that they would select them now. She rushed Nora off her feet after depositing Conny Beg in his cradle with much tucking and chuckling and, with calculated generosity, said that she would leave it to Nora to pick the items to be retained.

"And you, Mike, can bring up those bags from the boat and that box you had in the stern, while we are collecting the things." She was in great fettle, was Maire.

In contrite mood Nora exhumed all that Conny had hidden under the floors and exposed upon the kitchen table the contents of presses and drawers. She withheld nothing. When Mike returned with the bags, she superintended the packing, supplied a box of her own to contain the ware, and retained for herself only a few indispensable articles, as Maire had anticipated.

"We'll all have a nice cup of tea together to celebrate the day," she exclaimed and, warm with new confidence in herself, began to sparkle and poke fun at Thahailen. But though she beamed good will on Maire, she did not attempt any levity with her formidable sister-in-law. Maire overpowered her.

"Wouldn't it be as well for you to see the priest today, Maire," said Mike after the table was cleared. "It would spare us another day's travel, if you catch him at home. I'll wait for you at Bill's."

"But we haven't talked to Conny yet about handing the money belt over to Father John," Nora objected. "Why not wait and make one job of it?"

"Never fear, Nora dear," said Maire with a Mona Lisa smile. "I'll see Father Miles today and settle all with him."

They left it at that and Maire set out for the presbytery, leaving Mike at Hannen's shopdoor. He had not told her of the mission he

had given to John Joe in the excitement of the morning at Nora's
and he wondered should he call her back and let her know.

"Ach!" he decided as he pushed in the swing door of the shop,
"surely I can manage that much on my own."

Big Bill was alone, polishing glasses and tumblers till they shone
like crystal. He took a personal pride in the glistening tiers of glass-
ware and carried on all his conversations to the busy play of towel on
tumbler.

"*De vahassa, a Mike, a vrahir.*" Bill always saluted his customers in
Gaelic. "*Cunas thahee go leir ar an Illan?*"

"*Go marish ivad, a Waushtir. Is mise an dhuine is massa urha. Cunas
thaoi hein?*"

The lorry, returning from Cahirsally with a load of Guinness casks
and sacks of flour, rumbled into the cobbled storeyard and interrupted
the swap of views on fishing, and prices, and the official restrictions on
honest fishermen and honest traders. Bill told Mike to keep an eye on
the shop while he himself was checking the goods in the lorry, and
handed him a used pint glass to polish till he came back. As Bill
went out the backdoor, John Joe came in the front, neat as he was that
morning and as quietly self-possessed.

"You're still here?" he remarked, pulling the knees of his pants
daintily before he sat down near Mike and flashing those faunlike eyes
of his in one comprehensive sweep around the premises.

"You're home early from the fair," said Mike, matching one obvious
statement with another, but appending a question which John Joe was
never known to ask. "What'll you have?"

"A glass of port," he replied as if he were conferring a favour and
added, to forestall any obligation to call for a second round, "just to
keep you company, Mike."

They sipped their drinks in silence, each waiting for the other to
open the discussion of Conny's movements in Cahirsally. Mike's innate deliberation in the use of words made waiting easy for him and
wore down John Joe's mere tactical taciturnity.

"About Conny," the younger man observed at last. "I watched him, like a cat watching a mouse, from the moment he left the lorry and went into the fair field, himself and the Gow. They stuck together and made no attempt to enter a house, private or public."

He watched the effect of that negative report on his listener's face and detected no change.

"But I did spot one queer move of Conny's which might mean something to you."

He broke the thread of his story again in the hope that Mike might reveal his interest in Conny's actions by dropping a word or two. Mike remained silent and unrevealing, so that John Joe had to continue.

"Conny slouched across the fair to Long Pindar, the cattle buyer from Lisarney, and asked him to change a £10 note. I know it was a £10 note because he handed Conny the change, note by note, and I counted them."

Again he scanned Mike's face and this time caught the glint of satisfaction in his eyes before Mike could dim it.

"That's my story for you," said John Joe in words, but his knowing smirk told the silent man who saw it that the best was to come and that he would have to pay well to hear it. Accordingly, he cast off his pretence at indifference and asked forthright.

"What happened then?"

John Joe seized his chance of a dramatic climax.

"This happened."

He produced a brand-new, Bank of England £10 note and exhibited it to Mike's intent gaze with a flourish of vanity at his own astuteness. If he had hoped to stampede his companion into dropping his guard or making a bid for possession of the £10 note, he was mistaken. Mike's natural reticence was fortified by his determination to keep his sister's troubles within the family, considerations which schooled him to conceal his real interest in the banknote. He relaxed his long limbs into an easier slouch on the wooden seat and looked quizzically at John Joe.

"What in the world picked you to do such a mad thing?" he asked with a note of paternal disapproval in his voice. "And where did you find the money to buy that note from Pindar? I know you wouldn't steal it from him."

John Joe's elation subsided under this cool reception of his dramatic exhibition, though he suspected Mike's indifference might be assumed.

"But didn't you tell me to watch every move Conny Shuckrue made at the—"

Mike cut in with a laugh, "Not at all, Johnny, my boy. What I asked you to do was to find out what houses Conny called at and you tell me he called at no house. That's what I wanted to know and I am more than obliged to you for the information. Finish that wine, my lad, and we'll have two more."

Discomfited but still dubious of Mike's statement of the case, John Joe pocketed the crackling banknote with much less display than he had shown in producing it, drank the second glass of port in one gulp, and went about his business. Mike remained in deep thought until a boisterous group of men, returning flushed and talkative from the fair, burst into the bar and dragged him to his feet to join them in a *"deoch an dorish."*

An hour later he returned to Nora's to wait for Maire.

CHAPTER 10 · *Retribution*

WHILE Mike was pitting his wits against John Joe's inquisitive intuitions, Maire was composing her mind and arraying her facts in the order in which she proposed to present them to the priest. This second interview was really, she said to herself, a sequel to the first, when she had suggested to him that he take no action if Nora should ask him to exercise his parochial powers against herself. In this resumption of their previous conference, her purpose should be limited to the terms of her promise to Nora, which were, that Conny be led or driven into the straight and narrow path and that the family's good name be safeguarded in the process. But Father Miles was a difficult man to handle. In fact, he couldn't be handled, or led, or driven. The only way she might induce him to see things as she saw them and to act accordingly was to present them to him, without comment, in the order of their happening and hope that his mind would operate on them in exactly the same way as her own had done. She was subconsciously aware of the similarity of their mental equipment and built her hope upon that similarity.

Thade Carey was washing the Ford near the stream which rose under the culvert at the presbytery gate when Maire accosted him to ask if the priest were at home.

"Bless my soul, if it isn't my friend, Mike Mack's darling young lady, all the way from Shark Island before the morning is rightly under way," Thade exclaimed, throwing the bucketful of water uselessly away and drying his gnarled fists on a flitter of his soutane, to shake hands with Maire.

Menial tasks lost their priority in Thade's daily round whenever he saw a chance for a really good gossip with a visitor from the outer limits of the parish. He thrust his unshaven prowlike jaw towards Maire with an ingratiating grin to invite her confidence.

"And how is himself? At the fair making a wad of money for you, is it?" When Maire did not respond, he continued his catechism hopefully: "He's out lobstering so?" And when that evoked only a neighbourly smile, he returned the smile with one of his own that hid his mouth under the promontory of his nose. He changed the direction of his fire.

"If you can't delay, you could leave your message with me and Father John will get it as soon as I see him, ma'am."

Seeing Maire turn towards the gate after releasing her hand from his detaining grasp, Thade shook down the tail of his soutane and hobbled beside her up the grass-grown avenue to the presbytery. He gave a tap on the sitting-room door, which he opened without waiting for any response from within and announced her.

"Mrs. Michael Mack from the island to see you, Father. If you'll be wanting the old bus, I'll be here in the hall." He retired, leaving the door ajar after a noisy pretence of closing it. Father John came to meet her, and completed the closing of the door before he spoke.

The huge room was so sparsely furnished that a ghostly echo enveloped any attempt at conversation and disconcerted Father John's parishioners, who were attuned to the stuffy intimacy of their overcrowded homes. It rendered them more tractable whenever he summoned them into his parlour for correction. Maire was too stout of heart and too fixed of purpose to be affected emotionally by such accidentals and, in any event, she was not here for correction.

The priest directed her by a wave of his hand to the chair he had just vacated and stood with his back to the empty fireplace, facing his visitor.

"Well, young lady?" His glance was much more friendly than his curt overture. It invited candour, even if she had not already decided to put all her cards on the table without reservation.

"You remember, Father, that I warranted, at our last conversation, that any scheme to recover our rights from Mrs. Shuckrue of Trabeg would bring no hurt to her and no scandal to the parish."

"Yes, I remember."

"Well, Father, I have got back the goods without hurting a hair of her head or losing a scrap of her friendship, but I'm afraid scandal will come to her. Not from me, I assure, but from—" She stopped short and made an apologetic grimace which the silent man at the fireplace observed with an impassive face.

"Perhaps you would rather hear what happened since Sunday and judge for yourself whether scandal is brewing for the Shuckrues or not," she resumed. When he nodded assent, she entered into an orderly recital of Conny's depredations, commencing with his raid on the Mack homestead during Mike's absence, in which his wife joined him, probably under duress or threats of duress. She neither suggested nor averred Conny's complicity in the midnight foray on Mike's lobster pots, though she did indicate the need for prior knowledge of their location to find them in the dark. Her description of the rescue of the Norwegian was as impersonally factual as a pupil's recital of a memorized history lesson.

"*Sin agat mo sceal, Ahair,*" she ended, lapsing into Gaelic, when her mind sprang free of the constraint which her narrative had imposed on it.

"Oh, no," Father John rejoined, breaking his judicial silence for the first time, "that can't be the end of your story. You haven't told me of the famous plan you had for compelling Mrs. Shuckrue to restore the goods you say she abstracted from her old home, nor how it worked."

"It was a very simple plan, Father, though you might not approve of it." And for the first time its crudity dawned on herself and made her blush. "I intended to kid—to take the baby from Nora and keep him on the island until she brought us the stolen goods."

"The word you shrank from is the suitable word for your extraordinary project, ma'am," he pronounced gravely, frowning at Maire as he spoke. "You proposed to *kidnap* the innocent child. What would you have done with him, you, an inexperienced girl, on that isolated rock, if Mrs. Shuckrue had called your bluff and left him on your hands?"

The severity of his tone and the implication that she had not the intelligence to foresee and provide for such a possibility, roused her to swift justification of herself.

"I installed a very respectable woman in my house before I made any other move and put in a supply of baby food. But, my dear Father Miles, there was no fear that Nora would leave the child on my hands. She couldn't even if she wanted to." She paused deliberately, as if challenging him to contradict her, and then continued, to satisfy the ruminative look which she saw coming in his eye. "Nora suckles her baby at her breast, Father. How long do you think she would stand the agony of breasts swollen with milk? After twelve hours she'd be racing out to the child, and she'd be afraid to come in an empty boat."

The priest stared down into the unwavering eyes as he registered this new lesson on the rarer functions of the female mind. He recognized both the honest directness of her admission and the courage which enabled her to make them. He explored his memory of cases cited in *Walsh on Human Acts* and in his Maynooth treatise on moral theology for guidance in this unusual case, now developing within his own jurisdiction.

"But did you not say, just now, that you had no need to put that immoral—perhaps I had better say *unchristian*—that unchristian plot into practice, and that Mrs. Shuckrue surrendered the goods in dispute voluntarily?"

Thade Carey, dispensing with the perfunctory knock, stuck his puckish face into the room, announcing:

"Mike Mack of th' island, Father, chasing after that woman of his."

He pushed Mike in and surveyed the setting around the fireplace with a contemplative eye before he retired. Maire's look was equally inquisitive as her husband drew near, making apologies for the unceremonious entrance Thade had forced upon him. She wondered why he had not stayed at Trabeg, or at Hannen's, till she returned and guessed that some new development had disturbed that arrangement.

"I'm sorry I have no chair to offer you, Michael," said the priest. "Perhaps you won't mind standing beside me—in the dock, as it were—before your very remarkable wife. She is setting me a very nice problem—one which transcends my previous experience, even *in partibus occidentalibus*."

Father John's verbose welcome and the jocose manner of it indicated to Maire's keen perception that her candour was having the favourable effect on his mind which she played for, while they reassured Mike, who had trepidations for having burst so rudely into the priest's sanctum.

"I beg your pardon, Father," he said, "but I have learned something Maire, my wife, would like to put before you. And I wanted to remind her about the novena for my brother, Tim, God rest his soul."

After addressing that explanation of his presence to the priest, he turned to his wife and asked if she had told what had happened to Ollsen's money.

"I was just coming to that when you arrived, Mike," she replied. Directing her voice towards Father John again, she took up his last question on Nora's affair as if there had been no interruption. She retold Ollsen's account of his money and described Nora's dismay at overhearing Conny's whispered conversation with the Gow, her reaction, and her resultant zeal in making amends. When she finished, Maire nodded to her husband an invitation to tell of the new developments which had brought him on her heels to the presbytery.

Mike's face puckered into the ingratiating grin of a boy caught in the act of raiding a pantry cupboard as he undertook to render an account of his private essay into the art and practice of detection.

"Although Maire, here, and myself were sure that Con Shuckrue stole the sailor's belt, we had nothing to show, no proof that would force him to admit his guilt and give the loot back to the poor man. Ollsen told us that the money was all in £10 notes, and I guessed that Shuckrue would find it hard to change such large notes in Hannen's without rousing suspicion. He would try to slip them to some stranger at Cahirsally Fair. That's exactly what he did, but he was caught in the act by a fellow I set to trail him."

"Ah, Mike, why did you drag an outsider into this business?" Maire exclaimed. "We promised Nora that we would keep it within the family. Who is the fellow you got to spy on Conny?"

Mike answered this interruption of his narrative and its implication of indiscretion quite calmly.

"It would have been foolish of me to follow Shuckrue myself. He doesn't suspect yet that you and I know he found any money in the boat. He doesn't know that we rescued Ollsen and he doesn't know that his wife overheard him and the Gow arguing about the division of the money. But if he saw me tracking him, he'd guess I knew something and he'd cover his trail like the thieving fox he is. That's why I set John Joe Barrett on his tail."

"And did you tell John Joe what it is all about, Mike?" Maire asked, less reproachful of mien after Mike's reasoned statement, but still jealously careful of the family's good name.

"I did not, Maire; I told him nothing; but knowing John Joe, as we all know him, for the cute shaver he is, I had to take the risk that he would be drawing his own conclusions. That couldn't be avoided, but I never dreamed that his cleverness would carry him the length it did."

And Mike told his hearers how John Joe's cupidity impelled him to exceed his instructions and go so far as to buy back the £10 note in the expectation of selling it to Mike for a good profit and of using it as a lever to work himself into Mike's confidence.

"It may be unfortunate that he had the note," Mike said in conclusion. "I don't know. You, Father, may induce him to part with it, that is, if you are so good as to bother yourself with our petty family troubles. In any case, Con Shuckrue hasn't the faintest suspicion that the note he went to so much pains to export to foreign parts, was home from the fair sooner than himself."

Silence fell on the group. Father John withdrew his eyes from his young visitors and gazed thoughtfully through the window into space.

He was savouring the rare aura of manly simplicity, which Mike created during the telling of his story, as a connoisseur savours a choice wine, before he addressed his mind to the sordid conduct of the two black sheep. Dismissing the protective maxim *Noli in primum nuntium credere* from consideration, he accepted Mike's statement without reserve and decided that the swift action he would take against the malefactors would be of such a kind as to take the matter out of Mike's hands. He would deal with it himself. It came under the "faith-and-morals" category and was a purely parochial responsibility.

Having made his decision, he braced himself and turned towards Maire.

"I am glad you were diverted from your very unchristian designs upon the innocent babe and that you now appreciate the enormity of your plan."

His severity of manner and language was assumed for the purpose of curbing Maire's matriarchal habit of mind and making her feel his own overriding authority. "I'm sure you will refrain from any further activity in this affair."

Closing his lips masterfully on that injunction, he turned to Mike.

"You were saying something about Masses for your brother, Michael? Allow me to sympathize with you, before we arrange anything in regard to the memorial Mass. 'Tis sad to hear death mentioned with the young, very sad. Please tell me all about him."

Maire was on tenterhooks. Once the date of the Masses was arranged, Father Miles would announce them from the pulpit on Sunday. It would never do to let the public announcement of Tim's death take his brothers and Nora unawares. But if Mike informed them beforehand, they would naturally want to see the letter which brought the sad news. Unfortunately, it also brought news of the legacy. As soon as they learned that Tim had cut themselves out, war would be proclaimed, and the bequest would go up in legal smoke. What an awful dilemma! Her characteristic contempt for lies, even white ones, rejected the idea of pretending that she had lost the letter and her common sense warned her—. A high note of surprise in the priest's voice broke in on her racing thoughts.

"It never occurred to me," she heard him remark in explanation of some preceding statement. "It never occurred to me that McGillicuddy is always shortened to Mack and that you are the person to whom the communication referred."

Catching the puzzled expression which came over Maire's face, he repeated for her what he had just told Mike: that the Catholic chaplain to the Boston City Hospital had written some time ago to say that a young man had died there after a fatal accident, that his name was Timothy McGillicuddy, and that he expressed the wish that his relatives be informed. The chaplain regretted that the man died before he could repeat the address of his relatives clearly enough to write it with certainty. The deceased might have belonged to this parish, he thought.

"It was bad enough for me," Father John said in conclusion, "to forget that your real surname might be McGillicuddy, but when Thade Carey, who boasts that he knows the names and family connections of every 'sinner's soul' in the parish, assured me that there were no McGillicuddys in the sacristy records, it is too bad."

Maire was so delighted at this answer to her unuttered prayer for a way out of the dilemma into which Mike's premature request for Masses for his brother's soul had run them, that she could have thrown her arms around him in front of the priest and kissed him.

She suppressed her exuberance, however, and, after repeating her promise to retire from further activity in regard to the shipwrecked sailor's belt, she left the presbytery with an arm linked in Mike's. Mike shook it off under the contemptuous stare of the parish clerk, who had returned to the gate, ostensibly to finish the swabbing of the Ford, but actually to make this secretive pair run the gauntlet of his displeasure. Anyhow, Irish benedicts loathe any public manifestation of their bondage to one woman and Mike obeyed the unwritten law of custom.

When out of earshot of Thade, Maire chuckled and suggested that they make a day of it.

"We can now tell your people about Tim's death without telling them that we got that letter from the court in Boston. After they hear of the chaplain's letter to Father John, we need not mention the one from the court."

She was so pleased at their unexpected good fortune that she jigged a two-step ahead of him as he walked lightly along. She sang:

" 'Tis better to be lucky than rich, my dear,
    Better be single and free,
    Better be stuck in a ditch, my dear,
    With a copper to jingle and thee."

"That's a nice way of going to announce a death," Mike observed solemnly. He was, of course, more deeply affected by his brother's death than Maire, who had never seen Tim.

"If you feel as gay as you act, we'll postpone the announcement and go home till you cool off."

She was at his side at once, full of contrition, pressing herself against his shoulder and switching her voice out of the lively lilt into a warm, wifely decorum.

"Of course we'll call on Dan and tell him the sad news this very evening; he can tell Con and we'll be seeing Nora again on our way to the punt. And Mike, dear, don't be taking it so hard; what can't be cured must be endured."

In this subdued mood they arrived at Dan's, had a cup of tea and an egg from Mrs. Dan, who undertook to relay the tidings to all concerned with an alacrity which showed her gratitude at being selected to have the gruesome delight of telling and retelling the sad story of Tim's premature death. Nora's grief was relieved by the assurance that her husband's case was in Father John's hands and that the good repute of the family was secure. Conny had not yet returned from Cahirsally to dispute the delivery of the domestic contraband so that Nora was free to help in transferring it to the boat. The relief she felt when the last bag was loaded set her talking and giggling excitedly. It kept her waving her apron to the boat long after it had disappeared in the gathering dusk.

His visitors were not gone five minutes when Father John called Thade, the clerk.

"I want a lively messenger to run an errand for me. Jacky Griffin will do, if he's not at the fair with his father."

"Wouldn't I do, Father? You can't trust them young gaffers to keep their mind for one minute on the one job."

"Never fear, Thade. Jacky won't fail you, if you ask him nicely. By the way, will the lorry be bringing us any parcel from town this evening?"

"Sure you know dang well it will, Father. Didn't we order a pound of rashers from Johnnie Shea, two packets of salts from the chimist's and two bottles of altar wine from Lashlie's? Amn't I watching for the lorry this very minute? Though it might be a shade late this evening on account of how delaytory the stragglers do be leaving the pubs on a fair evening."

"I shall collect the parcels myself, Thade. You find Jacky for me and then go on to Mrs. Nolan's. Tell the poor woman I shall say Mass at the house at seven tomorrow morning without fail."

Though Thade understood that he was being sent out of the way for the evening, he could do nothing about it but grin in vexation. When he had gone, the priest sat down to the desk and wrote:

THE PRESBYTERY, MANISTIR

DEAR JOHN JOE:

You will oblige me by putting the £10 note you acquired from Mr. Pindar today into the enclosed envelope, which you will seal and hand to the bearer to return to me.

You will get the note back in due course.

I remain, my dear John Joe,

Yours sincerely,
JOHN MILES, P.P.

Jacky arrived panting from his cross-country run to the presbytery. Thade had rushed him with threats of the priest's anger, to make up the time he himself had lost ambling around by the laneway. Taking to the fields again, Jacky made a beeline for John Joe's and was back before Thade had left on the long tramp to Nolan's. Father John patted Jacky's head in payment for the service and told him he was a good boy, which Jacky probably suspected already.

When the messenger was gone, the priest, alone in his room and safe from Thade's prying for at least two hours, took out the note, crackled it, scrutinized the microscopic details of the design, noted the serial number, and then placed it carefully in the inside pocket of his soutane. It took him some time to find the key of the room and fit it in the lock. When that precaution was taken, he took his breviary off the overcrowded mantelpiece and walked slowly to the gate which cuts the avenue off from the mainroad along which the lorry was due to pass very soon. There was just light enough to read the familiar lauds, as he paced up and down the road, waiting for the drone of the heavy vehicle.

It came at last and stopped with a lurch which jostled the unsteady passengers against each other and interrupted their dissonant singing. Paddy Brown sidled out of the cab with muttered complaints against parish clerks who were too damn grand to bring their damn parcels from town in their own damn cars. He proceeded to dump the presbytery consignment on the roadside when he recognized the priest in the gloom. Tipping his cap and bobbing in every joint, he stammered:

"Beg pardon, Father, beg pardon. My peepers are failing me terrible to say I didn't know you. 'Tis foreshowing to me I must get specs, Father; 'tis so, then."

While Paddy was picking up the three packages again and dusting them with his sleeve, Father John located his man in the truck and beckoned to him to alight near him.

"Perhaps you would give me a hand with these parcels up to the presbytery, Cornelius?" he said to Shuckrue, who had climbed out of the lorry at his bidding. "Thade Carey is away and I have to do duty for him this evening."

"Sure, Father John, sure." Shuckrue replied obsequiously. He was unusually sober for a man returning from a fair. "Let me carry the three of them for you, Father; they're no load at all and I'm in no hurry home."

He ran to open the gate and followed the priest up the long avenue, a respectful yard behind, and through the hall into the room. He deposited the parcels in a corner in obedience to the pointing finger which the cleric levelled ominously after he had locked the door and withdrawn the key.

"Well, sir?" Father John imparted a judicial severity to his words which were intended to penetrate Shuckrue's habitual guard. "You have committed a hideous double crime against the law of God and the law of the land. You thought, and perhaps you foolishly still think, that you had escaped detection and eluded pursuit, but your sin of double iniquity has cried aloud and now demands retribution and chastisement of you, the wrongdoer."

Shuckrue's initial shock under the unexpected charge changed to a look of puzzlement at first and then hardened in a sullen glower to meet and resist the particular charge the priest must make if he was to justify his action.

"I don't know what you mean, Father," he growled sulkily.

"Yes," said his accuser with contempt in his voice. "You are wondering which of your many misdemeanours has come up for settlement.' Taking the banknote from his breast pocket, he showed it face forward to the staring Conny.

"This exhibit may indicate what I mean."

The mere thought that the note before his eyes could actually be the note he had disposed of so secretly only a few hours ago, seemed impossible. He would brazen it out.

"I don't know what you are trying to pin on me, Father. I never saw that note in my life," said Conny in a less pugnacious tone.

"Even if I bring Mr. Pindar of Lisarney to assist your sight?"

The priest snapped out the words like bullets and stepped towards the stunned and crumbling creature aggressively. Pindar's name crushed him. With downcast head he asked, as a whipped dog cringes and begs:

"What do you want me to do, Father?"

"I want you to place there on that desk all that remains of the ten notes you had from Mr. Pindar and to account for the rest."

From an inside pocket the broken-spirited man drew a grimy linen bag from which he extracted five £1 notes, saying, with a ludicrous logic which pricked Father John's impish humour:

"Two of them are my own, Father."

"If you can satisfy me which two, I shall consider the point."

The priest's eyes crinkled momentarily as he took possession of them and continued, "Meanwhile produce all the silver you have on you."

From his pockets Shuckrue collected 13 shillings and a fistful of coppers to make a gross disgorgement of £5 14s. 3d.

"That leaves £4 6s. 9d. to be accounted for," said the relentless prosecutor. "What did you do with it?"

"I gave—lent £3 to a friend," muttered Shuckrue.

"That friend being the Gow, of course, your accomplice?" the priest asked and, not waiting for an answer, added, "And ye drank the rest to celebrate the unsuspected robbery at sea."

Shuckrue drew a premature breath of relief, thinking the humiliating ordeal was over. He got a rude awakening.

"Strip off your coat and waistcoat," he was ordered.

This utter, bitter completion of his overthrow stung him to venture a trial of strength with his ruthless inquisitor. Buttoning his coat tighter, he crouched to withstand any attempt to coerce him physically. The young priest laughed at him and took the key out of his pocket to place it beside him on the mantelpiece.

"If you think you can take that and open the door, take it."

The manner of the challenge, its cool assurance, supported as it was by the vigour of the challenger, recalled to Shuckrue's mind the memory of Brohul's undoing, at which he was present.

Conny surrendered unconditionally. He took off both coat and waistcoat and, with an incongruous sense of decency, turned his back on the priest to pull his shirt free of the pants and take off the belt— the belt which neither had mentioned during the whole cross-examination, but of which each was keenly aware from the very outset.

While Shuckrue was resuming his garments, the priest was probing into each separate pocket of the belt and extracting its neatly folded £10 note until he had five of them.

"All present and correct," he observed as he hung the belt over his neck like a stole. "But we have not quite finished our business yet. Would you rather recover the loan you made to the Gow now and be done with it, or collect it in the morning and bring it to the Sacristy to me before you go fishing?"

"Tomorrow, Father, if you—" Conny hesitated and the priest finished the sentence,

"If I keep the disgraceful story secret. For your good wife's sake I shall make no public pronouncement about your iniquitous conduct, if you have the good sense to do all that I may require of you to redeem it. You may go now and ponder on the painful ways of the transgressor of God's commandments."

CHAPTER 11 · *Ollsen Prospects*

KNUT OLLSEN spent that Wednesday very busily, too. Feeling well and almost fit again, he left the house after breakfast to get a good look at the island upon which fate had thrown him and to seek out any chances it might offer him of repaying the good people who had picked him off the very toes of Death. Full of energy and of the Nordic urge to bend or mould his environments to his needs, he knew no better way of discharging his debt than creative work which would benefit his benefactors. He had lost his money and words were ever a poor substitute for work.

His first intention was to climb to the Lookout from which he could get a comprehensive view of the island, but the sight of the two large boats lying at their moorings in the cove drew him towards them. Those would surely present to his professional skill the very chance he sought: a cracked rib, a broken knee, or a faulty strake, anything that needed skilled attention. If they were carvel-built, and by the look of them they were, they might want a touch of a caulking iron to stop a leak.

But when he reached the slip, he could find no handy skiff to ferry him out to the heavier craft (the Macks had gone off with the two-oar punt), so that he had to look elsewhere for material to work on. The pile of timber, salvaged and thriftily stored by Mike and his predecessors, caught the carpenter's eye and set him off at once to gauge its possibilities and classify the various scantlings for future use. He ticked off in his mind the count of twelve-foot baulks, and planks of mahogany and deals, standard and whole, of Oregon and Norwegian pine. This was heavy stuff which needed a powersaw to cut it and was, for the present, of little use to him. The lighter stuff, three by two, nine by one, and four and a half by three, was plentiful, as was the miscellany of hatch covers and spars. But what could he make of them without the tools of his craft? They must wait until he got the tools.

He sat on the butt-end of a baulk to think, sticking his hand in an automatic way into his pocket for a cigarette and shrugging his shoulders when he found it empty. The gurgle of water falling on shingly gravel made no more than a background to his ranging thoughts at first, but its persistence worked the sound into them until at last it claimed his direct attention. The curious phenomenon of the Well Rock was just the sort of thing his inquiring mind had been seeking. It fascinated him. He tested the pressure of the spout on his open palm and admired the irrepressible lances of water which spurted through his fingers when he tried to block the aperture with his hand. Here was something to control, to bend to his wishes, and to turn to the benefit of his friends. He would have shouted "Eureka" if he knew Attic Greek and were addicted to the use of worn-out allusions. Being a plain man, who did not declaim memorable phrases under emotional stresses, he began scenting around for further knowledge of the issue of water from this particular rock. The rock itself, he saw, was the seaward end of the ridge that ran down from the hill to the south of the house and formed one side of the hollow in which it stood.

Ollsen saw possibilities in that. The subterranean stream, which fed the spout, probably threaded its way through a fissure in the length of the ridge and might be tapped near the house. Looking around for a large shrub from which he might cut a forked branch to serve as a divining rod, he found a sallow bush standing alone, its drooping branches seeming to emphasize its loneliness. With the rod held in outstretched hands, he zigzagged slowly along the crest of the ridge from the rock to the house, hoping that he might find in himself the not uncommon faculty of dousing and, through it, find the course of the feeder stream. The result was indefinite, because the rod remained dormant and he could not say which was at fault, his dousing or the stream's behaviour.

Joany had been watching his very strange progress along the ridge from the kitchen window, near which she had laid the table for their midday meal. Seeing him stand as if baffled like a hound at fault, she went to the front door and called him in that high-pitched long-distance hail which is heard at mealtime on the prairies and llanos and open spaces of the world. Instead of waving a hand to signal that he had heard her summons, he beckoned her to come and join him on the ridge. Dubious of the wisdom of approaching a strange man who was acting so oddly, she made great business of climbing the steep rise in the ground and kept a wary eye on him as she neared him.

"Don't be afraid, Mistress Joany," he said, when she was near enough to show the apprehension on her usually placid face. "I only want you to try this little rod for me; it is going against me."

Placing it in her hands in the approved way, he showed her how to grip it firmly and to resist any tendency it might get to twist out of control.

"Now, follow me and hold your grip," he said as he started to walk backwards so that he might keep an eye on the behaviour of the sallow rod. Joany had not stepped a dozen short paces when she exclaimed:

"Oh! Oh! Oh! Sir! I can't hold the mad thing. Look! 'Tis winding itself right out of my hands."

In her alarm at the dead branch's unnatural vitality, she flung it from her and turned to run for the safety of the house, but Ollsen restrained her and laughed a hearty laugh to reassure her.

"Don't be afraid. I told you it might twist; indeed, I wanted it to twist." He marked the spot on which she was standing when she screamed, before he retrieved the rod and placed it in her hands again. Joany soon lost her fears and joined in the "game" which was so easy to play and produced such novel results. In an hour Ollsen had marked all the points at which the rod became active and got a thrill when he observed that the marks lay in a straight line which ran direct to the

Well Rock. Then he threw his arms around the old woman and smothered her protesting clacks in his tawny beard.

"Mrs. Joany Cronin, you are the most wonderful woman in the wide world." He kissed her noisily. "You can see through stone and smell out the hidden water."

Joany wriggled out of his arms, flushed and elated by this renewal of long-lapsed experience, and dug up from the remoter depths of memory the phrases appropriate to the occasion.

"Conduct yourself, sir. Keep your hands to yourself or I'll go straight off home."

The implication that she was prepared, under conditions, to stay with him, tickled her fancy so much that she laughed in good humour at her own inconsistency and told the good man to follow her to the house if he wanted his dinner. He linked her arm to the house.

"Joany, dear," he told her in a voice muffled by the bite he was chewing, "the water refused to obey my namesake Canute, who commanded it out to sea. Let us hope it will not refuse me when I direct it into the land." To which cryptic allusion Joany responded by pouring out another cup of tea for him and for herself, and nodding her head.

After dinner Knut went up to Carrigard to discover from that commanding position what further latent possibilities the island had for his eager hands. The beehive huts at the north end he marked for closer investigation in the afternoon, while he estimated the number of households the island could maintain in modest comfort if the arable land was fenced and reclaimed. Three, at least, in addition to the existing one, he thought, but these projects required money and tools of which he had neither and which he would not ask of his friends.

Leaving the rock, he moved northwards along the cliff tops to the Cealluragh, his eyes combing everywhere for uncommon or favourable features in the terrain. He stood a long time to guess at the cause of a deep-green stain which picked out one whole cliff face from the universal red of its fellows. The discolouration seemed to issue from a level stratum of darker rock lying a man's height below the upper edge of the precipice. Copper ore, he hazarded, and a rich vein, too, if appearance counted for anything. He made a mental note of a distinctive tussock on the cliff top and when he reached it, crawled out to examine the lode. It was too far down for him to get a sample of the ore, but he did succeed in measuring the four feet of conglomerate that covered it. He would come again with Mike and bring spades and ropes.

An antiquarian would have revelled in the early Christian cells of the Cealluragh. Ten minutes were enough to satisfy Ollsen's utilitarian mind that the place and the habitations were "no damn good." The weed-covered well was the only thing worth a second look, the well and the flight of fifty steps cut broad and deep in the solid rock from low water to the plot on which the cells crouched like tortoises. The deep water and shelter would make the Cealluragh a fine alternative harbour to the cove.

Joany had tea ready when he worked his way back home along the low gravelly banks which formed the eastern boundary of the Shark, more exhausted than he would admit to her solicitous inquiry. He slipped off to bed to be free to dispose the items of his schedule of improvements in order of priority and was dead asleep when Mike and Maire got back in the dark after a day full of fruitful activity, which they were too tired to review. The house was resonant with sleep when Joany smoored the fire and padded away to bed.

CHAPTER 12 · *Mr. Mathew*

M AIRE always woke before Mike and spent the first luxurious moments of returning consciousness on her back, with her arms folded under her head, before she prodded him out of his wrapt slumber. She did her clearest thinking and made her best decisions in that delightful dawning of the spirit which lights up the dark places in the mind, and she let Mike sleep on so that she might enjoy it undisturbed by his intimacies.

On the morning after their visit to the presbytery, she lay longer than usual in thought, holding her breath at times as if listening or timing some interior experience. Soon she relaxed and her face melted into an aspect of blissful satisfaction that seemed to transform and amplify its girlish lines into a maternal maturity. Her hand sought Mike's under the blanket and clasped it warmly. She shook the sleep off him with the other.

"Thahailen, *a stor*," she whispered in his ear when she felt him slip quietly into full life, as men who are used to being roused from sleep in the open air usually do. "Thahailen, *a stor*, we'll soon be having company in this lovely bed of ours." He turned towards her, drawing her gently closer to kiss her.

"How soon, *a haisge mo chree?*" and he whispered too.

"Would Small Christmas Night suit you?" She nibbled at his ear when he chuckled at her lighthearted quirk.

"Oh! No, ma'am," he said in mock dismay. "Not Small Christmas." Slipping into Gaelic he quoted the old-time contempt for the minor feast of the Epiphany:

87

"Nodlaigh na mban,
Nodlaigh gan mhait,
Nodlaigh gan riar gan rath."

"I'm afraid it's too late to change the fixture now, me lad. You should have thought of that months ago," she said and snuggled deeper into his arms.

"Welcome be the will of God," he said in pretended extenuation of a serious lapse of foresight which entailed such disastrous consequences. "Sure, if it is a girl, we can do with another washerwoman in the house, and any time between the Christmasses is blessed."

They fell into an intimate silence in each other's arms until they heard Joany noisily reviving the kitchen fire. The mundane sound brought Maire back to earth and to immediate problems, and when Mike turned from her to swing out on the floor, she held him back.

"There are a few things we must get done while I'm able to move about, dear. That Boston letter is one and the island freehold is another, and both of them call for an attorney. That means a run to town for us."

Mike interrupted her to say that she could do the law business without him, and anyhow, he had lost too many days from the pots already. They must be full of lobsters by now, choked with them.

"Myself and Knut can ferry you in and bring you out in the evening. If you miss the lorry, you can hire Bill's Ford for the run to town."

With that suggestion she finally agreed, and they got up to join the others at breakfast.

Ollsen was eager to lay his projects for improving life on the island before its owners but Mike told him that they would have a better opportunity of discussing them on their way to the mainland. As Maire had a long day before her, he and Ollsen would prepare the two-oar boat while she was titivating herself for The City. The prospect of a visit to an inhabited place, where he might find tools and materials for the great schemes, reconciled him to this diversion from them, if it really were a diversion, and he almost ran to the cove to hasten their departure.

This was Maire's first real chance of wearing her best clothes since her wedding day. For the first time she would be a passenger with no obligation to row an oar or wade ashore, and she made the most of an occasion which might not come her way for many a long day. How lucky, she thought, as she took her finery from its tissue-paper envelopes, that she should be relieved of physical exertion on the very day that she had confided to Mike that such relief was necessary. She took her time about selecting what she should wear in view of the need for matronly camouflage. She had almost exhausted the men's patience when she did appear, stepping short in overstrained shoes and easing suede gloves dangerously on her toil-distended hands.

The simple-minded men stared at her magnificence, their patent admiration supplying the best proof they could have devised to assure her that she looked good to the eye. And she did look good, there in the stern sheets of the grimy fish-stained boat like a rose in a coal truck, her legs resplendent in rayon silk and her eyes gleaming in a face as freshly radiant as a baby's just out of the bath. The breeze plucked at her tawny tresses when they cleared the mouth of the cove to turn into the north wind. It blew the flimsy blouse into the rich curves of her breast, exciting in Mike's mind a proud glow of possession and in Ollsen's a bleak, lonely longing.

It took the Norwegian some time to accommodate his blue-water sweep to Mike's short fisherman stroke of the oar, and no one spoke until he picked up the timing and the boat settled into a steady course for the Old Quay.

"I was thinking, Mike," said Ollsen, "that you have a lot to do on the island, too much for one man, and that I could help you out if you'd let me." Mike, still full of the glad tidings Maire had whispered in his ear, thought the man in the bow was hinting at the loss she would be when nature would compel her to stay ashore.

"Oh! That'll be all right, Knut. Herself can carry on until I get one of the Black Head lads to come and give me a hand. Can't you, Maire girl?"

Blushing at her husband's innocent misunderstanding and its inept rending of the curtain which excludes strangers from marital secrets,

Maire kept her eyes fixed dead ahead, pretending not to hear. Ollsen, more embarrassed even than she by the revelation, stole one inquiring look at her figure and dropped the subject he had been so eager to open. They completed the crossing in silence and landed at the quay with great care, lest Maire's finery should touch gunwale or bollard and be defiled. The five-minute walk to the shop gave her a warning of agony to come from the tight court shoes and the inelastic brassiere which had fitted so trimly at her wedding. But the sight of the lorry waiting at the door promised relief and eased her mind.

Big Bill was, as always, burnishing tumblers busily while he gave last-minute orders across the counter to Paddy Brown, who stood leaning against it, his eyes watching a fly wriggling in the flypaper over his head. He seemed lost in a daydream as Bill rapped out the miscellaneous agenda: a lodgement in the Provincial Bank, a bolus for Murphy's blue heifer at the vet's, and a half ton of Guinness at the railway.

When the haphazard list came to an end, Paddy woke up, took the bankbook and the roll of notes off the counter without a word and slouched to the door, where he was held up by a straggle of people who had further commissions for him in town. One wanted the child's "bottle" renewed at the chemist's, another an umbrella she left in Reidy's to be reribbed; to all of which he listened in silence as he made his way to the lorry like a man in a permanent trance.

Bill beamed on Maire when she asked for a lift in the lorry to town and tendered the half-crown fee.

"Not at all, ma'am," he said. "Put that in your pocket; the pleasure is mine."

He came outside the counter, bowing and burnishing, to shepherd her to the cab of the truck and hand her over to the care of Paddy.

Maire opened her purse to make sure that she had the two documents she would need in town, while Paddy was stowing the outgoing goods in the truck and climbing into the driver's seat. His spare ascetic profile, facing straight ahead, did not invite conversation, but there were a few things she must ask him before she reached Cahirsally.

"Could you tell me the best place to get a bite to eat in town, if you please? I have never been there."

"Well, ma'am," Paddy replied without taking his eyes off the road. "There's two excuses for hotels in the hole they call Cahirsally." He dropped the corners of his mouth in his version of a smile and continued. "But what am I saying? It isn't a hotel you'll be wanting, ma'am, but a clean eating house where you'll get the run of your teeth on good sound vittles, like Maggie Mingawn's in the market lane. If you care to slip off those toe-twisters to ease your feet, don't mind me; Mrs. Bill always slipped off the shoes, going to town. When we topped the school height she used to put 'em on again. If you mention my name, Maggie will treat you decent, ma'am."

He broke his monologue to pick up a passenger by stopping the lorry, waiting with "eyes front" for one minute, driving on and saying after a glance at the side mirror, "The blasted fool couldn't make it! As I was saying, ma'am. Mrs. Hannen used to make a couple of calls to the chapel during the course of the day to ease her corns and cool her feet on the cold tiles for as long as she'd be saying a decade of the Rosary. The chapel is handy to Maggie's if your shoes start pinching you."

A detour off the main road to deliver a bag of sugar to a huckster's shop kept Paddy busy and silent until he returned to the cab. Maire addressed her second question to him before he could get under way again.

"Who do you think is the best solicitor in Cahirsally?"

"Well, ma'am," he said without casting her a glance, "that depends on the sort of business you might be having with a solicitor."

He stopped long enough for Maire to declare the nature of her affairs, but when he got no rise he resumed the stream of his discourse on the special aptitudes of the town solicitors.

"If it is a court case of assault and battery, or drunk and disorderly or a compensation case, Mr. Maurice is your man. If it is a writing case, of a will or a marriage deed or a mor'gage, or anything touching money, Mr. Mathew is the man you want. Poor Mr. Maurice has no hold of money, but he can talk you out of the gallows if you are after murdering half the parish. Mr. Mathew couldn't say boo to a goose, but your money is as safe as the bank with him. So take your choice, ma'am, and pick your fancy between them."

Changing into second gear for the school height, he looked Maire in the face for the first time and said:

"Get into your shoes now, ma'am, and I'll drop you at Maggie's in two shakes of a ram's tail," which he did while remonstrating with her for slipping a shilling into his coat pocket.

She let him drive off before she inquired where Mr. Mathew's office was and followed the direction she was given, down a side street. Like most solicitors' offices in country towns, it was shabby outside and gloomy inside, as if to emphasize the sad fact that the law of the land is a sorry affair, born of man's inhumanity to man, designed to frustrate his natural appetites, and administered by anatomies who work in an unreal world of John Does and Richard Roes, of torts, trovers, and forfeitures.

Even Maire's stout heart quailed temporarily during her passage from the light of day through a dim hallway past two desiccated clerks into Mr. Mathew's inner catacomb, where he sat at a square table behind a redoubt of paper files tied in bundles.

Following the timeworn procedure for parboiling new clients, he ignored her entrance and continued to write industriously for some time before he raised his head halfmast to look at her over the black-rimmed glasses.

"What's your trouble, young lady?" he asked throatily, clearing his gullet with a grating noise.

"I have no trouble, thanks be to God." She looked him straight in the eye as she answered. "But I have a few things I would like you to do for me, sir."

Maire's directness of speech and look woke Mr. Mathew out of the mental abstraction in which he transacted the routine scrivenry which comprised the greater part of his practice. Shifting his spectacles higher on his sparsely covered pate, and rubbing his eyes into focus with the palms of his podgy hands, he leaned across the desk towards her and took a good look at her. Apparently he liked what he saw, because he worked his fleshy features into a smile and motioned her to sit down.

"What are these things you want me to do for you?" he asked.

Maire took the Receivable Order, on which all the data regarding Mike's right and title to the Shark were recorded, out of her purse and handed it to the solicitor.

"I am Mrs. Michael McGillicuddy—Michael is my husband, and we want to buy out the island from the Land Commission. We were given to understand that we can buy it out, sir."

Mr. Mathew read the order through, laid it on the desk, and peered across the table through a comical grin.

"So ye want to buy the Shark, do ye?" he asked. He was great at asking questions. "Well ye can't buy it, and the Land Commission can't sell it."

His dogmatic statement of the law was intended to shake the overconfidence of this new client of his and to assert his absolute control of the matter in hand.

"But," he continued, making a basket of his fingers to impress her further, "if you can't buy the Shark, you can buy the skin of the Shark."

He paused dramatically to enjoy her amazement.

"I don't understand you, sir," said Maire.

"How could you, ma'am, when the pundits of the legal world don't yet see what a pup the Irish landlords sold to the leaders of the Irish-Race-at-Home-and-Abroad, when they sold the land but reserved the mineral rights for *saecula saeculorum*."

Maire sat patiently, waiting for light, while Mr. Mathew rode his hobby.

"Yes, my dear young woman, the poor misguided farmers paid their hardearned money to buy the top eight inches, the skin of the land, and let the landlords keep their grip on the carcass. When old Mike Mack, and all the other Mikes allowed Sir Brabington Grabington to retain the mineral rights, they made him a present of all the inorganic substances which God created for their use and benefit. They handed over, according to the *Oxford Dictionary*, all ores, precious stones, precious metals, coal, iron, copper, and even the quarries of which they build their houses."

Maire's innate good manners alone saved her from smiling at the notion of precious metals being found on the scraggy island. She allowed Mr. Mathew to blow off his obsession on land purchase and come back to her business when he felt relieved. When he did, she asked him if she could buy out the place for a lump sum instead of making half-yearly payments.

"Of course you can, if you have the lump sum to spare."

"And how much will it be?" she asked in her practical way.

"H'm, let me see now. Twenty times twice eighteen and ninepence will come near it. Say £40 in round figures."

"Does that cover your costs and all?" she queried.

"What a hard-headed haggler you are! Still, that's the way I like to do my business, my dear. Shall we say £50 to complete the transaction?"

"Yes, sir, if these are your usual fees."

"Now, it will be well for me to know that the money will be available when the Land Commission demand it," he said with more tact than he wasted on ordinary clients.

"That question brings me to the other matter I want you to do for us," said Maire, drawing the Boston letter from her wallet and passing it across the barricade of parchment files to the lawyer.

Before he attempted to read it, Mr. Mathew made great play with his spectacles, removing them from his head, peering through them at arm's length for smudges, and breathing upon them with mouth agape to moisten them for the voluminous handkerchief with which he proceeded to polish them. When they were secure on his squat nose, he perused the American registrar's letter thoughtfully twice before he spoke.

"Too bad about your brother-in-law, of course, but I must congratulate you and your husband on your good fortune. Am I to understand that you are granting me power to act for you in this matter, ma'am?"

"Yes, sir," said Maire.

He wrote a formal note to that effect on folio-size paper and showed Maire where to sign her name.

"That is a simple document which gives me the power of attorney to act for you in this matter and no more. Read it, please, before you sign."

When she had read it as carefully as he had read the originating letter, she signed it and handed it back to Mr. Mathew, who stood up to indicate that the consultation was ended. Then he did a thing which made the clerks in the outer office stare at Maire. He actually escorted her to the street and shook hands with her, an honour reserved for the canon and for Mrs. O'Connor, whose business ran into thousands of pounds. They did not hear his parting assurance.

"Don't bother your pretty head about that £50 redemption money. I shall look after that and we can make a general accounting when our American ship comes in. Good day, ma'am."

Maire's feet shrieked remonstrance as soon as she started to walk to Maggie's eating house and they set her wondering how far the chapel was. She wanted to go there, in any event, to thank God for everything: for Mike, for her unborn baby, for Tim's favour, and for having sent her to Mr. Mathew to handle her temporal affairs. It was not far and she treated herself to fifteen minutes of spiritual and corporal comfort before she left its soothing atmosphere and went to Maggie's for a good solid meal.

Paddy had the lorry at the door when she came out, prepared to do the shops to buy presents for the three at home. His impatience to be off was so apparent, however, that she got in at once and toed off the penitential shoes so that she might enjoy another of his monologues in comfort.

"Did you get all your business done, ma'am?" he asked her when they were clearing the outskirts of the town. "I didn't hurry you?"

"Not at all, Paddy, and I followed your advice in everything."

His austere profile registered the wry smile which indicated his conditional approval. Producing a large paper bag of mixed sweets from the pocket into which she had dropped the shilling, he placed it in her lap.

"I suppose Maggie gave you no sweet after your dinner," he said through the near corner of his mouth. "Those rainbow dewdrops will banish the taste of the strong tea she gave you."

"Thank you kindly, Paddy, and did you get all your own business done, too?" she asked, remembering Big Bill's long list of sundries and the odds and ends of messages entrusted to him by the neighbours.

"By Gor, ma'am, 'tis the way I'd be afraid of my life to face home without them. If it should prick the Divil to send rain next Sunday and I after forgetting to bring Mary Goggin her old concertina of an umbrella, her prayers at Mass would souren to curses on her. And, sure, I couldn't sleep the night thinking of Breeden Lahy crying for the cough bottle and her mother promising to plant the old cough on me to pacify the poor creature."

An untidy magpie fly-skipped across the road in front of the lorry as it complained noisily under its heavy load near the top of the school height.

" 'One for sorrow,' ma'am," said Paddy. "See would you see his partner, to knock the harm out of the one—ah, there she is, waiting for the villain in that old furze bush—'two for joy,' " he quoted in relief. The lorry had just surmounted the hill when he saw a third magpie fence-hopping across the fields and exclaimed for Maire's benefit: " 'Three for a girl,' and if you don't want a boy this time ma'am, keep your eyes closed till we get home."

"I'll take potluck, Paddy, and keep my eyes open," she said, and, be it confessed, declared her preference for an heir to the Shark rather than an heiress, by telling Paddy to watch his side of the landscape for the fourth magpie. That would augur the advent of a boy. They were so intent in their search that they were in view of Hannen's and the end of the journey before they spoke again. Together they exclaimed, " 'And four for a boy!' "

Paddy distributed the messages to the waiting recipients and laid those belonging to the lazier ones, who hadn't bothered to turn up, on the earth fence for them to collect that evening or tomorrow. No one would touch them, except to read the names and conjecture the why and the wherefor of each individual parcel.

Maire went into the shop to see if Mike were there and found Bill's daughter, Betty, in charge and as active as her father in the pursuit of cleanliness. Seeing the new Mrs. Mack for the first time in the shop, Betty got rid of the bottle of Lysol with which she had been sprinkling the floor and embraced Maire in the traditional manner of welcoming a permanent addition to a circle of old friends. To complete the ritual, Betty bustled her through the flap door into the overheated kitchen for "a nice cup of tea" to warm her for the boat. Maire accepted the kindly attentions as her due (she would have done the same for Betty on the Shark) but cut them as short as tact permitted to ask if Mike were on the premises.

"He's out in the big store with Daddy. Come and I'll show you the way, so you'll know it yourself for the future."

Maire discovered Big Bill seated on a cheeselike coil of new rope superintending Knut's hunt through a mixum-gatherum of marine stores for this and that which he handed to Mike to add to a pile near the door. Though she was eager to learn what was afoot, she was too wise to ask or to stay and find out. The prejudice against women who stick their noses in men's affairs was not lightly defied. Anyhow she would hear it all on the way home.

"I'll wait for you in the shop, Mike," was all she said, and she soared higher than before in Bill's regard. To satisfy the curiosity he knew was eating her and, perhaps, to enlist her support in a deal he had suggested to Mike without definite result, Bill called her back.

"These two men of yours are picking out everything good in the way of hammers and saws and sledges and chisels that only a mechanic would look at. I'm after showing them a thing more in their line and they won't touch it. Come and I'll show it to you, to see if you can persuade them to do what's good for them," he said as he joined her and led her down to a strongly built boathouse at the seaward end of his long range of outhouses.

"Look at her. Isn't she a beaut?" he asked her, shooting a six-inch forefinger at the largest of three boats ranged side by side on trestles. "Thirty feet of copper-fastened teak from stem to stern, built on the Clyde for the Anchor liner *Halifax*, and lost overboard in a gale last year. She'd make a darling fishing boat. Give Matty Shea a week's work on her, putting an eight-horsepower engine and a deck for'ard of the mast, and she'd lick the best boat that Salter ever sent out to Baltimore."

"I'm sure she's all you say, Mr. Hannen, but what has my husband to do with it?" she asked him.

"That's what I'm trying to tell you, ma'am. I'm ready to hand her over, lock, stock, and barrel, fully fitted with engine and nets, to your good man, Mike. All he'll have to do is to work her instead of leaving her idle on her bottom as she is," said Bill in his most beneficent voice.

"And Mike refused you?" she asked. "Did he say why?"

"When I explained how we'd work it, on a fifty-fifty share-out, me supplying the boat and oil and he supplying the men and the work, and the two of us making fair halves of the takings, he said he'd think about it."

Maire knitted her brows in thought. She imagined a catch of a thousand mackerel of which Bill would get five hundred after a fine night's sleep in a warm bed and Mike would get five hundred to share with his crew after a night's hard work in a rough sea. No wonder Mike put it on the long finger.

Before she had time to tell Bill that she would help Mike to consider the proposal, Paddy Brown stuck his head in the boathouse door to say that Father Miles was "above" at the petrol pump.

"When he heard that ye were here, ma'am," he said to Maire, "and that ye had a stranger with ye, he told me to ask ye come up to him."

Bill never forced a situation to suit his own designs. The present opportunity for enlisting Mike in his service had passed and he would wait for another, as a spider waits for a fly.

"Let you go ahead, ma'am," he said helpfully. "I'll collect Mike and your friend and bring them along at once. Father John isn't good at waiting. He has too much to do, poor man, keeping us in order, I suppose."

The priest was in great good humour, flexing his arms and pouting his chest in sheer enjoyment of himself and the world he lived in.

"Ho! Ho! Michael," he shouted to them as they came near. "Hello, Bill, what are you planning for the good of your neighbours today? And bless my soul, if it isn't Dame Maire, in technicolour!"

The wordly-wise Bill slewed off into the shop as soon as he had paid obeisance to the parish priest, leaving him free to say what he had to say to the others. He saw through the pretence at fortuity in the meeting, and he knew how to mind his own business.

"If you are going down to the Old Quay, Michael, I can give you all a lift. I'm passing that way on a sick call," the priest said before Bill was out of earshot, so that he might hear. Mike started to say that they would rather walk and spare him the trouble, but Maire cut in.

"You'd imagine, Father, that you knew the shoes were killing me," she said with a perfect semblance of guileless gratitude. "I was just thinking of taking them off and walking along the road to the boat."

They got into the Ford and Father John drove her out to the last bollard on the quay without saying a word. When they got out, he sat on the running board of the car and beckoned to Maire to sit beside him, leaving the men on the bollard.

"You must be Knut Ollsen," he said to the young Norwegian, whom he submitted to a searching glance.

"Yes, sir; I'm Knut." The answer displayed a respectful reserve.

"Would you care to describe the belt you used to wear?"

"Well, sir, there are hundreds like it all over the world," said the sailor. "Untanned kidskin, no buckle, pressure grip and six pouch pockets, three on each side. I punched K. O. on the inside but the letters wore off in use."

"That K. O. was ominous, even if they are your initials," said Father John, with a humourous glint in his eye. Stretching out his leg to ease the pocket of his voluminous soutane, he produced from its depths the soft leathern belt which he had seized from Shuckrue the night before. He held it up by one end to hang free, so that the sailor might examine it with his eyes.

"Is this it?"

Ollsen stared in amazement at the priest, who had by some magical legerdemain brought back the precious belt, the intimate repository of all his hoarded savings, which he thought were lost forever. He started from the bollard to touch it, to verify with his fingers the incredible evidence of his eyes, but Father John waved him back to his seat.

"You seem to know it, but we must guard against 'error and omissions' as good businessmen do," he said, holding his free hand palm outwards to quiet the Norwegian's evident eagerness.

"Perhaps you may have noted the serial number of the banknotes, which you claim to have secreted in this belt when you told these good people about it."

He embraced Mike and Maire in the nod he made to indicate them.

"I remember only one of them, sir—the lowest number. The rest ran without a break from that on to the last one, just as the teller in the Limehouse Bank gave them to me. It was 12SK243648."

He smiled at Maire's surprise that a rough fellow like him should be able to recall so long a string of figures with certainty.

"All I had to remember was: one dozen, two dozen, three dozen, four dozen," he pointed out with a slight trace of smug satisfaction at his own cleverness in seeing the mnemonic sequence of the figures.

"And to foresee," said the keen-witted priest, who loved to put others in their place for disciplinary purposes, "that you would be cast ashore on the Shark."

Maire, alone of his audience, saw the connection between "SK" and the word "Shark." Mike's semi-illiteracy and the seaman's unfamiliarity with printed English blunted the point of the priest's wit on them.

"How did you remember the letters SK?" Maire asked him to know if there could, by any chance, be any substance in Father John's suggestion that Ollsen was foredoomed to be cast away on their little island.

"Well," the Norwegian replied, "my old grandmother was very

fearful for me when I went to sea for the first time, and she placed me under the special care of Skuld, the kindliest of the three Fates. Skuld controls men's future and likes to be asked to use her powers mercifully. I thought of Skuld when I saw SK on the notes. That's all there is to it."

Father John stood up from the running board and gave the belt to Ollsen.

"You'll find the ten notes, all present and correct just as you left them. You should be very grateful to Providence that you fell into good hands, and I wish to impress on you that the best way in which you can show your gratitude is to refrain from all talk about your belt while you remain with us. Your friends, here, want to hear no more about it; neither do I."

Ollsen had too delicate a sense of propriety to feel for the money just then. Lowering his fair head in respect for the capable young priest, he passed the belt into Maire's hand for safekeeping.

"I shall neither talk about it nor wear it from now on, sir," he said. "It is enough for me to know that that is how you and my friends want it. But how can I ever show you how thankful I am for the trouble you have taken to get it back. I don't know much about clergymen like yourself, sir, but you may know some poor chap who needs a helping hand. Would you take one of the notes and pass it on where it will do some good?"

"Yes, Ollsen, I do know such a one, and I'm glad to get it with such good will," said Father John.

Maire fished one note out of the belt and gave Knut the pleasure of handing it to the priest, who had meanwhile recklessly swung the Ford round on the narrow width of the quay. With a noisy racing of the engine and a wave of the hand in which he held the note, he went off on the sick call, pressing the accelerator to make up for lost time. The others stepped down into the boat and rowed off to the south'ard where the afternoon light was beginning to accentuate the fishlike shape of the Shark with lengthening shades.

CHAPTER 13 · *Père Gourin*

ON the way home from the mainland, Knut did all the talking, he was so full of his plans to develop the natural resources of the island and so elated by the recovery of his money which put him in a position to carry out those plans at his own expense. Bill Hannen's proposal to equip the lifeboat for deep-sea fishing added still another proposition to those which had occurred to himself, all of which he laid before Mike and Maire with the force of his own enthusiasm.

They listened intently to it all, at least Maire did. She was refreshed by the novel experience of meeting another questing mind like her own and hearing it work. Mike seldom initiated new undertakings or new ways of doing old ones. His first remark deflated the Norwegian.

"I'm wondering how Father John came by John Joe's £10 note. I wouldn't wish it for the world that the young lad would be at the loss of his own money through me."

Maire welcomed the diversion, though she regretted the maladroitness which brought it about. She wanted time to consider all the implications of Ollsen's proposals, and, as we know, she did her best thinking at dawn.

"Never fear, Mike. Father Miles wouldn't see John Joe stuck for the whole £10, but I'm not too sure that he wouldn't like to make that cute shaver pay something for overreaching himself."

The business of landing at the slip and hauling the boat above high water kept the men engaged while Maire was getting back into her working clothes. Eating the solid meal which Joany had ready for them and catching up with the daily chores wore out the day without offering a chance for discussing Ollsen's schemes. Maire took care that they went to bed early, to make sure that there would be no premature discussion before morning.

Waking earlier than usual to the call of her subconscious mind, Maire had plenty of time to see around and through each of the sailor's projects; to arrange them in order of priority, and to deduce from a general survey of them all the one overriding requisite which was common to them all—the need for men to carry them out. She was about to shake Mike into wakefulness to tell him her conclusions when he suddenly came awake and started to listen to something which was sufficiently strange to his sleeping ear to rouse him.

"The Frenchman is dropping his anchor in the cove," he told Maire, and jumped out on the floor. "He'll be knocking us up if we don't look alive, and I wouldn't give him that satisfaction for all the crayfish in the Bay. Hurry up and call Joany. I'll run down to the slip and halt him."

By the time breakfast was ready, there was enough light outdoors to see the cove from the house and to distinguish the masts of a topsail schooner which lay well out in the deep pool near the mouth of the little harbour. In a background of creaks and rattles, main and mizzen topsails were furled and stowed by human insects which seemed too puny to handle the huge flapping sails. Jib, flying jib, and mainsail were lowered at speed to a succession of hoarse, high-pitched orders which the gusty morning wind brought, faint and fitful, into the kitchen of the house. The mizzen alone was left standing to steady the vessel while at anchor.

Knut Ollsen trotted down to the slip at Mike's heels and gave a hand in launching the punt and rowing out to the French schooner. He was eager to feel the firm smooth deck of a ship under his feet again and to run his hands along the oily round of a boom.

Close up, the schooner had the disreputable, draggletail appearance of a moulting duck which had given up preening herself. The original black of her sides was bleached to a drab motley and the red oxide of her bottom stained with blotches of green weed which waved to the motion of the water that lapped them. Only her name and port of registration had been painted recently in a vivid, villainous yellow, under her counter.

L'AURORE
SAINT-BRIEUC

A sturdy, grizzled old pirate stood at the port quarter to catch the boat's painter and peer into their faces as they scrambled aboard.

"Michael Macque! *Soyez le bienvenu,* Maicque," he exclaimed in a throaty bellow and thumped Mike's shoulder vigourously. "You are vaire velcum. Is it that you not sleep that you come of so good hour?"

It was evident that he knew Mike well and liked him. The stocky old Breton exuded good will through the thick woollen garments which enveloped him, and kept up a run of ha, ha's and bilingual ejaculations as he shepherded his visitors to the companionway. It was there Ollsen first noticed that the skipper had a peg leg; the cheery old fellow had to nurse it down the steep ladder which gave access to the stuffy cabin.

When their eyes adjusted themselves to the gloom, they sat on the lockers which served as seats around the cabin table. The Breton produced a half-full bottle of cognac and glasses which he had started to fill before his guests persuaded him to postpone the drinks until after breakfast.

"It is waiting for you in the house," said Mike. "You and the crew. Call them and we'll go ashore before Maire gets mad at us for delaying."

"Oh! *Vous avez épousé une* . . . Pardon, you are married?" asked the Frenchman chuckling and seizing the bottle again. "Ve ought drink a *vot' sante.* How you say it? *Shlainte, n'est ce pas?*"

"Too early, Captain Gourin," said Mike, using only essential words to accommodate the skipper whose English was very rudimentary, except in bargaining. "Bring bottle ashore. We can have a chaser after grub."

"*Soit!* Vaire well, Maicque. Ve go and I call *les autres.*"

His sons, Yves and René, were still aloft snugging the sails, and his nephews, Jacques and Pierre Carlaix, swabbing the deck abaft the foremast. Like the old man, these were dark, thickset fellows, swaddled in grimy blue woollens and wearing rubber seaboots. They came on the run to the skipper's call and, from the clutter of sails and chains about the bow, came a fifth young man. He was taller and fairer than the others, but like them in everything else.

"Vous resterez ici, Jean," the old man said to the fifth sailor. "Nous reviendrous tout'suite, mon vieux."

The fair-haired seaman leaned on the gunwale and smoked a cigarette as he watched them row ashore in the overcrowded boat.

"He Jean Driscole—man of Clear Island," the skipper pointed a thumb over his shoulder from his seat in the stern. "He brave fellow. Clear Island too small for him. He sail *dans L'Aurore* six, nine months."

Joany rushed out to the henhouse for more eggs when she saw the seven burly men coming up the path, while Maire pulled the table from its usual site under the kitchen window out to the middle of the floor. The Frenchmen couldn't take their eyes off her as she moved busily from hearth to table. When all were served and she was seated at the head of the table, their ardent stares became so embarrassing that she called Joany to sit beside her and share their attention.

"Well, Maicque," said Père Gourin, putting the bottle on the table. "It is not early now. Ve have a drink now, *oui*? And you say how many *ganguille* you 'ave and *langouste*, how many?"

"Six dozen crawfish," said Mike, "and eight and a half dozen lobsters. None caught more than three weeks and no cripples in the tally."

"How much you want, Maicque?"

"The market price," said Mike, "30 shillings a dozen."

"Ho! Ho!" The shrewd old Frenchman laughed paternally. "I see my cognac work against me. It give you courage to rob me. Ho! Ho! Ho! You say £1, Maicque, *n'est ce pas?*" he spread his hands and flashed his eyes in appeal to Maire.

"I place £14 in your—vat you call it—in your lap, madame, and a note of 10 shillings for yourself."

"If you put £8 on top of them, she might take it," Mike said to test the old man's grasp of mental arithmetic.

"Ah, *mon cher* Maicque; *vous vous moquez de moi*. You make mock. But we are friends; I give you *dix-huit*—£18."

"Call it the even £20, sir," said Maire, with a cleverly graded ogle in her eye. "I'm sure my husband will agree to the round number."

"Vat can a man say to a lovely woman but *oui*, yes. I will give you £20 and Maicque, you will bring your *belle ménagère* out to *L'Aurore*. She never see tank ship."

He stood up from the table and wheeled the peg leg stiffly in a circular sweep like one arm of a drawing compass. Seeing Joany's eyes fixed in wonder on the stout wooden leg, about which the tattered pants flapped loosely, he swung it face-high towards her, so that the iron ferrule passed within an inch of her nose.

"You like it, *oui? Moi*, I like it. Vaire vell. *Un coup de feu dans la jambe* and you will have a nice vood leg *aussi*."

Joany screamed like a frightened hen and ran to the back door to the loud guffaws of the rude old sea dog. That was his way of concealing his touchiness about his disability. Mike, who had grown fond of Joany, resented the rough treatment the dear old soul was being subjected to and turned a grim face towards Gourin to check him. But Maire read through the Breton's blustering and saw the raw wound on his masculine pride, which Joany's simple-minded curiosity had rubbed and hurt.

"Joany is all right, Mike," she said, touching his tensed arm to restrain him. She smiled around on the rest of the company, but addressed the captain who was simmering down.

"What is that you called me? *Belle ménagère?* If it is something nice, I shall be nice to you. You will tell me going out to the ship. We will go together; come along."

He and Mike walked beside her down the path while he gave her his concept of *la belle ménagère*.

"The woman who keep beauty after she have baby, the woman who change her man's passion to love, the woman who is *patronne*, who sail his house like a ship, she is *belle ménagère*."

Pivoting on the wooden pin before her, he tapped her lightly on the bosom.

"Maicque's vaire lucky man. He have *très belle ménagère* when his son come at Noël. *N'est ce pas, mon ami?*"

He took Mike's hand in a friendly grip as he directed his wrinkled grin from the blushing Maire to the no less embarrassed young man.

"*Allons, mes amis!* Jean Driscole think ve come nevaire."

The four young Frenchmen were gone off by themselves somewhere, nor was the Norwegian to be seen when Maire and her escort reached the ship. Ollsen had stayed behind to comfort Joany, and to let the others go ahead of him. He had the old Nordic antipathy to Latins, whom he classified as Frogs, Dagoes, and Wops, following the Lime-house terminology, and despised heartily.

Seeing the young "Froggies" hang back and whisper among themselves and then slip furtively off behind a hummock inland, he decided to watch them. He had heard that sheep were known to disappear whenever French and Spanish trawlers came to fish these waters. Perhaps the Bretons were prospecting the lie of the land for a future night raid on the island flock.

They had not come unprepared, he saw. Halfway to Carrigard, they laid snares of looped brass wire on rabbit paths as they met them, but did not stay hid in the heather to watch them. They climbed to the cairn at the Lookout and took cover while they combed the north end of the hill with their eyes for the slow-moving white spots that were grazing sheep. When they located the sheep, they stood up boldly and walked along the sky line in plain view like sight-seers. Ollsen paralleled their track northwards and lay hidden in a beehive cell when they arrived at the Cealluragh. He guessed the meaning of the excited talk and gesticulation, when the four scouts discovered the steps cut in the cliff face and saw the deep water below.

He kept them under observation as they retraced their steps to Carrigard, where they picked up the solitary rabbit which had been foolish enough to venture forth in broad daylight. Swinging it ostentatiously, they made a beeline for the slip to find Captain Gourin and his companions silently awaiting them, too full of impatience to talk. Ollsen strolled down the path to join them, and they all went back to the ship as aloof as passengers on a ferryboat.

Mike had often been aboard *L'Aurore*. A lobster ship was no novelty to him, but Maire and Ollsen were seeing one for the first time and their interest in its unusual features revived the friendly intercourse which had lapsed during the long wait on the boat slip.

At first sight the schooner's deck looked like any other deck amidships, with its wide, square hatch and narrow gangways by the gunwales. But when Père Gourin got his huskies to remove the hatch covers, the similarity vanished. Instead of a dark yawning hold, smelling of bilge water and ancient malodorous cargoes, Maire saw a tank full of clear ocean water and through it, as through a bright glass, she saw the sea bottom on which the taller seaweeds grew as beautiful as flowers in a well kept garden. The ship had no keel or bottom amidships but a metal grille which admitted the salt water but caged in the shellfish and kept them alive. The old *L'Aurore* was an aquarium under sail.

"I see no lobsters nor crawfish below," said Mike. "You'll be picking up mine when you are coming back, I suppose."

"Yes, Maicque. I go nord; I gather fish there first and I gather all fish on the way back. The *estomac* of *L'Aurore* will be full when I come back."

Mike got one of his rare inspirations.

"How long will that be, Captain?" he asked.

"Vell, Maicque. Le Bon Dieu, He know. Vone veek, two veek; *qui sait?* Why you ask?"

"I have cows here but no bull. Will you take two heifers to the mainland for me and bring them back when you return?"

"Vill you make round number of fourteen and half dozen? *La belle ménagère*, she like round number."

His love of haggling shone in the glance he threw at Maire, who had manoeuvred him into paying the £20.

"O.K. You'll get the fifteen dozen when you come back. I'll go ashore now to collect the cattle, while you bring the schooner closer inshore. We'll have to swim them out."

The islanders went off in the punt, the two men striking across the fields, after landing, to round up the two heifers. They drove them into the cowhouse, where they fitted rope slings under the forequarters and one loop over the back to take the iron hook of a pulley block. In that harness the heifers were driven down to the shore nearest to the anchorage.

Meanwhile, the Frenchmen had launched their own punt and kedged the vessel to within fifty yards of the strand to spare the beasts too long a swim. When all was set, Mike hailed Père Gourin to send two men ashore with a couple of light lines to help with the heifers.

The lines were tied to the forequarter slings, passed under the dewlap and out to the boat, where they were half-hitched to a thwart. The beasts took a lot of shouting and pushing before they were driven beyond their depth, but once their feet lost bottom they swam confidently after the boat, blowing heavily through their muzzles like grampuses.

The skipper had swung out the main gaff and tackle in readiness to grapple the slings as soon as the heifers came alongside, and stood by the gunwale with a boat hook to make the tackle fast in the loop of the sling. The first heifer was hooked and hauled aboard before she knew what to do about it, but the second had time to panic. Thrashing wildly in the water, she went under and came up, mad with fright and choking with sea water. Like an old cowhand, Père Gourin calmly dropped a running noose over her horns and made fast to a cleat after he had jerked the beast's head clear of the water. It was easy to hoist her aboard after that.

The tedious business of working *L'Aurore* out into deep water and hoisting a jib and foresail for the short run to the Old Quay gave Mike time to go ashore for his own boat. He would need her for the return home, after he had placed the heifers on a suitable mainland farm.

When the sluggish old schooner was well clear of the mouth of the cove and on the course for the quay, Maire persuaded Joany to climb the hill to watch her till she reached the mainland.

She looked more like a duck than ever, a duck with two ducklings trailing after her, as she nosed her beaklike jib to the swell in the Sound and towed the two boats in her wake.

"She's a regular Noah's Ark," said Joany in a meditative way, her eyes following the almost imperceptible progress of *L'Aurore*. "What with Frenchmen and Norwegians and Clear Islanders," she continued in careless overstatement to suit her mood, "poor Mike Mack is the stranger aboard of her. But for Mike being in her, I'd wish she never come back to this island."

"So you haven't forgiven the skipper the fright he gave you," said Maire with a laugh in her voice.

"That old rowdy. Augh! That for him and his bawdy tongue." She snapped her fingers in contempt. "He's as harmless as myself." And turning to look Maire in the eye she asked her:

"When is that Norwayman going back to where he belongs? He's as sound as a bell again and well able for his journey home. He'll be causing trouble between you and Mike soon, mark my words for it. Sure, it's against nature to have two men living on the one island with the one woman and that woman in full bloom as you are."

Maire was amazed by Joany's outburst, which had begun on a quiet, serious note but grew warmer as she spoke, and ended in an intensity of feeling quite foreign to her natural tranquillity. It was so unexpected and opened up a line of thought so new to her own limited experience of men that she did not know what to say. She held Joany's eye in silence for a full minute while she hunted through her own mind for reasons for the older woman's fears. She could find none. But, of course, Joany was older than she and so much the wiser in such matters.

She lay back against the huge bulk of the rock to explore the disquieting prospect with closed eyes. Was there any substance in it? She ran, in retrospect, through every action and every word in which she and Ollsen were connected since the rescue and could remember nothing to justify Joany's forebodings. Nor could she find anything in Mike's demeanour to show even the dawning of suspicion against the sailor.

But when her trenchant mind examined the general problem of two men, A and B, functioning naturally in the orbit of one woman, X, it recognized the dangerous possibilities. And because her mind was never satisfied with mere contemplation, it began to work out a practical solution; a rearrangement of the pieces on the board, or the withdrawal of a piece or the introduction of new pieces.

Joany would solve it by removing Ollsen. Maire shook her head to that, as a retrograde, negative treatment of the case. Ollsen had both the will and the capacity to improve life on the island. To banish him on suspicion and to lose all the benefits of his good will and craftsmanship shocked Maire's sense of justice and her instinct for progress. No, she would not entertain that solution.

What about new people for the Shark? New men? U'm, yes, Mike will have to hire a hand in the boat during her own growing incapacity, if Ollsen is to be free to carry out the plans he outlined to Mike and herself. And, of course, he could not even start the heavy manual labour they entailed without one or two hands to help him. So that, if Joany had never voiced her premonitions of trouble to come, at least three new pawns were due to come and create a new disposition of pieces on the board. With five men on the island, the chances of discord over herself would be considerably reduced. In fact, the more men there were, the less provocative her presence would be. So, the sooner they came, the better.

She had held Joany's hand in a warm clasp while she diagnosed the case the old woman had put to her. As soon as she made her decision on the best way to handle it, she squeezed the gnarled hand affectionately.

"There will be no need to drive Knut away, Joany. He has work to do here which will keep him busy and out of harm's way."

Standing up and bringing Joany to her feet by the hand which she still held, Maire took a last look at the schooner, now halfway across the Sound, and went down the hill to the house.

It was an hour short of high tide when *L'Aurore* approached the pier where Hannen's lorry was waiting in readiness for any job the skipper might have for her. That gave Mike plenty of time to scull the punt to the steps and arrange for a location for the heifers.

"That's easy to fix," said Paddy Brown, to whom Mike told what had brought him to the mainland. "We have as healthy a laddo of a bull as you'd find from here to K'llarney. Drive you maidens into the field with him and divil a fear they'll leave till you call for them."

The field and the bull belonged to Big Bill, but Paddy was so long in Bill's employment that he had become one of the family and used "I" and "We" in regard to Bill's concerns, as freely as Bill himself.

"Thanks, Paddy," said Mike who recognized Paddy's jurisdiction. "I won't leave them there a day longer than I must."

"The pleasure is mine, Mike," said Paddy, who made his own of Bill's mannerisms as of his wordly goods. "And if you have any notion of buying the lifeboat himself was showing you, why not have a shot at her. We're always ready to make a deal. If you won't go shares in her, we'll sell her to you."

Mike thanked him again and when Paddy learned that *L'Aurore* had no cargo to discharge but the cattle, he started his engine and drove off. It took the best part of the hour before high water to bring the schooner into her berth and drive the heifers across the gangplank on to the pier. Gourin selected Sean Driscoll this time to go ashore with him.

Having driven the animals into the field which lay beside the road to the shop, the strangely assorted drovers went on to Bill's for something to take the smell of the cattle out of their nostrils.

"Welcome, captain," Bill exclaimed as he deftly swung the glass-towel over his shoulder and stuck out a long arm to shake hands across the counter. They were old friends and had enjoyed many a dicker about lobsters. "I hope I see you well, sir."

Most of the big man's conversation consisted of ready-made phrases picked up from coast guards and trawlermen. He had over a hundred dozen crawfish and lobsters to sell the Frenchman—half of them caught by his own boats and the others by the small fishermen, who needed ready money and held lobsters on call in their own store boxes after selling them to Bill. The bargaining between him and the wily old Breton followed the conventional lines, which each knew well. Before it started, each could have told the other to within a shilling what the ultimate price would be, but they would rather have helped each other to throw the twelve hundred fish back into the sea than forego the profound pleasure of matching cliché with cliché, scorn with contempt, mocking laugh with provocative sneer.

While the action was being fought aloud to the accompaniment of repeated drinks in which everyone shared, except Bill who never drank in his own bar, Mike figured out that the hundred dozen should fetch £133 at the rate at which he sold his fifteen dozen. When Bill had worked Père Gourin up near that figure, the old man thumped the bar counter with a huge fist.

"All you people like round numbers. I like round numbers too. I give £130; take or leave."

Bill caught the "cease-fire" note in the Frenchman's voice and closed the bargain at £130. Taking the soiled pound note which Gourin gave him as earnest to clinch the deal, Bill lost all interest in lobsters and switched his mind to the matter of the lifeboat.

"Well, Mike Mack," he said, and he seemed to transmit a beam of selfless benefaction with his words, "I have been thinking of you ever since we had our chat about the boat. I was hoping you would have the good sense to work her with me. It will make an independent man of you. Are we going to be partners in her, Mike?"

"I'm afraid—" Before Mike could finish the sentence, Bill intervened. He preferred to leave his proposals in suspense rather than hear No.

"Don't say it, Mike. Let's leave it lie for a while. Sure there is lashings of time. We're in no hurry, are we?"

Knowing his man, Mike saw through Bill's strategy. Bill was only having a last shot at inducing him to work the boat on a share basis before beginning the business of selling her outright. So he said nothing. He knew the value of deliberate silence in business deals as well as any negotiator on Wall Street. All countrymen have that advantage over townsmen.

"Would you sell her?" he asked, after he had called for another round of drinks for his party.

"As she stands?" Bill asked in turn.

"If you like," said Mike. "But I'd be easier to deal with if you throw in with her that old second-hand Kelvin engine and a half-set of herring nets; new nets, of course. Old nets are worse than no nets."

"What'll you give me for the lot: boat and engine as they stand and the nets—brand-new from Gale's?"

"Ah, no, Bill! That trick is so old, there's moss growing on it. Let you name your price, then I'll talk to you."

"Very well—£100 for the lot, and I wouldn't lay them as cheap as that for any one in Erin's Isle but for your own four bones," said Bill.

"I'm sure you wouldn't. You got that half-train of nets from Gale's for £30, and less, if you paid for them within a month. You paid the receiver of wrecks £10 for the boat. That's £40. The Kelvin has seen the last of its days and is fit only for ballast. You'll be throwing it in for luck, Bill, free, gratis, and for nothing. But to show there's no ill feeling between us, I'll allow something for it and pay you £45 for the lot."

Ollsen, who displayed intense interest in the bargaining, was shocked by Mike's temerity in making so ridiculous a bid for articles on which his own heart was set. He feared that Bill Hannen would feel so insulted that he would drop the deal altogether. Bill's hearty laugh and the approving smile which spread over the faces of the packed circle of interested listeners eased his mind.

"I see, Mike," said Bill, simulating friendly concern for Mike's circumstances in the hope of stinging his pride into rashness, "I see you are suiting your bid to the length of your purse and not to the value of the goods. Very well, to show you how willing I am to meet you and to put you in the way to make a decent bid for things you might be wanting from strangers at some future time, I'll lay you this lot for— Here, show me your hand, friend."

Mike made no move to hold out his hand until Bill grasped it.

"Here, I'll lay them to your father's son for the miserable sum of £75. I know you don't believe your ears, but I'll say it again—£75!"

"No good, Bill; you must come again," said Mike, as cool as an archbishop talking to a mountainy curate who had boggled his answers in conference.

Bill made his next move, which the audience recognized as quite orthodox, but which Ollsen took at its face value and stampeded. Bill rose to his feet and left the company in high dudgeon.

"That's my last word—£75."

Bill's bluster was the accepted cue for the group of outsiders to seize his sleeve and hold him back, but the Norwegian jumped in prematurely.

Bill made his slip at that point. He thought Ollsen was only following convention and giving him a chance to say another "last word."

"Very well, sir. I will not be miserly with a guest of ours. You can have the lot for £60 as Mike Mack doesn't want them."

"But I do want them," said Mike unperturbed, "and I'm not giving you a penny more than £50 for them."

Pats Kelly, as the soundest man in the crowd, stepped in for the kill.

"I'll tell ye what ye'll do," he said, taking Bill and Mike by the hand and bringing the hands together. "Ye'll make two fair halves of the £10 between ye and call it £55. That's what ye'll do."

A buzz of approval came from the bystanders, who awaited the closing lines of a familiar play performed by talented actors.

"Fifty-five, clear to pocket?" Bill looked Mike in the eye as he asked his last question.

"A pound off for luck," said Mike without batting an eyelid.

"Leave the luck to Bill," said Pats Kelly. "He'll treat you decent."

"Righto," said Mike.

"She's yours," said Bill.

The crowd had swollen to fill the shop before the health of the principals in the sale of the boat had been properly drunk at the expense of the principals. They became so full of loving-kindness and so supercharged with energy to perform good works that a stray proposal to launch the boat forthwith was received with boisterous acclaim. There was a general exodus from the bar and a scramble to the boathouse. The wide double-door was thrown open, the boat itself was emptied of the flotsam and jetsam which had been stored in it, and rollers were got ready to smooth her passage down the strand to the water.

"Avast, there, ye blasted sons o' blazes!" Pats Kelly roared above the noise of competing orders. "Do ye want to burst her asunder? Clear out there to the slip till I pick six sober men out of the lot of ye. Clear out! The rest of ye stand by until she leaves the slip."

Pats selected six good men, including his own son, Johnus's nephew, and Tim Carey, to ease the boat off the trestles and haul her on her own keel down to the seaward edge of the concrete slip. From there she was handed over to the eager crowd who dragged her on the rollers to the water's edge, where reckless volunteers took over and pushed her out to deep water which reached over their belts.

Caught in the wave of activity, Bill and Paddy loaded the Kelvin engine, drive-shaft, propellers and all, on the lorry and had them ready on the quay when the lifeboat came alongside. In half an hour they were transferred to the boat, together with the tools Ollsen had chosen out of Bill's store, and the crowd of helpers were stretched in varying stages of exhaustion, wondering what dog had bitten them, at all, at all.

A fair wind, which had backed to the north during the day, saved Mike and Knut from the exhausting task of towing their purchase behind the punt. An improvised lugsail, fitted for'ard of the lifeboat's bow thwart, left them free to sit together in her stern sheets and discuss the alterations she needed to convert her into a nobby. They had them all cut and dry when they steered her to the moorings in the cove and paddled ashore in the punt to tell Maire all about her.

CHAPTER 14 · *The Launching*

THE two men were so full of their plans and so eager to set about them at once that Maire had not the heart to relegate the boat to its appointed place in the list of agenda she had decided on during her chat with Joany at Carrigard.

For ten days, from dawn to dark, they slaved and sweated. Their heaviest job was to winch the huge boat, foot by foot, above the high-water line of the beach and raise her with rough shear legs on to a building-slab of baulks. Maire and Joany were conscripted to help in that overpowering job, and, later on, in launching the transformed vessel; between those two major operations Ollsen was the chief executive and Mike the carpenter's mate.

Together they took down the engine, refitted each component after a patient overhaul, and tried her out on an improvised base block. She ran well enough but was tricky in reverse and rather noisy. Ollsen would have fitted the engine bed too far for'ard if Mike had not shown how necessary a large hold was to a mackerel boat. A thousand October mackerel took a lot of stowing, without counting the space required for a train of water-logged nets. Ollsen was firm on taking seven feet in the bow for a decked cabin and two bunks for the crew of three. Mike saw no reason for sleep, since the fishing would be done at night, but waived the point when Maire agreed with the Norwegian. She went further and recommended that a small cooking stove be installed in the cabin just abaft the stem.

With the engine aboard and the weight of the added beams and planking, the boat was almost twice as heavy as she was when they hoisted her up on the building slabs. To launch her presented a problem which worried the builders towards the end, until Mike, of all people, solved it in a very simple way.

"Let us haul the tackles of the shear legs till they are taut and then make fast. Knut and myself will shovel out a channel through the sand and let the tide flow in under her and melt away the sand she's sitting on. Two tides should make a job of it and all we'll have to do is lower her into the channel."

The *Nautical Almanac* assured them that the moon would lend a hand in launching their ship. The afternoon tide on the 29th of November, a spring tide too, would be at its top at 14 hours 37 minutes, Greenwich mean time. That would give them two clear days to excavate the channel and time after high water to float the boat and pole her out into the cove.

It worked like a clock. Maire and Joany sat high on the pile of salvaged timber, which gave a grandstand view of the miracle, while Mike and Knut stood by, with shovels ready to hasten the dissolution of the sand in the advancing tide, and to manoeuvre the baulks from under the keel. At two-fifteen the boat hung in the air, clear of the water which filled the channel, and by two-thirty she was sitting trimly on it, waiting to be pushed, stern first, out to the deep water on which she was to spend the rest of her existence.

"All aboard," Mike shouted as he took Maire in his arms and lifted her to the reinforced gunwale they had built into the boat. Knut swung Joany clear over it, she was so light, and landed her on her feet beside the engine, too breathless to protest. Two on each side, they poled the wonderful ship into the cove until she was well afloat, and the men had room to work the sweeps. By three o'clock she was back at her moorings, swinging slowly to the pull of the outgoing tide.

"I don't like her trim, Mike," Ollsen observed, viewing her with critical eye as they paddled back to the slip. "She's sitting too deep on her stern, I think."

"Yes, she has her bow a bit in the air," Mike admitted. "But wait till she has the nets aboard and has a full haul of mackerel amidships, and she'll sit the water as neat as a seagull."

"Seagull," said the Norwegian thoughtfully. "Wouldn't that make a right good name for her? *The Seagull.* What do you think, Maire?"

"Sure that's no sort of a name to call a boat belonging to a good Christian," Joany exclaimed with some heat. "If she is ever caught in bad weather, and that's sure to happen to her, or if the fish avoid her, and that could happen too, it would be little use for Mike to start praying to the seagulls to help him. The poor creatures have enough to do to help themselves."

She stopped suddenly when she became aware of her own volubility and blushed to the roots of her grey hair.

"And what would you call her, Joany dear?" Maire leaned against the old woman affectionately. "We'll let you christen her; she's as much your boat as mine or Knut's or Mike's."

"Well then, as you put it up to me, I'd find out a saint who knows something about the sea and call her after him. That's what I'd do," Joany replied with less heat but no less conviction.

"Let us make a list of them between us two," said Maire. "The men know nothing about saints or angels, God help them. I'll start with St. Peter. He was a great fisherman."

"Ah, no!" Joany rejoined quickly. "He's too big a saint for our little boateen. Anyhow, he was an Italian or a Jew or something. Why not choose an Irish saint, who would be near at hand when he'd be called? St. Brendan was a great sailor by all accounts and he comes from Tralee."

"Oh, if its neighbourly saints you're looking for, why pass over St. Finian? Sure it was Finian who built the beehive cells on the Shark, Joany. He's like one of the family."

"We'll leave it to the men to say," said Joany. " 'Tis the men will be needing the help; 'tis they should pick their choice."

Ollsen laughed and denied any acquaintance with saints of any nationality. He left the selection to Mike.

"I suppose the saint you know is better than the saint you don't know," said Mike. "But I always thought boats were 'she' and not 'hes.' Couldn't ye call e'er a woman saint to mind? One with a nice short name that's easy to spell. 'Tis I will have to paint it on her."

"There's St. Bride, St. Ita, and St. Dympna, all Irish and proud of it. But I never heard that any of them wet their feet in salt water," said Maire, voicing the woman's natural bias against another woman's claim to special attention. Joany agreed with her and said she saw no reason to pass over St. Finian, who had won his heavenly crown here on this very island.

"God bless and save us! The good, holy man may be listening to us now," she said in an awed whisper. "Maire, my girl, can you remember what was his mother's name? I used to hear the O'Sheas boast that she was one of themselves. Mór Ni Shea, they called her, but they never claimed that *she* was a saint. Perhaps St. Finian would be pleased if we called the boat after his mother."

"Divil a fear we will," Mike said abruptly. "Any Shea I ever knew, and I know a lot of them, has as much a chance of being canonized as I have. No, we'll stick to St. Finian and be done with it." And on second thought he added:

"You'll christen her yourself tomorrow, Maire, after we give her a trial run to the Old Quay. We'll bring a bottle of Jameson and a bottle of Sandeman out of Bill's for the job."

"Nobody will christen her and bless her but Father John Miles," said Maire. "It is only a fortnight now to the 12th of December, the feast of St. Finian. You'll arrange with Father John to bless the boat on her own feast at her own moorings."

CHAPTER 15 · *Sheepstealing*

TWO days later *L'Aurore* beat into the cove under the same old jib and mizzen, more sluggish than ever under the weight of her strange cargo of crawling shellfish, and anchored alongside the floating store boxes to facilitate the transfer of their contents to her own capacious womb. It does not improve lobsters to give them too much air.

"The skipper has stolen a march on us this time," Mike admitted to his wife as they strained their eyes to see if the two cows were aboard. "I was expecting to get word from him in time to have the cattle at the quay. Still, he's too sound a man to come without them."

"I hope so," said Joany with a hopeless shake of her head.

She saw no good in the coarse fellow who had made a pass at her with his wooden leg. Thoughtfulness was the last virtue she would associate with him, but she wronged Père Gourin.

"Oh, Maicque!" he called through his cupped hands towards the slip. "Oho! Oho! Is it that you sleep?" And when he saw the punt coming without the slings, he laughed loud and hoarse.

"Ha, ha! You think I come with no cow. Ho! Ho! Ho! You go back again for sling and I give you *les vaches*."

"We won't need slings, Captain. All we have to do is push the beasts overboard amidships. It won't hurt them; they're young."

The Breton's national thriftiness and care for domestic animals rejected Mike's rough-and-ready way of handling the heifers. Slipping a short length of sailcloth under their bellies, he had them hoisted over the gunwale and lowered into the water with their heads faced to-

121

wards the shore inside of ten minutes. Side by side they swam home
with their backs awash and their black muzzles held high, as sure of
themselves as if water were their natural element.

"Bravo! *mes petites vaches*," Gourin shouted after them. "You have
two jolly calf next year for Madame Maicque."

When the cows had scrambled ashore and bellowed to announce
their arrival to the beasts on the island, the men turned to the business
of transferring the lobsters and crayfish to the tank. The skipper stood
by, keeping tally with matches which he took from a full box and put
into an empty one. When all were in the tank, the count came to
fifteen dozen and three, all alive and sound of claw.

"Let me make you a present of the extra quarter dozen, Captain,"
said Mike. "You have saved me more than that by bringing the cattle
along."

"Thank you, Maicque. And may I make you happy also? See here
two bottle cognac. Take them for the great day; Madame Maicque and
you will drink *mon slainte* when your son comes, *n'est ce pas?*"

"Why not give them to herself? She's expecting us for breakfast,"
said Mike.

"Very well. *Allons!*" The old man straddled the gunwale to drop
into the island punt and beckoned to the crew to follow him, but the
elder of the two Carlaix, a swarthy fellow with a bold roving eye,
called him and said something in French. It rattled Gourin and drew
from him a gruff answer which could mean nothing but "Do you as
you damn well like."

Only Sean Driscoll followed him into the punt, the other four going to the stern of the schooner to haul on the painter of their own
boat. Ollsen watched them get into her and row out towards the Bay
at an easy stroke. The skipper ignored them and maintained a grim-
faced silence until the punt reached the boat slip.

"*Cochons!*" he muttered throatily as he stumped up the uneven
stones of the rough landing place. "They want fresh fish; they have
estomac très delicate. Agh!"

He spat noisily to relieve his disgust and strode stiff-legged into the
house ahead of Mike.

If Maire's hospitable welcome mollified him, the homely smell of hot scones and fresh butter routed the black mood which the defection of his young men had cast upon him. Producing the bottles from the folds of his woolen jersey, he presented them to Maire with an elaborate French bow.

"*Madame, je vous prie*—pardon, Madame will accept cognac. She vill guard it for the short time her child come. You will drink *une petite verre* to Père Gourin. *Moi*, I will be *chez moi*, at home at Saint-Brieuc, but I think of *la belle ménagère*."

When he sat at the table, Maire looked around for Ollsen and the Clear Island boy to show them their places, but they were gone. Mike whistled for them from the door but got no answering call.

"Everyone wants fresh fish this morning," he said, "but this nice little breakfast can't wait for them. Sit down Maire, and you, Joany. We'll go ahead and they can have the leavings when they turn up."

The Norwegian's old suspicions had been aroused by the furtive movements of the young Bretons and he decided to keep a close watch on them. Pretending to go and have a look at the heifers, he walked openly to where they had landed. But as soon as he was lost to view of the house, he took to the sandhills which ran from the cove to the Cealluragh, and wound his way at speed through the hollows between the dunes. Only once did he expose himself to view from the Bay, when he peeped through a tuft of sea holly to locate the Frenchmen's boat. As he had anticipated, it was proceeding in a wide arc northwards, which would bring it to the foot of the stairs rising up the cliff face to the beehive cells.

He was not aware, as he ran with lowered head to reach the cells ahead of the Frenchmen, that Sean Driscoll was loping along a parallel course further inland, and taking as much trouble as he to hide himself. Sean, too, had his suspicions of his shipmates and wanted to know what they were about. He knew, what the islanders did not know, that *L'Aurore* was on her last voyage home. She was old and slow for modern methods of handling crayfish, and it was only Gourin's affection for the old lady made him postpone the day on which he would strip her spars and run her hulk on a French mudbank to disintegrate.

Jacques Carlaix's misconduct, into which he had led his comrades, forced his hand. A night raid on a lonely Shannonside farm for a few scrawny chickens had humiliated the old man so much that he declared his intention to return home at once and do away with the ship.

Sean, who had not been admitted into their secrets by the others, intended to intervene if the latest foray entailed loss to Mike Mack, whose way of life was so like his own on Cape Clear Island. How he would stop it he did not know; circumstances would suggest the way.

He kept an eye on the boat as he worked his way north, wondering what was afoot. It was not long till he caught a glimpse of Ollsen's head bobbing up at intervals where the cover was light. Guessing that the sailor's mission might be similar to his own, he decided to join him. He increased his speed and edged his course towards the sandhills to bring him ahead of Ollsen so that they might meet before they left the dunes to face the rise to the cells.

The Norwegian froze like a pointer when he saw Driscoll waiting for him in a deep sandslide, with a friendly smile on his freckled face and the palms of his hands spread outwards in a gesture of peace. Ollsen neither moved nor spoke.

"Hallo!" said Sean with a friendly nod of his head.

"Hallo!" Ollsen echoed in a noncommittal monotone.

"Maybe you and me are thinking the same," Sean hazarded. "If we are, we could get together, maybe."

"What are you thinking?"

"I'm thinking those boys out in the boat are up to something. If it is more of their barefaced robbery, I want to block it if I can."

"Oh, no," said Ollsen. "We are not thinking the same. I think you are spying for them."

That unexpected charge shook Sean's sense of fair dealing. With some heat and bringing his hands down to his sides as if lowering a flag of truce, he raised his voice.

"If I was spying on you I could have signalled to the boat that you were on their track. I spotted you ten minutes ago and waited here to talk to you." He clenched his fists and advanced towards his man.

"If I am a spy, why do I show myself to you? Tell me that."

"All right! All right! No need for shouting." Ollsen, now turned friendly, held out his hand to Sean: "I believe you and I *were* thinking the same about those Froggies. Perhaps I know what they are going to do, too. Sit down and I'll tell you."

Driscoll accepted the handshake, but climbed the sandhill to get a sight of the boat before they had their conference.

"We haven't too much time, you know. Can't we do our talking while we move on?"

Ollsen agreed and told him, as they resumed their way north, of the sheep and the easy way the cliff steps afforded for taking the plunder off the island. When they reached the nearest of the beehive cells, they took cover at a point which gave a clear view of the steps and of the hillside where Mike's sheep were grazing.

"Here they come," Sean whispered in Ollsen's ear. They saw the boat back in under the steps and three of the four occupants land on the lowest one, which was just wide enough to hold them. It was clear that Jacques Carlaix was in command, for it was he who motioned to René Gourin to stay with the boat, which he tied by the painter to a tooth of rock beside the steps. He led the way up the sheer face of the cliff and gave instructions to the other two to round off a good sheep from the flock.

"Now," said Ollsen, as soon as the raiders had gone past the cluster of stone cells. "Go down to the boat alone and keep young Gourin busy till I come. He knows you and will let you get into the boat. When you do, grab him and don't let him shout. Quick and good luck to you."

Sean Driscoll was halfway down the steps before Gourin looked up from the shoe on which he was strapping his jackknife.

"Hallo, René! mon vieux! Comment ça va?" He kept on talking as he went down the steps. "Jacques m'a dit de venir ici pour t'aider à garder le bateau. Lui, il gardera les troupeaux; le bon berger garde ses moutons, n'est ce pas?" He laughed gaily at the joke.

His cheery, carefree manner quieted the youngster's doubts so that he made no objection to Sean's entry into the boat. He got a rude shock when Sean grabbed the back of his woolen scarf and pulled him backwards across the thwart on which he was sitting and proceeded to choke him. Ollsen saw how well things were going and wasted no time in joining Sean. Throwing the painter into the boat he pushed her out with a powerful thrust of his leg as he jumped in.

René was thoroughly cowed when Sean loosed the scarf and ordered him to the stern sheets, from where he fixed his eyes on the cliff top watching for the appearance of Jacques and the others.

"We better get a move on, Norway," said Sean, dropping an oar between the tholepins in the bow.

Ollsen followed suit without speaking and they soon had the broad-beamed old boat going south to the cove faster than she came out.

"We'll drop this bloodthirsty pirate into the schooner as we go in," said Ollsen. "He can cool his heels there while we take this skiff ashore and let Mike decide what to do with him."

A change in René's face drew Sean's eyes in the direction of the cells. The raiders had come into sight and halted on the cliff top. One of them bore on his shoulders what looked like a huge white cape, which he threw to his feet with a twist of his body.

"Ha! Ha!" Sean shouted. "Jacques et Cie have missed the boat. That's going to be the dearest mutton they ever ate, if they do eat it, which I greatly doubt."

"Save your breath and keep this tub moving," said the less excitable Norwegian. "If they have the guts and the brains to run to the boat slip before us, they can make things tough for us all."

But the discomfited trio made no move and the boat reached the landing-slip without incident, after putting René on board the schooner.

"We'll hide all oars and take out the spile plugs from the two boats, so that the buckos can't use them while we're away," said Ollsen. "With the youngster out of the way, we'll be three against three. I don't think the skipper knows about this robbery. We ought to be able to teach them a lesson they won't forget."

Joany met them at the door with a tart welcome.

"If you two think you are going to get breakfast at this hour after a morning's gallivanting around the place, you're greatly mistaken. I had it ready for eight men, as much as they could eat, and only two sat down to it. Now you two come in, expecting me to wet fresh tea and boil another half dozen eggs. . . ."

"But we're not looking for breakfast, Mistress Joany."

The serious tone in his voice stopped her housewifely upbraiding more effectively than an excuse or a smile could have done. She retired to the table and busied herself preparing their places for the meal.

"What's wrong, Knut," Mike asked, reading Ollsen's face.

"A lot."

The Norwegian remained by the door as if he would call Mike out of hearing of the others. Instead, he went over to Père Gourin and laid a hand on his shoulder.

"I'm afraid what I have to say will hurt you bad, Skipper."

"C'est les garçons. Qu'est ce qu'il y a?"

The old man guessed at the bad news and rose to his feet to face it. Mike got up too, but Maire stayed in her chair at the head of the table, where she remained after breakfast chatting with Gourin and Mike.

When Ollsen had finished his story, all heads were bowed in silence: the Breton's for shame that his young men had requited Mike's hospitality with open daylight robbery, the others out of sympathy for an honest old man, betrayed by his own flesh and blood.

Gourin shook himself together.

"Come. Show me where they are. I fix them."

Ollsen led the way along the beaten path to the cells, but they had not gone far when Sean's sharp ears heard the hollow sound of a boat being dragged over cobblestones. Mike started to run towards the cove but Sean called to him.

"They can't get away, Boss. We fixed the boats in a way they can't use them. Let us keep together."

When Mike's party gained the strand, they found the crew hunting around for a wooden peg of some sort to serve as a spile for their boat which they had pushed halfway into the water. Sea water, spouting into her through the plug hole, had put an end to launching her. On the floorboards lay a young ewe with its trotters tied together and its throat cut in regular butcher fashion. It was plain that Jacques Carlaix had elected to brazen out his crime, thinking that, even if his uncle were not with them, the ship's crew could oppose five men against the two islanders and defy them. He had not reckoned on Driscoll's going over to the enemy nor on René's being confined to the ship.

He and his two accomplices retreated to the off side of the boat before the determined advance of the skipper and stood sullenly awaiting a violent explosion of his anger. But the essential meanness of their misdeed had hit him too hard for words. Pointing at the dead sheep, he turned to Mike.

"How much? Vone pound? Two pound?"

"One pound ten, I suppose," said Mike.

"I pay you £3. I keep t'ree from his vage."

He bent his head scornfully towards Carlaix and ordered his son, Yves, to take the carcass to the house.

"But she's yours now," said Mike, "and you may as well eat her."

"*Non.* It would choke me." To Yves he snapped out.

"Portez ce mouton-là à la maison tout'suite," and pointing an accusing finger at Jacques Carlaix: "Cette affaire-ci n'a pas reussi, mais je m'en prends à vous. Restez ici."

He swung round after Yves, who was making a bad job of his load, and took hold of one end. Mike's party followed father and son up the path to the house to Maire. Before going in, they slung the sheep by the hind legs to a rafter in the potato house.

"Well, this is bad job, *mes amis*," said Père Gourin when all except Yves were seated at the table. Yves had obeyed a whispered "*Vamose*" from his father. "It is worse because *L'Aurore* come here no more. I come not back. But you shall not say bad vords of me when I am gone. I pay for ever'thing, the fish, the *mouton*, and the damage to *mes amis*."

Pulling a long canvas pouch from underneath his woolen guernsey he counted out twenty notes and pushed them across the table to Mike, saying "Pour les langoustes," and then three other notes, "Pour le mouton."

His actions and the money translated his French commentary better than words would have done.

Mike made no move to touch the money, but raised his eyebrows and looked a question at Maire. Understanding, she nodded in agreement and Mike pushed back the three £1 notes.

"My wife and I think that the £20 covers all." He smiled as he added, "We have the sheep, you know, ready for the pot."

Gourin stamped his sound leg on the floor and reached for the pile of notes into which he slid the three, one by one, and then shuffled the lot like a pack of cards.

"No, Maicque. You will please take what I give."

When Mike shook his head, the shrewd old fellow placed the notes beside Maire's hand on the table.

"If you find the three I give for *le mouton*, I take them. If you not find them, you take them, Madame."

Even Joany joined in the general laugh at the old man's clever trick. The laughter relieved the tension, which Mike dispelled by taking the money and asking Maire to get four glasses and the bottle which had been opened earlier that morning.

Père Gourin mellowed in the hospitable atmosphere, which should have been actively hostile to himself as well as to his unruly crew. He would not be outdone in generosity by these simple island folk.

"I have tell you, Maicque, that *L'Aurore* is finish. I sell her spars and break her up. Vell, I have pay you for the fish and the *mouton*, but I have not pay you for the damage my boys make. Vell, I give you two coil of new rope for your new boat."

Ollsen saw his chance to forward his scheme to bring water to the house. *L'Aurore's* stores might have tools and spares for the pump.

"Perhaps if we went aboard we could see other things to buy," he suggested.

"*Oui, Oui.*" The skipper glowed with good fellowship. "*Et la belle ménagère*, she come too. She find what she want, too."

They trooped down to the shore, replaced the hidden oars and plugs, and went aboard. Ollsen saw that the peculiar construction of the ship required two pumps, one for'ard of the tank and another aft.

"One pump will take her home, sir," he said. "We'll buy the other."

When Gourin made no objection, he proceeded at once to dismantle the afterpump, leaving Mike to settle the price of it. Maire set her eyes on one of the brass-hooped water barrels and on the ornate cabin lamp; Mike was interested in the French lobster pots, which were sturdier and more capacious than his own, and a ship's riding lamp which was just the thing for the new boat.

While they were prowling around, the skipper got the elder Carlaix to bring the topsail and the coils of rope amidships, and when the Macks named their selections, those were placed with them, the six lobster pots covering one side of the tank hatch. The imposing array raised qualms in Mike's thrifty mind and set him fingering the wad of notes, which Gourin had paid him, in the house. When Ollsen and Sean added the dismantled pump to the collection, Mike began to wonder how deep he would have to dip into Maire's fortune to eke out the £23 he had with him.

"Is the new boat working, Maicque?"

"Yes, she is; good enough."

"Bring her to *L'Aurore*. Ve put these things in her, eh?"

"But we have not bought them yet."

"*La belle ménagère*, she buy them. You bring the boat, Maicque. She buy them before you come back."

When Mike and the Norwegian were gone off in their punt, the old man rolled the two coils of rope into the skuppers and placed the cabin lamp carefully beside them.

"I not sell these. I give them," he said, waving them out of bounds with his hand. "The others I sell like the Hollanders sell."

Maire's face showed that she did not know how the Dutch carry on their auctions.

"I show you. I say big money, you say nothing. I say not so big money, you say nothing. I descend always till you like what I say. Then you say, *Oui*—Yes. You *savez*?"

"Yes. I *savez* now, Captain. Go ahead." She smiled into his face and said, "But I won't know when to say 'Yes.' "

He held up his hand and started to speak at high speed.

"*Maintenant*, ve commence. Vone hundred—no, that too big money. Ve commence again. Thirty, twenty-nine, twenty-eight, twenty-seven, twenty-six, twenty-three, twenty-vone, twenty-twenty, ninetin', eightin', seventin', fiftin', thirtin', tvelve, eleven, ten. You like say *ten*, Madame? Yes?"

"Yes! Yes! Yes!"

The Dutch auction was over and the goods sold for £10.

A gusty noisy *rat-a-tat-tat* came from the new boat as she slipped her moorings and gathered way in a wide circle which brought her close alongside the schooner. They kept the engine running while the purchased articles were being transferred by Mike and the skipper, who would not allow the crew to lay a hand on them. Ollsen and Sean stowed them in the boat.

"What did you and Maire agree on?" Mike asked the old man when the transfer was completed.

"She tell you, Maicque."

"I am ashamed to tell you," said Maire and Mike's heart skipped a beat. "The good man is giving them to us at half the value."

Mike's heart picked up the dropped beat when he found how unfounded his fears had been. He counted out ten notes from the roll and tendered them to the smiling Breton.

"*Gura mile maith agat, a duine chroi*. Thank you, Captain. We're sorry you are leaving us and we wish you a safe voyage home."

"We do indeed, sir," said Maire. "And we hope you will forgive your boys as we do. You were young like us once. Let ye all come to the house and forget it in a good dinner." She threw him a whimsical glance from the corner of her eye and dropped her voice to say, "We have lovely mutton for dinner, sir."

"Madame is always *la belle ménagère*. I am happy that you and Maicque forgive *les vauriens. Ainsi termine l'affaire*."

He kissed Maire's hand as he helped her into the boat and made Mike blush by embracing him and rubbing cheeks as women do.

"*Pardon, Monsieur le Capitaine*." It was Sean's voice coming from the stern of the boat. "*Je resterai ici. Vous n'aurez pas besoin de moi sur la navire*. I'm staying in Ireland where I belong."

"*Mais mon garçon*—Vaire vell. You leave ship, you leave pay."
French frugality was asserting itself. "You vere good man, Jean. Adieu."

He waved his hand to the boat as she bustled noisily off to the
shore and then swung his peg leg round to shout orders which set the
crew running to make sail. Soon the old ship was clear of the cove,
and before the winter light failed she was lazing along to the southward,
well off the Fang.

CHAPTER 16 · *Heart Tremors*

ALTHOUGH Sean Driscoll was a welcome addition to those on the Shark, he raised the housing problem for the Macks. If the five of them had been members of one family, it would have been easier to accommodate them. As it was, Sean had to share Knut's bed.

Maire was glad that the problem had arisen, because it afforded a sound reason for furthering the long-range strategy she had decided on to counter the dangerous possibilities to which Joany had referred in their chat at Carrigard. Her scheme comprised the building of a second house on the island and the bringing of other young people to help Mike at sea and Ollsen on land.

"Did you ever build a house, Knut?" she asked.

The Norwegian halted the sweep of the jackplane along the base of the stillion which he was making for the newly acquired water barrel, and looked at Maire. She was polishing the brass hoops till they glistened.

"No one man ever built a house. But I have helped to build many houses in many places."

"Could you build one here on the island?"

"Yes, if I had the material. That would be hard to get and harder still to bring here."

"It must have been harder still for Mike's grandfather when he built this house."

"I was not thinking of a mud-wall house, Maire. I was thinking of the beautiful timber houses of Norway and Canada."

133

"Oh, we must forget beautiful timber houses for this bare, rocky old island. We must do with what we can get here. This houseen isn't too bad, is it Knut?"

"We'll see what we can do." He chuckled as he turned back to the stillion. "When do we want the new house? Tomorrow?"

"Or sooner, if you want to get Sean's cold knees out of your back."

"If you had the Cohul Driochta, you could wish a new house into being," said Joany, who always managed to find some job to keep her near Maire whenever Ollsen was about the house. "But as you haven't, you'll have to build it in the sweat of your brow, like the Gobban Saor."

The Norwegian ignored the tartness which Joany reserved for him alone; he attributed it to the distrust which natives always feel for foreigners.

"What is this Cohul Driochta?" he asked with a friendly inflection in his deep voice. "And where can I get it?"

"No fear you'll ever handle it. The Colg Fola is more in the line of a Sasanach, or a Norwayman, than the Cohul."

The acidity was becoming so marked that Maire intervened.

"Don't mind Joany, Knut. She got out at the wrong side of bed this morning. The Cohul was Aoife's magical wand, made of a branch of rowan. The fairy queen could cover this island with beautiful castles with one wave of her wand and wipe them out with another. The only mortal man that ever came near her in building castles was the Gobban Saor. He could roof a castle without using any timber rafters. They say St. Finian learned a bit of that trade from an old Pagan mason before he died. The cells at the Cealluragh are roofed that way."

"As you are so good at explaining what every Christian should know for himself," said Joany, "why don't you tell him about the Colg Fola?"

"Because it has nothing to do with building houses, Joany," Maire replied as casually as a teacher setting a child right.

"No, but because it had more to do with knocking them down," said Joany, who refused to be placated. "And as you won't tell him,

I will. The Colg Fola was the Bloody Sword, the Sword of Destruction which the Sasanachs, and the Norwaymen before them, fed with blood."

Ollsen winked at Maire and straightened his back. Flight was the only answer to a woman who was at cross-purposes with herself.

"Where would you like me to place this stillion before I go out looking for a rowan tree, ladies?" he asked, and getting no answer he left it in the middle of the floor and went out. Climbing on the long low ridge along which he and Joany had tracked the subterranean water, he sat and viewed the dwelling with a professional eye. It was about forty feet long, eighteen wide, and not more than eight foot high to the wall plate under a low-pitched roof, thatched with reed, through which the chimney barely emerged. The doorway and window opes showed how thick the walls were—two feet or so. The door itself and the windows were low, deep-set, and narrow. Not a stone to be seen but the wide flag at the threshold and the cobbled causeway which ran from the threshold under the windows to each gable. It was a retiring unpretentious thing, but it looked snug and warm and lasting and very much at home in its rounded hollow.

Everything in it was got on the island, except the glass of the windows. Driftwood made the rafters and doors and the dowels which knit them together. The original Mack had risen above his shortcomings.

"Maire shall have another like it and I will build it for her," he mused. "But I have to discover how the walls were stiffened. Earth is a crumbly thing."

Maire appeared in the doorway and called to him.

"I see you have put on the Considering Cap. That's what the Gobban Saor did when Aoife refused him the Cohul."

"Good old Gobban," Ollsen shouted back. "I bet he had some good Norsk blood in him, too. Wait for me," he called, as he stood up and scrambled down the slope towards her. "I want you to show me where you are thinking to build the house."

"Oh, anywhere near the cells you choose."

"As far away as that?" he asked in surprise.

"Certainly," she replied. "Didn't you ever hear what St. Patrick said to St. Shaughlin? No, of course not. They were never in Norway. Shaughlin was St. Patrick's favourite disciple, and when he asked where he would build his new church the wise old saint advised him well. 'Build it,' says he, 'near enough for our love for each other, and far enough for our respect for each other!' "

"The old boy had something there," said Ollsen. "Let's go and see the place you have in your mind."

Maire slipped the knot of her kitchen apron and balled it up to throw in the open door, but thought better of it and tied it on again. She needed it for camouflage.

"Joany, dry your hands and come along till we show Knut where to put the new house. 'Tis we will have to keep it after he has built it. So, who has a better right to say where we'll have it?"

She knew that the old woman would be hotfoot after them as soon as they set out from the house, in any event. The invitation might deceive the Norwegian and ease the situation. In consideration for Maire's condition, Joany took the lead and kept the pace down to a crawl with many stops for this and that.

"Anywhere hereabouts will do," said Maire when they reached the circle of weather-worn cells at last. She sat down on the hip of one of them and, with a comprehensive sweep of her hand which took in the Bay and the receding ring of mountains that encompassed it, she drew Ollsen's attention to the magnificence of the prospect.

"The saints were very fond of God's creation. They never built their monasteries in holes or corners, but on hilltops and clifftops from which they could see the wonderful works of the Lord."

"Yes," rejoined Joany, whose mind was still soured by her suspicion of the sailor, "the poor holy men lived in peace and plenty until the plundering Danes came out of Norway with the Colg Fola and reddened it in their blessed blood."

"But, Joany dear, that happened thousands of years ago, when every man—the Cronins, the Macks, and the Horgans as well as the Danes and the Sasanachs—went round like roaring lions seeking whom they might devour. Sure, you know those are the very words of the *Catechism*."

Ollsen's imperturbable calm took the sting out of Joany's petulant nagging. He went and sat beside her on a tussock of heather.

"You are too nice, Mistress Joany, to be going around with a gang of corpses that should be put back in their graves. . . ."

"Me? A gang of corpses? What do you mean, man alive?"

"Not with their bones, Joany. I don't mean that. But you are dragging their minds around with you. Their dead memories should be buried with their dead bodies. Forget them. Tomorrow has no memories to vex us and no corpses. It is for tomorrow Maire is building her house. Trying to bring back yesterday is like an old man who had his day but wants to carry on among young men. Forget the yesterdays and let them rest in peace."

He brought his arm around her old shoulders, as a son would comfort his mother, and when he finished he tipped her face and gave her a kiss straight on the mouth.

"How dare you, sir!" she exclaimed, but it was clear from the gleam in her eye that she was mollified. She stood up, patting dry sprigs of withered heather from her skirt.

"What's keeping us here, Maire girl? Knut knows where you want the house. He can stay here and look around. We have our jobs calling us."

"I'll come back with you," said Ollsen. "Mike will like to look over the site with me after dinner."

"Tell me, Knut," said Maire on the way home, "how did you get to know English the way you do and you a Norwegian?"

"Oh! Everywhere. Ashore and afloat. Don't you know that English is taught in Norwegian schools? We find English very useful when we go to sea. All my schoolmates are at sea."

Joany was making more speed back than she made on the way out and fewer stops for breath downhill. Perhaps her mind was easier about the stranger after his filial kiss. Maire smiled to herself and wondered at the simplicity of her companion, who seemed not to see what Joany's worry was.

"Perhaps you will tell me," said Ollsen, directing a disarming blue eye into her grey ones, "how you come to know English so much better than Mike and Bill Hannen and the rest?"

"I don't know that I do. But if I do, it must be from my mother I brought it. We had but four books at home and my mother had them by heart. The *Catechism*, the *Sacred Heart Prayer Book*, *Moore's Almanac*, and the *Story of Ireland*. I have them still and can say them blindfold from cover to cover. Try me any time you like."

"And is your mother a good singer? I have heard no singing on the island since I came."

"No. Mother cannot sing; neither can I, though we love to listen. It was Mike's singing voice that first told me what a true heart he has—kind and generous, too. His mother sang like a bird, I hear."

"So did mine."

"And yourself?"

"So, so. I have been told that my voice is true," he laughed. "But no one has told me that it reveals a true heart."

"Let me hear it now and I'll tell you."

"A song of Norway?"

"Yes. I can judge the heart better when the words don't interfere."

"Very well. Here's our national anthem." He craned his neck to see if Joany had gone out of earshot. Her unburied dead would shriek at the sound of a Norsk song after all these centuries.

> "Ja, vi elsker dette landet
> Som det stiger frem
> Furet värbitt over vannet
> Med de tusen hjem.
> Elsker, elsker det og tenker
> Pa var far og mor
> Og den saganatt som senker
> Dromme pa var jord."

He had begun diffidently but the vision of the distant homeland, knit into the words of the anthem, recalled old memories of youthful gatherings at which it was sung loud and high. His voice swelled and his eyes grew bright with feeling. For one short moment he forgot

Maire and the Shark and let his vibrant baritone resound at its fullest power. The end of the song brought its anticlimax of silence as songs do. He turned to Maire.

"Well, have you read my heart?"

"How do you say 'Thank you' in your language?" she parried.

"*Mange takk skal De ha.*"

"*Mange takk skal De ha,* Knut," she repeated. "I would love to hear it in English. It moved you deeply."

"Your wish is a command, Madame." The stilted phrase, though spoken airily, showed that he was still elated beyond his wont. "It sings well in English too. Listen.

> "Yes, we love with fond devotion
> This, the land that looms
> Rugged, storm-scarred, o'er the ocean
> With her thousand homes.
> Love her, in our love recalling
> Those who gave us birth
> And old tales which night, in falling,
> Brings as dreams to earth."

"*Fad saol!*" said Maire. "*Is go dtuga Dia slan abhaile thu.*" It would never do to forget the Gaelic on an Irish island which has often heard both Norse and English raised in anger. "*Go dteir slan!*"

She kept on talking to still a dawning disquiet which Ollsen's singing had raised within her, and quickened her pace. She wanted to leave his disturbing proximity at once and gain the safety which a third person would afford her. Joany above all. Joany's fears were not as baseless as she had thought. The vigour and virility of this man from outside vibrated through his song and woke within her an answering chord which warned her to build up her defences. A diversion was urgently needed.

"How long would it take to build the house?" she asked.

He chortled at the artless simplicity of the question which has been curtailing the night's sleep of architects and builders since man ceased dwelling in caves.

"With plenty men and material on the site and good weather, it could be done in a fortnight. Here, without men or material or any hope of good weather, it might take six months."

That startled her and jumbled her neat arrangement of work in order of priority. The need for a second house was still the most urgent of all her needs, if only to restore the precious privacy of her home. To remove the menace to her peace of mind which Knut Ollsen's presence in her home provoked, made it more urgent than ever. But the very building of the house would aggravate that menace, if it should take six months. He would be around and about at all times, opposing his quietly forceful personality to Mike's easy-going serenity. She dare not risk dear old Thahailen's happiness, nor her own, for a house, which, after all, was only part of a scheme to improve life for him and herself on the Shark. The house must be relegated to the bottom of her list or dropped altogether.

"And how long would it take to bring the water into the house, our house, I mean?"

The abrupt switching from anthems to houses and from houses to pump-sinking deranged Ollsen's methodical process of thought. Shaking his square head like a yearling colt which resents a tug on its rein when in full career, he snorted.

"Agh! How should I know? One day, two days, a week. Who knows how deep the water runs?"

This first manifestation of impatience, of dislike for control, confirmed Maire in her new decision to reconsider her plans. Fortunately they had reached home, where Joany's voice was keeping up a lively chit-chat in a rattle of pots and pans. When they came in, Mike was shaving laboriously and emitting wry-mouthed "U'ms" and "Ahs" in pretence of following Joany's inconsequent chatter.

"Come over here, Knut, and lather your puss while the water is hot. I'll strop the old razor again for you when I'm done skinning myself with it. Maire girl, we have to run in to Bill's in the new boat. He sent out word by Johnus that there's a couple of urgent letters in the post for me. I met Johnus trying his pots out north in the Sound."

He spoke between the short finishing touches of shaving.

The dinner was a sketchy affair, which Joany prepared as soon as

Mike returned with the news, tea and fresh whiting Sean had caught on a line trailed after the punt as he went from pot to pot.

"You had better arrange with Father Miles about blessing the boat, as you are going in," said Maire. "I have a list of things you'll get in the shop for the great day. Give it to Betty and she'll pack them for you. Ask Thade what the priest will be needing besides what he brings himself."

"Easy, easy, woman. How do you think a poor divil of a man can think of all those fal-lals. Come with us yourself and see after them."

"And why not?" said Joany. "Knut and Sean have jobs to do at home."

She countered every argument with a better until she had her way and saw Maire safely aboard with Mike.

CHAPTER 17 · *An Orphan*

THE run across the Sound in twenty minutes without the stress of rowing was a great treat to Maire, who had so often laboured like a galley slave for an hour for the same passage. The walk from the Old Quay to the shop was a pleasure, she felt so fresh, but the two-mile trudge to the presbytery was out of the question.

"Certainly, ma'am," Bill assured her when she asked if the car were free to take her there and back. "Paddy will run you up in no time, and, as for the charge, the pleasure is mine."

Going into the end of the shop which served as the post office, he called Mike and handed him the two letters of which Johnus had told him.

"I'd have given them to Johnus for you, if I hadn't a sort of notion that they might be important and the old fellow might drop them overboard and he wrastling with the pots. Mr. Mathew's name is printed on the back of one of them and the Land Commission on the other. Sit here near the light of the window and you can read away at your ease."

Mike by-passed Bill's invitation to discuss the purport of the letters and gave them unopened to Maire, who was in conference with Betty on the list of requirements for the priest's visit to the island.

"Ye'll be having Mass in the house, too, of course," he heard Betty say, "and ye'll be wanting the altar things. I can lend you them. Let me see: a large crucifix, two brass candlesticks, two vases for the flowers —I have some lovely escallonias in full bloom—and a large white-linen tablecloth to cover the altar. That'll be all. Of course, you'd rather buy the wax candles and have them in the house; you'll always be needing blessed candles. I'll pack a half dozen 6½ per cent candles along with your own order and pack the things I'm lending you in a box by themselves. Thade Carey can bring them back when they are returning from the island. I'll have everything nicely boxed by the time you are back from the presbytery."

"Thanks, Betty, and we'll take good care of them. But you need not lend me the tablecloth nor the crucifix. I have those already." Then Maire lowered her voice: "Could you tell me, Betty, *a chroi*, if Father Miles has good warm shirts for the winter?"

"I think he has, Maire. Deb Sweeny, Brohul's sister, made him a grand pair last week and the poor man needed them badly. Mary Conway keeps him in socks, but I would say that his bed could do with a heavy quilt."

"Pity I didn't know that before I left home. I could have brought him the spare one we have and leave it on his bed this evening."

"Take one of mine, Maire, and I'll take yours."

Paddy pushed in the shop door and walked to the middle of the floor where he stood and looked up at the ceiling.

"Beg pardon, ladies, but anytime you're ready now, Mrs. Mack."

"One minute, Paddy, till I run upstairs for a parcel of Mrs. Mack's," said Betty.

Betty was not much more than a minute parcelling the quilt and handing it with a conspiratorial smile to Maire, but Mike and Paddy had time enough for the small quick one which Bill served with the speed and skill of a conjurer. Mike joined a group of blue-guernsied fishermen, who shouldered their way in as Maire followed Paddy out to the baby Ford. These were mackerel men and their talk was Mike's talk, the rich racy Gaelic which fitted their thoughts as easy as the clothes they wore. He stayed with them.

Paddy maintained complete silence during the short run to the presbytery gate, but broke it, as he drove through, to inform Maire that the parish priest was at home.

"I see Thade, the clerk, in his shirtsleeves in the back kitchen, wetting

the tea for the dinner. The pair of them are poisoned with tea. Will
I wait or will I come back, ma'am?"

"Better wait, Paddy. Five minutes will do what I have to do."

She entered the huge empty hall quietly and stood at the foot of
the stairs, listening. Hearing no sound of movement, she tiptoed upstairs and found the bedroom, the only room but the oratory which
was not absolutely bare, and spread the quilt on the narrow bed. She
reached the hall again just as Thade had finished his fruitless questioning of Paddy.

He frowned on Maire. She had proved herself already to be an un-
confiding doxy, a touch-me-not from outside the parish. Without opening the door, he shouted through it.

"That one from Shark Island is here again, Father. Will I tell her
wait till we have our dinner?"

Father John came to meet her and led her to the solitary chair.

Now, why didn't I think of getting him a second chair instead of the
quilt? she asked herself. But, sure, I can get the chair too.

"Well, ma'am. Have you settled down to a quiet life with us yet?"

As either Yes or No would be too equivocal an answer to his question, Maire contented herself with a smile.

"Is the Norwegian still with you?"

"He is, Father, and he is, in a way, the cause of this visit. He and
Mike have built a fishing boat and we would be glad if you would bless
her before she goes fishing, this week or next."

Father John consulted his notebook and found Tuesday, 10th December, free.

"Could you make it the 14th, Father? That's St. Finian's day and
we are thinking of calling the boat after him."

"Yes, I can bring forward the Mass fixed for that day and give St.
Finian his own. Let us pray for a fair wind and I shall be with you at
seven o'clock in the morning. I'm assuming that I shall say Mass on
the island that day, of course."

"Thank you, Father. Mike will have the new boat at the Old Quay
at six, rain or shine. She has a cabin to cover you if it rains."

Mrs. Cotter, the district nurse, was waiting in the hall when they left the room and the priest introduced the two women to each other. The older woman's professional interest prompted her to ask Maire if there was any other woman on the island with her, and when she heard that Joany was there she warmed up at once.

"Perhaps, Father, the island is the very place for Mai Hogan. What do you think?"

The priest put his elbow on the newel post of the bannister against which he leaned, chin on palm, considering the nurse's question. Nurse Cotter, tall, gaunt, and wiry, waited for his answer as eager for action as a setter at point waiting for his master's word to go. Her very clothes looked ready for action, the dark blue tam drawn tight over her crisp iron-grey hair, and the neutral grey coat and skirt closely buttoned and belted to her spare figure.

"Perhaps the island would be the right place for the poor girl, Nurse. But—" and his eye ran from the nurse's expectant face to Maire's perplexed one and back, "Mrs. Mack has the last word in deciding that and Mrs. Mack, I'm afraid, doesn't know what you and I are talking about. Tell her what it's all about."

"Your dinner is stone-cold again, Father, and I haven't e'er another egg in the house." Thade Carey shouted his plaint from the kitchen end of the passage and banged the door to express his opinion of loitering lady visitors.

"If that awful man would only let me into the kitchen," said Mrs. Cotter, "I could . . ."

"Now, now, Nurse. Thade has his own troubles and I am not the least of them. I'll tell you what you'll do. Go in the car with Mrs. Mack around by Mai's place and let her see for herself. I'll stay and take Thade's bicocted egg and his special black brew."

Though Maire jibbed at being disposed of like a piece of portable property in this manner, her interest in the unknown Mai Hogan was quickened to make her fall in with Father John's suggestion.

Paddy nodded assent to the nurse's query if he knew where Mai lived and made way for Maire beside him in the front seat. But Mrs. Cotter led her into the back of the car and started to talk in a tense whisper.

"Mai Hogan will soon be presenting a serious problem to me and the parish priest. Her grandmother is dying, and when she goes, Mai will be alone in the world. That's nothing new, you'll say. I was left an orphan myself and am none the worse for it. But Mai Hogan's is a peculiar case. She's a Yank. She's nineteen and she's a good-looker, like her mother before her. The mother must be a sweet doxy. Ten years ago she sent Mai home to her grandmother with a label round her neck like a prize puppy, and a trunkful of clothes, and a letter in the trunk containing £100 and her birth certificate. The father's name was given as Thomas Hogan, Gentleman. A nice gentleman, that never showed up, either before or since."

Her pause was heavy with innuendo.

"Mrs. Lee is the grandmother. A great old battler. She took in the child as she would have taken in a princess. The expensive clothes, the abundance of money, and the beauty of the child made her do that, perhaps. Perhaps, too, the child's American way of talking helped, for Mrs. Lee can talk nothing but Gaelic. Anyhow, the old woman became her willing slave. Wouldn't let her wet a finger. Dolled her up in the posh clothes the mother sent from America and put by every penny that came with them, year by year, until the supply stopped suddenly last year. The mother died, I suppose. Anyway, the grandmother is pegging out and the young girl will be left more helpless than a canary you'd let out of a cage."

The motorcar stopped near a wicket gate that hung loosely open on a grass-grown pathway, which led to the closed door of an ill kept farmhouse. The nurse ignored the wicket and took to the rough cart road which went to the backyard and the backdoor, where a Kerry cow and calf were bellowing their hunger to inattentive ears. A disconsolate pony stood silent and apart, woebegone in every bone. Closed doors, like drawn blinds in a dead-house, proclaimed the presence of the Reaper as clearly as if a wreath of black crepe were tacked to the wooden wicket.

The matter-of-fact Mrs. Cotter lifted the latch and walked straight into the kitchen, followed by the no less self-possessed Maire, and headed for the canopy fireplace. Close beside it the settle bed sprawled wide across the hearth, its feather tick bulging under the weight of the occupant. Mrs. Lee looked ghastly, staring upwards as if waiting for a call. Her hard horse-face, soon to take on the aloof dignity of death, but still repellent with ebbing life, was the only part of her that showed in the huddle of bedclothes. She made no sign that she was aware of the newcomers or of the girl seated in the shadow at the far side of the kitchen.

"This is Mai," said the nurse to Maire. "Stay with her while I see how the patient is getting on."

"*An tu san, a vanarla?*" Only the lips moved as the sick woman asked who was there.

"*Sme cheana.*"

"*Scriobh m'uacht dom.*"

Mrs. Cotter thought for a moment and then asked the young girl to get a writing pad, or copybook, if there were one in the house.

"Your Granny wants me to make her will. Do you mind if I do?"

"She has been asking me to make it, but I don't know how."

Maire had a good look at Mai Hogan while the nurse was writing the will on her knee beside the settle bed. Despite the drawn weariness of her face, the girl seemed strangely alive and colourful in such drab surroundings. Her large dark eyes shone as clear as Maire's grey ones, but without their steadiness. Her hair, eyebrows, and eyelashes, lush and black as a Spaniard's, gleamed where the light from the murky window touched them. Her well rounded features were rich with the bloom of youth. Her hands and her expensive clothes bore out the nurse's foreword about her secluded upbringing. The palms of the hands were as soft as a baby's; not calloused by housework like Maire's and the nurse's, nor by farm work like those of the young girls of Manistir. The clothes were of expensive cut and chosen to match the girl's rich colour, but they put her as far apart from her setting as Broadway is from Manistir.

"You must be worn out, poor dear," Maire said to cover her own quiet scrutiny as much as to comfort a lonely girl.

"It is terrible." The very relief of speech broke down the rigour of hours of watching and waiting. The girl threw her head on her arms and sobbed her heart out among the teacups which stood unwashed on the rough deal table.

Maire let her cry to a finish and the nurse, after one quick glance, continued to write uncomfortably. The dying woman stared upwards without a move. At last the writing was done and Mrs. Cotter touched the old woman's shoulder.

"*Eist leis seo,*" she said to attract her attention.

"*Leig e.*"

The order to read the will was quite clear, though the blue lips barely moved. It was a simple affair, couched in straightforward Gaelic, leaving everything, land, stock, and money, to the granddaughter. When the reading ended, the nurse asked in Gaelic:

"Is that what you wanted?"

"Put my hand to the pen."

The nurse groped and brought a stiff bony hand out from under the clothes, placed the penhandle between the fingers and drew a cross at the foot of the page. After writing "Mor Ni Laoi" beside the cross, she signed her own name as witness and got Maire to sign it, too.

The old woman spoke again.

"Mai's money . . . Bill Hannen has it in the bank."

For the first time her eyes closed and her cheeks sagged. The nurse's diagnosing gaze noted the change and estimated the time left for making immediate arrangements for death. Maire must be got away at once. Proximate birth and proximate death are unnatural associates; synchrony would be revolting.

"I will go for help, Mai. You'll come with me, Mrs. Mack."

She bustled Maire out to the waiting car and gave her the will.

"Give that to Father Miles, if you please. I must stay and do the needful for this grand old woman. Good-bye, dear, and think out what can be done for that poor, defenceless girl."

The priest was waiting in his room and listened in silence to Maire's account of what happened at Mrs. Lee's. He waited, after she had finished, like one seeking for the answer to a question which had been asked already. Maire read his look.

"The island would be just the place for that friendless, helpless girl,

Father. I see what you and the nurse fear for her: that all the wild, unprincipled young blackguards in the three parishes will dog her night and day, till one of them gets her and her money to ruin and squander. A year on the island would teach her how to protect herself as well as train her how to work. But there is one big snag, Father."

"What snag that can't be removed?"

"It will sound mean to your ears, perhaps, Father, but it is there all the same. Mike and I had enough food in stock for us and Mrs. Cronin, but we have two more mouths eating into it, since Ollsen and Sean Driscoll joined us. The island is far out and—"

"That snag is easily removed. Have you any other in mind?"

"None, Father. If we had potatoes and bacon for the extra months, I would take the child home with me today."

"In fact, ma'am, you welcome the lucky chance which sends Mai Hogan to solve a problem of your own." He smiled knowingly down at her and continued. "It doesn't require much experience in a confessional to foresee the difficulties which the presence of three young men, however decent and well bred, create for a more than usually attractive young woman. Mai Hogan will help you as much as you will be helping her."

"Yes, Father John. You are a good priest for us all, the good and the bad of us, and you read our hearts."

Tears, comforting tears, flooded her eyes. Powerful emotions had stirred her soul since Ollsen sang his triumphing anthem and Death laid his summons on Mrs. Lee's forehead. It consoled the lone-traveller feeling of the human heart in her to know that Father John understood and forgave. Maire Mack nearly dissolved into a good cry.

"Be off home with yourself, ma'am. The November evenings are short for sea crossings. I'll be at the quay at six on Thursday. *Deo volente.*"

She was glad to be released and gladder still to sit relaxed beside Mike in the gathering dusk as the boat thrashed noisily across the Sound towards home and rest. She was too tired to read the letters which they had come so far to get and Mike was too understanding to expect it. Even Ollsen, who had got one of his projects well and truly started during her absence and was eager to tell her all about it, saw how exhausted she was and held his report over till the morning.

Before she fell asleep, she told Mike of the date fixed for the blessing of the boat and of the priest's proposal in regard to Mai Hogan.

"By Gor, Maire, the day we landed here we thought we'd be doing fine if there were three of us on the island in twelve months' time. At least, them were my calculations. But the way things are shaping, we'll be asking for a polling booth of our own on the island at the next election."

CHAPTER 18 · *Money to Spend*

Breakfast was very early next morning, the two men having started the fire before even Joany had reached the kitchen. They were so keen to resume their outdoor work with the first dawning of the short December day, that they woke at the unearthly hour when foxes turn in their dens and jackdaws withdraw their heads from the downy warmth of their wings before composing themselves for the last spell of their night's sleep before day.

The kitchen glowed warm and yellow in the light of the French cabin lamp which hung high over the hearth when Maire followed Mike to join the others around the table.

"*De 'ur mbeaha-sa!*" Sean Driscoll was proud of the advantage a knowledge of Gaelic gave him over the Norwegian in his contacts with the island folk.

"*Go maire sibh i bfad,*" said Maire as she took her place at the head of the table which Mike had resigned long ago to dodge the little services which outdoor men find so irksome and women delight in.

Breakfast was a meal as devoid of gastronomic delight as stoking a furnace, though the food was both tasty and ample—bread baked by Joany with sour milk supplied by Drummin, golden butter churned by Maire from Drummin's cream, and a dozen brown eggs which the native brown hens laid under the intensive urge of quern-crushed oats. When it was finished, the men belched unashamedly and sat back in their chairs to ease the heavy food into their stomachs.

Ollsen was the first to speak, he was so full of constructive fire.

151

"The waterworks are under way at last, Maire. Wait till it dawns outside and you'll see what Sean and myself have done already. If all goes well—"

"Ha, ha. The Norwegian makes a joke of our hard labour." Sean was as quick to see a pun as to perpetrate one. Ollsen stared at him for some time before he, too, saw the lapse and then laughed louder than Sean.

"Anyway, if all goes 'well' we ought to have water running to the door before the week is out. What do you say to that, Mistress Maire? No more waiting for the tide to fall."

"That's great, Knut. We won't know ourselves, we'll be so pampered and puffed up. But, while we are waiting for daylight we'll have a general chat about other things."

Joany cleared the table as they settled down to hear what Maire had to say.

"We have another visitor coming to live with us." She stopped to watch the effect of that statement on their faces and then went on to tell of Father John's solicitude for Mai Hogan and his request that she be given sanctuary on the Shark. She repeated the priest's assurance that there would be no difficulty about food.

"But," she continued, "there will be considerable difficulty about housing us all."

She faced Ollsen, whose face had lit up at hearing a point in support of his pet project of building the new house at the cells.

"A new house will not solve it, Knut. The new building will take six months. You said that yourself and Mai Hogan will be with us within a week. I have a suggestion to make but I would like to hear a better one, if any of ye have it."

"That'll be three women and three men to provide for," said Joany, squeezing in between Mike and Ollsen to reach for the unfinished last loaf and take it away. "I'd say to have her sleep with me, but that young and old don't make good bedfellows."

She pottered off to let them consider what was really a veiled objection to having Mai foisted on herself.

"If we had another bed—" Mike ventured, and left the possibilities of the fourth bed undeclared.

"Where would we put it?" Sean asked more to keep himself within the discussion than to further the inquiry, but Ollsen's practical mind saw something in his question.

"We could put it in the dairy and you and I could sleep in it, Sean. Two days of patching and painting would make a fine bedroom of the dairy. We would have our own bachelors' bunkhouse and the women would have this house to themselves."

He looked to Maire to approve of his plan; so did the others, to whom no better suggestion had come, though it did occur to Sean to oppose Mai Hogan's intrusion into their already overcrowded quarters. He stifled the ungenerous thought at once and ranged himself with Ollsen. Maire did not let them know by overeagerness or overdelay, that Ollsen's solution was what she had already worked out for herself.

"What do you think of that, Mike?" she asked.

"Only that it looks as if we are pushing the lads out in the cold."

"Oh, no," said Sean. "We'd be happier outside." He blushed at the false implication of his words and made matters worse by trying to correct it.

"That's all right, Sean. We know what you meant," Maire soothed him with an understanding smile to support her words. "Well, Knut, I think you have settled our problem for us. Mai Hogan can bring her bed with her and we'll set it up in your room. Mike and Joany can prepare the dairy, so that you and Sean can finish at the waterworks."

She made the last suggestion to allay the worried look which she saw coming over Ollsen's face. She had discovered only yesterday how badly he took sudden alterations in his lines of thought, and sensed the wrench it would give him to switch from well-boring to house decoration. They rose from the table, filed through the door into the grey light outside, and climbed the crest of the ridge.

All Maire saw was a ten-foot square of level rock from which the thin cover of heathery turf had been removed. In the centre of the square was a small round hole from which the top of a crowbar protruded, and near the bar lay a light eight-pound sledge. Ollsen's excitement provided a very meagre visual display, she thought.

"See, Maire," he explained, "the ridge falls a bare two feet from here to the top of the Well Rock. The spout is only six feet below the top of the rock, so the feeder stream can't be more than six feet under our feet where we stand. It is probably much less, say five feet. Sean and myself will bore at least one foot per day and reach the stream before the end of the week."

He drew the borer from the hole and showed Mike and Maire the chisel point of Swedish steel. Squatting on his rump, with his legs around the hole, he dropped the drill into it again and clasped it lightly between his hands.

"Show them how 'tis done, Sean."

Sean held the sledge short, with one hand near the head, and began to strike the bar quick crisp blows which made it ring on the rock. Ollsen gave the bar a quarter turn in his hands after each blow, keeping it plumb as it turned.

"Slow but sure," he said. "Of course, a power drill would bore the hole in a couple of hours, but we'll get there in time."

"How do you get the powdered rock out of the hole?" Mike wanted to know.

"The old *Aurore's* pump will do that when we go down a bit deeper. We'll flood the hole with water and pump it out again as white as milk with the crushed rock."

"And if the hole goes too deep for that bar?" Mike pursued.

"We'll rig a small derrick and work the bar off a rope sling. But I think we'll strike water before that."

Mike and Maire left the two men to the monotonous task and walked along the ridge to the Well Rock, where they sat down facing the Bay to read the letters at long last.

"The Dublin one first, I suppose," said Maire as she weighed them in her hand. It was from the Land Registry Office and she read it through from address to signature for Mike's information.

NOTICE OF APPLICATION
To Register a Dealing with Registered Land
LAND REGISTRY, CENTRAL OFFICE, CHANCERY ST. DUBLIN
Folio 11036: County Kerry
Registered Owner: Michael McGillicuddy   2. 12. 1930

You are hereby informed that application has been made to me for registration on above Folio under the Deed specified in the Schedule hereto.

This notice may be disregarded if the Deed was executed by you. If it was not executed by you, you must notify me within 3 days from the receipt by you of this Notice which will be deemed to have been received by you within 3 days of the date hereof.

Schedule:

Deed of Release dated 28th of November, 1930.

L. O'BYRNE, *Registrar of Titles*

A second reading satisfied them that the letter was sent direct to themselves to check the validity of Mr. Mathew's application to redeem the land on their behalf.

"That needs no answer," said Maire, putting it back into its envelope and secreting it in the bosom of her blouse.

"This second one is postmarked in Cahirsally and must be from Mr. Mathew. He is checking up on me, I see, because it is addressed direct to you, Mike."

"Dear Mr. McGillicuddy," she read:

In pursuance of instructions given to me by your wife, Mary McGillicuddy, on the 20th ultimo, I have instituted proceedings in the two actions to which those instructions referred, with results as set forth hereunder.

1. I have, on your behalf, redeemed the annuity payable on your holding on the Shark Island for the sum of £32. 14s. 1d., the amount as calculated in the Office of the Irish Land Commission and the receipt for which payment I hold in my chambers for your inspection. You will receive formal notification of this transaction from the Central Office of the Land Registry in due course, and also from the Land Commission.

2. *Re: Timothy McGillicuddy (decd.)—Case 2758*

I am in receipt of a rescript of the final certificate in respect of the estate of the deceased Timothy McGillicuddy, from the Register of the Probate Court of Suffolk County in the State of Massachusetts, U.S.A., which certificate sets forth that the estate, both real and personal, reached a total value of $3,550.21. At the current rate of exchange of $4.85 to £1 sterling, the estate is worth £717. 8s. 5¾d.

The Register has accepted the proofs of identity which I furnished to him and has forwarded to me for transmission to you a certified bank cheque for the sum aforementioned of $3,550.21, which I hold here awaiting your instructions.

If, however, you think it preferable to have an independent inquiry made in Boston into the value of the estate of the deceased, I would be obliged if you authorize me by letter, or by a visit to my chambers, to undertake such independent inquiry.

I do not recommend that course. My considered opinion is that you should accept the Court's valuation and take delivery of the cheque as it stands.

3. We can settle the account of my disbursements and costs in these two actions when you call to collect your money.

Yours truly,
MATHEW O'CONNELL, Sol'r.

"Great news, Maire," was Mike's commentary. He took off his cap and added in Gaelic: "May the good God, who watches over us all, grant poor Tim, who remembered us in his dying hour, a warm place in Heaven this day and for ever."

"Amen." Maire blessed herself and took Mike by the hand.

They sat looking out over the Bay in a silence punctuated by the ringing tap, tap of the sledge on the boring iron. The possession of so much money suffused them with confidence in themselves and in their future. Their world was become a happy place, full of good people and good things, and their future was assured. The island was now their very own, to work as they would, and they had the money with which to work it. Mike's mind ran to an up-to-date nobby with a mile-long train of nets and a crew of five. A new boat, staunch enough to weather the heaviest gale and bring in her ten thousand mackerel when the prices ranged high. Maire was transforming the island into a well ordered farm, fencing the lowland from the hill and parcelling it into sizable fields, drained, limed, fruitful, and loud with the mooing of cows. Each was being true to upbringing.

"How much have we now, Maire?"

"Is it money you mean?"

"What else?"

"After we pay Mr. Mathew and give back to Knut what he loaned us to buy the *St. Finian* from Bill, there will be a good hole in Tim's money. I suppose we'll have about £620. Along with that we have my fortune of £170 and the lobster money. You might say that we are worth £850 in dry cash."

"Maire, girl, I'm a bit afraid of all that money. Don't let it get a grip of you. Don't keep it in the house. You'd be hiding it like a bad sore you couldn't heal and you'd be suspecting me and the children, when they come, of stealing it. And if you put it in the bank, it would be calling you to add to it and add to it in a way that you would be driving us like slaves to work for it. Let us spend it, Maire *a stor*."

He put his arm about her waist and pulled her close to him in his overpowering will to make her think as he did.

"Father John is a great priest and he sets no store in money. Father Denis before him was full of God's wisdom too. I'll ever remember a sermon he gave us against setting our hearts on money. In Gaelic he said it, and one word of it stuck in my mind. 'Money is good only at the moment you spend it. It is a dead thing the moment before you spend it and it goes into death the moment after.' When Father Denis died, he left no dead money after him. All he had he spent buying happiness for unhappy people."

He looked into her eyes and rejoiced in what he saw.

"Thahailen, *a chroi*, I have half of it spent already in my mind. You can do what your heart tells you with the other half."

He helped her to her feet and they returned, hand in hand, back along the ridge to the well sinkers and down the slope to the house.

The next few days were busy ones for them all. The dairy was transformed into a clean sweet-smelling bedroom inside, though the outside still looked its own rough weather-stained self. Ollsen and Sean had bored deep into the sandstone rock and were stopping more frequently to test the bottom of the bore for seeping water.

CHAPTER 19 · *Mai Hogan Arrives*

Between dark and dawn on the morning of the 13th, the islanders sat at breakfast. Mike cocked his ear.

"There's a boat making for the cove. Pats Kelly's old smack by the sound of her," he said.

The men gulped what remained of their breakfasts, pulled on rubber thigh-boots and hurried down to the sea to meet the incoming boat. She loomed very large in the dim morning light and seemed to sit deep in the water. Two figures moved actively about the deck; a third sat motionless near the helm. A big-bellied man peered shorewards under his hand when he heard the crunching of feet on the gravel of the strand.

"Ahoy, there! Ahoy, the slip!"

"Ahoy, Pats Kelly! We're coming aboard."

Mike had never seen Mai Hogan but he guessed that it was she who crouched over the heavy oak helm, watching him fearfully as he clambered into the smack. He threw her a welcoming smile but made no effort to speak to her until he had heard what old Pats had to say.

Pats was standing wide-legged on a heavy tarpaulin sheet which covered the maw of the hold and making great play with a letter which he held like a precious thing in his tar-stained fingers.

"Father John told me to give this to your missus. He said it explains everything."

Mike stuffed the letter into his breast pocket without pretending even to read the address on the envelope. The shrewd eyes of the man, who ranked Mike with himself among the illiterates, would have turned to scorn had Mike attempted the idle pretence.

"And I suppose he left it to Pats Kelly to explain the rest to me."

"Give me a hand with this tarpaulin, Mike, and you can see for yourself."

Ollsen and Sean lent a hand in rolling back the stubborn sheet and exposing the cargo—as miscellaneous a collection of luggage as ever a passenger on a ferryboat brought along. Potatoes, ten sacks of them, five full bags of oats and a sack of flour were ranged side by side across the forward end of the hold. Aft, near the cased-in engine, were stowed a polished oak bedstead, with springs, hair mattress and bedclothes, all neatly disposed to keep them from scratch or dunt. Four large American trunks filled the space between the agricultural produce and the bedding.

Mike looked from the cargo to the shrinking figure in the stern and scratched his head ruefully.

"And there's more to come," Pats chuckled.

"To come here?"

"Yes, Mike—to come here this very day." His capacious belly shook in enjoyment of the problem Mike had to solve in the matter of landing the cargo at a shallow-water slip.

"How much do you draw?" Mike referred, of course, to the smack.

"Three foot six aft, with this load, and a foot less for'ard."

"We'll manage it easy, Pats. 'Tis two hours till high water. We'll snake the smack in till she grounds, bring my boat alongside and shift the oats and bedding into her. That will lighten the smack, so she will float in nicely to the end of the slip."

"Oh, no, Mikey, me lad. You're not going to hole my bottom planks as simple as that. Not on your life. Out here in deep water you'll bring your boateen alongside and 'tis the spuds you'll shift into her. Get a move on and bring your liner alongside. The day is wearing away."

"Righto," said Mike. "But, first of all, we must see our passenger ashore."

"I'll see to that," said Sean, who had been keeping an unobtrusive eye on the girl in the stern. "I'll run yourself out to the *St. Finian* first, to save time, and I'll be back to help ye with the cargo in two flips of a cod's tail."

Mike and Ollsen tumbled back into the punt after Sean, who took the oars to himself and rowed around the stern of the smack under the girl's eye, feathering the oars with a great flourish of wrists and elbows. He picked up Mai on his way back and landed her on the slip without having uttered a word, when helping her either from the smack to the punt or from the punt to the slip. He was tongue-tied in the presence of the rare other-world creature who seemed a composite of starlit eyes, gleaming hair, and soft warm contours. Making a great demand on his reserves of courage, he controlled his voice, and spoke to her.

"Mike told me to tell you—to tell—to give this letter to Mrs. Mack."

He stood stock-still and so did she. Of course, she had no idea where Mrs. Mack might be and, because Sean's mind had gone dead on him, it did not occur to him to tell her. After a minute of awkward silence, Sean's enravishment actually spoke to him.

"Where is Mrs. Mack?"

"Oh, I forgot. I'll show you." He paced sidelong before her, like a moonstruck page conducting a damsel of high degree to her bower, until they got view of the roof of the house.

"We live there. You'll find Mrs. Mack there."

The girl lingered, undecided whether she would stay with the unknown she saw or face the unknown she did not see.

"I'll go with you," Sean said. "Come along."

The women saw them hesitating on the path and came to meet them with hands outstretched to welcome the bewildered girl. Impelled by her life-long dependence on an old woman, she turned towards Joany and clung to her arm as to something she understood and could trust. Maire and Sean were outside her experience; she had been allowed very little traffic with young people and shrank from association with them.

Driscoll stood with Maire until Joany had led the girl into the house, his whole being concentrated in his eyes. Maire had to bring him to earth.

"Won't they be wanting the punt, Sean?" she asked.

Throwing her a startled look, he wheeled about and ran down the path. He was too excited to walk or, when he had leaped into the punt, to sit on the thwart and paddle. He had to work off his surcharged emotion in violent action, and stern-sculling with one oar gave him all the action he needed. The punt danced like a mad thing as his body swayed to the sweep of the oar and came near to throwing him overboard when she crashed blindly against the side of the smack.

Maire was disturbed in mind, too. Not so much about Sean Driscoll as about Mai Hogan. Sean would cool down, but Mai's plight was worse than she thought. The girl was little better than an automaton, devoid of initiative and completely dependent on external direction, even in regard to her own actions. If physical excellence were the sole measure of perfection, Mai Hogan was as nearly perfect as a girl could be. Yearlings attain that sort of perfection; horse trainers cultivate it and suppress all initiative in their thoroughbred fillies.

Mai's mother must have been a wayward filly, Maire thought as she worked towards an explanation for the girl's subnormality, and old Mrs. Lee must have set herself deliberately to kill in Mai every natural impulse, lest she grow up as high-spirited as her mother and kick over the traces as she did. Father John gave me a nice job of work to undo what that old lady did to the poor girl.

"Joany will show you around the house while I'm reading this. Make yourself at home, dear."

The letter was short and uninformative. She read:

DEAR MRS. MACK:

I am sending Mai Hogan sooner than you expected, perhaps, but circumstances forced my hand. We buried her grandmother yesterday and, rather than transfer the poor girl to a temporary lodging, I thought it better to make one job of it and put her under your wing at once. God bless her and you.

Yours sincerely in Xt.,
JOHN MILES, P.P.

"Not enough guidance in that," she said to herself in her judicial way. "But sure the day's needs are all the guidance we want. The Lord knows we'll have our hands full of needs today preparing the house for tomorrow's Mass."

She called Mai and Joany back into the kitchen to plan the best way of transforming it into a chapel, with the altar to the east, as tradition requires, and a convenient place of privacy for the confessions before Mass. She took Mai into the conference as a matter of course, but took care to ask her no direct question and to give her no direct instruction.

Down at the cove the men worked with the breathless haste of men salvaging precious goods from a sinking ship. Sean Driscoll and young Kelly, in the hold, hoisted a sack to the gunwale where Pats held it for Mike and Ollsen to lower and stow it in the converted lifeboat.

"Ha, ha!" Pats kept a running commentary going with the sacks. "You'd imagine this Hogan filly was emigrating to foreign parts." A sack came up from the hold. "Needing all this grub for this short run." Another sack claimed his attention. "If she was emigrating to the States, now—" again a sack—"in a coffin ship like my Aunty Biddy." Another sack. "Old Biddy took a barrel of spuds with her—" a sack— "a barrel of salty ling. And a piggin of corned butter. And a dozen oatmeal griddle cakes. And she was two months on the sea. And all this grub for Miss Mary Hogan. Thank God she has but the one mouth."

With the ten sacks aboard, the smaller boat motored off to the slip, discharged them, and returned to the smack for the bedding. Pats followed her in with the oats at high tide, his keel showing six inches clear of the sandy bottom when he slowed into the slip. After unloading he reversed out, swung round in a wide sweep, and opened the throttle wide for the run home to the Old Quay for the second load.

It was low water when he returned with the most extraordinary cargo the island had ever received, to wit, one pony, wearing its leather harness to quiet the animal in disquieting circumstances, and one farm cart with the wheels dismounted for convenience in stowing them. The unloading was crude but effective. The pony, stripped of its tackling, was forced overboard to swim ashore. Père Gourin was too far away to protest as he had protested in favour of the heifers. The wooden body of the cart was dumped into the water and towed in at the end of a rope by the punt. The wheels, being less buoyant in their heavy iron bands, were transshipped to the new boat and remounted under the body when brought ashore.

The Kellys came with them. Maire had sent word that their belated dinner was ready for them with her own three men. They did not object to eating off their knees, because the tables and chairs had been scrubbed white and rearranged to suit the early morning Mass and, anyhow, as Pats put it: "We're starved with the hunger, and hunger was invented before tables." He promised Mike to remind the Macks and Shuckrues of the mainland that tomorrow was the day fixed for Tim's memorial Mass and to give them seats in the smack with Father John if they were coming out to the island.

CHAPTER 20 · *Blessing the Boat*

ST. FINIAN'S morn filtered through tattered rags of sea mist that trailed along the island, swathed the Lookout, and drenched the lowland with their saturated tails. It was still dark when the new boat nosed her way through the drifting fog across the Sound to the Old Quay to pick up Father John and the guests invited to the memorial Mass. As soon as her side grated against the steps of the pier, Dan Mack grabbed the gunwale and stooped low to allow Nora, swaddled in double shawls, and Thade Carey in two layers of overcoats, to stumble awkwardly aboard.

Father John ignored Dan's proffered arm, and stepped, confident and erect, off the greasy stone step to the greasier rail of the gunwale: too confident and too erect, for his landsman shoes failed to bite into the timber and shot him, heels foremost, into the hold on the flat of his back. His voluminous clothes saved him from bodily hurt but not from shock to his estimate of his athletic ability.

Stung by the indignity of his fall, he rolled over on his tummy, picked himself up as quick as a forward in a collapsed scrummage, and then moved towards the bow as nonchalantly as if his were the approved manner of boarding a fishing boat. Dan pushed off after his brother, Con, and stepped aboard with the certitude of long practice, carrying the heavy leather cases into which Thade Carey had packed the vestments, altar stone, and other precious equipment.

Although there was a lazy ground swell coming in from the west, the bow rode high and the boat made good time across the Sound.

Nora took refuge in the small cabin as soon as they lost the shelter of the quay and the men shook down into pairs for a chat, Father John joining Ollsen in the bow.

"This must be a novel experience for you, Ollsen."

"Oh, no, sir. Raw mornings like this are nothing new to me. Try an open boat in Narvik Fiord, some day, and you'll learn what hard weather really is."

"I wasn't thinking of weather. Did you ever cross a fiord on a morning like this to attend divine service?"

"No, sir, I never did."

"Are you a Catholic?"

"No, I'm not. If I'm anything, I'm a Lutheran, but it is a long time since I went into any church."

"What about attending my Mass this morning?"

"I was wondering what I ought do. I would like to do the right thing: the thing my good friends would wish me to do. But I do not want to butt in, if I am not welcome."

"You'll be as welcome as the flowers in May. If you feel at sea during Mass, do as the others do." Father John laughed quietly. "I do not mean that you make your confession as they will, but you might furbish up your forgotten prayers and repeat them during Mass. It will do you good, especially if you pray for someone dear to you."

"Thank you, sir. . . . May a heretic say 'Father'?"

"Sure. That will do you good, too."

Halfway across the Sound they overtook a boat pulling strongly through the dark towards the island, the occupants clad in their Sunday clothes. When they drew level with her, Mike bent towards his brother Dan and whispered in his ear.

"That's Katie Sheehan sitting on the stern sheets, the girleen that her father stopped of marrying Tim. He had no farm of land for her. Go for'ard and tell Nora to invite her into our boat. She'll be drier here."

They helped Katie aboard and took her boat in tow, leaving her two boatmen to enjoy the sensation of lively speed free from the labour of rowing. The fog still hung low when the crowded boat made the cove and the passengers ferried ashore in the woolly darkness.

A surge of warmth, backed by the blaze of lamps and candles, met them at the door of the busy house. The rich smell of simmering fat came from the crackling fire of driftwood which was surrounded by black pots each bearing a crown of glowing coals. The family table stood by the east wall, ennobled by a stiff white linen cloth hanging in starched folds to the floor. At its mathematical centre Maire's large brass crucifix held pride of place, between Betty Hannen's shining candlesticks and matched vases, resplendent with plumes of escallonia.

The rows of chairs and wooden forms filled the kitchen floor, leaving a gangway by the walls for the busy womenfolk. Just inside the door of the bedroom, which used to be Ollsen's but which was to be Mai Hogan's for the future, the best chair in the house was set ready for Father John to sit on during the confessions before Mass. Just outside the door a length of sailcloth was spread for the unshriven to kneel on while awaiting their turns. The formal Sunday clothes, in which all but Ollsen were dressed, gave the brilliant interior a very festive appearance.

Thade Carey was not impressed. He was used to *private* Masses and gala kitchens. He took charge at once and dived into the leather trunks, from one of which he took the surplice and stole and handed them to Father John. Thade placed the linen-covered altar stone in position midway on the glistening white tablecloth, and on the near end he laid chasuble, maniple, alb, and amice, one on the other in that order. After balancing the three altar cards precariously against the crucifix and candlesticks, he stood back, checked the setup, and retired to engage Joany in a good fruity gossip. She barked him away. She was too busy for gossiping.

While Thade was speeding through his familiar task, confessions went on like clockwork. The women took precedence, for household rather than for weaker-sex reasons, and each of them hurried back to the job which had been assigned to her, as soon as she emerged from the confessional.

The men were slower in their movements and in the ritual than the women and much more conscious of the solemnity of the sacramental occasion. Ollsen stood apart by the back door, marvelling at the informality and the assured confidence of the Catholic at prayer. When the last confession was heard, Father John brought his chair with him into the kitchen and carried it to where Ollsen stood, like a stranger at the feast.

"Here, use this. Sit down when the others do and kneel when they kneel. Say the prayers your mother taught you. Pray for her and for yourself."

He picked his way to Mai Hogan and patted her on the head.

"Say a prayer for me, child," he whispered and passed on to vest himself for the Mass in full view of the kneeling people. Looking very like a medieval stained-glass saint in the lustrous chasuble, he turned towards the little congregation.

"My dear brethren, you know the intention for which I am celebrating this Mass. It is for the repose, the eternal repose, of the soul of Timothy McGillicuddy, who was born under this roof and who lived a good Christian life until it pleased the Almighty God to call him in his prime. You will join me in offering this Mass for that intention."

The Mass ran its solemn course through a whispering hush that was broken at intervals by explosions of blazing sparks on the hearth and the grating of boots and chair legs when the people rose to stand during the reading of the Gospels. Unlike Thade Carey, the Norwegian was deeply moved by the intent devotion of his friends and by the colourful dignity of the Mass, which the unfamiliar Latin raised above the level of mundane affairs. The homely scene recalled the fervours of his early youth when he joined in the family recital of the Lord's Prayer and the Creed. The once familiar phrases welled up from the depths of memory and, bowing his head, he recited them again in his native Norwegian, fresh and full of meaning after long disuse.

In front of him he heard Mike and Dan whisper their prayers in Gaelic to the thumbing of brown beads and saw Mai and Katie Sheehan following the new fashion of reading English prayer books. The polyglot nature of the service struck his mind when the first fervour of his own prayers was waning and set it free to observe and appraise the strangeness of the scene.

" 'Tis well that God reads the heart rather than the tongue and that the Recording Angel writes all languages. This little kitchen is giving him a queer old blend of Latin and Norwegian, Gaelic and English this morning." His thoughts ranged freer than usual under the stimulus of the emotional atmosphere.

"Catholics seem to be very sure of God and the afterlife, particularly of the afterlife. They pray for the *souls* of their dead and think so little of their *bodies* that they neglect the graveyards in which the bodies lie."

Thade Carey's bell tinkled at the Consecration and heads bowed low in reverence. Ollsen's thoughts ran on.

My people plan garden cities for the empty bodies of our dead and refuse to have any further dealings with their souls. Strange—I wonder who has the right slant on things—I d'n'o; but there's something in the Catholic way of handling it.

He frowned at the elusiveness of a satisfactory answer and shook his head.

I wish I had a fixed faith like these people. No doubts, no fears for the future. Ah, heck! What's the good at guessing or wishing.

His decision coincided with Father John's *"Ite missa est."*

Soon the women left their places and got busy preparing the breakfast and restoring the kitchen to its normal uses. Breakfast was as substantial a meal as a dinner. It had to be, because everyone had been up and doing since the small hours and had worked up the appetites of hawks.

Joany was the self-appointed liaison between the pots and the table. To everyone she gave a plateful of sizzling plaice, fried a golden brown in home-made butter, a brimming cup of tea, which would have been scalding but for the generous "drop" of cream in it, and buttered scones piping hot. When they had dulled the keen edge of appetite and began to loiter over the meal for a long leisurely gossip, Father John stood up and turned off the light of the cabin lamp.

"We don't need this. See, it is broad day and we have more to do before I go home."

Thade took his cue and started the exodus from the house to the sea. Two by two, the company walked, bareheaded down the path to the cove, led by Father John in surplice and stole. Thade came close behind, bearing the asperges brush and a deep bowl of holy water, which splashed as he stumbled on the uneven stones. Mike stepped forward a pace and whispered in the priest's ear. "One decade of the rosary will take us to the boat, Father." Father John led the prayers in a tone pitched well below the usual ecclesiastical chant. The processionists responded at speeds as various as their steps; some thoughtfully and others perfunctorily. Only the women maintained a decorous concentration on the content of the prayers to the end.

The men eyed the transformation which had come over sea and sky while they were indoors. The fog had lifted off the water and thickened into a low ceiling of cotton-waste cloud as level as the black water over which it brooded, silent and impending. A cathedral twilight filled the still air. Hundreds of seabirds, whiter than usual on the dark water of the cove, sat motionless as if wondering at the strange constriction of their flying space. Even the tireless little sand waves ceased their fingering in the breathless calm.

The rosary came to an end at the slip, where the new boat lay waiting to be blessed and christened. She echoed hollowly when the priest mounted to the foredeck and took a stance overlooking the boat, the group of men and women on the little pier, and the still water beyond them. Placing the asperges brush and bowl near to his hand he opened the *Rituale* at the page he needed: Benedictio Solemnis Navis Piscatoriae.

"*Adjutorium nostrum in nomine Domini*," he began and swung immediately into the sonorous Latin of the eighth Psalm, magnifying the greatness of the Lord. The triumphant song of the psalmist gripped his imagination and thrilled his voice.

" 'The fowls of the air thou hast subjected to the feet of men and the fishes which pass through the paths of the sea. How wonderful is Thy Name over the universal earth.' "

He paused on the last vibrant verse to compose his voice for the long narrative gospel of St. John.

" '*In illo tempore* . . . Jesus showed Himself a second time to his disciples by the Sea of Tiberias. . . .' "

At the blessing, which closed the ritual, he took the brush and dipping it deep into the bowl, sprinkled the blessed water on stem, stern, and hold. He named the boat "*Sanctus Fingenius*," which is Saint Finian, and invoked the blessing of the Almighty on her and on all who in her would be, thereon to remain for ever. "Amen," quoth Thade.

The ceremony was over and the group on the slip fell apart, the men fumbling for pipes and matches and the women running their fingers through straying wisps of hair, patting them into place. A great black-backed gull spread his wings, taxied with hanging legs till he was airborne, and croaked hoarsely. In discordant squawks and screams the others scurried with flapping wings to follow him, streaking the smooth surface of the cove with rippling wakes like speedboats at a regatta. For the fog had lifted and dissolved under the miraculous alchemy of the sun and the birds were the first to observe it. They whirled and screamed overhead till they gained height and fell silent to glide off on widespread pinions, north, south, east, and west, scanning the fringes of the island for things of nauseous smell.

Mike sidled towards Maire and whispered wry-mouthed.

"Take the priest away with you, Maire. Any old excuse will do, but give us a chance to sample the drinks you brought from Bill's. The men won't touch it while he's around, though their tongues are out to wet the christening."

Mike need not have whispered his plaint in her ear. Father John, wise man, knew he would be *de trop* until the customary libations had been drunk to the Macks, to the new boat, to Tim, God rest his soul, to the stranger from Norway, to Mai Hogan, and to as many more conceivable toasts as the bottles at the house were good for. Removing his stole, he invited Maire to sit beside him in the *St. Finian* and dismissed the rest with a wave of his hand towards the path.

"My letter told you why I planted the girl on you without notice. Perhaps 'twas better that way."

"It was, Father, now 'tis over."

"The potatoes and oats and things will tide you all over present needs. Consider them as Mai's entrance fee to the Shark Academy for Young Ladies."

He crinkled the corners of his shrewd eyes in appreciation of his own quirk and stayed Maire's incipient protest with a lift of the hand.

"Mai is comparatively well off and can pay her way independently. It is to let you know how her affairs stand that I held you here after the others. She has, as it were, two accounts—one of which will remain where it is until she comes of age. I mean the money her mother sent from America year by year and which Mrs. Lee lodged in Mai's name in the post office. I have told Mai that I am holding it for her. But I did not tell her how much stands to her credit nor am I going to tell you, beyond saying that it is a considerable sum, according to the standards of Manistir Parish. You don't mind?"

"I do and I don't, Father." Maire did not like pigs in pokes nor half-revealed secrets, and was resolute enough of mind to say so, even to the masterful parish priest.

"Then wait until I have laid Account No. 2 before you. We'll call it the Working Account, over which I propose to give you full control in Mai's interest. I have had Mrs. Lee's farm and stock valued for immediate sale. It is a smallish place and will fetch, at auction, about £250—not more than £300. With the bishop's assent and the approval of his Lordship's solicitor, who has read Mrs. Lee's will, I shall deposit the proceeds of the sale in the joint names of Mai Hogan and yourself in the National Bank—"

"Isn't Mai under age, Father?"

"Yes, but it can be—"

"Bank it in your own name, Father, and let Mai draw on you for what she will need from time to time."

Father John's jaws clamped tight and his lips zipped straight across his face. It would have been bad enough, had Maire been hesitant or unhelpful in accepting his considered arrangements. He had come prepared for feminine indecision, for objections and hypotheses, and had been sure of overcoming them either by blandishment or by guarantees of profit in cash or in kind. But to be met, not alone by direct opposition to his plan but by a positive order which ran counter to that plan, was intolerable.

"My good woman, do you understand that I have worked this matter out with the greatest care?"

"I am sure you have, Father."

"Then please listen to my instructions about the disposition of this girl's money. I leave everything else—how you will train her, how you will expend the money on that training—I leave all that to you, absolutely—"

He stopped irresolute. He could not go on because Maire was subjecting him to a kindly, tolerant, but searching scrutiny. She was looking deep into his eyes and into the mind behind them for the sources of his implacable decisions. She smiled hopefully when he went silent.

"You are vexed with me, Father Miles."

"And haven't I a good right to be displeased?"

"You have not, Father; no more than I have a right to be vexed with you for wearing blinkers while you are doing your good works. You see very clearly what lies ahead of you but you don't see what runs beside you."

She watched his face for signals. It was still severe in outline but the eyes were less domineering than they had been. She decided to risk his anger and carry on.

"You do not know the fear Mike and myself have of money. Only yesterday we opened our minds to each other about some money which is coming to us soon. Oh, I forgot. Sure, you know about that already, the money Mike's brother left him. Well, Father, neither Mike nor I wants to hoard it or have it on our hands. We're going to spend it at once."

His eyes telegraphed a deprecatory query.

"No, we're not going to squander it, but to put it working. And we have barely made up our minds to get rid of our own money when you come along with this money of Mai Hogan's, to plant it on us. Do you wonder that I won't accept it?"

"Um?" The blinkers were slipping off.

"That is why I ask you to bank it in Mai's name or in your own. I'll let you know whenever she wants to draw on it."

"Very well, Maire."

His use of her Christian name for the first time told her not alone that he would scrap his own plan for hers, a notable achievement in itself, but that she had lost none of his respect. Indeed, it told her that his respect had turned to regard, and she became so elated at the signal success of her daring that it required a pronounced effort of will power to suppress the impulse to renounce her victory and accept his original plan with whatever discomfort it would entail.

"Thank you, Father John."

She had always used his surname to round out the obligatory "Father," rather than the more intimate "John."

"Quits," he replied, and helped her to leave the boat.

CHAPTER 21 · *Ollsen's Rage*

THE house party came down the path in great good humour after their libations. Dan and Con Mack linking arms with Katie Sheehan's ferryman and singing their approval of God's good world in cheery discord. Mike followed them at a distance nicely measured to associate him with the party but to dissociate him from its uproarious behaviour. He had drunk a little less liberally than they, just a little.

"Where's Knut?" Maire asked him. "Isn't he going to the mainland with you?"

"I d'n'o. He's back at the well-sinking again. That man doesn't know how to enjoy life."

"I'll talk to him. And, Mike, you may as well make a day of it and run in to Cahirsally after landing Father John and see Mr. Mathew. Draw as much from him as will buy a new rig-out for Knut. The poor man must have been agonized this morning to see us all dressed up to the nines and he as ragged as a scarecrow. Wait for him at the boat, but don't tell him about the new suit until you get him into town."

She left the path to pick her way diagonally up the ridge towards the boring from which the familiar tap-tapping of the drill reached her ears. Ollsen was working alone and from the black look on his face as he plied the drill with a savage expenditure of energy, it was evident that something or someone had broken his habitual self-control. He threw Maire one flashing glance of his eye without breaking the rhythmic heave of the powerful oak lever, which he and Sean had rigged up to work the drill when the hole became too deep for sledging.

"Where's Sean from you?" she asked.

He ignored the question and went on working the lever with a greater bunching of his powerful shoulders. Insolence was so alien to the Norwegian's behaviour, as she knew it since he came to the island, that the deliberate display of bad temper and bad manners struck Maire more violently than a physical blow. The studied insult, striking her in the full tide of elation at her beneficent victory over Father John, stung her to the quick and provoked her fighting spirit to one of its rare explosions into blind unthinking counteraction.

"You ungrateful wretch," she hissed.

The revulsion of emotions overcame her. A tremor of faintness ran through her whole being. She sank down on one of the rigging timbers in utter collapse and passed out of consciousness.

Ollsen released the lever at the top of its throw so suddenly, that the drill dropped into the cavity with a violence that shattered the highly tempered point deep in the vitals of the rock. Seizing the bucket of water, which he kept for flushing the bore, he soused Maire's face and arms until she gasped her way back to awareness of her surroundings. Grim and forbidding, he glared at her with water trickling through his fingers while she struggled to her feet and leaned against the lever to regain her balance. Her mind was already in full operation.

"What happened us, Knut?"

"What happened me, you mean?"

"Well then, what did happen to you?"

"Whisky happened to me, the damn stuff. It burned me up; it twisted me inside; it— Oh! Av veien, av veien!"

Maire guessed there was more to his madness than whisky, but she knew it was worse than useless to argue with him until he had worked it off without outside interference.

"Hush," she cautioned. "There's someone coming. Forget it and calm yourself. I'm going into the house."

It was Father John, looking for Ollsen to sail the St. Finian back with Mike.

"Hello!" he called cheerily to announce his approach. The Norwegian turned his back on him and, pulling the broken drill from the bore, flung it clattering on the rock and began to tackle the spare one to the lever. The priest recognized the hostility of his reception but stooped to pick up the drill and examine the splintered point, waiting for an opening for talk.

"Drop that."

Ollsen grabbed for the drill as he snapped out the angry words, but Father John's grip on the iron bar tightened instantaneously and held firm against Ollsen's vicious one-handed pull. Ollsen heaved with all the weight of his body and dragged the priest stiff-legged as far as the timber framework of the lever. Father John braced himself against the timber and, working his hand to the ends of the drill to gain the maximum purchase, he proceeded to twist it out of the Norwegian's grasp. Under the insistent pressure, Ollsen dared not loosen his grip on the middle of the bar to seek the greater leverage which Father John had secured at the outset. He opposed all his strength to the relentless turning movement, trying to reverse it and force the bar out of the priest's hands. For one short moment he gained a perceptible advantage, but the deadly pressure came back again and he knew that the best he could hope for was to hold on and make it a stalemate. He had no use for stalemates and, anyhow, his madness was ebbing away and he let go.

"You win."

The very words of surrender released the last dregs of the frenzy which the strain of the silent combat had been wearing down. He was in his own mind again, an abject, abased mind, which waited for the angry indictment its turbulence had incurred. But the contest had drawn deeply on Father John's energy too. He leaned against the rigging, where Maire had leant after her collapse, drawing deep breaths of the December air and gazing blankly at the drill which he now held in his hands, the neglected spoils of victory. At last he drew away from the support and balanced the weighty drill against it.

"Well, my man," said Father Miles, "don't you think you owe me an explanation for your extraordinary behaviour?"

"What good are explanations or excuses? I have shown Mrs. Mack and you what sort of a mad dog I really am. I will make no objection if both of you kick me out. I deserve no better."

He made to collect the tools, like a workman who had been dismissed in the middle of a job, but the priest intervened.

"The explanation can wait, but you need not be a quitter as well as a 'mad dog.' Why not finish the job in hand?"

Ollsen toothed his lip in thought and then looked into Father John's eyes for the first time since he came on the rock, a reenkindled enthusiasm in his face.

"I'd like to. We are so near a finish but . . . well, I beat up Sean when I was out of my senses. You'll hear all about it when you go in. I can't expect any help from him now."

"Carry on. I'll have a look at Sean when you are started."

Father John wished to let Ollsen regain his self-confidence before he called him to account and he knew no quicker way to that end than exacting work which required concentration. He could not condemn him unheard and it would be unfair to hear him before he was in a condition to make his case.

Ollsen resumed where he had broken off when the priest arrived on the ridge. Fitting the unbroken drill to the sling, he dropped it into the hole to test it for truth in the fall. An unfamiliar sound made him cock his ear and try another fall. Instead of the dull stubborn thud of steel on powdered rock, he heard the plash of squashed mud at the bottom of the hole. Father John heard it too and moved toward Ollsen who was pulling up the drill by hand in suppressed excitement to examine the point. It was stained with a thin grey smear, which was so watery that it ran off under Ollsen's finger.

"*Vi har det! Her kommer vannet!*"

He realized suddenly that he had broken into Norwegian in his elation.

"Don't you see, sir? We have struck the water. The drill I smashed did the trick. All we want now is to widen the cut it made into the stream."

Father John caught the excitement and ran to the lever to have a hand in the completion of the task. Up and down he worked the heavy beam while Ollsen stood over the bore to see that the drill ran true in the guide and to watch the happenings in the hole. The thuds and creaking noises reached the house and brought the women to the door to gaze at the priest's pumping arms and flapping soutane silhouetted against the sky. Maire saw by Ollsen's expectant pose that his black rage was gone, and that he was working in harmony with Father John for some urgent and immediate result. She sent Mai running to the boat to bring Mike on the scene while she and Joany sidled up the slope of the ridge to the two workers, who were so dissimilar in everything but their absorption in the joint task. The women took their stand beside Ollsen and fixed their eyes on the mouth of the hole through which the drill shuttled faster than they had ever seen it move. Mike and his brothers joined them, silent as huntsmen watching the dying struggles of a stricken stag.

"Oh!" The women screamed in unison and ran backwards to escape a wetting when the throat of the bore filled with a swirl of water which gushed up at the centre and fanned out over the rock. All the men jumped clear to the cross timbers and up the rigging—all but Ollsen. He stood by, estimating the volume and force of the upflow and waiting for it to reach equilibrium.

Wading through the spreading water, he extracted the drill and, taking a long oaken plug, which he had rounded to the size of the bore, he calmly proceeded to drive it down the hole and choke off the welling water. When the overflow dried off he rose to his feet, flushed with pride in the justification both of his forecasts and his unremitting toil, and turned to Maire.

"I'll have this water to your hand in the kitchen before the week is out, ma'am."

Mike, who was wondering at the oak plug, fingered the top of it and looked for an explanation.

"We'll build a concrete tank around it," said Ollsen, "and then draw the plug. The tank will feed the house."

"We're all very thankful to you, Knut," said Mike. "It has been a great morning altogether, between Mass and the blessing of the boat and now this well of spring water."

Neither Father John nor Maire said a word, though Ollsen looked from one to the other for a word in praise of his achievement, nor did they show any visible sign of approval. Speech might imply that they condoned his unpardonable outbursts. He might construe approbation of his well-boring into a general forgiveness of his transgression.

"Remove your caps," said Father John, "and join me in a prayer of thanksgiving to Almighty God. You need not go on your knees; the rock is still too wet.

"Almighty God, the giver of all good things, we humbly thank Thee for all Thy favours and particularly for having of Thy bounty granted a goodly store of beneficent water to this parched rock and for having led among us an unknown servant to release the waters to our use. Amen."

CHAPTER 22 · *Lloyd's Agent*

THADE CAREY grew tired of waiting and crawled into one of the bunks of the *St. Finian*, placing his precious leather bags in the other. They were his only care. The excursions and alarms of his neighbours were, to him, material for subsequent gossip but not for present action. He never attended whist drives or regattas or draghunts, because the people who watched them became too wrapped up in the contests to talk or be talked with. And Thade lived for talk. He did, however, frequent wakes, not because he took a sadistic pleasure in grief or pain, but because wakes and funerals were talk-fests on a high level. No subject but the frailties of the silent dead was taboo. The sombre setting and the convention of subdued voices and subdued lighting gave pregnancy to platitudes, point to inanities, and freshness to ancient anecdotes. Thade scintillated at wakes.

But alone on the slip with no one to talk to and with no desire to share in the excitement at the well, life offered nothing to Thade and he crawled into the bunk to suspend it in sleep. His punchinello face relaxed and soon the boxlike cabin was booming to the snores of his mighty nose.

He opened a selective eye when the return party came noisily aboard and woke him. He wanted to pick out the likeliest reporter of the doings at the house and attach himself to him during the crossing to the Old Quay. Father John, of course, he dared not approach, but when he saw the priest coming forward to the bow to join someone overhead on the foredeck he closed the roving eye and pretended to be asleep. His ears missed nothing when the priest spoke.

"Well, Ollsen? Feeling better?"

"Yes, Father John, much better but not too happy about things."

"Why not try a good confession. It will do you a world of good. There's this difference between it and a cross-examination. A confession is voluntary and you retain the initiative while you make it. But under cross-examination you are a cockshot; you confess against your will and gain no thanks for what you confess."

"Does that mean that you are offering me a choice between confession and cross-examination?"

Father John did not answer but his eyes said Yes.

"What makes you think I have anything to confess?"

"Well, a young Norwegian of more than ordinary intelligence, who is found unconscious in an empty ship's boat, who makes no effort to get in touch with Lloyd's or his shipowners or his own people and who —who is prone to frenzies of ungovernable rage, surely he has something to confess."

"To confess to whom?"

"To the good people who rescued him from certain death and took him to their bosoms without thought of reward and without question."

Ollsen considered the case, presented so stark and clear-cut in Father John's crispest manner, and made his decision.

"Shall we call Mike from the helm?" he asked.

"Yes, that would be better," said the priest. Stooping his head into the cabin, he spoke quietly to Thade.

"Tell Mike Mack to hand the helm over to Dan and come here. You can stay with Dan and keep him company or finish your one-eyed snooze in the stern."

Thade did not pretend that he was asleep or that he did not hear the quietly uttered instructions. His subterfuges never availed against Father John's omniscience. Reluctantly he scrambled to his feet and made his way aft, mumbling dissent.

"No rest for the wicked or for crucified parish clerks. 'Tis nothing but 'Come here, Thade,' 'Go there, Thade,' morning, noon, and night.

Divil a word of thanks Thade gets from clergy or laity, nor ha'pence, ayther, but kicks; oh, yes, plenty of kicks. 'Tis well our poor backside isn't made out of a pane of glass. . . ."

His grumblings died down when he reached Mike, at whom he shouted a garbled version of his orders.

"They want you to make a quorum up there in the bows; a secret conference behind closed doors, if you please. Listen here to me, Dan Mack, and you, Con Mack—we'll have our own conference here in the stern, all to ourselves and the gulls and the gannets. "

Father John heard Thade's high-pitched travesty of his orders but made no remonstrance. Parish Priests, shrewd parish priests, bow to tradition for peace-sake and never remonstrate with one of the ancient guild of parish clerks, however eccentric. Indeed, free speech is the birthright of the guild, retort its badge, and eccentricity its hallmark. The Clerk and the Church are the constants, the immutable substance of the parish. Priests come and go. Who are *they* to curb the clerk who sees them come and go and commemorates their struttings in caustic phrases? Father John shut his ears and waited for Mike to join them on the foredeck coaming.

"Our friend, Ollsen, has something to tell us, Michael."

"Is that so, Father?"

Mike's thin, dark-skinned features betrayed neither curiosity nor surprise, but the intelligent eyes changed from their set meditative continence to guarded awareness. Mike was nobody's fool. How could he be, accustomed as he was to working alone on the sea where keen observation and quick decisions made the whole difference between success and disaster? No change in the shape of a cloud, in the behaviour of a bird or in the translucence of the water escaped his sensitive eye or failed to convey its portent to his mind. He had, accordingly, been keenly aware of the surcharged atmosphere on the ridge and of Ollsen's suppressed excitement. He had noted Maire's silence after his own eulogy of the Norwegian and Father John's prayer of thanksgiving. But he suspended judgment until he had concrete facts rather than vague inferences.

The island was dropping astern and Ollsen slewed his head around towards the Old Quay, measuring the time it would take them to get there.

"We'll be ashore in less than ten minutes and I'll need more than that to say my say. 'Tis a long story, I'm afraid."

Father John pondered over the idea of postponement and looked to Mike for his opinion of the suggestion. Being a firm believer in the efficacy of the "long finger" in the solution of the problems of his simple life, Mike merely shrugged his shoulders.

"Where's the hurry? Knut and myself are going to Cahirsally on business. We can drop in to the presbytery on our way home in the evening, if that suits you, Father."

"Better still," said the priest, "our friend can tell you his story on the way to town. It is more for your ears than for mine, I assume. You can tell me all about it later on, if you think my advice is needed."

The Norwegian nodded his agreement with that arrangement and stood upright again on the small triangle of foredeck. High over the others he cut a fine figure, balancing his tall frame on the giddy platform with an easy flexing of the joints. His straw-coloured hair, which had not been cut since his rescue, rippled to the breeze and showed, as plainly as did his outworn clothes, how badly he needed a general tidy-up. But Mike did not like the arrangement; he would prefer that Maire was present to hear Ollsen's statement and observe him while he made it. But, true to his habit, he said nothing and turned to the job of conning the boat in to the Quay.

Bill Hannen's lorry was already gone to town with a load of empty Guinness barrels and a small consignment of turkeys for the Christmas market in Cahirsally. The women, who had reared the birds, went with them to make the sale and collect the price of them for their own private and personal use. Turkeys are the perquisite of the womenfolk, their sole source of income, into which the men dare not pry, though many a stone of precious oats goes to fatten the delicate birds.

"Sorry ye weren't here to get a lift in the lorry," said Bill when he heard that the islanders were going to town.

"Ye lost a buckshee drive, but that's my luck. I'll drive ye in the Ford and I can do my own business in town at yer expense. Ten bob a head."

John Joe Barrett waited at the dark end of the shop until Mike had agreed to pay £1 for the car and called for a drink for himself and Knut. Then turning the full radiance of his gazelle eyes on Mike, he brought his dapper figure into the light.

"Perhaps I am in luck, too, Mike. Would there be room for me? I'm very small."

"Small in more ways than one," Bill cut in sarcastically. He had a special contempt for petty cleverness and took delight in thwarting it. "Six and eightpence is small too. That will be your share of the fare to town; that is, if Mr. Mack wants your company. The car is his for the day."

Mike was half glad to have a third party in the Ford to postpone Ollsen's confession. He still wanted Maire to hear it with him and to make any decision which might arise. To ensure the postponement, he went out to the Ford and sat in the front seat beside Bill, leaving the other two to finish their drinks, lest John Joe, with his customary consideration for his own comfort, preempt the front seat and throw Ollsen and himself together in the back.

Bill was a bad driver. He pressed the accelerator fully down at all times, steered erratically with one hand on the wheel, and kept up a lively conversation with whoever sat beside him in the front seat. Mike gasped as Bill sheered miraculously from instant destruction against a telegraph pole and charged recklessly across the road towards a solid stone gatepost, which he skimmed with the front wheel in his sinuous progress.

"A miss is better than a mile, Mike. You're never killed till you're dead and we're not dead yet. I was expecting some boxes of mackerel from you every day since you made a nobby of the lifeboat. Is it short of a crew you are? Johnus's nephew is only waiting to be asked. He's a good lad and I'd advise you hire him. You can't sell fish if you don't catch them, and they won't come in and give themselves up. You must go out for them."

The high-speed monologue stopped for Mike's reply.

"I could do with young Johnus, all right. I'll see him this evening—
Look out! The geese! You'll massacre them."

"Never swerve for a dog or a goose, Mike. They're not worth it.
Anyhow, Biddy Cremin— Wow! I got the gander, I think. Yes, there
he goes with his watch and chain hanging from him."

The poor disembowelled bird flew high in a dying effort to reach
safety and dropped dead at Biddy Cremin's feet.

"As I was going to say, Mike, before I killed the gander, Biddy drives
the old birds out on the road and takes the number of any car that
hits them. She gets a price and a half per goose and keeps the dead bird
for soup. She'll be down to the shop this evening to collect the money,
without fail."

As they careered past the presbytery gate, Bill waved his free hand
derisively at Thade Carey, who was hurrying with a parcel under his
arm to intercept the Ford.

"That's a 'thank-you' job escaped by inches—a pair of his own
brogues for patching by the look of the bundle. He'd expect me to wait
till dark, till Patsy, the cobbler, had them mended for him and blame
me, instead of Patsy, if they were a bad job."

Entering the town, they passed Bill's lorry drawn up outside Paddy
"God's" fish and poultry store. Paddy was surrounded by a crowd of
turkey women who goggled suspiciously at the graduated steelyard,
held high to show the weight of each bird. Paddy is an O'Donoghue,
but there are so many O'Donoghues in Cahirsally that nicknames are
necessary for differentiation. The initials stencilled by his father,
Garrett, on the firm's fish boxes were a godsend to a people who have a
genius for nicknames. They could not resist G. O'D. Thenceforward
Garrett was "God" and his son, "Paddy God."

Bill drove through the crowd without casting a glance at the lorry.
Paddy Brown resented supervision of any sort, he knew, but would give
him a tediously detailed report of the day's happenings in his own
good time and render a scrupulously accurate account of all takings
and disbursements. Bill valued Paddy highly and nursed his little
foibles.

"Where will I drop ye, Mike? I'm going to the bank myself."

"The bank will do us nicely, Bill," Mike said in a noninformative tone, mindful of John Joe's cocked ear. He knew his way around Cahirsally and would shake off John Joe before he bent his steps towards Mr. Mathew's. The less that shaver knew of his business the better.

"We'll all meet at Spitton's at four, if that suits you," Mike suggested to Bill when they alighted. "That will avoid the usual round-up of scattered passengers for the run home in the afternoon." Bill agreed and sprinted up the bank steps without another word, switching instantly to the next job in hand. John Joe, sensing that he was not wanted by the other two, made a gesture as near a bow as Irish distaste for posturing permits and went his way as daintily as if his pants were flounced skirts and he a ballet dancer.

"Will we have a drink before we start business?" Mike asked the sailor.

"Better not, Mike. I'm off it for keeps. Show me where Lloyd's agent hangs out and I'll wait there for you."

"Righto."

Ollsen's rolling gait and tattered seaman's clothes drew all Cahirsally out to doors and windows to stare stonily at him as he gained the agent's office. Corner boys winked at each other and left their points of vantage to slouch towards him with much loin-scratching and squirming of shoulders. Frowsy children clustered about his legs and threw their heads back to gape up at him unblinkingly. The unusual drift of loafers up the street and the dropping fire of questions across the doors and alleyways woke a Civic Guard from his somnolent lookout at the Corner House and sent him sauntering with exaggerated unconcern in the general direction of the drift.

"G'on ou' that; scoot," he barked as he drew near.

The loafers did not scoot at the guard's curt command; they merely rolled their eyes and writhed their mobile lips to show their contempt for policemen who interrupt promising beginnings. Then they idled back to their old haunts, like carrion seagulls retreating with reluctance from a tidbit of jetsam at which they were disturbed. The children backed to the middle of the street and re-formed in a semicircle, with heads aslant and hands behind their backs.

Ollsen seethed within but he kept a calm front. He had no objection to displays of local curiosity; he had been in too many half-dead seaport towns for that, but he did have the merchant-sailor's deep-seated antipathy for policemen. Policemen take advantage of solitary seamen to exercise the disciplinary powers which they have to curb in their dealings with townsmen. To avoid an encounter with the approaching guard, Ollsen turned towards the brass-plated door and knocked loudly.

A finger on his shoulder stiffened every muscle in his body, but remembering his outburst of mad rage on the ridge that very morning, he clenched his teeth in a supreme effort at self-control and clattered the knocker again.

"Can I help you, my man?" the guard asked him in a tone which intimated a severe interrogation to come.

Ollsen wheeled and confronted the self-satisfied policeman so abruptly and so forbiddingly that the startled man leaped backwards with mouth agape. The children leaped backwards too, and clapped hands.

"I'm not your man or any man's man. What do you want?"

"No need to bite a man's nose off," the guard stammered in temporary discomfiture. "A civil question deserves a civil answer, any day," but when Ollsen dismissed him summarily by turning towards the door again, the guard's native trigger-temper broke and routed his discretion. Grasping the sailor's arm to wheel him round, he pulled imperatively just when the door opened and Bill Hodge's red grizzled face stuck forth aggressively. Bill was a peace commissioner of ancient standing, a Protestant who had once exercised the overriding powers of a justice of the peace under the British regime. He still employed the quasi-judicial voice of authority in the new dispensation which barely tolerated those of his kind who had not fled from the stage on which they once strutted so outrageously.

He glared at the two men jostling on his doorstep.

"What's this? What's this? Brawling in the market place?"

His flat croaking voice brought the guard to his senses. Releasing the Norwegian, he raised his hand smartly to the visor of his cap to salute the outraged Mr. Hodge.

"This man rejected my offer to assist him in a manner which was likely to provoke a breach of the peace, sir."

The P.C. turned his cairn-terrier face on Ollsen.

"Well, my man. What have you to say to that?"

"So, I'm *your* man now. *He* claims me as his man. Am I a lost pup or what?"

The agent took a slit-eyed look at the big Norwegian, who spoke so assuredly and, with a single phrase, put himself and the guard in the wrong.

"Um, yes. Um. Oh, it was you who knocked. Come in, come in. That will do, guard. I'll look after him."

The door closed, leaving the guard discomfited, and the children disappointed by an unfinished action-play. Hodge preceded the sailor into the comfortable well worn sitting room, which he used for private and public purposes, and gave him the chair allotted to undistinguished visitors.

"Well, then, what's the trouble?"

"I am here to report as a shipwrecked sailor to you as Lloyd's agent."

Hodge pulled out a drawer from the desk at which he was sitting and placed it, with its neatly arranged papers, on the top between him and Ollsen. Beside it he spread a folio sheet of writing paper.

"What ship?" he asked with pen poised.

"The brigantine *Bernadotte*, of Trondheim, Norway."

Hodge entered that answer carefully, writing with stiff forearm jerks.

"Owners?" he asked.

"Norwegian Sails, Ltd., of Tromsö and London."

"Cargo?"

"Salt cod and Swedish iron for Bilbao."

"Captain and crew?"

"Gunnar Skelde, captain; crew of twenty."

"Your own name and rating?"

"Knut Ollsen, bo'sun and ship's carpenter."

"Are the ship's papers available?"

"How should I know?"

"Any other survivors?"

"I don't know. I was picked up unconscious and alone in one of the ship's lifeboats."

"When and where?"

"On 12th November last, off Shark Island."

"Why!" exclaimed Hodge, "that is more than a month ago. Why didn't you report sooner? You know it was your duty to your owners to report the loss of the ship."

Ollsen eyed him coolly.

"I told you I was unconscious and in bad trim when I was rescued. It took some time for me to come around, and Shark Island is not easy to get at. But what about it? I am here now."

Hodge laid down his pen and took from a compartment of the drawer a cardboard file containing the year's issue of Lloyd's *Siren and Shipping*, and a dozen or so of loose typewritten sheets bearing Lloyd's heading. He scanned the sheets first, laid one aside, and then picked up the bundle of *Siren and Shipping* to search for a particular issue. He found it and read a marked paragraph intently. A knock at the street door deepened the frown on his face.

"Would you see who that is?" he said to Ollsen and returned to his search, barely looking up when the sailor came back with Mike Mack.

"Ah, I thought so," he said at last and laid the pamphlet, face down, on the single typewritten sheet. Smacking his lips he leaned back in his chair and directed at Ollsen one of the masterful judicial glares he used to turn, in the good old British days, on a "drunk" he had trapped into prevarication.

"Now, my man. You said you were a shipwrecked sailor."

"I did."

"And that the *Bernadotte* was lost at sea."

"I did not say that."

"How dare you contradict me! I have it here in black and white from your own lips," Hodge barked as he clapped his open palm down on the folio of written answers.

"It can't be there. Unless, of course, you wrote more into my answers than I actually said. Why not read it through?"

Hodge snorted with indignation and read the answers aloud. He bit his lip at the end and read them a second time to himself, looking for the incriminating statement. With diminished truculence, he still sought to justify himself.

"Did you not say you were shipwrecked?"

"I did and Mr. Mack here can prove that I was."

"And you knew when you said it that the *Bernadotte* was not lost at sea."

"I know nothing of her since . . . I myself was lost off her."

The two angry men came to an impasse, glaring at each other until Mike intervened as peacemaker.

"You seem to have some information, Mr. Hodge. Perhaps you could let Knut know what it is, then ye would have both sides of the story and understand each other better."

Hodge had cooled off sufficiently to welcome Mike's suggestion. It was a handy ladder for climbing down with some salvage of dignity from the false position he had taken with Ollsen.

"Perhaps I had better to read what the *Siren* has to say about the *Bernadotte*. The report was so unusual that it stuck in my mind. Here it is: 'Our Bordeaux agent reports that the brigantine *Bernadotte* bound for Bilbao, has put into Bordeaux for repairs to her hull. The owners are sending a captain to replace Captain Skelde, who has been transferred to the Mariner's Hospital, suffering from head injuries. The boatswain is reported missing.' What do you make of that?" he asked them.

Ollsen said: "None of my answers contradict anything in that report. I am the missing boatswain and, as you say, the *Bernadotte* is not lost."

"But a blind man can see that the Board of Trade or Lloyd's or the owners will hold an inquiry into the whole thing. An injured captain, a missing boatswain, and a sinking ship simply shriek for an inquiry,"

Hodge countered and then added as an afterthought: "And you must report in person at Lloyd's without any delay."

"That is why I am here," said Ollsen. "I understand that you have funds to assist distressed mariners."

"Ye—es, but I must satisfy myself as to their bona fides. Have you any money on you?"

"Not a penny," Ollsen shot in, lest Mike commit himself by promising to help or by telling Hodge that the St. Finian had been bought from Bill Hannen with Knut's money. "And as you see, I am in rags. I will need a full rig-out and travelling expenses to London. The owners can stop that out of my wages."

"If I defray these charges, you must be ready to travel by the next train."

Mike demurred at such short notice, there were so many things to do, but Ollsen surprised him by accepting the agent's conditions with unexpected alacrity and by quietly pressing on his foot to tell him to defer his objections until they were alone again. Hodge got the sailor to sign an official receipt for £3 sustentation money and then handed him a voucher to present to the stationmaster for a through ticket to Euston.

"Which draper do you prefer?" he asked Mike before he entered the clothier's name in a voucher for the sailor's outfit.

"The Blue Seas," said Mike and the agent, understanding, wrote "W. C. O'Donoghue" in the appropriate place. Passing the voucher across to Ollsen, he rose, shook hands with his clients, and saw them to the door. As soon as they were gone he put a long-distance call through to Lloyd's to inform them of the reappearance of the Bernadotte's boatswain, and of his immediate departure for London.

"What's all the rush for?" Mike wanted to know when they reached the street. "The train leaves in two hours' time. You can't get clothes and your dinner and run out to the island to say good-bye to Maire and the rest in two hours. Take your ease, man, and go tomorrow if you have to go at all."

"I'd better go now, Mike. That report from Bordeaux means trouble for me if I do not get my story in before Skelde returns to London. He's fit to concoct a tale to put me in the wrong and himself in the clear. The sooner I get to the owners, the better for me and the ship's crew."

"Things done in a hurry are never done right," said Mike. "I don't know what's up but surely another day won't make it worse. Maire will never forgive me or you, if you clear out without seeing her."

Blue Sea (W.C.) fussed out on the shop floor to meet, with outstretched hands, the two men whose appearance brought the cleansing breath of the sea into the heavy, fusty atmosphere of tweeds, woollens, and strong leather. His bulging eyes, set in dead-white pendulous features, peered upwards over the top of his steel-rimmed spectacles at them and finally rested on Mike.

"*De vahassa, a chara chroi.* How are ye all, out Manistir way? Is the wifeen in town with you? I hear she's a great girl—but, sure, what else could she be? The Horgan's are old stock. . . ."

He chattered on, assuming the part of a host welcoming a valued neighbour on a friendly visit with no thought of business. Mike would have taken his cue and carried on the charming make-believe, if he had time for it, but Ollsen's need was pressing.

"My friend, here, wants a full rig-out from shirt to overcoat. Can you manage it in a hurry?"

Blue Sea snapped into action at once. He swivelled his eye over the Norwegian's stalwart figure, pulled the six-foot tape from his shoulders to measure sleeve, breast, and leg lengths, and then leaned back against the counter to think out his stock with closed eyes and folded arms. He knew the value of suspense for reducing a customer's bargaining power and delayed his answer as long as he could.

"I don't think your friend can be fitted at such short notice, Michael. He's a very big man, you know."

"We must try elsewhere, so?" said Mike turning towards the door.

"That's no good. You won't find his fit in the whole town, if I can't fit him," said Blue Sea still leaning against the counter and smiling at Mike with the smug assurance of a purse-proud small-town shopkeeper.

Mike knew that Blue Sea's boast was well founded.

"Well, show us what you have then."

Blue Sea led them into the storeroom, told Ollsen to strip to the pelt,

and returned to the shop where they heard him rapping out orders to
Maura of the haberdashery counter, Mr. Murphy of the Manchester
department, and Michael John in the boots and ready-mades. No shipmaster could beat Blue Sea at curt snappy orders when business was
adoing. In half an hour Ollsen emerged from the back room like a
huge butterfly freed from his chrysalid skin of grubby seaman's clothes.
The dark Burberry raincoat was a shade tight for his bulging shoulders,
but the brown pinstriped suit was a good fit. Blue Sea rubbed his hands
in satisfaction with the transformation he had worked on the sailor
and beamed over his spectacles on his handiwork.

"You're a grand figure of a man, sir," he said as he backed into the
shop before them, leading them with shrewd intent towards the pay
office. Slipping inside, he elbowed the girl accountant off her seat and
made out the long bill with surprising speed.

It made Mike gasp when he pushed it through the aperture in the
glass panel. Sixteen guineas seemed a lot of money for a suit of clothes
and trimmings. But when Ollsen handed in the voucher Hodge had
given him, Mike came up for breath and grinned widely as he watched
Blue Sea read the voucher with pursed lips.

"Show me that bill again, till I check it," the draper said without any
trace of satisfaction in his voice. His gruff tone indicated that he
thought Mike had tried to outsmart him. Taking a blank billhead from
the tray he recast the account and presented it through the peephole to
Ollsen.

"Sign that, please," he said, as dry and matter-of-fact as you please.
Mike peeked over Ollsen's shoulder at the revised total and read
"£18, 10s. 9d"! Blue Sea ignored the wry-mouthed comment of his
customers and showed them to the door.

Leaving the old clothes in a bag to be called for, they went to Maggie
Mingawn's eating house in a sort of silent communion of thought
which lasted through the dinner and the walk to the railway station.
Neither of them had much small-change conversation and neither of
them wished to open the subject which filled their minds. Mike led
Ollsen into the waiting room and held out the £50 he had drawn from
his account at Mathew's.

"Here's your money, Knut. You'll be wanting it in your travels."

"No, no, no! I owe you and Maire more than that. I owe my life to both of you. Put it back in your pocket."

"Orders is orders," Mike quoted. "Maire wants you to have it. We surely must do that much for her, the way she is. 'Tis bad enough for me to have to tell her you went off without a good-bye to herself."

The train backed noisily into the station and a handful of passengers climbed into the one grimy carriage assigned to human freight. Ollsen followed them, let down the window, and leaned on his elbows to look down on Mike.

"Tell Maire I'll write from London."

Mike nodded that he would.

"I'll be back as soon as the inquiry is over, Mike."

Mike took that as the sort of comforting assurance one gives to a child and smiled dubiously.

"That's gospel truth, Mike. I have a debt to pay and I'll pay it on the Shark."

The engine coughed asthmatically, jolted forward with a great clanking of coupling chains, and began to drag its heavy load from under the platform-roof. Mike trotted alongside, grasping the Norwegian's hand, gave it a great squeeze and let go. Ollsen waved his hand once and withdrew his head as the train drew away to rumble slowly across the suspension bridge and gather speed for the climb through the hills that fenced Mike and his people from the outer world.

CHAPTER 23 · *Winter Nights*

THE year went out in a succession of southwesterly gales which drove heavy seas battering against the sheer cliffs of the Shark and smothering the Lookout in a driving mist of salt spume. They filled the Sound with an interminable procession of humpbacked rollers, racing on to some urgent rendezvous at the head of the Bay, and cutting off all communication between the island and the mainland. The islanders were marooned and thrown on their own resources for work and for the pleasant relaxations of Christmas. They did not mind the enforced internment very much. They expected prolonged bad weather to see the old year out and were prepared for it. Maire had secured ample supplies of candles, paraffin oil, and matches to ensure a bright kitchen in the long nights, and had put in a store of tea, sugar, and flour to eke out the supply of native food which the island and the more generous sea had given them in good measure.

Mike and Sean Driscoll hauled a two months' supply of turf from the bog, with Mai's pony and cart, and stacked it near the kitchen door for Joany's convenience. Nearer still they piled up a great pyramid of short wood blocks. These they had sawn off the old ships' timbers which the sea disgorged in stormy weather. The straight-grained ones they had split into thin splinters and placed near Joany's hand by the hob to toast.

A gammon, a ham, a half-head and odd slabs of bacon still hung high under the smoky thatch; two firkins of pickled herrings stood side by side behind the backdoor, under a dozen salt ling, nailed stiff as boards to a rafter. A long hank of onions was festooned between two couples, just clear of the fumes of *L'Aurore's* gleaming cabin lamp. Food, fuel, and light were assured till the gales blew themselves out.

The islanders missed Ollsen's strong personality and tireless energy. Maire missed him more than the others for reasons which she voiced and for reasons which she smothered as they formed in the depths of her mind. She joined freely in praise of his thoroughness in doing things that made life easier on the island and kept reminding Sean to carry on with Ollsen's plan of building a concrete tank about the well bore to store the water. But she hid, even from herself, every resurgence of the emotion which the sailor's virility had stirred in her breast when they were returning together from the cells. The mere idea of thinking emotionally of any man but Mike shocked the puritanical code in which she had been reared. Realistic though she was, she was yet too inexperienced in erotic phenomena to know that women, as well as men, can love more than one at a time. Her vulnerability alarmed her.

The household rose late during the dark days of December that were too short for serious work. Mike and Sean fended for the cattle morning and evening and, between times, hammered out of oddments of timber the casings into which they would pour the concrete mix for the tank. Maire sat in a sugan chair by the fire putting the finishing stitches in the baby clothes she had cut out in preparation for the newcomer. Joany baked fruitcakes for the Christmas feasting and plucked geese which she would stuff with mashed potatoes and onions and roast in the basting ovens for the Christmas dinner. Mai polished the delft, scoured the sycamore mugs snow-white with fine sand, and installed the huge Christmas candle in its place of honour in the embrasure of the kitchen window.

The nights closed in early with roaring wind and smothering rain, but the house was too low and too snug in its hollow to suffer from the gales. Once the doors were closed and bolted, all exterior sounds were excluded and nothing was heard indoors but the cheery crackle of firewood, the intermittent conversation of the women riding lightly on the subdued boom of the wind in the chimney. The men took off their boots after supper and joined the barefoot women around the fire of turf and driftwood. Maire stowed wool and knitting needles away for the night and settled herself snugly in her chair. Mai took her accordion out of its case and fingered it lightly in jigs and reels which set the bare feet beating time. The accordion was almost the only dissipation her grandmother had countenanced in her upbringing.

When she had run through the best of her dance tunes, Mai slid into the long cadences of Mike's favourite "Bean an Fhir Rua" (The Red-Haired Man's Wife). Maire used to love the way Mike's deep-chested voice flowed with the feeling of the song. She once told Ollsen that it was Mike's singing that first showed her the softness of his heart and made her love him. She thrilled to it still, but compunction for her secret fallibility in regard to the fair-haired Norseman was turning her against the song. It pointed a finger at her hidden transgression of the law of monogamic loyalty. To cut off discussion of the "Red-Haired Man's Wife" and her frailty, Maire asked Joany to tell one of her fairy tales. Joany came from a family of great storytellers who knew the Seven Major tales, the Seven Minor tales, the saga of Finn in verse, of Cuchulain in prose, and the anecdotes and satires which enshrined the history of the Barony for more than ten generations. She had heard them all many a time at her own fireside and could recite them in the professional style which forbids the transposition of a phrase or the substitution of a word.

"What kind of tale do ye want?" asked Joany. "Giants or dwarfs, maidens or witches, love or treasure?"

"Love," said Sean, stealing a glance at Mai.

"Treasure," said Mai, who caught the furtive glance and, with woman's innate guile, thwarted the lover's wish in order to stimulate his desire.

"Why not give us a mixum-gatherum of giants and dwarfs and treasure?" said Mike. "And if you work in a little love here and there, these youngsters won't object."

"Very well, Mike. Giants and dwarfs and treasure it is. Put some more logs on the fire. And you, Mai, turn down the lamp, so as we can see the fairy faces glowing deep in the fire, and the golden castles rising and changing into dungeons."

Joany closed her eyes, leaned her head back against the breast of the fireplace, and linked her fingers on her lap. The low firelight, striking upwards on her homely face, lit the under surfaces of chin, nose, and brows and sent strange shadows flitting across her features. When she broke into the sustained monotone of the shanachie, she was transformed into a Druidess sitting in the gloaming under her oak tree at Belltane.

"This is the tale of Raha the Runner. One day of many days that Finn and the Fianna went hunting, the hounds woke from her bed among the rowan trees a hind which had outslept the dawn. . . ."

The tale ran its long course through an eventful sequence of miraculous pursuits and escapes, vanishments and metamorphoses to the final triumph which Raha the Runner shared with his fairy princess. The organ boom of the wind in the chimney and the flutter of flames in the fire accompanied the tale from beginning to end, giving it a weird unearthly dignity. Joany closed it with the traditional formula.

"That is my story for you. I did not make it or mar it but told it as I heard it. If it is true, it is a great story; if it is not true, it is still a great story and great is the man who made it. May he find a warm place in heaven near Matthew, Mark, Luke, and John, God's own storytellers. Amen."

"Amen," said her audience together, as Joany sat up in her chair and smiled her homely smile upon them.

"Raha must have been the fastest creature in the world, if he was faster than the wind," said Sean.

"There are a lot of things to beat the wind," said Mike. "Didn't you ever hear the old rhyme?

> "The Hind, the Hare, and the Hound,
> The fastest to run on the ground;
> The Seal, the Skate, and the Ray,
> The fastest to swim in the say."

"I did," said Joany, "but my old father used to say that the fastest thing in the world is the thought of a man's mind. Quicker than a flash it flies from Hell to Heaven, from here to the sun and stars. The one

thing it can't reach is the end of eternity. Only God's mind can reach
that."

Mai began to yawn; so did Sean. Healthy young people cannot fight
sleep as old ones do. Joany stood up to smoor the dying fire and hummed
the old mocking bedtime verse.

> "Come to bed," said Lazyhead;
> "Wait a while," said Slow.
> "Put down the pot," said Greedygut,
> "We'll eat before we go."

On Stephen's Day the wind backed to the south, blowing across the
ocean rollers and breaking them up into an insane tumult of jostling
water. The Lookout lost its wreath of flying spindrift and the Bay,
though still restless, eased down in the shelter of the southern circle of
mountains. Scuds of rain still flogged the island but they came inter-
mittently and at growing intervals, which gave Mike Mack chances to
go down to the cove and see how the boats and gear had weathered the
Christmas gales. He found everything shipshape and secure there and
made a circuit of the dunes and lower fields to count the sheep and
cattle which had to fend for themselves outdoors. The ram and two old
ewes were missing, blown off a cliff, perhaps, or gone to ground somewhere in a brake of brambles. One of the black bullocks had a slipped
shoulder, but a pitch plaster would cure that as soon as he and Sean
could get the beast into a byre.

He returned to the house for Sean to climb with him to the Lookout;
anything might happen to a lone man up there in a gale. They stood
in the shelter of the grey rock of Carrigard to scan the Bay and the
water-logged fields beneath them for any untoward results of the storm.
They found nothing of note in the woebegone prospect but a few up-
rooted bushes and a dark brown rope of seaweed which the gale had
piled above high water along the strand, the whole way from the Cove
to the cells.

Sean shouted in amazement when they left the rock to climb the
short steep rise to the top on hands and feet.

"Look, Mike! All the herrings!"

"Good God Almighty," was all Mike could say.

Scattered over a wide stretch of heather were hundreds of white-bellied fishes lying limp with gaping jaws and opaque staring eyes. They strewed over a wide acre of hillside.

"Only once before did I see the like of that," said Mike. "A shoal of herrings caught in the crest of the wave and flung clear over the cliff when it broke. Poor devils, they got the hell of a death."

They went among them, taking one here and there to examine the gills and scales and to get the feel of the flesh.

"They're as fresh as daisies," said Sean. "Talk of manna from heaven; this beats it bad. I'll run down to the house for the fish basket and I'll bring Mai with me to help to gather them."

"No need to run, Sean. You'll be tired enough by the time we have them home and gutted and salted and packed in the barrels. Take your ease, man. They won't run away."

"All right; all right. But I'll take a dozen of the biggest with me for the dinner. Joany will have them fried in the pan to make our mouths water when we have the lot basketed home."

They were wracked with toil before they brought the last of the herrings to the house. After the odoriferous dinner, all but Maire tucked up their sleeves to split the herrings down the back, open them out flat, and pack them between layers of coarse salt into the special barrels used for herrings and mackerel. It was a slimy job, followed by much sluicing of water to clean up the mess of offal and fish scales. But no one grumbled. A gift of herrings from the sky was too miraculous for any words but of thanksgiving.

To Maire, who was reared on a hill farm on the mainland, fish-curing was a new experience, promising much profit in the future when the St. Finian started to hunt for spring fish. She did not know that all but the late October hauls were sold by auction at the pierhead, straight from the nets, and shipped on ice by special trains to Billingsgate.

She was too big to stand, knife in hand, and help in the work, but she had her chair placed at the head of the table to watch the dexterity with which Mike, Sean, and Joany slit the fish from snout to tail in one slash of the knife and removed the entrails featly with crooked fingers. Mai was a novice too. To her was assigned the job of keeping the table supplied with whole fish and removing the split ones to the salting tables at the end of the kitchen. Mike would not trust her with a knife lest she lose a finger.

It was still broad day when they were finished and washed up, and they were too full of the holiday spirit and of the thrill of the God-sent herrings to call it a day. Moreover it was Stephen's Day, a great day of mumming on the mainland, of re-acting the pre-Christian folk play of the wren. If Maire had remained on the mainland, she would have enjoyed the boisterous invasion of her home by the Wran Boys, would have paid them their traditional dues of food and money, and joined in the noisy dance which winds up the mummery. But on the Shark there was no tradition of the ancient mime and Maire would have to go without and cut another of the ties that bound her to her old home.

Mike guessed at her nostalgic regrets and planned a pleasant surprise for her. Out in the byre he and Sean had secretly switched from carpentry to costumery, from making casings to contriving masks and disguises from sundry garments and plaited straw. These they hid in the byre, letting none but Mai into their plan. Her assistance was needed to supply the music which is an essential part of the play.

Normally, the Wran Boys set out on their rounds in the forenoon and Mike had arranged for an early start for his little troupe, but the discovery of the herrings threw his schedule out of order. It was nearing four o'clock when he gave the prearranged nod to Sean and Mai to slip out and get busy. Sean led the way into the byre and up on the hayloft where the costumes were hidden: straw helmets and buskins, oakum whiskers and trousers made of strips of cloth. He separated the sets, placing Mai's at one end of the loft and his own at the other, and proceeded to remove his outer garments to get into the grotesque mummer's costume. He was in great good humour and kept up a running commentary with Mai. She answered his lighthearted banter at first, but soon Sean sensed a hesitance in her responses and looked across the hay at her. She was finding unexpected difficulty with her costume. Her working skirt was too thick to stuff into the trousers and her hair too long for the straw helmet to cover.

Sean let her alone for a while and went on with his own transformation into a bewhiskered warrior clad cap-a-pie in straw.

"What's the trouble, Mai? Can I help you?"

"My skirt won't fit into these old pants."

"Throw 'em off, then."

He got no answer to that facile suggestion, but a shrug. Mai turned her back to him and stood still with bent head, wondering how she might make her prime difficulty known to Sean.

"Go outside till I try it," she said at last.

"Sure, I won't look at you doing it; I promise you that."

"Go down off the hay and wait till I call you," she said.

Sean slipped down to the floor of the byre and waited out of sight.

"Come up now and help me to fix these other things on me. They are flapping around every which way."

"Oh!" she exclaimed when Sean appeared, grizzly and awe-inspiring, in the gloom of the hayloft. "You put the heart across in me, you look so frightful."

Sean gasped, too, but not in terror. Mai's rich figure, clad only in light underbodice and improvised pants, took his breath away. Her glossy hair hung loose to the smooth white arms she had folded under her breasts, swelling round and provocative under the clinging bodice, as she stood in the hay facing him. He could neither speak nor move. Hot blood rushed to his head and ebbed again, leaving him in a tremor of emotion. Mai caught the infection and stared with lips parted and arms hanging by her side, wondering what had come over herself and Sean. Under the urge of an overriding mutual impulse, they leaped into each other's arms and relieved their pent-up ecstasy in a fierce silent embrace that left them breathless and unnerved, excited and unsatisfied.

"Hist. Listen." Mai whispered her warning and pushed Sean out of her arms, under the dictates of the female subconscience, which is never totally submerged, even in the wildest emotional storms. Woman keeps one ear cocked for noises without, for the rustlings and faint creaks that threaten intrusion or eavesdropping on her lovemaking. Her surrenders are never complete; she is rarely taken unawares.

"Quick," she said urgently. "Fix up this helmet and jacket. Mike'll be wondering what's delaying us."

Sean helped her to bind the flimsy straw trappings in position and slid down the hay with her to the cobble floor, where they stood a moment listening for suspicious noises with bated breath. Hearing none, Mai stepped out of the byre and across the farmyard to the kitchen door at her normal pace and waited there for Sean, who had gone back for the accordion they had forgotten in their disconcerting ebullition of passion.

"Am I a show in this awful rig?" she asked in a low intimate tone, which thrilled Sean with its suggestion of secret fellowship.

"You couldn't look a show in anything," he whispered warmly in her ear. "You're fine."

But they did look prehistoric and aboriginal with their heads hidden in straw beehives which tapered to a pixie point on top and opened in front to show the beards of teased rope. About their bodies they wore cuirasses of twisted straw and cloth puttees about their legs. Mai hugged the accordion to her breast and Sean carried in his right hand a branch of furze, showing a tiny dead bird in a flourish of gaudy ribbons. Mai's accordion, a gross anachronism which accentuated the antiquity of their crude garb, was the only false note in the picture.

"We'd better make a start," Sean said. "Get that old gadget going, Mai."

Drawing the accordion wide on a loud brassy chord, Mai swung into a simple jigging tune, which both of them took up, to sing the traditional "Wran Song" in its original Gaelic.

> "A dreolin, a dreolin, a Ri nan ean
> Ce mor do vuirin is beag tu fein.
> Eiri suas, a vanatee,
> Toor duin uv na circe dee
> Ata ag breh ag bun do hee."

Knocking loud on the door, Sean led Mai into the kitchen through which they sang and danced their way to the hearthstone. Thence they danced, in turn, to Joany and Mike and Maire, before whom they stood and sang again.

"The Wran, the Wran, the King of all birds,
On Stephen's Day was caught in the furze.
Although he is little, his family's great;
Stand up, Landlady, and give us a treat.
Hang up the kettle, put down the pan,
Give us a shilling and let us be gone."

The unexpected continuance on the sea-girt island of the old mainland tradition filled Maire's cup of Christmas happiness. Now she knew that her marriage to Mike had not cut her off from her kindred as completely as she feared. The Shark was no longer a place of exile, but a part of the familiar countryside which, to her, meant home. Her heart warmed to the kindly thought that had prompted the younger pair to make that Stephen's Day as homelike as last year's. Of course, she saw through their disguise and recognized their voices. That was no blemish in the presentation of the play. Folk got their big thrill in guessing at the identity of the mummers.

She turned to tell Joany to "put down the pan," but that knowledgeable lady was already in action. Lemonade and generous cuts of currant cake appeared from nowhere on the end of the table. Beside each glass Maire placed a bright shilling to clear her own and Joany's dues, and on each cut of cake Mike laid the scot of the man of the house. The mummers gulped the drinks and danced backwards to the door and out into the darkness. There Mai gave Sean his second lesson in female tactics. Dropping the accordion at her feet, she sped like a snipe into the byre and bolted the door against him and the world. It was late when they returned, separately, in their own clothes to the kitchen, half proud and half ashamed of their mumming and very conscious of each other.

"Strange," Mike observed in continuance of the conversation which developed while the pair were outside, "strange that for 364 days of the year we are fonder of the little brown wran than of all the birds in the sky, but on Stephen's Day we start out on a mad hunt to murder them in thousands for no reason at all. Isn't it strange?"

"Don't they say," Sean ventured, "that it was the wran betrayed Our Lord to the Jews?"

"Nonsense, man alive!" Joany's voice was full of contempt for Sean's ignorance of a well established fact. "Sure everyone that knows anything knows that it was the *daol duff* did that bit of dirty work, that black beetle that cocks his tail at you."

Sean conceded the point and proceeded to register a good mark for the wren's supremacy as a builder of nests, but Mike, noting a weariness on Maire's eyelids, drew his rosary beads from his pocket, turned the back of his chair to the fire and knelt down, with his elbows on the seat. Maire remained seated, reciting the Five Joyful Mysteries from memory and leading the Paters and Aves over the heads bowed around the fire.

The synchronized responses gave no indication that the minds of the little community were going their separate ways, following the thoughts nearest their hearts. Distraction is the great defect in communal prayer.

Mike began to wonder what had happened to the few lobster pots he had to leave in broken water when the gale started. Were they gone adrift and lost or smashed beyond repair? He feared so. It could be worse. Anyhow, he would not be doing much lobster fishing for the future. Mackerel would be more in his line when he got the third man for the *St. Finian.* He must see Johnus's nephew. . . .

The first decade came to its end.

"Glory be to the Father, the Son, and the Holy Ghost," said Maire. "As it was in the beginning, is now and ever shall be. Amen."

It was Mike's turn to lead in the second decade and concentrate on fingering the beads carefully lest he undercount or overcount the Hail Marys.

While Mike's voice droned on, Sean tried manfully to tie his mind to his responses, but after a few perfunctory attempts to shoo away a set of new lascivious thoughts, as insistent as buzzing bees, he surrendered his whole being to recapture the exquisite physical thrill of Mai's body in his arms, as vibrant and responsive as his own. He succeeded so well that a cold shudder ran through him and shook his dangling beads and made him mumble the responses lest his chattering teeth betray him. Mike's "Glory be" brought him back to earth and the obligation of leading the third decade with fitting decorum.

Led into distraction by the sound of his voice, Mai surveyed the new world of wondrous promise opened to her by Sean in the hayloft. At last she knew whither the vague yearnings and physical appetites of the past year led to. She had found out that Sean could satisfy them and that she had the power to enthrall him as she willed. She recalled the scene, the look of amazed, hungry desire on his face when he saw her, standing exposed in half clothing in the half light. She imagined again the wholly delightful quiver of abandon that suffused her when he crushed her to him. This was a wonderful thing she had discovered, but a secretive thing of the dark, to be controlled and used with circumspection. She pulled the rein on her thoughts when her subconscious timing warned her that Sean was nearing the end of his quota of "Hail Marys" and that her turn to lead in the fourth decade had come.

Joany's mind did not wander far. Tomorrow was Friday, a fish day. Would the herrings be fresh enough for the dinner? Only two hens were laying and, of course, the two men must get the eggs. Men have to be fed, whatever the women do. That's what her old mother used to say to her when food was short and her young brothers clamouring for tidbits.

She had passed on the law to her own three girls and Maire would teach her daughters, when the time came, to stint themselves to preserve the full vigour of the men. A puny man is worse than no man. Sure, every woman knows that. But a strong lusty man, now, like Mike or . . . Unbidden, Ollsen's powerful figure, virile and dominant, forced its way into her mind, disturbing its pleasant ambling progress through familiar ways, and frightening it into a prayer, a real heartfelt prayer, that God might keep the Norwayman away from Maire and Mike Mack. . . .

"Joany dear, you're wool-gathering. It's your turn," said Maire. "Fifth Joyful Mystery, the Finding of Jesus in the Temple."

The old woman straightened her back with a jerk and composed her face in the prim austerity of solemn prayer, the eyes unfocussed and the brow drawn to a frown. Maire watched her with amused affection as she thumbed her beads nervously. What a comfort it was to have Joany on hand when her hour came! That hour was near, very near, if the flutterings under her heart meant anything. How would she have faced the ordeal alone with Mike? When they took possession of their island home, they had both accepted with light hearts the prospect of complete seclusion until children would come to share it. The Shark was to have been the inviolate sanctuary of their love. Vain hope. Perhaps it was a foolish hope. Anyhow, the Lord ordained against it. One by one, Joany and Sean and Mai had invaded their sanctuary. No, their coming was not invasion. They were too welcome to be called invaders and too firmly established to be deemed visitors. But Ollsen's coming was different. He himself was different and dynamic and disturbing. His very presence on the island disturbed their quiet pool of life. It was an invasion, an intrusion, an insurgence against easygoing habitude. Moreover, he was an alien in race and in his outlook on life. Everything changed when he came. Even her deep-seated love for Mike had felt a tremor at its foundations. He said he was coming back. . . . God forgive me, she thought. I'm not sure whether I want him back or not.

Joany's voice, rising in the crescendo of the closing prayer, broke into her wandering thoughts. They all blessed themselves as demurely as if their communings had been with Heaven and of heavenly things, and took their chairs from the hearth to range them by the wall before they went to bed.

CHAPTER 24 · *The New Curate*

Father JOHN had an easier Christmastide than he had looked forward to. The bishop, with kindly understanding, sent him a young curate to shoulder some of the duties which accumulate around the Feast of the Nativity, more than at any other period in the ecclesiastical year. But curates are a mixed blessing, be they zealots or journeymen. Zealots run riot on a free rein and sulk on a tight one: journeymen operate only from an outside impulse, as void of initiative as the parish priest's horse.

The Reverend Father Patrick Boyle was a by-product of the new Gaelic education, which tends to create a lopsided mentality in children. He started with imperfect English into an intensive Gaelic curriculum and emerged with his English still imperfect. He used a bookish brand of Gaelic, but made no attempt to limber it up by converse with the old people who speak it fluently. He read no English but the headings of the daily newspapers and the reports of football matches and had no English books but the lives of Casement, Pearse, and De Valera. Vannoort's *Dogmatic Theology*, Prummer's *Moral*, Walsh's *De Vera Ecclesia*, and the current *Ordo* stood on his table to testify to his knowledge of Latin.

He made it a practice to read his breviary along the main road at the peak of its traffic, bowing remotely, with eyes fixed on the printed page, as the carts rumbled past him. Thus he fostered the common belief that Father Boyle was a saint and a scholar, God bless him. He was no zealot. For him religion was as fixed, certain, and commonplace as arithmetic and daylight and farming. He grew up in that happy state and preserved it inviolate through his seven-year course in Maynooth. The résumés of competing religions, of schisms within the Church and of debatable points in Catholic tradition, which were traversed seriatim in the theological classes, woke no sympathetic doubts in his complaisant mind. Rather did they provoke him to wonder at the tolerance of the Lord with doubting Thomases and inquisitive cranks. What possible purpose could He have had in creating them, let alone permitting them to blaspheme the truth?

No, he was no zealot. The daily round of Mass, and sick calls, the weekly sermon and confessions and the annual retreat discharged his whole duty as a priest. The parish priest could plan the weekly timetable; he would carry it out.

But Father Patrick was a healthy, vigorous young man, albeit small in stature. He was in a position of authority, subject, of course, to Father Miles's overriding jurisdiction in parochial affairs. His vigour and his authority had to find expression in corporal activity, and football lay ready to hand. By the end of his first month in Manistir, he had usurped Jim Brehony's position as chairman of the parish club, ousted Jim's cronies from the committee and set himself up as director, manager, and coach to the team.

Of course the noise of his cyclonic activities reached Father John's ears. A parish priest hears everything, from the creaking of a bedpost in the dark to the colloguing of gossips in the day. But he was biding his time until he had Father Boyle under the presbytery roof. When the bishop's letter came to announce the appointment, he had to make hurried arrangements to house the newcomer in Hannen's Hotel until the presbytery had sufficient furniture to seat him, feed him, and bed him.

And he had to get a housekeeper. Thade Carey's stewed tea and hard-boiled eggs would provide ample cause of complaint to summon him before the Ecclesiastical Court for cruelty to curates.

The afternoon Father Patrick drove his Hillman Minx up to the presbytery door for the first time and quick-stepped into the hall with his hat on the back of his sandy head, his squirrel eyes looking everywhere but into Father John's, he placed himself outside the fold. With an effort, the parish priest suspended final judgment, showed him around the empty house, and suggested that they proceed at once to Hannen's Hotel. On the way he gave Father Patrick the lie of the parish and of the two churches that served the separate parochial units of Manistir and the Coombe, and after tea he handed him a written list of his duties for the week.

He repressed an impulse to reprimand the younger man for the off-hand way in which he took the list, folded it in four without looking at it, and fobbed it, as slick as a waiter palming a small tip. It was early days for correction, but Father John did display some curtness in refusing Father Patrick's offer to drive him back to the presbytery.

He borrowed Big Bill's Ford and drove her hard over the pass to Brohul's cottage in the Coombe where Debby Sweeny still lived in solitary independence.

She met him at the door with welcoming eye and waited respectfully for him to speak.

"May I come in, Debby?"

"Sure, Father John. Come in and sit down near the fire."

"Have you had any news from your brother?"

"Not a word. But I wasn't expecting any."

"You must be finding it hard to make ends meet, my child."

"The fowl keep me going, Father, them and the knitting. The neighbours are good to me, too. And you don't forget me yourself, Father."

"Would you do me a good turn, Debby?"

"Anything under Heaven, Father John."

"Will you come and keep house for me? Wait!" He raised his hand to cut off the hasty answer that sprang to her lips. "Wait till you hear what I have to say. I got a new curate today. Thade Carey managed all right for myself, but he is too old and set in his ways to look after two of us. We will be needing a woman about the house and there is no one I would rather have than you. What about it, Debby?"

She studied the problem quietly for a while and then raised her head to look around the kitchen and its familiar things, the table, the dresser, the press bed, and the array of pots and pans, caressing them with her eyes.

"You could bring them with you," he suggested in an encouraging tone. "Room is the one thing we have in plenty at the presbytery."

She considered that carefully and nodded a sort of provisional acquiescence.

"I could bring the hens with me, too, I suppose. But what would I do with the house?"

"Sell it," he hazarded, though he knew no one would buy it in that wilderness. She ignored the hopeless suggestion.

"It is very old," she said. "It is only the heat that keeps it together. In one month after I put out the fire, that my mother's mother lit ages ago, it will fall asunder. But that would be kinder than to pull it down or to burn it. I'll let it die decent of old age. Death is natural."

Though her eyes filled with tears, she turned them bravely to the priest.

"How much time can you give me, Father?"

"I can send Bill Hannen's lorry to bring whatever you decide to keep, any day you name."

"Tomorrow then. I won't have time to mope if Paddy Brown comes with the dawn for us."

She stood up with an assumption of sprightliness to remove the depression into which the chat had fallen.

"Will you join me in the last supper—" She gasped when she caught the sacrilegious implication of the question. Father John laughed loud at the slip of the tongue to put her at her ease and sat by the fire to drink a cup of tea and to discuss life in the presbytery under the new dispensation. The short winter day was dying into premature darkness in the shadow of the mountain by the time they were finished.

"We had the last supper together," said Father John. "We shall now say together the last of the long chaplet of rosaries that have been said in this old home since the day it was built, and we shall say it for the souls of the good people, your people, Debby, who spent their lives under its roof."

"You won't forget poor Brohul, Father John?"

"No, Debby. We shall not exclude him from this last prayer."

When they were done, Debby saw him to the door and out past the pitfalls in the yard to the comparative safety of the boreen. Long after his footsteps were lost to hearing, she stood in the gloom looking at the dark bulk of the old cottage that had been the biggest thing in her lonely life, and sighed and went in.

Betty Hannen was waiting at the garage door when Father John came back with the Ford and invited him to the family sitting room upstairs. She closed the door and lowered her voice to a conspiratorial undertone.

"Congratulations on the new curate, Father. 'Tis time you got help in this prairie of a parish. Sure, you were killed from it. The travelling itself would kill a horse."

"Thanks, Betty. Yes, I shall have more time now to keep the young women in order. They badly need a sheep dog."

"G'long with you. 'Tis the boys that need the watchdog. 'Tisn't that but this, Father. You won't mind me saying it, will you? You'll be wanting a few sticks of furniture; bedding and ware and things, for Father Boyle. Myself and the Nurse and Mrs. Mack of the island have got the things for a good while, but we didn't know how to approach you. We were waiting for a chance of slipping them into the presbytery when you'd be away at the Retreat. But it is urgent now that Father Boyle has come. Sure, we couldn't lift our heads for shame, if he saw how bare your house is. He might imagine that we don't like you and that would be a lie, Father. Sure you know that, yourself. We're afraid of you, right enough, afraid of our lives, but we know you are for our good. We're fond of you, too, if you would only let us show it. 'Tis no use giving you money. It would burn a hole in your pocket if you didn't give it away to the first hard case you met. . . ."

"Mercy, mercy!" cried Father John in mock dismay under Betty's precipitous character reading. "Spare me my self-respect and tell me, in slow measured words, what's in your mind."

"We want you to come and stay here for twenty-four hours and leave us free to furnish a couple of rooms in the presbytery at our ease."

"When?"

"Tomorrow. We have the things ready for the lorry. Two runs will take them from here to the presbytery."

"No can do. I am taking the lorry tomorrow for another job. Debby Sweeny has agreed to keep house for Father Boyle and myself and we have arranged to bring her and her things home tomorrow. She is packing them up even now. It would be unkind to disappoint her, wouldn't it, Betty?"

That unexpected development silenced Betty. In her managing way, she had been making her own arrangements for providing the presbytery with a housekeeper. Indeed, she had the very girl for the job, picked and labelled, in her own mind, and ready to install with the furniture. She dissembled her disappointment, but did not surrender without a last effort to salvage her plans.

"Debby is a grand girl, Father John. No better in the two parishes. But did she say she could cook a three-course dinner and run a ten-room house?"

Father John stiffened at once against interference with his own dispositions, however well meant that interference might be.

"Debby is my housekeeper, Betty, and she enters on her duties tomorrow. We can't overlook that, can we?"

The priest's set lips and precise utterance, though tempered by a crinkling smile, cooled Betty's ardour and drew the line past which she dare not step. With the wordly wisdom she derived from her father, she knew when to jettison an unpromising project and switch over to a new one.

"Shall we say the day after tomorrow so, Father? You can come here after morning Mass and have your meals in the private room with Father Boyle while we are getting the rooms ready in the presbytery."

He winced at her persistence in trying to manage him, to applot his whereabouts, to control his movements, even though it was only for a day and in furtherance of his own interests.

"Please forget about me, my child, and carry on with your other arrangements. If the day after tomorrow will suit them and you want the presbytery clear, go ahead in God's name and God bless you." Then he thought of a submerged rock in the sea ahead which might wreck Betty's benevolent intentions—woman's inhumanity to woman.

"And Betty dear, leave Debby to herself in the kitchen. She will be in no humour for taking orders on her first day in a strange house. Try to carry on without her, like a good child."

"Very well, Father," she replied with just a snatch of impatience in her voice. Betty had a trigger temper too. "I'll bring a girl with me who *can* take instructions for the day."

"Jaikus Jack," Thade Carey exclaimed on Saturday night when all the imports had arrived and been duly installed. "Th'ould presbytery is turned into a bedlam o' blazes in its old age. Mileses and Boyleses and Sweenys all over the place, tripping over fal-lals of furniture that no one knows what they are for. An armchair, if you plaze, for his nibs the curate, and the kitchen range for Mistress Deborah Sweeny. For Brohul's sister, that has the alphabet burnt on her spindle shanks from nursing the ashes on a mud hearth. And nothing for Thade Carey but the outside of the house."

CHAPTER 25 · *Rough Justice*

An east wind had brought a spell of hard dry weather and smooth water, stirring Mike to active preparation for the mackerel fishing. With Sean, he had spread the nets wide along the levels on the north shore of the cove to examine them, mesh by mesh, for soundness. Mice have an irritating habit of gnawing new nets, and the nets themselves a habit of heating if put away for the winter before they are bone-dry. Fermentation rots them irreparably.

While the two men were leading the footropes before breakfast on the eve of the Epiphany, Joany and Maire held an intimate conference, with noddings and whisperings to cheat Mai's eager ears of details they deemed too grown-up for her. With rural purity of thought about the function of child-bearing, they admitted the young girl, as a matter of course, into their confidence as to the imminence of the event and assigned to her the minor duties that fall to assistant midwives.

After breakfast Maire simulated keen interest in Mike's activities at the cove.

"Is it long till the *St. Finian* will be ready for sea, Mike?"

"Any day now. We have mended the mouse holes and replaced the missing floats on the headropes. All we have to do is to string the nets together and put them aboard."

"How many nets will you have in the whole string?"

"Only seven. The *St. Finian* is a bit small for mackerel fishing, but she'll do for a start. At thirty-three fathom the net, the string will stretch more than a quarter of a mile."

"Isn't that too much for the two of you?" said Maire, very casually to conceal her design to lead the conversation to the need for outside help in handling the whole train of nets. "Don't you think you ought to bring out young Johnus and his uncle or Tommy Fitzgibbon to help ye?"

"I don't like to go off and leave you alone these days." Mike spoke into his empty teacup to escape her eye as he made his explanation. "Don't you remember what *Nodlag na mban* means to you? Tomorrow is the women's Christmas, you know."

"Have sense for yourself," Joany laughed. "Sure isn't there a houseful of women here, if we are wanted. Do as Maire tells you. She knows."

Their cheery assurance slackened the bond which had been tying him to the island, even though he was eaten up with eagerness to get among the mackerel while they were thronging for the taking.

"Righto! Off we go. We'll be back before dark, but don't wait up for us if we are a bit late."

He called out the good news to Sean and trotted down the path; Maire waved a hand to him from the door as they disappeared on the dip to the cove, and went straight to bed.

The Old Quay was full of noise and loud voices when the *St. Finian* chug-chugged into the only empty berth she could find. The five mainland boats had just come in with heavy catches. Big Bill had phoned the good news to the Cahirsally fish merchants and they had come pell-mell, chasing the auctioneer's noisy Ford in their Dodges and Buicks in a mad race against time. Fish trains leave early on the long haul from Manistir to Billingsgate. Speed is the essence of fish-dealing.

The auction was in full swing when Mike climbed up on the quay and joined the circle of merchants around Whispering Donal as he started to sell Pats Kelly's catch at the quayside. The boat was smothered in fish, their glistening white bellies and satin-blue backs creating a false gleam of sunlight in the grey winter morning.

"How many thousand have you, Pats?" Donal's low-pitched question was barely audible in the din of hammers and of voices calling the tally of fish.

"Five and half, more or less," Pats told him in the raucous shout he

usually kept for bad nights at sea. He wanted everyone to know how
well he had done.

"Well, gentlemen," said Donal, "you see the fish and you know the
count. What am I bid per hundred for the lot?"

No one spoke. Fish merchants are more chary than fish.

"Am I bid 12 shillings a hundred?"

Johnny God wiped his nose with the back of his hand.

"Twelve shillings I am bid. Twelve shillings I'm offered. Fourteen,
sixteen, sixteen, seventeen—time for you to say it—seventeen, seventeen. Who'll say the seven half dollars and close it? They're sold—sold
at seventeen and six the hundred to Mr. J. G. O'Donoghue. Next boat,
gentlemen."

Pats and his crew of three put their heads together to figure out the
total in the mysterious way of the illiterate, which is never taught in
the schools.

"Fifty-five hundred is £55, all but 55 half crowns," said Pats. "That's
£7 off, all but a lone half crown. That's £48 and the lone half crown.
What do you make it, Mickeen?"

Mickeen Murphy was Pats's tallyman and engineman. He nodded
his agreement with the result.

"Righto," said Pats when he got forty-eight pound notes from
Donal's clerk. "You can keep the half dollar you have in the heel of your
fist for luck."

He found a stone bollard to sit on, thumbed twenty-four notes off
the bundle and shoved them deep into his groin pocket.

"That's for the boat."

He dealt out six notes, like hands of cards to each of the crew, spreading out his own six for them to see.

"Not a bad night's pay," he said to Mike Mack who stood by, looking on. "Why don't you make the *Finian* pay for herself while the
fish is running?"

Before Mike could answer, loud angry voices broke out above the
hammering and the shuttle of the fish boxes at the landward end of
the quay, where the sale of the last catch was in progress. Whispering
Donal jumped off his box pedestal to back out of the melee of thrash-

ing arms that suddenly erupted about him. But only just out of range. Quiet though he was in his ways, he enjoyed a rough old-time fracas as well as any of the alerted crowd who had dropped hammers and ice and fish at the first battle cry and swarmed into a wide ring around the belligerents. He was held up by the sudden dispute that had sent two crews at each other's throats and put a stop to the sale of the *Blue Bird's* catch. He could not go on until the point at issue was settled.

Mike elbowed himself to the front and tried to sort the struggling men into sides. They resolved themselves into the crews of the *Blue Bird* and *Realt na Fairge*, pummelling each other in a heavy slow motion imposed on them by cumbersome sea boots and many layers of woollen jerseys. The two skippers fought with a vindictive intent that betokened a deep-rooted personal antipathy. Standing toe to toe, they punched each other ponderously and grunted at each blow. The bystanders, scenting a needle fight, made a clear ring for them by summarily seizing the two crews before they had got out of hand and keeping them apart until their tempers cooled down. Unheedful of this intervention the skippers fought on, as grim and purposeful as ever.

"Let them fight it out to the end," Tommy Fitz whispered to Mike, who suggested that they separate them. "They have been brewing bad-mind to each other since Shrove, ever since Andy Keating of the *Realt* stole Black Tom's girl from under his nose and married her out of hand. They have been watching each other like two fighting cocks with the steel spurs on. Any excuse would do."

"And what brought it to a head this morning?"

"Something that happened out on the mackerel ground last night. We'll hear about it soon. See, they have themselves fought to a standstill."

Still toe to toe, swiping blindly at each other and panting heavily, the two men slowed down like windmills from which the breeze was withdrawing. Heaving great breaths, they turned from each other at last to grope their separate ways through the crowd and sit on the gunwales of their boats.

Whispering Donal beckoned Big Bill and Pats Kelly towards him.

"Ye had better settle the dispute quick if the fish are to catch the train. Andy is claiming that Black Tom cut through his string of nets last night and did him £50 worth of damage. He wants me to stop the £50 out of the *Blue Bird's* money as compensation."

Donal directed his words at Pats, who was the accepted authority in such matters, and the circle of faces converged on the old man expectantly. Squaring his shoulders, he walked across to Andy Keating and tapped the bowed head.

"Stand up and make your case, Andy." To Black Tom he said, "Stand up, Tom, and defend yourself."

Leading the way towards the curing shed at the neck of the quay, Pats seated himself on an upturned barrel in the sheltered lee of the shed and, with a sweep of the hand, directed the crowd to sit on the stunted grass in a wide half circle around him. When all was quiet, he recited the set preamble to summary trials.

"*Go dtuga Dia ciall agus eagna duinn chun an cuis seo to phle agus chun brchunas coir do thuirt innte,* Amen."

Then in stentorian tones he addressed the complainant.

"Andrew Keating, I am calling you to the stand. Make your case and keep to the truth. The truth is the best in the sight of God and the hearing of your neighbours."

Andrew stood forth on the right of the open-air court and turned his battered face towards Pats. He spoke with a strong sense of grievance and his swollen lips, by slurring his utterance, added an odd significance to his words.

"I have no need for lies."

Pats addressed Black Tom.

"Thomas Walsh, I am calling you to stand and defend yourself. Listen to the charge against you without let or hindrance. Let your answer be the truth. The truth is the best in the sight of God and the hearing of your neighbours."

Black Tom took his stand to the left, uncovering his dishevelled head and speaking with the handicap of a split lower lip.

"I have no charge to answer," he said sourly.

Pats lifted his hand towards Andy Keating to begin.

"He *has* a charge to answer," said Andy. "I'll prove it to you and the crew will prove it too. Listen. We put out in the *Realt* with the ebb tide last night. We were the second boat to leave the quay. There was no sign of the *Blue Bird's* crew when we left nor any sign of Black Tom himself.

"We went to the south'ard, following the gulls, and spread our string of nets in a patch of likely water about four miles dead south of Black Head. It came down pitch-dark at the turn of the tide, dark and dead calm, so that we could feel the weight of the fish filling the nets. Just when we started to haul them in, we heard a boat coming full pelt from the nor'ard off our port bow. We could hear her plain and she could hear our engine starting to move up to take the slack of the nets. We raced the engine to make sure the other fellow would hear us and give us a wide berth.

"Divil a hell he cared. He kept on his course as bould as brass and struck our string with a wallop that tore the slack out of our hands. We heard his engine plugging away in the dark for about ten minutes till he shut her off to shoot his string. When we finished our haul, we had only nine nets instead of the eleven we came out with. The other two were carried away by the *Blue Bird* and sunk by the weight of the fish on them.

"Before coming home, we ran to the south'ard to have a look at the boat that hit us. It was the *Blue Bird* all right. I told Black Tom that he wouldn't get away with his highway robbery, but he only laughed at us."

Andy looked at Black Tom's puffed eyes and bloodied mouth with a wry attempt at a grin.

"Let him laugh now . . . if he can."

Pats raised his hand for Black Tom to open his defence. The big man made an attempt to hold his split lip together with his fingers but the pain made him wince. Dabbing the sleeve of his blue jersey on his mouth to stop the fresh issue of blood, he shrugged his shoulders to belittle the case Andy had made. His defence was a blank denial.

"I told you I had no charge to answer and I tell you so again. The *Blue Bird* struck no nets last night. We saw no boat on our way to the grounds or heard a boat's engine. We had a quiet, peaceful night's fishing until the *Realt* hailed us about dawn and Andy Keating began to bellow at us."

He, in his turn, grinned painfully at Andy for a parting quip.

"You were in no laughing humour last night. You may laugh now . . . if you can."

The air cleared with a general guffaw of approval of the manly way the two men were taking their wounds. When the laugh died down, Pats took off his sou'wester and looked into it thoughtfully as if seeking inspiration in its greasy depths. He sat for five minutes, framing the questions which would probe to the truth without betraying any bias towards Tom or Andy.

"Was the *Realt* showing a riding light, Andy?" he asked in a light casual tone, as if it did not really matter.

"Sure, you know she wasn't. You don't show a riding light yourself, nor any other boat, either," said Andy.

"What about the *Blue Bird*, Tom? Did she show a light?"

"She did. Ask Andy. He saw it."

Tom's voice jubilated at scoring that strong point against Andy, but Pats's face maintained the judicial calm he had imposed on it from the beginning of the trial. Not by the quiver of an eyelid did he reveal that, to his mind, the riding light pointed at guilt in Tom's behaviour. Why did he show a light last night above all nights? The legal obligation on drifters to show lights was ignored by all the Manistir boats. Few of them had the lamps to light.

He paused a moment to import special significance to his next question to Andy.

"Have you anything to *show* that it was the *Blue Bird* and no other boat—nor yourselves—that cut the net? The night was dark and you could not see what happened."

Andy shook his head impatiently.

"How could I have anything to *show* but the torn nets? Aren't they show enough for you?"

"No, Andy. They only show that they were torn. They don't say by who or by what. Have you anything to tie it up to the *Blue Bird*?"

Andy shook his head again and uttered a curt "No." A murmur ran around the seated listeners in anticipation of a decision against him in Black Tom's favour. They craned forward, eager to hear the verdict and return to the urgent jobs awaiting them on the quay.

"*He has something to show.*"

All eyes turned on Sean Driscoll, sitting beside Mike in the centre of the semicircle. He blushed to the ears at his own temerity in intervening so dramatically. At a sign from Pats he rose and advanced to stand midway between Tom and Andy.

"Tell me what it is he has to show that the *Blue Bird* cut the nets," Pats asked in level tones.

"Come down to the quay and look at her propeller. The neck of it is showing the meshing of a mackerel net."

The court dissolved at once and trooped back to where the *Blue Bird* lay at the quay with her stern to the bow of the *St. Finian*. Pats followed in his slow duck waddle and went down on his knees to peer under the *Blue Bird's* counter at the bronze propeller, showing clear in the luminous water against the sand below. Around its shank he saw a thin cord of chocolate coloured twine from which short strands waved free, like a fringe, to the flow of the water. Dusting his knees as he laboured to his feet, he jerked a thumb downwards for Black Tom to see for himself and looked around for something to sit on while he prepared his judgment.

When everyone had had a look at the propeller, they crowded around Pats, carpenters and lorrymen downing tools to join them. Only the seagulls, squabbling for offal and broken fish, broke the new silence that had come over the quay.

"What did you pay for the nets, Andy?"

"Big Bill can tell you. He's there to your elbow. Ask him."

"Ten guineas the net," said Bill without waiting for the direct question. "One hundred and ten pounds for the string of eleven nets, with leaded footropes and cork floats, complete and fitted, from Gales of Bridport."

"How long were they in use?" Pats continued.

Andy and Big Bill replied together, "Two seasons."

Pats called for the auctioneer's clerk and asked him what Andy's catch had fetched.

"Three and the half thousand at 18 shillings. Thirty-four pounds."

Pats closed his eyes for mental calculation, and then cleared his throat to deliver judgment.

"Andrew Keating and Thomas Walsh, stand together and shake hands before you hear my judgment."

They shuffled closer, each watching the other to make the first move and neither willing to make it.

"Aw, damn it, men," said Pats, "shake hands and have done with it. Haven't ye bate sense enough into yerselves yet? You, Tom, take Andy's paw. . . ."

They shook hands, grinned hideously at the bruises they had given each other, and turned towards Pats again.

"That's more like it, boys." The old man raised a finger and beckoned to Whispering Donal to join them.

"Well, Donal, you will stop £15 out of Tom Walsh's money and give it to Andy Keating. You can give it to him now and go home as soon as you like. I know you are in a hurry to get away."

Black Tom eyed the notes sulkily as Donal dealt out three fivers. He made no demur and accepted the diminished balance the auctioneer counted into his own hand without question.

"Now, men, here's how the case works out," said Pats. "Andy lost two nets that cost him £21 two years ago. And he lost the fish in them. A thousand of them according to what the rest of his string caught. That's £9. But they were second-season nets." His fat face crinkled into a sly grin at Andy and he went on with his judgment. "And the *Realt* was showing no riding light. That's against the law and she must bear half the blame for the damage. Half thirty is fifteen and that's that."

Even Black Tom appreciated the rough justice of the decision and joined in the laughing approval of the bystanders. Pats waddled off to complete the boxing of his take of fish and soon the busy din of hammers, voices, and engine exhausts was as loud as ever. The summary court proceedings had interrupted it for a scant half hour.

Mike and Sean Driscoll clambered onto the tail of the last lorry away, to drop off when she slowed passing the post office and join the boisterous crowd of blue-jersied, sea-booted men in the bar.

Mike elbowed through the close-packed groups to Tommy Fitz and young Johnus who were already halfway through their second pints of Guinness and getting nice and red "about the gills." All workers in chancy occupations which alternate between amazing luck and dismal failure fling their money away with divine abandon. When fortune smiles, they laugh outrageously and drink until they collapse; when their luck is out, they endure privation with divine patience and work till they drop in their tracks. Be they soldiers, punters, or fishermen, they are all akin. The Manistir fishermen were celebrating their lucky strike.

"Two more pints, Bill, for Mike and his friend," Tommy shouted loud to ride the confusion of noisy jibes and laughs. With a flick of his glass-cloth Bill signalled that he had heard and that the drinks would follow at once.

Embracing the four glasses in his capacious hands without spilling a drop, Mike backed through the kitchen door and beckoned the others to follow him away from the crowd. He saw that Tommy and young Johnus were ripe for a business chat as they were; in ten minutes they would be overripe.

In the comparative quiet of the kitchen, Mike laid his proposition before Tommy, which in his mellow mood he accepted at once. The four were to work the St. Finian on the usual terms, with the temporary emendation that Tommy would get a share and a half, as skipper and mentor, for the first month. Mike ordered another round to clinch the deal and, to bind it fast, made the terms known to Big Bill when he brought the drinks safely through the milling crowd.

"Ye'll have to bunk in the boat at first," Mike informed them, "but ye'll have yer grub in the house with ourselves."

"O.K.," Tommy replied. "There'll be no hardship in that."

Father Boyle, coming quietly from the dining room into the kitchen to order a mid-morning cup of tea, caught the restatement of the agreement to Bill. His voice, saturated with disapproval, broke in on their discussion.

"What's that I hear? The best forward and the best fullback in the Manistir team reneging the club! Speak up, Thomas Fitzgibbon. Speak up, man, and explain why you, our vice-captain, make a hole-and-corner plan to desert us in the middle of our training."

Tommy's hackles rose at the charge made so peremptorily and so suddenly. Hot repudiation of both "desertion" and "hole-and-corner" surged to his lips, but Mike gave him a furtive kick on the shin to restrain him. Quick as a flash, under the inspiration of the imp that lives in Guinness, Tommy seized the opening to divert the curate's ire from himself to Mike. He writhed as if in pain.

"Jaze, Mike Mack, who are you kicking? You are not a member of our club. What right have you to interfere between Father Boyle and us?"

The little priest swallowed the bait whole. Clothing himself in his own version of "the grand manner," he turned upon Mike to deliver a cold ultimatum.

"Who do you think you are to interfere with my men? Mark my words: if you attempt to wangle them out to that island of yours, I'll see about it in a way you won't like."

Leaving the astounded Mike to guess at the mysterious punishment he would bring down on their devoted heads, he directed his indignation on Tommy.

"I will expect to see the two of ye turn up on Saturday and Sunday, as usual, for training. Good day to ye."

Like Pilate, he did not wait for an answer, but strutted off in high dudgeon, forgetting to ask Molly for the cup of tea she had prepared for him. The poor girl stood openmouthed, looking aghast at Tommy for daring to provoke the priest to anger. Such irreverence was rash and unlucky. Taking a swig of his pint, Tommy waited only for the door to close behind Father Boyle to leap into action. He threw an arm around Molly's stocky waist, forced her backwards on the kitchen table, and silenced her protestations with wet beery kisses.

Mike dealt him a friendly smack on the buttocks and followed the priest to put himself right with that potent personage. He was barely in time to catch him entering the Hillman which was parked outside the post office.

"I beg your pardon, Father. Can I have a few words with you?" Mike removed his cap from his head to his oxter as he spoke.

"Well, what have you to say for yourself?" said the little man, going stock still, half in and half out of the car. Neither of them saw Father John, who had called for his letters and stopped at the counter when he heard the familiar voices outside.

"My boat will be left idle if you take Tommy and Johnus from me. It is for them I came ashore," Mike said respectfully.

"You can't have 'em. You should have known that I want 'em for the team."

"And leave the boat and four men idle when the fish are running? Sure, that would be flying in the face of Providence, Father."

"How dare you bring Providence into it, sir? My mind is made up. Don't attempt to interfere with those men. They can get work here as they ever did."

He was pushing Mike's hand off the open door of the car to end the discussion, when Father John approached them from behind.

"I am glad to see that you and my old friend Michael Mack are getting acquainted, Father Patrick, and I'm sure you will both become as great friends as we are. Could you spare Michael to me for a few moments? You can resume your conversation later on. You get around more than I do."

Father John quietly closed the car door and waved his hand to dismiss his disconcerted assistant. Neither by word nor by aspect did he show that he had overheard the heated discussion. The car drove off.

"How is your good wife, Michael? And Mai Hogan? I hope they are very well. As soon as the weather picks up, I shall make it my business to run out to the island and see you all. Let me see, now. What day of the week is it? Thursday? Yes, Thursday. You'll be making your first shot at the fishing next Monday, I suppose. Good Monday, good week, you know, Michael. Start on Monday like a good man, and all will be well."

With that injunction Father John left him and walked back towards the presbytery, reading the letters he had collected at the post office. Mike stood looking after him, wondering if the parish priest had not heard Father Boyle's impatient words after all. Father John was very deep, he thought, as he returned to the kitchen to inform Tommy and young Johnus of the favourable change in their timetable. But they had gone back to the bar and joined the uproarious celebration of the arrival of King Mackerel off the coast of Manistir. Mike and Sean were quickly absorbed into the joyous throng and steeped in its riotous spirit. The sun was long past its meridian before unstable heads and weak stomachs succumbed to the fumes of drink and strong tobacco. By dusk the weaker brethren were snoring in stupor outdoors in the chill evening air whither the hardier ones had carried them, one by one, as they fell.

It was pitch-dark when Mike and Sean stumbled into the *St. Finian* and worked her awkwardly out of her berth and headed her homewards across the Sound. The night wind sobered them up, but they were still bemused when they groped towards the mooring in the cove and paddled the punt to the slip. They sluiced their heads under the Rock spout to freshen up before facing the women and then proceeded up the path to the house with a studiously careful gait. The house was lit up, fore and aft, the door closed and a curious silence about the place.

A vague fear clutched at Mike's heart and sobered him instantly when he entered the hot, brightly lit kitchen and saw it empty. But the sudden change from the frosty air to the heated atmosphere of the house melted Sean's more susceptible reflexes and intoxicated his joints again. Grabbing at the dresser to save himself from falling, he missed and brought a big delf jug crashing to the floor with him. The bedroom door opened, Mai looked at them once with questioning eyebrows, and shut it again without saying a word.

Her secretive look and the closed door augmented Mike's fears that all was not well on the further side. But his natural habit of biding his time while things took their course and of turning his hand to the nearest job of work in the meantime prevailed. He haled Sean to his feet and half carried, half led him out the backdoor to his sleeping quarters and stretched him on his bed.

He reentered the kitchen, still conscious of dark forebodings, to find the stage transformed. The bedroom door stood wide open and from the threshold Joany beamed upon him like an abbess receiving the Lord Bishop on visitation. Exuding good will, good cheer, and benevolent welcome, she invited him up to the bedroom with a wide sweep of her arms.

"Come up, Mike, and welcome your son to the island!"

He followed her into the room and stood at the bedside, looking down at Maire's face, pinched but triumphant, in the halo of yellow hair which Mai had brushed wide over the pillow till it shone like gold.

"Dear old Thahailen," she said as she drew the counterpane down to display their treasure. "Isn't he a darling?"

The red, wrinkled little anatomy that lay in the curve of its mother's ivory arm shocked Mike as profoundly as firstborn children have shocked first-time fathers since begetting began. It was so small, so blind, so parboiled, so animal, so unlike the man-child he had expected, that he felt that there was some awful mistake, that an enormity had thrust itself upon Maire and himself and thwarted their love.

"Why don't you kiss the pair of them, you great big booby?" Joany pushed him from behind. "Are you afraid they'll break? They are not made of glass."

Maire put out her free hand and drew his head down to her bosom and kissed him on the mouth. With the other she eased their son's face up to join their own and heaved a breath of deep joy as she encircled her two men in her protective arms. Joany drew Mai away and closed the door to leave the Macks to the enjoyment of life's greatest hour.

FATHER BOYLE whizzed up the drive, slammed the door of the Hillman, and sped to his chair in the dining room with the rhythmic action of a halfback scoring a try under the bar.

"Sorry, Father John. I didn't feel the time passing. It took me near an hour to show Brehony how a team should be trained. Obstinate chap. He don't take advice from people that know. Very obstinate."

Father John laid aside the book he was reading while waiting for his curate and rang the hand bell to let Debby Sweeny know that she might bring in the soup. With deliberate calm he ignored the affront the younger man had given him by his unceremonious entry, his careless grammar, and his offhand condemnation of James Brehony. It was his intention to *lead* the unlicked cub the bishop had wished on him along the path to wisdom and good manners rather than *drive* him. Father Boyle was his first curate, to be handled with circumspection, if he was to evade the risk of getting a bad reputation among the junior clergy. Cohabitation at its best imposes a severe strain on two bachelors when one is very old and fixed in his ways and the other very young and greedy for variety. When both are young and pulling in different directions, as he and Father Boyle were, only the greatest tact prevents a catastrophe. Whenever he had to impose his will upon the curate, to give him definite instructions, the restraint he had to put upon his natural impulses almost made him ill. On such occasions he resorted to heavy reading to slow down his mental processes. The book he laid aside when the little red-haired man bounced into the dining room was the second volume of the *Summa Theologiae*. He thought that the Divine Doctor's placid and impersonal ratiocination provided the best preparation for a reasoned attempt at inducing the curate to restrict his football activities to their proper province and, particularly, at convincing him that Mike Mack's fish were more important than Tommy Fitz's goals.

Debby sailed in with the soup tureen held bosom-high in time to save Father John from the obligation of a direct response to the curate's flippant excuse for being late.

"St. Thomas was a mastermind," he said, patting the huge tome which lay beside his bread plate. "He is a veritable thesaurus of philosophic knowledge. You have a copy of the *Summa*, of course, Father."

"I have not, then. Vannoort is my man, every time."

Father John could not resist the urge to flick a little dart of sarcasm into the insensitive cuticle of the curate.

"Ah, yes, Father. You remind me of Dr. McNeice's favourite tab: *Timeo unius hominem libri*—I fear the man of one book."

Lest the shaft might reach the quick, he ran on, in a reminiscent vein, to salve the smart.

"The doctor was a profound scholar, but he talked too much, even in the lecture hall. Did you ever hear the epitaph his caustic colleague, Dr. Sharp, composed for him?"

"No, then. They were before my time in college."

"And mine, too, Father, but good stories outlive the actors. When Dr. McNeice died and was buried in the college cemetery, Dr. Sharp volunteered to provide what he called the epitaphic eulogium. Here's what his malicious muse inspired him to write.

> "*Hic jacet Joannes McNeice*
> *B.A., B.L. atque D.D.*
> *Vitam egit in loquendo*
> *Multa magna proponendo*
> *Nihil autem faciendo. R.I.P.*"

"Sounds great; great swing to it," Father Boyle observed.

Being better at construing printed Latin than catching the drift of the spoken word, he confined his appreciation to the metre for safety.

Father John diagnosed his trouble and proceeded to ease it, not without a whisper from Dr. Sharp's impish muse.

"Yes, indeed. Like you, the doctor had an ear for rhyme, Father; and for reason too, be it added. Of course, the executors turned it down, but Dr. Sharp maintained that they did so because they did not understand Latin and presented to them this English version.

> "Silent at last, poor John McNeice
> Sleeps 'neath this stone of stale degrees.
> He spent his life in dreary prosing,
> Many mighty schemes proposing,
> Nought to the end achieved but posing. R.I.P."

"And you tell me they cut that on his headstone?" said the curate in obtuse wonderment. "Sure, that would be a sin against charity, Father John. Wouldn't it now, I ask you?"

Having achieved his object and captured the elusive interest of his assistant, Father John left the innocent query in mid-air and returned to the *Summa*.

"My edition of St. Thomas is old and lacks a good index. I have been hunting up his thesis on Authority. For you and me, who are set up in authority, it is most important to have a clear concept of what it is and what it empowers us to do."

"I tell you it is. Couldn't be more so," the curate said in the weighty manner of one acceding a grave premise to a serious discussion. "*Quid est auctoritas?* That's the stuff."

"Yes, Father," Father John agreed. "A strict definition is essential at the outset. Your friend Vannoort would, I'm sure, define authority as *the right and the power to act*. Is not that so?"

"*Immo, Domine*," said the curate, using the classroom Latin rather than the vulgar "Yes" to show that he was accustomed to the high levels to which the discussion was rising.

"We may assume," Father John continued, "that God, being the supreme power, is also the supreme authority. His authority is *absolute*; it ranges over the whole universe and over all activities."

He smiled whimsically at the younger man. "Your authority and mine range less wide, I fear, and cover fewer activities."

"*Concedo, Domine,*" quoth the curate sententiously.

"Ours is a limited authority then: limited in range to this little pinpoint parish, and, in activity, to purely spiritual matters. To be explicit, our authority is limited to the faith and morals of the people of Manistir."

He caught the curate's eye and held it in his own level stare, while he repeated the explicit statement of the case. "Our authority is limited to the faith and morals of the people of Manistir."

Warned by his pastor's intent look and studied utterance, Father Boyle played safe and merely nodded a suspensory assent. Father Miles noted the nod and went on to develop his thesis.

"But, Father, the people of Manistir have temporal activities as well as spiritual ones. They work and they play, and there exist temporal authorities to control both their work and their play. The state exercises its authority over their various mundane activities through the police, the judges, the doctors, and the engineers. On each of those it devolves a limited authority of circumscribed range. Central associations exercise authority over their games. The G.A.A. controls football; the I.T.A., tennis; the N.C.U., cycle racing, and so on."

He paused to hand the curate a cigarette and light one for himself and then resumed his survey of the picture he had drawn.

"Now, Father, all these parallel authorities have clearly defined areas of jurisdiction. They work side by side, without friction or collision, in normal circumstances. It is only when circumstances become abnormal that trouble arises. Dual authority is abnormal. If the superintendent of police happens to be elected as chairman of the golf club, he will have to move carefully lest he unwittingly carry the authority he exercises in one domain across the boundary into the other. For example, he might use the information he gains as chairman of the golf club to proceed against the club for a breach of the licensing laws."

At last, Father Boyle saw whither the parish priest's Socratic method was leading. A guarded look entered his eye. He hunched his shoulders for the impending rebuke against which he had no answer, much as he resented it, and began to fiddle impatiently with the spoon Debby had placed in his saucer. Father John saw the change but went on as impersonally as if he had not.

"A priest, especially a young priest of zeal for both worlds," he smiled benignly in acknowledgement of the zeal of his assistant, "a priest vested with dual authority is in great danger of carrying the august authority of his holy office into the club room and overbearing his fellow members with it. His zeal obscures from him the unfair advantage he exerts over them. Worse still, the same zeal carries him into fields in which his authority does not run."

The fiery little redhead could stand no more.

"Cut the head of it, Father, and say what you mean. You are alluding to what happened at the post office this morning. Sure, the team would fall asunder if I let the players do as they like."

Father John maintained his judicial calm, undisturbed by the ebullition.

"But observe what you were actually doing when you threatened Michael Mack. You were imposing your authority as a footballer upon his authority as a boat captain. That was wrong in itself, but you aggravated the wrong by clothing yourself in the sacerdotal authority, too."

"I beg your pardon. I did not work the priestly influence on him. Far from it."

"How could you avoid 'working the priestly influence,' to use your own words, while wearing the priestly garb? No, Father, it won't do. It would have been wrong for James Brehony, a layman, to interfere with the livelihood of his players. For you it was a gravely culpable transgression."

"Why didn't you say so on the spot, then?"

"The very question reveals your unreadiness for the answer. In time, please God, you will come to understand why I withheld my lecture for the privacy of this room. But in the meantime, I suggest that you call on Tommy Fitz and young Johnus and set matters right."

"Is that an order?"

"It was a suggestion, Father, and is still a suggestion. I don't like orders myself and hate to give them to others."

"Very well, I'll see them."

"Thank you, Father Boyle. You can win much grace for yourself and for those young men, by the manner, or rather by the Christian spirit, in which you handle them. It takes a bighearted man to say *peccavi*, but a bighearted man always says it."

He pushed back his chair and they shook hands.

CHAPTER 27 · *Norwegian Sails, Ltd.*

EARLY on the third morning after he had parted with Mike Mack at Cahirsally railway station, Ollsen set out from the riverside lodging house in which he had slept his first night in London to find the head office of Norwegian Sails, Ltd. He had decided to report himself there rather than at Lloyd's. He walked slowly, marshalling in the order of their happening the salient incidents of his voyage in the *Bernadotte* and wondered how his own share in them would be received. A seaman, even though he be a bosun, who comes into conflict with a master mariner on his own ship in blue water, has a poor chance of vindicating himself with the owners.

Shrugging his shoulders to dismiss these forebodings of certain condemnation, he stepped out to meet the ordeal like a man.

Norwegian Sails had their head office in one of the huge grimy warehouses that line the north bank of the Thames below Tower Bridge. They had made a good job of remodelling the bald face of the ramshackle building and had applied to the old side door in Fen Lane a decent surround of cut granite, surmounted by a pseudoclassic pediment. They must have gone to great expense to commission the sculptor who carved the Viking galley that filled the whole triangle of the pediment. The brave barbaric ship struck a note of defiance amid the roar of steam sirens and the clangour of donkey winches. It seemed to proclaim the firm's proud allegiance to the sailing ship in a world which had basely deserted it.

Ollsen entered the doorway into a vestibule from the ceiling of which

hung lamps of copper beaten into the shapes of brigs and brigantines
in full sail. Pushing through the swing door at the further end, he found
himself in the counting house, a spacious room ribbed and beamed
with heavy timber and lit through portholes like a ship's saloon. On
each side of the central gangway ran a mahogany counter portioned off
into sections for the various clerkly departments, each section distinguished by a brass plate bearing the name of one of the company's ships
inset in red enamel.

Ollsen stopped at the counter marked "Bernadotte" to ask for the
manager's office, and was led to the glass door at the end of the gangway by a cheery snub-nosed clerk, who knocked and waited for the call
to come in. When he went into that inner sanctum, Ollsen felt that he
had come aboard a full-rigged ship and, by some magic, had been
ushered into the luxurious aftercabin of the shipmaster. The sides and
ceiling, curved to the streamed lines of a racing ship, were overlaid with
warm polished satinwood. Marine maps and charts covered the far wall,
and lockers fitted with brass knobs and hinges broke the smooth expanse of the sidewalls into panels. In the centre of each panel hung a
picture of a ship of Norwegian Sails, done in oils by an artist of a high
repute.

Ollsen saw none of those beauties after their first assault on his eyes.
The big bearded man seated at the green table in the centre of the
room drew his gaze to the exclusion of all else. Even in his chair he
looked a giant of a man, a giant gone in years but still dynamic and
powerful. Wide, loose-shackled shoulders and long arms ending in
masterful hands testified to great physical strength preserved beyond
his prime.

But Ollsen merely sensed the imposing structure of the man. His
whole attention was drawn to the magnificent Nordic head, the san-
guine face framed in a sheen of snow-white hair, and the searching blue
eyes. He stood silent, hat in hand, waiting for the extraordinary man to
speak.

"*Hven er du?*"

The voice came slow and smooth, with a deep chesty resonance.
Ollsen's reply was full of respectful confidence.

"Jeg er Knut Ollsen av skipet Bernadotte."

Only the blue eyes flashed their appreciation of all that the seaman's answer implied; the deep voice remained calm and unhurried as the old man told Ollsen who he was.

"Og jeg er Eric Skunder," he said.

The simple announcement startled the sailor. He had asked for the manager and had been ushered in to the owner, unwitting and unprepared. To Ollsen, as to every sailor that manned the ships of Norwegian Sails, Eric Skunder was a mythical figure as remote and legendary as a hero of Valhalla. His proven skill as a shipmaster, his resource and enterprise as a shipowner, and his impregnable faith in the sailing ship were boasted loud, ashore and afloat, by every sailorman from Hammerfest to Oslo. Instinctively, Ollsen drew himself to attention and clicked his heels like a man-of-war's man.

Skunder, waving his hand towards a chair, got up, strode across the room to the panel bearing the picture of the *Bernadotte*, and opened the topmost locker. It was full of folio ledgers, all showing the ship's name on the leather spines and numbered in sequence. He brought the last of the row to the green table and ran his finger down the list of names on the first page till he reached Ollsen's. Following the index number to the middle of the ledger, he read the seaman's dossier thoughtfully, closed the book, and took from a drawer of the desk a typewritten document which he ran through more quickly, as if to refresh a recent reading. At last he raised his eyes to look at Ollsen.

"You have come, I suppose, to report on how you came to leave your ship."

"Yes, sir."

"Before you begin, I must tell you that I have received a written report from the mate of the *Bernadotte*, and copies of the ship's log, manifest, and shipping articles. Her captain lies seriously ill in a mental hospital, with little hope of recovery." After a significant pause he went on. "With these facts in mind, do you still wish to make your report or would you prefer to take time to consider it?"

"I prefer to make it now, sir."

The owner lifted the desk phone to ask Miss Pederson to come to his office, and replaced it to assure Ollsen that she was a very discreet young woman. When she came, she seated herself at the end of the desk with pencil and notebook.

The old man, with a quiet gesture of the hand, told the sailor to begin his story.

"I suppose you know my rating in the *Bernadotte*, sir. I was her bosun on her last two trips. Before that, I was ship's carpenter on her sister, the *Ingrid*."

The owner nodded that he knew.

"Well, sir, she lay for clearance in Trondheim on a Tuesday. The last Tuesday in October, I think it was. We had a mixed cargo, dried cod and horeshoe iron for Bilbao in Spain, but we carried two hundred coils of Manila and hemp rope for the Faeroes, too.

"Captain Skelde was ashore on Monday when the iron came aboard and there was some argument about the way it was stowed. Early on Tuesday morning ten wagons of potatoes came along side us and we spent the day loading them. Most of them had to be stacked on the main hatch as the hold would not take them."

The old man reached for the ship's manifest and looked through it for an entry of potatoes. There was none, but his gaze was calm and unrevealing as he placed the document, face upward, before him on the desk.

"We went out with the night tide and the captain clapped on all sail to make up for lost time. The potatoes sunk her very near the Plimsoll line and slowed her down a couple of knots, I'd say. So we had to drive her hard, but in spite of our best, we were still behind time when we sighted the Faeroes. They have no proper unloading gear on the island nor experienced stevedores. So we lost more time and the captain lost his temper with every one. He went mad, out and out, when he found how the loading was mismanaged at Trondheim. We had to remove the iron to get at the rope that was stowed under it. By the time the potatoes and rope were on the quay, we had lost another day and the main cargo of cod and iron was thrown every which way in the hold. We did our best to stow it and batten it down, but the skipper wouldn't give us the time to make a job of it. Half the crew were below in the hold when he took her out to sea.

"All went well the first two days. With a fair wind and the ship in better trim, she made eight knots with skysails and spankers drawing— the best she ever did while I knew her. But the old man wasn't satis- fied. Something more than lost time was eating him. When the wind swung round to the south'ard off the Rockalls and rose to half a gale, he wouldn't take a stitch of canvas off the old lady. The fore skysail was carried away before he gave orders to reef the topsails. He wouldn't do more than take in one reef, he was in such a hurry.

"When the gale struck her, good and proper, the poor old *Bernadotte* was in a bad way, rolling and pitching and shaking herself like a wet dog whenever the sea broke over her. Something had to break loose. And something did. The top layer of bar iron worked out of the battens and began to slither around the hold with every roll. The mate spoke to the captain about it and got his nose bitten off for interfering. I slipped down myself to see what could be done but was ordered back on deck to take in another reef. I had seen enough to know that the ship was doomed if the iron was left free to batter a hole in her side.

"I followed the port watch to the fo'castle when they went below to their bunks and asked them to give me a hand with the shoe iron on the quiet—their lives and all our lives depended on it, I told them, and dog-tired as they were they came with me.

"It looked an impossible job, sir. The bars were bound together in bundles of twenty, every bundle twelve feet long and three-hundred weight. Three of them were shooting like shuttles to every roll of the ship and kicking up a hell of a clatter. They had splintered the casing timbers already. One head-on dunt on the ship's outer planking would open a hole that would swamp her.

"The eight men in the watch and myself made nine. That meant three men to each bale. I divided the men into three teams and told each of them which bale to go for. We decided the only chance we had was to catch them when they were dead at the end of a run before the ship canted for the swing back. I gave the word when they started to slither to port in the next roll and my party went after our lot and smothered it, just when it struck the casing. It was child's play to hold it for a few seconds, but when the ship fell away to the next sea, it came alive. It threw all its weight on us and started to roll sideways. But Ole Thorsen was as strong as a bull. He slewed round on his back to get a purchase for his heels and set his shoulders against the bale. That left me and Boorsen free to get a bight of rope round its two ends and make it fast to a stanchion.

"Trig Grieg's crowd cornered their bale, too, and tied it down, but Per Wessel caught a tartar. It bucked and charged in all directions. It kept the whole lot of us dodging and dancing to hop out of its way, but we got a hitch on it at last and put an end to its tantrums. By degrees we levered the three of them back to their beds in the cargo and battened them down with the slats of fish crates that got smashed in the battle."

Ollsen broke the narrative to draw breath and throw a whimsy that showed he had got over his awe of Skunder.

"I'm afraid, sir, we used up a lot of the dried cod for packing. The place was littered with them, sound and broken; they made grand stiff packing."

"Well, sir," he continued when the old man made no response. "My own troubles started just when we had everything secure and shipshape. I was stooped down over the last batten when Per kneed me on the rump and said, 'Hist! the old man.' I stood up and before I was properly facing him the captain rushed at me.

" 'You spying bastard! I'll teach you to mind your own bloody business.' That's all he said, but he gave me a skelp in the ear that threw me up against the casings with my head singing. I went mad, sir. After all my trouble with the shifted cargo to get only a clout on the lug! Captain or no captain, I let him have it. I hit him a wallop on the chin and he went down like he was poleaxed. Not a move out of him.

"The rest of the watch skidooed and left me with him. Small blame to them. Mutiny is worse than murder and they wanted no hand in it. When I cooled down, I took him by the shoulders and hauled him back to his cabin by the small hatch, the way he came.

"In the morning I knew I was for it and stayed in my bunk till I was sent for. The call did not come until late in the evening and it was the mate that brought it. He brought a mug of coffee, too, and something to eat with it. Mr. Kregg is a fine, understanding man that knows the ways of ships and crews, though he does not talk much.

" 'Get this inside you, Ollsen,' he says. 'Take your time to it. At seven bells I'll come for you.'

"He came when he said and we went aft to the officer's quarters. The captain was sitting in a big chair in the doorway of his cabin with a wicked look in his eyes. All the crew but the helmsman were standing with their caps off in front of him. He made short work of me.

" 'Knut Ollsen,' he said, 'you are guilty of the foul crime of mutiny. I could put you in irons to meet your punishment ashore, but the ship would stink with you on her. You will leave her at once, and be damned to your spying mutinous soul.' He pointed at where the dinghy used to hang in her davits till a spar fell on her and crushed her gunwales. 'Mr. Kregg, put him overside.'

"The mate looked sorry for me, but what could he do? He walked me to the side and whispered in my ear as he pointed down to the dinghy below. 'The Irish coast lies thirty miles due east of us. Good luck to you.' I slid down the painter into the dinghy and the mate cast it off without looking at me any more. I sat on a thwart and let the boat drift until the *Bernadotte* was lost to sight to the south'ard. I was too dumb to do anything but to gaze after her. It was well for me there was no breeze worth talking about and no broken water. The dinghy wouldn't live five minutes in a lop with her gunwales as they were. All they gave me with her was a spar, a small sail, a pair of light oars, a gallon of water, and one bag of biscuits. I threw the spar overboard, but I kept the sail to lie on.

"I slept through the night and made a rough guess at my bearings in the morning and took to the oars. It was killing work on an empty stomach but I kept at it till midday. After a swig of water and a few biscuits, I went at it again till nightfall. I slept that night in the bows under the sail and woke in a calm with fog all round me. As there was no hope of getting a bearing, I curled in under the sail again. I woke with a terrible thirst and crawled aft to the water can and drank it dry.

My senses must have gone, or my courage, to do such a mad thing. I went on my hands and knees back to the bows and got under the sail somehow. I know no more. I was picked up, dead to the world, by the two best people in the world—Mike Mack and his good wife Maire. They brought me to their home. They nursed me back to life and made me one of their own. I can never repay them."

During the recital Ollsen was sustained by the vivid remembrance of each incident as it followed in sequence, but when he reached the end and sat back in his chair he felt deflated, as slack as a purse that had given up all its treasure. Eric Skunder watched him subside, but the veiled blue eyes soon turned introspective in a train of thought which would lead to a comprehensive decision.

"Miss Pederson," he said at last, "type your notes in triplicate and let me have them as soon as you can."

When the secretary had gone, he stood up to his full height, sent his chair sliding aside with a swing of his thigh and took a spread-leg stance against the wall opposite Ollsen. Stopping the bosun's movement to get to his feet with an impatient throaty growl, he took out a short-stemmed pipe and got it going before he spoke.

"Young man, your own story convicts you of the most serious crime known to the law—the crime of mutiny on the high seas. The mate's report bears it out in every detail and the captain's entries in the ship's log for the 8th and 9th of November confirm you in your guilt.

"Your crime placed you absolutely and completely in the captain's hands, without appeal or redress against the punishment he meted out to you. That is the law. He dismissed you from his ship as a dangerous criminal and the law supports his action. So must I."

He stopped to let his statement of the case sink into the bosun's mind.

"All that occurred three months ago," he continued. "How do you stand now? I shall tell you. You stand in the same position as any other criminal who has served his sentence and survived. You are a free man in the eyes of the law, but a man with a black mark on his papers.

"You may wish to know how you stand with me—with the company."

The stern judicial lines in which the florid face was set to state the legal aspect of the case softened into a friendly smile.

"For me and in the company's books your name bears the white mark of loyalty. You are still bosun of the *Bernadotte*. She lies here now, filling up for the return run to Trondheim, and you can go aboard today."

He came around the table with outstretched hand as he spoke and drew Ollsen to his feet in a powerful handclasp.

"Guts, loyalty, and push are fine things. Most fellows have one or other of the three, but few men have all three. You have them all."

His exuberance died down as he observed a hesitance in Ollsen's reception of his wholehearted approval. Pushing the young man to arm's length, he searched his face sharply.

"What's wrong? Are you nursing a grievance?"

"Oh, no, sir. If you kicked me around this office, I would have no grievance. It isn't that is worrying me. But . . . I can't join the ship."

"Why not?"

"I'm going back to Ireland. I promised the Macks I would. I'd go back, anyhow, to pay back some of what I owe them. If you'll have me when I've done that, sir, I'll report for duty on any ship you name."

"Sit down and tell me about these Macks and what you have in mind for them."

"They are a young pair, just married, living on a small island no bigger than a hill farm at home. Look, sir! There it is on the map, in the mouth of that round bay facing west. Mike is a lobster man, but he wants to tackle the mackerel and herrings while he is young. We fixed up a small boat before I left, but I know his heart is set on a fifty-foot drifter of the latest type, with a brand-new engine and a full train of nets."

"But that will cost money—good money."

"It will, sir—£500 or more. Mike has the money to buy her, but I want to save him the expense, if I can, and I believe I can."

"How?"

"I haven't worked out any plan yet, though I have a couple of good notions in mind."

The shipowner turned his back on Ollsen and walked across the room to the leaded window looking on the river, crowded with shipping. He stood there in thought for a while and then wheeled round.

"You are a poor sea lawyer and a rotten businessman. Did you ever hear of a maritime lien?"

"I'm afraid I didn't."

"And I am a rotten businessman to be telling you. You are a maritime lien on the *Bernadotte* since you joined her. She is responsible for your pay and for any damage you incurred in the course of your duty on her. Suppose we say that both pay and compensation amount to half the cost of this mackerel boat of yours, would you sink it in her, if Norwegian Sails put up the other half?"

"If the company agreed to sell us their share, at cost, within twelve months, I would, sir."

"You are waking up, young man. Very well, buy your boat and good luck to her."

He sat down and phoned Miss Pederson again. To her he dictated a form of release of all claims and charges that Knut Ollsen had, or might have, against Norwegian Sails, Ltd. for service given or damage incurred, for the consideration of £250. He passed it across the desk for Ollsen's signature and then drew a check for £500 on the company's account, which he exchanged for the release.

Ollsen was encouraged by the friendly atmosphere to make the request he had held at the back of his mind during the whole interview.

"Would you mind asking Miss Pederson to type a short statement that I am clear of all blame for anything that happened on my last voyage, sir? Rumours travel far and a man has to protect himself."

"Still wide awake," Skunder remarked with a grin as he proceeded to dictate the testimonial to the poker-faced secretary.

"Norwegian Sails, Ltd. hereby acknowledge and publish to whom it may concern, their indebtedness to Knut Ollsen, boatswain of the brigantine *Bernadotte*, who, by his courage and initiative, preserved his ship from becoming a total loss at sea.

"Eric Skunder, *Owner and Director*

"Here," he said after he had signed it with a flourish, "I don't believe in half measures. A bald acquittal from blame would be worse than nothing; this is better."

He rose when the secretary left them and accompanied Ollsen to the door with a paternal hand on his shoulder.

"Don't waste your time in Ireland. You are too good a man for that. Take out a master's certificate and I will give you a ship. Whatever you do, don't miss your chances or undervalue your services."

"That reminds me, sir," said Ollsen. "I must insure the drifter, seeing that she will be half yours till we clear her. Who will we insure her with when we buy her?"

"Laxton & Lee of Fenchurch Street do our business. Good firm."

"Thank you, sir." Not by a flickering eyelash did the younger man betray the sudden inspiration that had come to him with Skunder's advice to take his chances. He would call on Laxton & Lee while the going was good.

"Good-bye, Ollsen. Have a good time."

"Good-bye, sir."

Fenchurch Street was just around the corner and there was still an hour until lunch. Full of elation after his propitious interview with the owner, Ollsen stepped out for Laxton & Lee's and swung into the building that housed them on its second floor as if he owned it. His impetus carried him past the outer offices to the senior clerk's room, where his career was halted by the senior clerk himself.

"What can I do for you, sir?" he asked and looked the sailor up and down to place him in a category for suitable treatment. But Ollsen saw a further door bearing a discreet brass plate with "Mr. Lee" inset in pale green enamel and strode towards it masterfully. Before the clerk could intercept him, he had opened it, entered Mr. Lee's sanctum, and closed the door after him.

Mr. Lee looked up. He was a spare sparrow of a man in the early fifties, a town dweller of the type that makes a fetish of fitness, carries the bloom of youth into middle age, and drops off suddenly on the threshold of retirement. Ollsen's brisk entry provoked in him a mere lift of the eyebrows, his reflexes were under such perfect control.

"Mr. Lee?"

"Yes. Won't you sit down?"

"Thanks. My name is Ollsen, Knut Ollsen. Perhaps it would shorten my business with you if you read this first."

The sailor passed Eric Skunder's testimonial across the second office desk he had sat at that exciting morning. Sigurd Lee ran through it quickly and then read it with more deliberation.

"Very nice, very nice indeed. May I congratulate you?"

He said no more, though he guessed what was coming and left the onus of opening the engagement on his visitor.

"You may also congratulate your firm on being saved a heavy claim for the loss of the ship."

"Um, yes. But, you see, she didn't become a claim."

"It would have hit you for—say £50,000," said Ollsen at a venture, ignoring the broker's disavowal.

"Nonsense, young man. Half that would have covered everything, ship, cargo, and personnel."

"Even the half would have hit you hard." Ollsen spread his hands wide on the desk and tensed his huge shoulders to come to close quarters in the contest. "I was not on the payroll of Laxton & Lee when I saved them £25,000. It occurred to me that they would put me on it now."

"Did Eric Skunder send you here?"

"I have come straight from him. I shall go straight back to him when I have finished here," Ollsen replied, telling the naked truth and implying an affirmative answer to Lee's explosive question.

"The bloody pirate! I wouldn't put it past him. Well, what did he tell you to gouge out of us?"

"I'm sure he would not be surprised if you allowed me a shilling in the pound on the policy."

"Nonsense, man. That's sheer blackmail. We are under no legal obligation to you nor to that bloody buccaneer, Skunder."

"I know," Ollsen replied as if conceding a point, but he went on to score a winner. "But only a formal inquiry could settle the matter definitely."

An inquiry would not suit Laxton & Lee; even if they won the case they would lose prestige. Finding that bluster was proving ineffective with the cocksure young man, Lee dropped his pretence of indignation and accepted the veiled ultimatum with good grace.

"Though I admit no legal lien, I am prepared, on Mr. Laxton's behalf and on my own, to express our appreciation of your very gallant conduct in a very substantial way. But, a shilling in the pound is preposterous."

"A paltry penny in the pound would be ridiculous," Ollsen cut in with a suggestion of contempt that he did not really feel. He guessed that the "paltry" penny would mount to £100 on the face value of the policy.

The broker shook a premonitory finger at him and dropped his voice to a serious undertone.

"Don't overplay your hand, young man. Be reasonable and you'll find me reasonable. If you don't, there's an end to the matter."

The finality in both word and utterance told Ollsen he had sounded rock bottom. He decided to put his cards on the table, face uppermost, and state definitely what he wanted. He told Lee of his intention to buy a fishing boat with whatever gratuity he might be granted—not for himself but for the Macks, who had snatched him from the death he had risked in saving the ship. He spoke of their loving care and utter unselfishness and of his desire to repay them if he could.

The tale gripped the broker as it had already gripped the shipowner. For the second time that morning it moved a great executive to open a folio-sized chequebook and draw a substantial cheque with a good heart.

"Take this with my best wishes, Ollsen. I wish you luck in your fishing, though I'm surprised that that rascal Skunder is letting you go. Good men are scarce."

He looked at his wristwatch in dismay and exclaimed that he must rush off to catch Skunder at lunch and give that bird of prey a piece of his mind.

"Would you mind telling him that I have already taken his advice about not missing my chances? I'm sure he'll be glad to hear it," said Ollsen as a parting shot from the door.

When he got back to his lodgings, he rounded off his first adventure into high finance by endorsing Laxton & Lee's cheque and posting it to Eric Skunder to wipe off the loan towards the cost of the boat. By a convenient fortuity, Lee's cheque and Skunder's loan were perfectly matched.

CHAPTER 28 · *The Share-Out*

A FEW days after her child was born, Maire was out and about again, as slim and vigorous as she was when she and Mike entered their new home for the first time. All her parturient lethargy was gone. She picked up the reins that had slackened during her own "expectancy" and the Christmas festivities and began to draw them tight.

The fishing was her prime interest, and she set herself out to keep the *St. Finian* and her crew in good trim for the heartbreaking work while the mackerel were running. She fed them like gamecocks, saw that they slept six undisturbed hours of the day, and put a large cask of Guinness on the kitchen stillion to induce them to satisfy their thirst for strong drink at home rather than at Big Bill's. Never before had fishermen been treated so well and never before had a drifter fished through a season as persistently as the *St. Finian*.

It was a record season. The mackerel came in from the west in massed battalions and solid divisions, a whole species on the move in relentless pursuit of its minute migratory food. There was no end to them. Assailed from the sky and ambushed from the depths, they still pressed hungrily on, heedless of loss while food was there to engorge.

In the dusk of the winter evenings the boats went out from the Old Quay to the slaughter, guided by the wrangling seagulls to the shoals packed fathoms deep and acres wide under the oily surface that betrays them. The *St. Finian* always led the procession from her seaward vantage at the cove and shot her short train of nets in the line of drifting fish long before the larger boats reached them. Shooting a long train of nets is a ticklish business. Paying them out free of twist at a regular pace while the boat backs slowly astern calls for perfect timing. But shooting them is child's play in comparison with hauling them in, heavy with sea water and with slimy fish. Galled hands and aching backs work to the inexorable rhythm of *heave, shake,* and *coil.* Heave the net up, shake the fish out, and coil each length of netting fair and free, lest it foul in the next shot. The engine joins in the medley of shouting and grunting to keep the boat's bow pushing slowly forward to take the weight off the men. It is a gruelling, heartbreaking business, though often sugared with luck and spiced with danger. Were there no sugar or no spice, free men would not condemn themselves, body and soul, to such hard labour.

The *St. Finian* did well, small though she was. She averaged fifteen hundred a night for the whole three weeks the mackerel were running and 15 shillings a hundred at the auctions. At Maire's suggestion, Mike postponed the division of the crew's shares until the end of the run. A share-out every morning on the pierhead would have left Tommy and young Johnus free to join the carousal at Big Bill's and drink themselves to forgetfulness of their aches and pains. The cask in the kitchen reconciled them to Maire's new dispensation, though they missed the license and the noise and the atmosphere of the crowded bar.

Mai Hogan was another and a more potent inducement to the young men to return straight to the island after the fish auctions. Among young men Mai was in her natural element.

Her experience with Sean Driscoll had opened the way into an enchanted Eden, where she could disport herself as she willed and taste the forbidden fruit for which her wayward mother had given her so keen an appetite. She burgeoned and blossomed like a plant transferred from the dark to the sunlight. The kindly atmosphere of the island home loosed the bonds her grandmother tied about her, set free her tongue, and taught her to laugh and make merry. This coming of the young men presented a glorious opportunity for satisfying her repressed longing for mixing with males. Mai was in her element at last.

She rose with Joany in the dark and bustled about the kitchen to have the early morning chores finished and everything in apple-pie order for the men's breakfast when they got back from the fishing. Hers was the first ear to catch the chugging of the engine in the Bay and she was the first to meet the punt at the slip when the weary men stumbled out of her onto the rough uneasy stones. One morning she would link arms with Tommy, press warmly against him on the way up to the house, and give his hand an intimate parting squeeze that kept him slinking after her for the rest of the day. Next morning Tommy was out of favour and young Johnus on her string, helping her at sit-down jobs that offered chances of amorous whispers and furtive digs at her softer parts. She gave Sean just enough intimacy to keep him to his allegiance and keep him guessing. Mike she left alone, not because she did not want him. She wanted him more than any of the others, but she feared Maire's keen eyes and implacable resolution. She knew that her shrift would be short if Maire got after her.

Of course Mai did not reason all those things into a planned campaign. Her procedure was purely instinctive. Her desire for males was as functional as her desire for food and drink and just as urgent. If Sean had not been available when it first moved her, she would have braved Maire's ire and sought satisfaction in Mike—furtively by preference, but openly if she were starved into it. She could not have helped herself. But with three unattached young men to work on, she felt as content as a cow in a cabbage patch.

Three moonlit nights and an offshore wind put an end to the orgy of fishing. The mackerel vanished as mysteriously as they had come, without flourish or fanfare, leaving the water free to the aboriginal tribes of cod, ling, hake, and haddock. The gulls returned to their monotonous longshore patrol and the fishermen to their patient round of long lines and lobster pots.

Mike spread his nets along the ridge to dry and he and Tommy went through them with their wooden needles, repairing rents in the meshing while Sean and young Johnus went aboard the *St. Finian* to sluice and scrub her clear of scales and slime from stem to stern. They took their time, breaking off for frequent spells of complete idleness to sprawl loosely on their backs and stare vacantly at the white clouds overhead. They were resting like soldiers behind the battle line, recovering the energy they had squandered so lavishly in prolonged action.

Maire knew their needs and adjusted the household hours to suit them. She let them sleep late, eat slowly, and dander at their work to their heart's content. She sent Mai to the ridge and to the boat with cans of hot tea between meals while she and Joany swilled shirts and collars in tubs of suds. She was bursting with happiness and was planning a feast of thanksgiving.

When Mike had at last dried the nets and stored them in a loft with a good sprinkle of salt between the folds against fermentation, and Sean had brought the paint pots and brushes ashore from the *St. Finian*, Maire called a council of war. She dragged the table to the middle of the kitchen under the copper lamp, planted Mike at the head of it, herself beside him, and the other men at each side as they willed. Joany sat by the fire rocking the cradle with her toe. Mai, silently moving around, swept the floor before she joined Joany to watch the men at the table. The scene was set for the great share-out of the *St. Finian's* catch for the season.

"Bring us the old bag, Maire, till we see what's in it," said Mike to open the proceedings.

Maire brought it from the bedroom, a cotton purse with a slip-string round its neck, and placed it on the head of the table near Mike's hand. Slipping the string, he took the purse by the bottom seam and spilled out on the table twenty small paper bags stuffed with banknotes. On each bag Maire had written the date, the name of the fishmerchant, and the amount of the takings for each night the *St. Finian* went to sea.

"Read them out for the lads, Maire. They'd like to hear what became of the fish they handled," said Mike.

Maire arranged the packets in the order of the dates and read the labels aloud. Each label started a discussion: "That was the night off the Fang when the engine stalled," and: "That was the night Mike Murphy of the *Blue Bird* boarded us for matches; they forgot to bring matches with them."

When all the bags were accounted for, the contents pooled and halved, and the halves quartered, the boat's share lay piled in front of Maire. Before Mike, Tommy, Sean, and young Johnus lay their personal shares, each containing twenty-eight single notes.

"Don't stir," said Maire when the men prepared to leave the table and secrete their money in deep-set pockets. "I stole one gallon of stout when the cask was full. Ye can drink it now as a *deoch an dorish* to wet the divide. Myself and Mai will wet it in tea; Joany, you old toper, go and fetch that little noggin from under your tick and join us."

They drank and argued and sang till the cows bellowed to be milked, but before they broke up Maire announced her program of thanksgiving.

"We had a hard month's work, boys, and we are entitled to one good blowout. Oh, you needn't laugh, Mike Mack, nor you, either, Tommy Fitzgibbon. You imagine woman's work is no work. Try it and see. Anyhow, we are all going to have our fling for one night—a dinner, a hop, and a singsong at the hotel to wind up the season."

"This pile," she said, shuffling the boat's share with open hand, "will stand the racket without feeling it. So, boys, sharpen your razors and mow that stubble off your jaws. They need mowing badly. Your shirts are scoured and your collars are stiff with starch. Take care and clip the tar out of your hair before ye put them on. Tomorrow evening we cross the Sound. So ye'll have a whole morning for titivating yourselves."

Mai and the boys raised the roof with approval and crowded round Maire in a rough affection that ruffled her hair and rumpled her blouse. Catching the riotous infection, she sprang from her chair, released her pent-up feelings in a loud "Yo-ho-o-o," and spun around the kitchen in a whirling dance that sent her golden fleece fanning out about her head. Some one pushed the table back to its place by the wall to clear the floor and let her dance herself to a standstill. But a yell from the cradle cut short her girations in mid-career. Her shrill Bacchante cries had roused the infant and, as Joany said, "put a stop to her gallop." The revel was over for the night; tomorrow was another day.

CHAPTER 29 · *The Dance*

IT was a busy morning of unaccustomed occupations. Mike trimmed the matted hair of his crew in the open air. They, in turn, painfully removed their bristling beards with Mike's German razor, the only razor on the island. Indoors there was great inspection and rejection of skirts and blouses, learned discussion of colours that "go" with each other and with the hair of the wearer, or that make a "lovely contrast." Dinner was a sketchy meal. There was no time to prepare a solid one. Everyone was leaving room for the "swell" dinner that awaited them at the hotel.

The men were ready first, splendid in Sunday clothes, shining collars, and the sharp-pointed light shoes that delight young men who work through the week in stub-toed hobnailed boots. They rowed the punt out to the *St. Finian*, placing their snow-white handkerchiefs on the thwarts with exaggerated care before they sat on them and smoked many impatient cigarettes while they waited for the women.

"Ah, here they come."

When they paddled ashore to meet them, the men stared in amazement. Joany was coming, too, covered in a woolly black shawl and bearing the infant, coiffed and ribboned, under one wing. She led the way followed by Maire and Mai, blonde Juno and brunette Venus. Instinctively, the two girls stood at the landward end of the slip and bathed themselves in the frank, open-eyed admiration that met them. Maire squared her shoulders and looked at Mike with glistening eyes, as if to say, "My wedding dress fits me again, Mike." Mai's eyes roved free, seeking admiration from each in turn, but resting longest on

254

Mike. Above the dark-red of her American costume, those dark lambent eyes gleamed alluringly, almost invitingly, as they roved.

Joany plodded along the rough causeway with her precious burden and squatted, wide-lapped, on the stern sheets of the punt, waiting stolidly for the young people to come down to her. They came at last, filling the small boat dangerously and talking little until they boarded the *St. Finian.*

"Look here, Maire," said Tommy Fitz, using her Christian name with the easy familiarity of their kind. "Myself and the lads here had a chat last night about you paying for this blowout. We're all for having the fun, but we won't stand for you or any woman paying for it. We're no Sheilas hanging to a girl's petticoats. We'd never hear the end of it if the boyos ashore came to hear of it. We'll stand the racket, the three of us and Mike. You and Mai and Joany can come on our invitation."

"But, sure," said Maire, "we settled that it would be my party—"

"Tommy is right, Maire," said Mike in his quiet way. He stooped to swing the starting handle of the Kelvin. "When, before, did you pay for your fella going to a dance? What do you say, Joany? Used the girls to pay the piper in your day?"

"Very well," said Maire. "And will ye do the ordering too? What ye'll have to eat, I mean, and the dances?"

"Ha! Ha!" Tommy laughed. "You watch Big Bill when we tell him we want a first-class feed and the use of the big storeroom for a hop, money no object. He'll rob us, of course. He'd rob you, too, but he'll give us a damn good time."

Sean and Johnus backed Tommy's fight for male priority in social finance with nods and grins. They felt male and opulent and masterful themselves. The engine roared into action to declare the matter decided, and sped the boatload of light hearts to the mainland and the joys it had to give. They created a great stir on the Old Quay where the crews of the mackerel boats were still lazing through net-mending and deck-scrubbing. Mike and Tommy and Johnus went among them telling what was up and inviting picked pals to get their girls and come along.

The women walked ahead to the hotel to hire the Ford to take them to the chapel and have the child christened and Maire churched. They could get those important functions performed while the men were "wetting their whistles" and Betty Hannen was preparing the dinner. If Father John was not at the chapel, they could go on to the presbytery. It did not occur to Maire that Father Boyle might be there, and she was taken unawares when she found him pacing up and down the chapel path, reading his breviary in assumed absorption. Hoping against hope that Father John might be in the sacristy, she shepherded Joany and Mai into the church and ran round the gable to see. The sacristy was empty. Her firstborn was to be christened by a bird of passage.

While she was groping for a stratagem to evade her predicament, the curate breezed in, donned his stole and surplice and took his stand at the font.

"Come along, ladies. Time is precious. Come along."

There was no escape. They came along and submitted the sleeping child to his efficient ministration and followed him, when it was done, to the sacristy to have it duly entered in the parish records that Donal Michael McGillicuddy had been baptized according to the rites of Holy Church and that John O'Driscoll and Mary Hogan were his sponsors. Father Boyle churched Maire with impersonal dispatch and acknowledged with a perky smile the substantial stipend she had intended for Father John. She smiled back but went out to the waiting Ford feeling little of the unction she would have felt if Father John had performed the ceremonies.

The bar was buzzing with friendly noises when she passed through to the kitchen to dispose of Joany and Donal Michael for the evening. The table was set in the kitchen; Betty knew that the crew would be more at home there than among the naperies of the dining room. The luscious smell of boiling bacon and cabbage filled the hot air.

It took all Big Bill's tact to catch the eyes of the St. Finian's crew and smuggle them into the kitchen without attracting the attention of those left behind in the bar, but he managed it.

Each of the islanders invited a mainland guest to the board. Mike brought his brother Dan; Maire, his sister Nora. Tommy led in Jim Brehony whom he had found at the post office. Mai picked up John Joe in the shop, natty as ever, as he sidled in to find out what was up. Joany sponsored old Pats Kelly and young Johnus showed his nepotal affection for old Johnus by placing him near Pats and Joany. Sean, being a stranger in Manistir, would have surrendered his right to invite a guest but that the number of the feast would then be thirteen. Mike quietly vetoed Conny Shuckrue and prompted Sean to invite Paddy Brown instead. When Paddy joined them, they were fourteen, just filling the table, with Mike at its head, Maire at the foot, and Mai snugged in between John Joe and Jim Brehony.

It was a mighty feast, drawn out with lusty stories and endless discussions of ups and downs on land and sea. It was Big Bill who put an end to it by announcing that the store floor was clear and waiting for the dancers. In a great clatter of chairs, the young people hastened away to the new excitement, leaving old Johnus and Pats to stay with Joany and decry at their ease the changing times. Maire turned back from the door and whispered in Pats's ear that she and Joany would be leaving for home before dark, but that she did not wish to spoil Mike's fun by asking him to run them across the Sound. She left it at that, but the shrewd old man guessed what she wanted of him.

"Of course, Maire. Myself and Johnus will run ye out to the island. If you don't find us here, we'll be down at the Quay. Have a good time while you're young, *a chroi*. You'll be old before you know it."

The big store was full of the noise of shuffling shoes and the reedy blare of the melodeon when Maire joined the others. They paired off for the "Waves of Tory" and worked themselves into a free perspiration in its jigging, bowing, weaving measures. With the shortest of intervals, they danced through "The Siege of Ennis" and "The Walls of Derry" until they could dance no more. To the last dying wail of music the men slumped, streaming with sweat, onto the crates and cases Bill had ranged along the walls for seats. They drew their partners to sit on their knees and pant for breath.

When she cooled down, Maire disengaged herself from Brehony's arms and went across to Mike who was supporting a redfaced bouncer who could not sit still.

"Joany and myself are taking the child home. Ye can stay on and enjoy the fun. Pats is running us out home and will bring the boat back to the quay for ye."

Mike dumped the bouncer without ceremony and followed Maire out to expostulate with her, but the sight of Joany sitting patiently with the child at the end of the kitchen silenced him. Going with them down to the quay to make sure that the old reliables were really there, he saw the boat safely started and returned with diminishing compunction to the dance. He reached the hall at the end of an old-time waltz when the couples were slipping out into the dark to cool and to cuddle in barns and outhouses. One pair was bickering in fierce whispers as he approached.

"I will dance with whoever I like," he heard the girl say.

"But Mai, dear, you didn't give me one dance yet, though you promised me all of them last night. Sure, that's not fair play. Even a tinker's trollop would keep her word."

"How dare you, Sean Driscoll! Compare me with a tinker's trollop! Take that for your impudence."

"That" was a stinging smack on the cheek which angered Sean into retributive action. Seizing her hand while still raised for another smack, he swung her into his arms and rasped his smarting cheek against hers until she screamed. Mike thought it time to intervene.

"*Bog brea a phaistini!* Take it easy and don't wake the childer." He laughed good-humouredly as he loosed Sean's arms and stood between the struggling bodies. "If ye have to fight, do yer fighting at home. No one but the gulls will hear ye there."

Mai seized her chance with intuitive speed. She linked her arms around Mike's elbow and pulled him possessively towards the store-room where the opening strains of another waltz were recalling the scattered dancers.

"Thank God you came, Mike. I was afraid you were gone off with Maire and Joany, leaving poor me all alone. Don't mind Sean. He can't dance the waltzes and you know I had to give John Joe the sets. It would be mean to refuse him after inviting him to the party, wouldn't it, Mike?"

This voluble, assertive young woman, so unlike the bashful Mai Hogan he had grown accustomed to, swept Mike off his feet. He had, of course, noticed in a general way that she had gradually come out of her shell and taken a normal part in their life on the island. She kept her end up in the housework and in the give and take of kitchen gossip as freely as Joany and Sean, but she never took the lead as she was doing now. This was a new Mai Hogan, a rather thrilling Mai Hogan.

"We'll dance this one together," she told him with a warm whisper and an intimate tug on his arm as she led him out on the floor. "Waltzes are great. You don't have to swop partners and you can talk as well as dance."

She was a born dancer and had no difficulty in steering Mike's uncertain steps through the swirling dance. Indeed, she was glad that he needed steering; she could draw him close without attracting attention and get him to embrace herself when the crowd pressed on them. Whenever that happened, she snuggled tight and whispered "Oh, Mike," into his ear. He was glad when the melodeon wheezed out the end of the waltz and the furtive embracing. With an arm around her vibrant waist he took command and steered her through the stream of dancers escaping into the dark. He wanted to hurry her out of the public eye to some place apart. He wanted—oh, he did not know what he wanted. He was deeply disturbed. Mai, moving quickly to his urgent lead and searching the darkness for a deeper dark, wanted nothing more of the dance. She thought that she had got a grip on Mike at last, had pierced the solid screen of kindly indifference that surrounded him on the island. Her vagrant heart was thrilled in the deep blackness of Big Bill's boathouse. She swarmed her arms around him with reckless abandon and pulled his head low to hers.

"I'm mad about you, Mike. I was always mad about you, but I was in dread of Maire. She'd kill me if she knew. But sure, we needn't let her know."

Mike said nothing in reply. The cool air and the mention of Maire's name cleared his mind. Removing her arms from his waist he took her by the elbow and urged her quietly towards the storehouse where the music was striking into the next waltz. She stopped halfway and shook herself in her clothes to make the gambler's last throw in her little game.

"Give my skirt a pull down at the back, Mike. It is all twisted on me. And Mike," she said in an access of womanly wisdom, "I'll dance this one to Sean, so that people won't notice us."

Mike tugged at the skirt but made no remark. He felt too mean and revolted to speak, but when they entered the hall the cheery babel and carefree atmosphere toned him up. He piloted Mai through the crowd and handed her over to Sean with a fair simulation of his old good humour.

"Here she is for you, Sean, sound of limb and broken to harness. Don't pull on the bit and she'll travel as sweet as a song. And Mai, dear, no rearing or shying, if you please. Show Sean the steps and he'll dance the waltz as well as me."

Tommy Fitz was sitting by the wall, surfeited of dancing. He called Mike to a seat between him and Jim Brehony, who was also sitting out the last dance.

" 'Twas a whale of a night, Mike. Tell Maire that, when you go home. I'll settle with Bill in the morning and we can fix up our share of the expenses any day. Bill won't be hard on us. He's a great old sport."

"He's all that, Tommy, and, whatever it costs, it was well worth it."

"Of course, you know myself and young Johnus won't be going back with you tonight. We'll stay ashore until you call us again. We'll come on the hop."

But Brehony had no ear for their chat. His eyes were fixed on Mai as she steered Sean skillfully through the eddying dancers. He had paced one of the Irish set dances with her, early in the evening, and had planned to have this last waltz with her. She had been so silent, so demure, so angelic in the presence of his own austere deportment and she had looked so like his mental picture of the lovely Deirdre, and the still more lovely Blanait, that she swept the innocent young man off his feet into the realms of romance for the first time in his secluded life. Mai Hogan was his dream maiden come to earth; she was so beautiful and her eyes said such wonderful things.

The dance came to an end at last and wound up in a round of cheers for Mike Mack and his crew. In twos and threes the dancers went off into the dark, huzzaing to let the world know how happy they were. Brehony went with the islanders on their way to the quay. He wanted to be near Mai if she should need guidance in the gloom or assistance at the boatside. But he was too awed, when his chances came, to avail of them. When she was aboard, he stood and gazed after the departing boat and listened. One by one the brave exultant huzzas faded into thin ghosts of sound in the hills behind him. At last the throb of the engine was gone out of hearing in the distance, and silent night dropped, black and mysterious, on the hills and the islands and the people who on them slept.

CHAPTER 30 · *Ollsen Returns*

THE clear skies and luminous nights that had sent the mackerel out into deep water persisted and threw the islanders back to inshore fishing. They were glad in their hearts to get back to their old reliable daylight rounds, the trolling for pollack, the leisurely visits in open boats to lobster pots that waited for them, the short runs to the whiting grounds where they dropped moorings and sat on thwarts to smoke and haul up the strangely unresisting fish.

Maire took to the water again more eagerly than ever after her long immurement. On calm days when the morning chores were done and Donal Michael was duly bathed and fed, she shouldered the oars down to the slip and helped Mai to bail out the punt and set the spillers in order. Calm weather made it safe for the two girls to fish around the Bay Rock, which lay a bare half mile due east of the cove and in full view of the house. But in any sort of a lop Mike always insisted that one of them go with him and the other with Sean; in heavier weather he left them ashore.

One morning towards the end of Lent, Joany sniffed contemptuously when she uncovered the barrel of pickled herrings to take out a half dozen for the day's dinner.

"Phew," she blew in disgust. "Nothing but salty scad in this house from year's end to year's end. Pity we don't live near the sea. If we did, we'd have fresh fish once in a while. But all we ever see in this Godforsaken place is crabs and lobsters and herrings poisoned with brine. Sure, this is no food for Christians."

She took the darkly discoloured fish by the tails and held them high in her fingertips to drip into the barrel before she put them to soak in a pan.

"That's one in the eye for us, Maire," said Mai. "The men are gone around the island setting the French pots and they won't be back for hours. It is up to us to find food for Christians."

Maire winked behind the old woman's back at Mai.

"It isn't right, they say, to deny a woman in a certain way anything she sets her mind on. . . ."

"G'long with you and your play-acting," Joany exclaimed, splashing Maire with pickle from a herring which she swung by the tail at her. "Maybe 'tis your own tale you're telling. But we want fresh fish, me lady. Go out there and get it."

Out they went and down to the punt in great good humour.

"Let me see if I can find the Bay Rock, this time, Maire," said Mai. "I know the bearings now, and if you let me row in the bow, I think I will make out the rock all right."

"Go ahead, Skipper," said Maire. "You're the boss."

When they cleared the mouth of the cove, Mai held the punt headed out into the Bay, keeping the Well Rock in line with the Lookout. That course would take them due east to where the Bay Rock lay, five fathoms deep and thirty fathoms long, somewhere ahead of them. A cross-bearing would show where. From time to time she shot a glance towards the northern tip of the Shark, which hid Black Head from her view, to take her cross-bearing as soon as it opened up.

"We're over the Rock now, I'd say, Maire," she said at the moment the sheer face of Black Head showed clear of the island. Maire checked the two bearings and nodded.

"Good work, Mai. Mind you don't get tangled in the line when you are dropping the mooring stone overboard."

The stone plopped with a hollow splash and sank out of sight, making the line hum on the gunwale like a cello string as it paid out to the seven-fathom knot. Seven fathoms gave just the right length of mooring for that part of the bay. When the punt settled down with her nose to the filling tide, the girls dropped their lines overside, letting them run through their fingers until they plumbed bottom, and then hauling in a half fathom to raise the baited hooks just clear of the weeds below.

"Thank God, it is whiting we'll be killing today," Maire called out to Mai, after each had caught a few fish. "I don't think Joany would have any welcome for gurnet. There's too much trouble skinning them."

"I'd rather a gurnet any day," said Mai. "They are more filling than whiting and a good deal solider under your tooth."

The fish were feeding freely, as is usual at the turn of the tide, and the girls were kept busy hauling, baiting, and running out the lines. They were working two each, one on each side of the punt. No sooner was one gone down than the other was coming up with a pair of trailing, docile whiting that had not the spirit to fight.

Maire called a halt when her heap in the stern reached Mai's spreading down from the bows. In an hour and a half they had caught over twelve dozen whiting, five dogfish, a small turbot, two brill, and one ugly monkfish. They slung the dogs and the monk overboard to the gulls that sat patiently on the water astern, waiting for the rejects they knew would come.

"We'll have enough for the dinner in the brill and turbot," Maire said after the count. "That means that Sean must run the whiting into the shop this evening. Whiting don't keep and they are not worth salting, the watery things. Would you like to run in with him, Mai? It would be a nice break for you. You weren't there since the dance."

"And row across the Sound and back, after this morning's hard work, too?" Mai responded with a high note of disapproval in her voice. "Not likely, Maire."

"You're taking me wrong, Mai dear. I was thinking of the *St. Finian.* You and Sean could manage her fine."

"If it was Mike now, we might manage." Mai made this suggestion with a studious hesitance to cover her secret delight in the prospect of having Mike all to herself for the evening. The hesitance, or rather the insincere overtone, caught Maire's ear and begat an embryonic query in her mind as to why Mai said such a simple thing with so much deliberation. Mai's "Sure, you know Sean is no good at engines" did nothing to smother the vague Why?

"Perhaps you're right, Mai. It would take the two men to work her if anything went wrong." Then Maire's face lit up with a new inspiration. "What's to stop us all from going? That is, if Joany will mind Donal for the few hours we'll be away. Come on, Mai, haul in the moorings and we'll go home."

Maire got into a skittish humour on the run home. The air was heavy with ozone. It exhilarated her. She felt emancipated and full to overflowing with energy. She put her back into the oar and pulled it with a swing that bent the pliant ash and forced the punt off her homeward course. Mai felt the swerve and put extra pressure on her oar to correct it. She succeeded at first, because the bow oar has more power over a boat than the stroke, but Maire would have none of it. She clamped her heels on the footboard and pulled against Mai with full-bodied sweeps to win back the advantage she had gained. Mai accepted the silent challenge with grim determination.

Bracing her right foot against the thwart on which Maire was sitting, she put the power of her thighs into her stroke and rowed with all her might.

The dour struggle settled into more than a mere trial of physical strength. It became a fight for supremacy, not in the realm of fishing and rowing boats, but in what matters most with women, the realm of love. Maire's vague suspicion of Mai's interest in Mike took substance. It filled her with a dull anger against this interloping girl who might challenge her power over dear simple-hearted Thahailen, as she was now challenging her power over the punt. She would die or let her see who was the better woman.

Mai's will to fight was more definite. She remembered Mike's tentative surrender to herself on the night of the dance and told herself that he would be absolutely hers but for this woman now in front of her, this overbearing woman, whose only claim to Mike was that she got in first. She would show Maire who was the better woman or die in the attempt.

Seething with unreasoning rivalry, they drove the stunted little craft forward in short froglike leaps. She was too short in the keel to run smoothly. Gradually Maire's stamina and deep reserve of strength asserted themselves. The punt kept rising to the north against Mai, though her very heart was bursting under the straining of her arms to check her. Suddenly her resistance broke. She was conquered. She dropped the oar and slumped off the thwart to the bottom of the boat among the whiting.

Maire gave one last pull on her oar that swung the punt around on her heel facing out the Bay. It was her "victory roll." She said not a word to the girl collapsed in the bows, but took her oar and rowlock to herself and paddled the punt slowly back into the cove. When Mai recovered her breath, she resumed her seat and took back her oar from Maire as if nothing had happened. On the slip they boxed the surplus whiting to the usual running chat on this and that and walked up the path together bearing the "food for Christians" that Joany had clamoured for in the morning. But their relationship was fixed for ever. Maire was still the boss and Mai knew it.

"Let one of ye go to the Lookout and call the men to their dinner," said Joany. "It will be ready by the time they get home."

Mai looked askance at Maire, seeking permission to go, thus revealing that the suppression of her recent revolt was complete. As she climbed the hill she took stock of the new situation. She must be very circumspect in her future dealings with Mike. Maire was dynamite. She might be suspecting them already. Why did she start that trial of strength in the punt? Maybe it would be safer to steer clear of Mike altogether and stick to Sean Driscoll. Or that sissy of a schoolmaster that was throwing eyes at her at the dance. He's nice and clean and he dresses well. But he has no more life in him than a schoolboy, big and active as he is. Where's the good in a statue, anyway?

She climbed up the cairn when she reached the Lookout and searched the languid swirls at the feet of the cliffs with her eyes. The boat was almost directly under her and the voices of the two men were barely audible in the subdued pervading sound of heavy water in motion. She called down to them, though she knew they would not hear her, and then stood erect waiting for one of them to look up that she might signal to him. Sean perceived her, at last, and acknowledged her signal by waving his cap with one hand. She saw them start for home before she turned to go down the hill to the house, sorting out the troubles that loomed ahead of her.

Mike jumped at the idea of an incursion on the mainland. The whiting would more than defray the cost of the run and the price of the drinks and cigarettes he and Sean were beginning to hunger for. A lick and a rub would get them ready, he said, and there was no need for the girls to spend much time on dolling up for a run to the shop.

They were just leaving the house in great spirits when Donal Michael gave vent to an unearthly long-drawn-out yell that brought Maire running back to the cradle with a clutch at her heart. His cries filled the house until Joany took him in her arms and soothed him to a restless silence.

"That puts paid to our run," said Mike. "We can't leave Joany alone with him now. You could never tell what might happen while we are away."

"Nonsense, Mike," said Maire. "There's no need for ye to stay. I'll stop with Joany and nothing will happen, please God."

"I'll stay, Maire girl, if you like. You didn't get the full value of the dance like I did. 'Tis your turn to go ashore." Mai imported as much sincerity into her offer as she could, but her attitude at the door betrayed her eagerness to be off.

When Joany added her assurances to Maire's, the trio at last departed with a seemly show of reluctance. Meantime, Donal Michael had calmed down to his own old gurgling smiling self and Joany was able to see how disappointed Maire was at losing her afternoon ashore.

"I'll put the darling back in his cradle, *a chroi*, and you can run off with yourself. Never fear; we'll be all right till you come back. If you hurry, you'll catch up with them."

Maire needed only "the wind of the words." Giving her heart's delight a kiss and a tickle she darted down the path like a deer. Alas! She was brought up in mid-career by another heartrending yell from Master Donal. She raced back to find the child in Joany's arms again, convulsed with struggles that purpled his face.

"Give him to me, and get a tub of warm water ready at once," she cried in the masterful way she assumed in times of crisis. She proceeded to strip the child to the skin, keeping an eye on each garment for safety pins gone adrift or for wrinkles that might have galled his tender skin.

"*Joa-ny!—Come here.*" Her voice was indignant as well as masterful now. She had the baby sprawled face-down across her lap in the seemingly callous but really skilful way that women have, and she pointed with accusing finger at the sprinkle of crusty breadcrumbs that showed between the undervest and its upturned back.

"They weren't there when I dressed him this morning," she snapped harshly, stressing the accents of the fortuitously rhythmic phrase that matched the surge of her anger. "No wonder the poor child was in pain."

Joany's cry of dismay was so real that it dispelled any suspicion that might lie against her in Maire's mind. But how did the crumbs get there? If Joany did not drop them carelessly down the child's neck, who did? The men never handled the baby; Irishmen are no good about the house and abhor weanlings. Only Mai was left.

Maire's mouth drew into a thin line at the thought and its implications. She handed the child to Joany to finish dressing it and went to the door to see if the *St. Finian* was still in the cove. It was gone. She went to the drawer in which they kept the ship's binoculars and took them with her out the backdoor and up the hill to Carrigard. Sitting down at the base of the old grey rock, she focused the glasses on the boat which was just abreast of the cell steps, less than half a mile away. What she saw brought a black, forbidding frown to her brows. Sean Driscoll lay prone on the short forward deck with his nose over the stem watching the bow wave beneath him. In the stern sat Mike with one hand on the helm and beside him, snuggled close with her head on his shoulder, sat Mai Hogan!

"The designing little wretch!" That was all Maire said. She lowered the glasses and leaned back against the rock to readjust her world. She looked straight ahead, high over the Bay and the mountains beyond, with introspective eyes, seeing nothing but the tangled skein which Father John's protégée was bent on making of her ordered life. She closed her eyes and sat as still as the rock behind her, searching for a plan of campaign that would untangle the mess without hurting Mike or offending Father John, but which would bring down on Mai Hogan's treacherous head the direst punishment she could devise. A deep breath marked the taking of her decision. She opened her eyes and, for the first time since she sat down, took in the familiar features of the scene. She even traced the course of the punt in their race home from the Bay Rock only two short hours ago. It was characteristic that she did not send one look in the direction of the *St. Finian* already shrunken to a small black speck to the northward, just off the quay.

Picking up the binoculars as she rose to go down the hill to the house, she saw another black speck to the southward, just off the Fang. Boats came so seldom from the south that she stood and watched the speck grow large, wondering who it could be. It was travelling fast and on a course that would bring it inside the Shark. Passing boats always kept well outside the island; perhaps this one was going to anchor in the cove. Maire caught her in the glasses and saw that she was a drifter of the Baltimore type, but larger than the Manistir boats, and, though still far off, that she was making for the cove as if she knew her way.

Curiosity about the approaching stranger banished, for the time being, the black dog which Mai Hogan's duplicity had planted on her shoulder. She walked slowly down the hill and stopped in the house long enough to see that the baby was sleeping and to set the kitchen in order in preparation for visitors. She knew she had plenty of time.

The drifter was circling confidently into the cove when Maire reached the slip and sat on the pile of driftwood to observe its further movements. She saw it run straight up to the punt at the *St. Finian's* moorings, saw a man boathook the mooring buoy as neatly as Mike ever did, and then saw him paddle the punt shorewards with an assurance that amazed her. She rose to her feet to meet this stranger who made his own of everything without "By your leave" or "May I."

He jumped ashore and saw her coming towards him, slim and erect in her shore-going clothes, with a light of dawning recognition in her eyes.

"Knut!" she cried, and ran with open hands to welcome him.

"Maire Mack. Dear Maire Mack." He held her at arm's length, gazing into her flushed face with undisguised affection. "At last I know what has been pulling me back to the island."

The spontaneous avowal, made in a deep tone that sounded like a caress, threw her into an alarming conflict of emotions. Her heart wanted to sing but her head, so recently exercised in planning retribution for Mai's disloyalty, forbade it. Tears welled to her eyes as she withdrew her hands and retreated backwards up the slip lest she betray her real feelings.

"Have I offended you, Maire? Forgive me. You know I couldn't hurt you for the world."

She shook her head, smiling wanly through the tears to reassure him. Her throat was too full for words. She had never felt so unstrung, so out of control before, experiencing for the first time in her life the alarm of one who is at the mercy of runaway forces. It was the forlorn, contrite expression on Ollsen's face that restored her self-possession. Pulling herself together, she flicked the tears out of her eyes with quick fingers and took charge of the situation with a gay laugh.

"You took me by surprise, Knut. I had no notion who was the cocksure stranger until you faced me and swept me off my feet. Do you wonder I got startled?"

"I would have hailed you, but I didn't see you against the baulks you were sitting on. But it is all right isn't it, Maire, and you'll come out to see my new boat."

He moved towards the punt, taking it for granted that she would be keen to go aboard to inspect the handsome boat in which he had returned and hear all about it. But she was on her guard, not so much against Ollsen as against herself. She was not sure that she could trust herself with him in another emotional disturbance, out there in the boat. In her subconscious mind stirred the thought that she would be no better than that wretched pagan slut, Mai Hogan, if she followed her heart's desire without a thought of the consequences.

"Not now, Knut. We'll all go aboard when Mike comes home from the mainland. Come up to the house for your supper. You must be starved with the hunger and Joany has a lovely brill for you—alive and kicking. Oh, I forgot. What about your crew?"

"Dan Donovan? He's all right. He'd rather stay aboard and look after himself."

They walked up the path together, but well apart, saying little because Ollsen was looking here and there for signs of new work done while he was away. He was glad to see that the concrete water tank was in position on the ridge and the tap at the backdoor, though he thought the workmanship rather rough and ready. He would put the finishing touches on it in his own good time.

Joany was stooped over the basting oven by the fire, testing the bread with a table knife when they entered the kitchen.

"Hallo, Joany! Still baking stampy?"

The old woman turned her head to look under her arm at the newcomer. Her mouth gaped oddly, showing the empty gums and the pale ball of tongue drawn back into the throat.

"*The Norwayman!*"

Her hoarse windy whisper was more eloquent than a loud cry. Drawing herself stiffly to her feet, she turned to face the sailor and stare at him blankly as at an apparition.

"*The Norwayman!*" she whispered again, reluctantly admitting the evidence of her eyes. She looked from Ollsen to Maire and back again, searching their faces for signs of collusion, of private understanding between them. The flush, which her cold scrutiny brought to Maire's neck, confirmed her suspicion and inspired her to take the only defensive action she knew. Going to the cradle, she took the sleeping child up in her arms and walked across the kitchen to Maire, as stiffly erect as a priestess performing a solemn ritual.

"Take Mike's child in your arms, *a chroí*, and there's no fear of you. He will keep you safe while his father is away."

Without casting a look at Ollsen, she walked off to her own room and closed the door behind her, leaving two very embarrassed young people to stand, bereft of speech, looking at the closed door. At last Maire spoke.

"I'm sorry, Knut, but perhaps it would be better if you had your supper on the boat. Joany will be over her . . . her notions, by the time Mike and the others get back. You can come ashore with them."

Ollsen went out. He did not see Joany's white face watching him through the room window until she saw him go aboard.

He made no answer when his man offered him a cup of coffee but climbed up on the afterdeck and sat leaning against the wheelhouse to think out the awkward situation that had arisen for him and Maire. He was still sitting there when the *St. Finian* came back and fussed up to find her moorings occupied by a strange boat.

Mike's shout of wholehearted delight at seeing him brought him to his feet with a jump and dispelled the fear, which Joany's hostility had created, that he might never again be accepted on the old footing by his old friends.

Mike came aboard and took Ollsen by both hands, drawing him towards him with a brotherly roughness.

"*De vahassa a bhaile, a bhrahair!* You're welcome home, cousin. Welcome as the flowers of spring. Let me have a good look at you to see did they treat you well in London. Ah, but 'tis grand to have you back."

When the greetings calmed down, Ollsen wanted to show Mike the new boat, but the islandman would have none of it until he had discharged his duty as the host in his own home.

"*Is tuisge deoch na sceal, a Knut.* You must eat before you talk. A hungry belly tells a poor story."

So they went ashore, all five together in the punt, leaving the new boat where she was and tying the *St. Finian* to the seineboat's mooring, a mere rope's length astern. After supper they could spend the evening inspecting the Baltimore boat. She would take a whole evening to size up properly.

As they sorted themselves out on the slip, Ollsen became aware of strained relations between the *St. Finian's* party. Mai lined up with Mike, but he edged away from her and took the Norwegian by the elbow toward the path. She then turned to Sean but he was preoccupied with Dan Donovan. Sean had found out that Dan was from his own country, fifty miles to the southward, and that they had a lot of news for each other which could not wait. With a toss of her lovely head, she stepped quickly into the lead up the path and headed the party into the house.

Even in the house the atmosphere was unusually tense. Though the table was laid and the fire burned brightly, it was evident to Ollsen's susceptive eye that Maire and Joany had had a heart-to-heart talk since he left them and that Maire was in command again. The old woman went through her jobs with none of the easy mothering of the household that became her so well. She performed them in silence like a helper hired for the day. Maire, on the other hand, was the conscious mistress of the house, brisk and bright and, in a flouncing way, assertive of her right to direct things.

Ollsen missed the old free and easy warmth of the islanders, the memory of which had sustained him during his short stay in London and through the long wait in Baltimore while the boat was being built to his specifications. Surely, he thought to himself, the slip I made in showing my feelings for Maire cannot be the cause of Mai's disagreement with Mike and Sean. Nevertheless he did feel unhappy in his "homecoming."

The supper was dispatched at speed and as soon as the ware was washed Mai slipped down to her own room, Joany took the baby into hers, and Sean took Dan Donovan out to show him the place. Ollsen would have followed Sean to escape the uneasy atmosphere had not Mike detained him.

"That's no way to act, Knut. Sure, you know we are dying to hear all that happened to you over in England. Sit down, man, and tell us all about it. Look, I brought a drop in the bottle from Bill's, though it isn't of you I was thinking when I got it."

"Take it yourself, Mike, but cut me out. Whisky and me don't agree. I drank it once on the island and made a show of myself. That once was enough."

But he stayed with them and told them of Eric Skunder and of the brokers, Laxton and Lee. He showed them with simple pride, which he made no pretence to conceal, the great owner's generous testimony to his services when the *Bernadotte* was in danger. He recounted the incidents of his long solitary journey from London to Baltimore and of his fights to get the boatbuilders to depart from their stock plan and accept his modifications. It was dark when he had finished and leaned back to relax and look around the silent kitchen. As if she had been waiting for his voice to cease, Joany opened her door quietly and brought the sleeping child back to his cradle. She looked towards Maire to come and help her to carry the cradle to the large bedroom and then went off to bed, leaving the smooring of the fire to Maire for the first time since she came to the Shark.

Ollsen took that as a signal for his own departure. He and Mike went together in friendly silence till the shingle crunching under their feet woke Donovan from his snooze on the pile of driftwood. Mike looked around for Sean.

"He went to bed an hour ago," said Donovan as he settled himself to the paddles. "There's something on that chap's mind." Mike pondered on that on his way back to the house.

Maire lay awake far into the night, teasing out the snarl into which her daily life and Mike's were thrown by the unexpected happenings of the day that had just closed. The day had begun so well, within and without, and everyone had been so gaily happy that its dismal ending, with everyone at cross-purposes, seemed all the more calamitous. She stared upwards at the web of rafters looming through the dark, and unravelled the tangle thread by thread.

She must, she decided, face up to her dangerous susceptibility to the Norwegian and either find some way of killing it or run the risk of ruining her life. Through the weft of her thoughts ran a thread of surprise that she, or any woman, could think emotionally of two men at the same time. It led her to compare her love for Mike with her feeling for Ollsen and to find how different they were. Her love for Mike was like himself, deep, safe, and reliable. In fair weather or in foul, in good report or evil, it would always possess her as completely as the air possesses the forest. It was part of herself.

Ollsen was deep, too, and reliable, but was he safe as Mike was safe? She knew he was not. She remembered his uncontrolled rage on the ridge the day they struck water and recalled his own account of the fierce fight with Captain Skelde. Perhaps it was the primeval ferocity, which he kept under leash deep in his being, that attracted her to him and begat in her a primeval emotion which she was beginning to fear.

Mike moved in his sleep and stretched himself luxuriously into another spell of untroubled slumber by her side. He seemed to intervene in her thoughts and bring her to a conclusion that would settle the problem that vexed her soul. She would tell him all about it. Open confession was good for the soul; healthy beings thrive in the sunlight, furtive things die in it.

She nudged him into wakefulness and took the hand near her into her own and laced fingers.

"Thahailen, *a chroi liom.*"

"Well, *a stoirin.*"

He had come wide awake at the first nudge, as seamen do, and knowing her way, waited for the weighty thing she had to say. She did not break his sleep merely to comfort her own wakefulness.

"Knut is back with us again and I am wondering . . ."

She paused to find words for her embarrassing case. Mike squeezed her hand to encourage her.

"We both know that he came back to try and make up for what we did for him. He bought that fine boat because he knows your heart is set on deep-sea fishing and he knows I dislike poking among the rocks for crabs and lobsters as much as you do."

"Lobstering in a small boat is a mug's game," said Mike to fill in another pause.

" 'Tis well we know it. That boat cost him a pot of money—money he earned at the risk of his life. As he told us this evening, he bought her for us, but . . ."

Maire stopped again, more to fix Mike's attention than to cover any hesitance she might have felt as she approached the core of the story.

"Ask yourself, Mike, why did he come with the boat. Couldn't he have sent the money or couldn't he have given his orders to the Baltimore people to build her and send her here?"

Mike clung to his impregnable silence. He knew that she did not expect an answer to what was really a statement put like a question.

"Listen, Mike Mack, and don't imagine for a moment that it is a giddy whipster just out of school is talking to you. *Knut Ollsen came back because he is in love with your wife*— Stop! Let me finish it. 'Tis hard enough for me to say it without having to parse it too. He just gave himself away when he came on me suddenly at the slip. He got a shock and so did I. But he got over it and I brought him to the house to Joany. She's no fool and she saw into his heart and told him so. Now you know it too. It is your right to know it. Only a fool that didn't love every hair on your head would try to hide it from you."

Mike rolled the strange revelation over in his mind at his ease before he broke silence.

"It is a story that no woman in Erin but yourself would have the pluck to tell her man up to his face at the dead of night. But I wouldn't expect anything else from you, *a chroi istig*. I can't blame Ollsen for getting struck on you. I got struck on you myself the first time I laid eyes on your yellow head and your dancing legs. I swore I'd marry you or clear off to the States to Tim, God rest him, if you wouldn't have me. No, I don't blame him for having a *gradh* for you, but if he dares to think he'll get you from me . . ."

He went no further, but the fierce grip he gave her hand said more than the unspoken words could have said.

"That'll never happen Mike, and you know it. Another thing you know, too. Knut Ollsen is a whole man, a decent man, that will never pay back what we did for him by getting between us. It slipped out of him in the shock of meeting me. He'll never mention it to me again. And I ask you, now, by the love you had for your brother Tim, not to show him by deed or word that you know his secret. Promise me that, Thahailen."

He gave her his word in the simple phrase he always used when he agreed with her novel points of view. "*You're* the boss," he said, and she needed no more.

They fell into silence, but Maire's mind was revolving its second problem very actively. Would Mike now be as candidly outspoken about Mai Hogan as she had been about Knut? He would never have a better chance. She was in the mood to forgive, and she was anxious to clear the air around Mike and herself completely. She waited on, but Mike lay so reposeful that she guessed he would soon relapse into sleep.

"Mike, *a chroi*, is there anything on your mind? Anything you'd like to talk over?" Her voice was invitingly loving.

"No, then, there isn't. What could there be?"

"Aren't you worrying about Mai Hogan?" She asked as a kindly confessor helps a hesitant penitent over the first style.

"About the way she's playing randy with poor Sean, is it?" He gave one of the tolerant laughs a settled married man uses for the affairs of courting couples.

"Well, yes," she said, "and the way she carried on in the *St. Finian* when you and Sean went in with the whiting."

"I'll admit she did put Sean's nose out of joint, however you came to hear of it. But the poor chap was asking for it. Any girl would take a rise out of him, he was so sheepish."

"What happened between them?" she asked with less of the troubled earnestness she had shown up to then. Mike's easy laugh at Sean's discomfiture and the absence of any sign of reservation in his manner suggested that her own interpretation of the grouping on the *St. Finian* might have been wrong.

"Ah, she'll tell you herself Maire. I'm no good at remembering what two kids like them say. Anyhow, whatever argument they had, Mai stuck out her tongue at him and flopped down on the stern sheets alongside me to grig him. He got mad at her and went off to the bows in a sulk."

Maire's main anxiety disappeared after Mike's simple explanation of what she had seen through the glasses, though she did not agree with Mike's last word before he rolled over on his side to sleep.

"Mai's all right. She's nothing but a young filly kicking her heels among the colts."

CHAPTER 31 · *The Snare*

In the morning Maire radiated good humour and jollied Joany and Mai out of the aloofness they were trying to bring over from the night before. She failed to soften Sean. He clung to his silence and hurried off after a quick breakfast just as Ollsen's figure came and cut off the morning sunlight at the front door.

"*Bail o Dia oroaibh*," he called out. Ollsen liked to show off the Gaelic "Good mornings" and "Good evenings" he had picked up on the island. Besides, he was in festive mood. There would be no drudging work today, he told the kitchen at large. Everyone was coming aboard the new boat to see her beauties and test her wonderful power in a long run across the bay.

His unselfish enthusiasm affected the household variously. It banished the last tenuous wisp of suspicion from Mike's mind. It warmed Maire's heart, now fortified against backsliding by her plenary confession. In Mai's predatory soul it woke the hunting spirit more strongly than usual, because she would be free to pursue Ollsen in the open. His affection was not bespoken as Mike's was. Joany, alone, withstood the Norwegian's high spirits. She eyed him coldly and withdrew from the company to look after the baby, while they got themselves ready for the great event.

Ollsen paddled the punt slowly around the new boat before they went aboard to show up her great size and her sweet lines. She dwarfed the *St. Finian* that had been their pride, and sat on the water as suggestive of power as a small battleship.

Ollsen backed water as they rounded the stern to let them see the bright orange lettering painted large across the top strake of her counter: *Mary Mack*.

"Oh, why did you do that, Knut?" Maire exclaimed in a vexed confusion of pleasure and dismay. It was grand to see her own name on such a gallant boat, but Knut's generous gesture might easily rouse Mike to the jealous suspicion which her voluntary confession was designed to forestall. She shot a quick glance at Mike to see how he was taking it and missed the veiled scrutiny Mai was directing on her and Ollsen. Mike's pleasure in the compliment to Maire was evident and sincere enough to reassure her.

"I wouldn't doubt your taste, Knut," Mike clapped Ollsen on the back to strengthen his approval. "I'm glad now that Joany picked a saint's name for the *St. Finian*. My own notion was to call her 'The Maire,' but Joany outfaced us. I'm better pleased now."

Mike's wholehearted approval having wiped out the disappointment that Maire's exclamation had caused him, Ollsen laid the punt alongside the *Mary Mack's* waist and led the party aboard. He showed them the three-bunk cabin forward for the crew, the capacious hold, divided into sections, one large enough to contain twenty thousand herrings, the other housing a full train of nets. He displayed a boyish pride in starting the powerful engine off the battery by a touch of his finger and racing her to a roar that echoed back from the Lookout. He reserved the luxuries of the aftercabin to finish the show: the neat lockers around the collapsible table, the twin electric lights set deep in the upper-deck beam, and, to cap it all, the radio receiver firmly anchored to its corner shelf out of harm's way. He showed Maire how to switch it on and dial Northern Ireland; it was too early for Radio Eireann. She was in luck. The station orchestra was playing Irish dances and Maire tuned in on "The Rakes of Mallow," which she recognized and tapped with her feet on the cabin floor. It was a wonderful experience for the islanders who had never heard wireless before: to hear it for the first time on the new boat at home was miraculous.

When, at last, they tore themselves from the cabin and came on deck, Donovan hailed them from the slip. Sean was with him, dressed in shore-going clothes and balancing a bag against his shin. He looked a very woebegone young man, even at that distance, and barely spoke to Mike when he ran the punt in for them. He went into the forward caboose as soon as he came aboard, without casting a glance at Mai Hogan, though she kept peering at him with a mocking complaisance in the corner of her eye. She knew his ailment and gloated over the visible effect of her allurements on him.

"Go for'ard, Mike, and slip the moorings," Ollsen said with a brisk assumption of command as soon as Donovan was aboard. "And you, Maire. Come and have the first go at starting the engine of your own boat. We'll run her into Big Bill's and have her registered today."

Maire caught the implication of "your own boat" and stiffened momentarily to protest until her quick mind saw the possibility that Ollsen was referring to the name of the boat rather than to the ownership. Mike caught it, too, but gave no sign as he moved quickly forward to the bows. He was great at suppressing outward signs of his inner thoughts and letting things declare themselves. Donovan took charge of the engine after Maire had had the thrill of waking it into exuberant life with her fingertip, and proceeded to show its power. In a wide arc that skirted the curve of the cove with growing speed, Ollsen steered the *Mary Mack* to the open bay and set her on a beeline for the old quay before he handed the wheel over to Maire. He was proud of the steering wheel, the first of its kind in the Bay, and of the weather-proof covering for the steersman.

They reached the quay in twelve minutes, three faster than Pats Kelly's fastest time, and tied up to the rings at the pierhead to make sure of having plenty of water under the keel at low tide. Leaving Donovan aboard to act as showman to the crowd that gathered to examine, criticize, condemn, and commend the marvels of the wonder boat, they went up the middle of the road to Bill's. Halfway there, their formation was split by Father Boyle, speeding the Hillman to the quay to find out what the crowd was gaping at. He threw them a short-arm salute as he flashed through, more in bravado than in apology.

Bill made short work of the registration. He phoned through to the registrar at Fenit, gave him the specifications of the boat, and then turned to Ollsen.

"How do you spell your name, sir?"

"I'm not registering her in my own name, Mr. Hannen, but in Mrs. Mack's. You see, sir, I am an alien. My name would not be accepted by the registrar, but hers will."

Seeing a puzzled look dawn on Big Bill's face, Maire intervened to prevent his sharp mind from pursuing suspicion to conclusions.

"Register her in the joint names of Mike and Knut," she suggested. "Who ever heard of a married woman owning a fishing boat or, for that matter, having a boat called after her. Cut out the Mack and christen her plain *Mary*."

The registrar got impatient at the delay and buzzed Bill for action. That riled the big man. Though he was a born hustler himself, he could not stand being hustled by another.

"Ah, keep your hair on," he bawled into the mouthpiece. "This is the first call you've had for weeks. When it is finished, you'll fall back on your bed for another snooze. Here. Take down the particulars, if you aren't asleep already. Boat's name, *Mary*; owner, Michael Mack, Shark Island. Got that . . . ? You needn't fear: you'll have the fee in the morning's post."

Neither Maire nor Ollsen demurred at Bill's quick decision to register the *Mary* in Mike's name alone. It saved the complications and explanations they wished to avoid and speeded up the matter in hand. They were relieved when the crackling voice of the phone ceased after saying that the boat's registration number was T333 and that she was licenced to fish in the territorial waters of Eire, without let or hindrance, and would continue to be so licenced on the payment of the appropriate fee on the due dates.

"The pleasure is mine," Bill said with a grin towards Maire when Mike offered him the cost of the phone call.

Maire pulled Mai by the sleeve as the party left the post office and beamed a bright sisterly smile at her.

"We haven't seen Father John since you came to live with us on the Shark. What about a nice walk to the presbytery while the men are 'wetting' the new boat? Father John would be mad if we went back without seeing him."

Mai's smile was no less sisterly and ulterior. She was an apt pupil and was beginning to wonder about her companion's moves and where they were leading. After Ollsen's proposal to register the *Mary* in Maire's name, she was certain that the Norwegian was in love with that immaculate dame and stored the knowledge away in her bosom for future use.

"Certainly, Maire, girl. I was going to suggest it myself." She said it so sweetly that the elder girl slanted a keen glance of suspicion on her. Mai did not leave an assembly of men so easily without good reason. What could it be? Mai, herself, could not have specified any more definite reason than the general idea of keeping Maire under observation.

In that unamiable frame of mind they went at a brisk pace up the road past the chapel and on towards the priest's house. Mai knew the district better than Maire and kept up a running commentary on the private lives of the people who lived in the thatched farmhouses standing in the fields that sloped down to the road. She showed no nostalgic regrets for her old home when it came into view, far away to the left in a fold of the hills. She merely pointed at it and passed on to retail a gossipy tidbit about Biddy Cremin and her geese.

Maire marvelled at the change a few months on the island had made on the dumb irresponsive Mai Hogan the priest had entrusted to her. She felt proud of her volubility in a wry grudging way of which she was half ashamed. She knew that, but for Father John's interest in the girl, she would not have allowed her to put her foot on the island.

"Is the priest at home, Thade?" she asked when the old clerk came to intercept them with an ingratiating grin on his grotesque face.

"Which of them would you be wanting, ma'am? The boss or his nibs?"

"Father Miles, Thade. We saw Father Boyle going west in his car a while ago."

"Splittin' the wind, too, I warrant," said Thade, twisting his lips sourly under the beetling nose. "Mark my words, ma'am; that young man will finish up with the shaft of a donkey cart stuck in his gizzard, if he doesn't take his aise going from nowhere to no place."

He hung on, waiting for a word or sign to indicate their business with the parish priest and moved towards the door only when they started in that direction for themselves.

"He's busy making up school accounts with Master Brehony," he said. "I doubt if he'll see ye, unless yer business is out of the ordinary. I could tell him for ye and put in a good word, too."

"Thanks, Thade. We'll tell him our business when we go in."

"Is that so?" he said, viewing Maire with a bleak eye, and added with a flash of bitterness, "Ye can find yer own way in too, I suppose."

Jim Brehony stood up to go when the two girls entered the study in obedience to the "Come in" that answered Maire's knock. He nearly sat down again in the confusion that swamped him when he saw the angelic Mai glide demurely in at Maire's heels. All three observed his plight. Father John smiled wisely, Maire looked past him with politely impassive face, and Mai conjured up a peach blush to emphasize her maidenly charms.

"You can carry on with the averages in the dining room, James. I'll call you when I'm free again— Oh, by the way, this is Mrs. Mack of Shark Island and this young lady is her protégée, Mai Hogan."

The young schoolmaster, who could charge gaily into a melee of battling forwards and emerge with the ball on his toe, mumbled his responses and backed out of the presence of the two women like a bashful child who had wandered into a strange house.

"Well, young lady," said Father John to Mai when Brehony was gone, "I'm delighted to see you looking so well. The Shark seems to agree with you."

"It does, indeed, Father." Mai loosed upon him a radiant, wide-eyed look which she modified judiciously when she turned to embrace Maire in her praise of the island. "I can never repay you, Father, or Maire for all you have done for me. I was lost till I went to live there."

Though Maire knew that Mai was playing up, both to herself and

Father John, she could not withhold her admiration for the young girl's artful performance. It was calculated to do credit to Maire's training and to justify the priest's judgment in selecting the right treatment for her deficiencies. His satisfaction at the result was evident. He beamed on both of them and drew Mai to speak of her newly developed interest in the people around her. Mai was entirely objective in her answers and gave him no inkling of her own thrilling reactions to certain of those people, though she was engagingly free in her description of their work and way of life. Maire sat back and admired her cleverness, marvelling, too, at the pliancy of even the ablest men in the hands of a designing female.

Mai would have gone on indefinitely if Father John had not felt the call of other affairs and brought the dialogue to an end.

"Perhaps, you would like to see the house, my child, while I have a few words with Mrs. Mack. Debby will show you around. You'll find her in the kitchen at the end of the hall."

When she was gone, he had a good look at Maire before he spoke.

"You are very silent this morning, Maire. One would imagine you were the pupil and Mai Hogan the mistress, you said so little and she so much."

"I thought that was the way you wanted it, Father John; to let her show the schooling we gave her on the island. What do you think of it?"

"It worked like a charm. I wouldn't know her for the timid frightened child she was when you got her, and I cannot attempt to tell you how grateful I am to you. And she seems to be grateful to you, too: very grateful. There remains only one further point to set my mind completely at rest. *How do you like Mai?* Did she fit in with your life on the island?"

"I know, Father John, you have no use for soft talk. No more than I. You asked me do I like Mai and you expect a straight answer. I do *not* like Mai Hogan. To her credit I must say she is the makings of a good housekeeper. She's intelligent, she's clean, she's willing, and she's good-tempered. That's more than can be said of a lot of your parishioners, Father John."

She took out her handkerchief, not to use it, but to mark with a pause the end of Mai's credit account, and then went on.

"I'm sure you guess what's coming, Father. You and the nurse hinted at it when you asked me to take her out of harm's way. Mrs. Lee feared it when she tried to rear Mai in blinkers. Mai is her mother's daughter. She is mad for men. She can see nothing else in life worth bothering her head about, and would risk her eternal salvation for an hour with a man she had her eye on. She can't help it, poor girl; it was born in her, but it is a terrible affliction."

She was watching the shadow spread over the priest's face as she laid Mai's soul bare to him, wondering whether it betokened sadness or unbelief.

"Perhaps, Father John, you find it hard to believe such a good-looking girl can be so depraved. You may think I am just a woman slandering another woman. Listen, Father. I am so sure of what I say that I will make a bet with you. You told her to go down to Debby Sweeny in the kitchen. Well, I bet you anything you like, that if you go straight from your chair to the dining room you'll find Mai sitting on Master Brehony's knee or doing her best to get there."

Whether it was the challenge in her words or the impelling conviction in her eyes that urged Father John to take up the bet, he rose quietly from his chair and walked out of the room without any suggestion of stealth. Maire heard him opening the dining-room door and speaking for a few moments with someone. When he returned, he closed the door behind him and sat down in the chair before he spoke to her.

"You win your bet. I found her standing by James's chair. She told me, quite convincingly, that she had missed her way to the kitchen and blundered into the dining room, but it was evident that she had wasted no time in bewitching the poor boy. He could only gape at me, tongue-tied and overwhelmed."

Maire knew how to hold her tongue as well as Mike, when she had made her point. She waited for him to continue.

"She's going to be a bigger handful than I bargained for," he said.

"She must be protected against herself, but *how* is the question. And she must be taken off your hands as soon as possible. She has caused you enough trouble already."

He looked at Maire for a suggestion but she held her tongue and let him think matters out for himself, unhindered by distraction from outside.

"Marriage is her only safeguard," he mused aloud. "She would soon settle down under the grace of the sacrament and the responsibility of housekeeping. But who will we find in the parish for her?"

He directed the question at Maire with an emphasis on the *"we"* that forced her to answer.

"You know best, Father. I don't know the young men of the mainland as well as you do."

"What about James Brehony? He's a grand fellow with tons of character and a mind of his own. I'd say, from his attitude out there in the dining room, that he would not be unwilling. Indeed, I'd say he'd be more than willing to marry her. She'd bring him a fine dowry which he would put to excellent use. Yes, I think a marriage with James would be the making of Mai."

"I thought you were fond of the master, Father John. If you are, surely you wouldn't dream of clapping Mai Hogan as a plaster on him for the rest of his life. She'd have his heart broken long before he would have broken her off her bad habit of chasing strange men. He's miles too good for her, Father."

"But we must think of someone, Maire. To leave her reclamation half finished would be a crime, a permanent blot on my reputation as long as I remain as parish priest of Manistir. Surely you know some young man who could face up to the job."

"You said just now that she has a good dowry," Maire said tentatively. "How much would it be, Father? Mind, I'm not asking you out of curiosity, but if it is worth his while, I think I know a bachelor who would marry her and make a good job of taming her in his own quiet way."

Father John drew his eyes away from Maire and looked past her out the window with a wrinkle of concentration on his brow. He was running the *quiet* bachelors of the parish through the sieve of his mind to find Maire's selection for himself. He slanted a whimsical smile at her when he had finished the roster and found his man.

"John Joe Barrett, of course," he said. "He's the very man to tame this bird of paradise in his own silky, persistent way. I must set about it at once."

"You'd better keep out of it, Father John," Maire suggested. "You would rush it too quickly and spoil it, and, anyhow, you must have heard the old saying that there's no luck in a match made by a priest or a nun. Leave it to me. I'll let you know how it is working. But," she added with a knowing twinkle in her eye, "you dodged my question about her dowry. I must know how much she will have, if I am to get John Joe going."

"She'll have more than any girl in Manistir except Betty Hannen. That ought to excite John Joe's fancy better than the warmth of spring."

"How much, Father?" Maire persisted with a mock pout to kill the curtness of her words.

"Fifteen hundred, between post-office account and the amount I hold in trust after the sale of the farm."

"Thank you for trusting me so much, Father. I assure you I will not break your confidence, but you must give me a free hand with John Joe."

"Now! Now! my lady. Blank cheques are dangerous things. You must give me some idea of your plan of campaign."

"It is a very simple one. It is so simple that you might think it foolish and condemn it. I'll manage to let John Joe ferret out that Mai will have thousands to her name when she gets married. He'll take it for gospel truth if he picks it up on the sly like that. The little weasel would suspect something if I told him straight out."

Father John nodded in agreement with the simplicity of the scheme. "But," he asked, "what do you expect John Joe to do then?"

"I expect him to manufacture excuses for going out to the island and playing up to Mai. Never fear, Father John. We might as well give him lodgings with us once he starts the hunt. He'll give Mai no peace till he gets herself and her fortune."

"Very good, my child. *Fiat voluntas tua.* Have your own way. If your plan fails, we can try another." He stood up. "Come. We may as well find the young damsel and let you go home."

Mike was full of news when the girls got back from the presbytery to Hannen's. Tommy Fitz had taken over the *St. Finian* on a share basis and would work for her from the mainland. Sean Driscoll had thrown in his lot with Tommy, but had persuaded Donovan to take his place on the island. Mike, in an aside, told Maire that Mai Hogan was the cause of Sean's desertion; he could not stand her hot and cold antics. Best of all, Mike thought, Maurisheen Bowler, the Dingle trawl-erman, had signed on to work the *Mary's* trawl. He knew trawling inside out and, better than that, he knew the bearings of all the foul grounds within a day's sail of the Shark. Counting Knut and himself, the *Mary* would have a picked crew of four for the season. Of course, they should have a fifth man for such a big boat, but they'd manage somehow.

Maire listened with half her mind; the other half was occupied in a search for John Joe in the thinning crowd in the bar. It was Mai who sighted him first, bent over the grocery end of the long counter, col-loguing with Betty Hannen. Mai and Maire joined them and chatted for a few moments.

"Excuse me, Betty," said Maire in a half whisper designed to make John Joe cock his ears. "Is your Daddy in the post office? I want to see him."

"Yes, ma'am, he is. He's making up the old-age-pension books, I think," said Betty.

Maire went out and around to the post-office door, listening like a hare to sounds behind her. She was gambling on John Joe's curiosity, that he would think up some excuse to follow her unostentatiously. Big Bill received her with a frown of irritation at first; she was in-terrupting him in the middle of a long tot that had gone astray more than once. But he summoned up his broad-beamed smile to greet her.

"What can I do for you, Mrs. Mack? Whatever it is, the pleasure will be mine."

" 'Tis about Mai Hogan's savings book. She'll be wanting to draw the interest on it for the odds and ends a young girl, like her, needs."

She heard quiet steps approaching the door behind her but gave no sign that she heard. They stopped outside just when she told Bill what she wanted.

"What makes you think she has any savings in the post office?" Bill asked her with a disarming smile.

"Mai and I have just come back from the presbytery and I may as well tell you between ourselves, that Father John himself told me come to you. You know, of course, he is looking after Mai's business."

"Um . . . Yes. That is so. But what do you want *me* to do?" Bill was still smiling but noncommittal.

"To tell me from the savings book how much the interest for this year amounts to. Father John will allow me draw that for Mai's use."

Bill fell into the snare she laid for him. Looking around the office to assure himself that he would not be overheard, he lowered his voice.

" 'Tis as much as my job is worth to reveal official secrets, but I know I can trust you. There's roughly £1,200 in one savings book. At 2½ per cent you can count on about £30 to spend on Mai Hogan's new outfit."

"Twelve hundred pounds!" Maire repeated aloud, as if in admiration, but really to make sure the hidden ears would hear her, "and £300 in the other book. My! Mr. Hannen, Mai is a millionaire."

Maire kept on talking to drown the faint sound of feet stealthily retiring from the office door and then thanked Bill profusely for his kindness.

"The pleasure is all mine, Mrs. Mack."

When she got back to the bar, John Joe was with Mike's party and in the act of asking them what they would have. Such unprecedented extravagance tempted practical jokers to leave their own groups to join them and tell him what they, too, would have. But John Joe never lost control of his impulses. Indeed, he never had impulses, all his actions being considered and objective. Turning a deaf ear on the interlopers, he bought four drinks and no more.

Through the corner of her eye Maire watched him exert all his charm to ingratiate himself with Mike and Ollsen. She knew that her ruse was working and began to guess his next move to get close to Mai and her money.

He's a cute little shaver, she said to herself in a glow of self-approval, but not cute enough.

CHAPTER 32 · *The Alchemy of Danger*

THE island settled down to uneventful workaday calm when the *Mary* was put to trawl the Bay. Trawling is the steadiest and most predictable kind of sea fishing, with which only the weather and the known habits of the fish that feed deep, interfere. The catch, though small by comparison with the harvest of the migratory herring and mackerel, is fairly uniform in size and the market fluctuates within narrow limits.

Maurisheen Bowler knew his job. He learned it in the hard days of the hooker and the heavy hardwood beam with its monstrous trawl irons that broke one's back to haul up from the weedy bottom with a hand winch. He was a chubby, redfaced ball of a man with a foot itch that drove him from post to pillar. He could not stay two seasons in one boat or one port, but he was a keen, canny little chap who picked up his trade as he went. It was the *Mary's* modern equipment that induced him to sign on with Mike. He had fished out of Arklow an otterboard trawl and power winch and was eager to show the Manistir men what he could do with the new gear.

The women went out, the first day, and enjoyed the slow steady three-mile drag through the middle of the Bay to its eastern shore. Once the trawl was shot, there was little to do aboard but sit around on gunwale or spar and swop yarns until it was hauled up. Maurisheen put his hand knowingly to the warp (towrope) now and then, as a doctor fingers a pulse, to find out how things were going below and kept an eye out for the bearings which would tell him they were nearing the submerged teeth of Carrigeer rocks. It took nearly two hours to reach them at trawling pace.

"Hard a-port, there," Maurisheen hailed to Ollsen at the wheel. "We'll clear the stones by twenty fathoms and pick up a few pair of black sole in the mud along the verge of them."

He gave Mike the cross-bearings for future use and then composed himself for a snooze on the straight drag home to the Bay Rock. There would be nothing for him to do till they reached it. The slow tempo of trawling and the ozonous effect of a steady sea breeze conduce to sleepiness. Even the girls got drowsy and sat down in the shelter of the wheelhouse, lazily watching the rise and fall of the dripping warp with heavy-lidded eyes. Ollsen alone kept a lookout. He was alive to everything, to the rhythmic swelling of the sea ahead, to the resilient power of the *Mary* on her maiden fishing trip and, above all, to the nearness of Maire Mack, relaxed in luxurious ease, just under his eyes. He was never happier and began to hum a slow Norwegian sea-song. The unaccustomed sound penetrated Mai's drowsiness and drew her to look up just when Ollsen was taking one of his quick glances at Maire's recumbent figure. She read the light in his eye and felt a sting of jealousy. It urged her to her feet in a light graceful motion that brought her face close to his in the wheelhouse window.

She peeked a knowing smile at him to let him see that she had surprised his secret and then looked deliberately over his shoulder towards Mike who was huddled with Donovan amidships at the engine controls. The look was as clear as a spoken warning.

"Stolen apples are sweet," she said in a stage whisper. "But look out for the appleman."

Ollsen repressed his first impulse to repudiate her impudent challenge and box her ears. He knew that such precipitate action would lead to a scene from which Maire would come out badly by the mere implication of complicity. That must be evaded at any cost and by any wile. He took his hands off the wheel and, cupping them about Mai's cheeks, drew her face towards his and kissed her full on the mouth. The suddenness of his counter action was too much for Mai's frail defences. She yielded herself to pleasurable thrills and returned his kiss with abandon while it lasted. Her wary subconscious mind retained control of her feet, keeping them from disturbing Maire from her doze.

A hail from Maurisheen woke them all from their preoccupations.

"Oilskins and mittens! Oilskins and mittens!" he piped in a high throaty voice. "Hoist her aboard and get meat for the kittens."

No one knew where he picked up his colourful slogans, but everyone learned them from him.

He was already halfway into his own oilskin pants, when Donovan cut down the engine to quarter throttle before he went to the locker for his oilskins. Ollsen pulled Mai into the wheelhouse, telling her to keep the wheel steady as it was, and called to Maire to follow him forward where they would find a job for her. Mike got into his oilskins without fluster, took the free end of the warp to the winch and wound a few preparatory turns around the drum.

When Donovan got the winch going and saw Mike instructing Maire how to take the incoming rope off the drum, he went back to his engine. Ollsen and Maurisheen stood looking over the lee rail for the mouth of the trawl to appear from the depths. The otter boards were the first to break the surface, like the dorsal fins of a pair of grampuses.

"Trawl awash," shrilled Maurisheen. "Come claw her in. Trawl awash, come claw her."

The call brought Mike and Donovan running from their jobs to join in the backbreaking task of hauling the sulky, waterlogged mass of net, weeds, and fish aboard with their naked fingers. Foot by foot they won it from the sea, Maurisheen synchronizing the pulls with "Heave—aaah; heave—oooh," until with a last long pull they brought the cod end aboard and flung it well in on the deck, to lie there until they drew their breath.

To Maire was given the honour of slipping the lace that closed the pocket of the trawl and letting the heterogeneous catch slide slimily out on the deck. It was a very mixed bag of cod, hake, and haddock; brill, turbot, and plaice; stealthy crabs and piratical dogs; stinging rays and flapping skate. Maurisheen surveyed the heaps, after the sorting, and appraised the result of their labours by the number of sole.

"Umm, fair enough. Four and a half pair of black sole and six of lemon," was all he said.

"But what about these and these?" Ollsen asked in surprise, pointing to the other flat fish and the heaps of round fish.

"The sole are the pick of the bunch. They're sold by the count, the coarse fish by the stone. A pair of black sole is worth more than a stone of cod or two stone of dabs."

Maire's business instincts got to work.

"Who fixes the prices and where's the best market for them?" she asked Maurisheen. "Hucksters on the quayside will be no good to us from now on. We will want a steady market."

"Bill Hannen could tell you that, ma'am," he replied. "He deals with Billingsgate salesmen direct. He found the Dublin fellows too chancy. Anyway, the Dublin Jackeens aren't given to eating fish like the English."

Maire turned to Mike who was taking it all in, without exerting himself with questioning. He knew most of it before, anyhow, but he had been satisfied to sell his small, infrequent catches of coarse fish to Bill or the hucksters. He understood Maire's unvoiced question and nodded reassuringly.

"I'll have a talk with Bill, when we take this fish ashore for the evening train. He has a standing contract with Stewart of Billingsgate and, maybe, he'd take our fish with his own. We'll fix up something between us."

That evening Bill agreed to accept the *Mary's* fish and send it with his own to Stewart's every day and to show Mike the daily advice telegrams as they came. He said the cartage fee for taking the fish to Cahirsally would pay him well for his trouble. They clinched the deal with a drink which Big Bill stood. He stalled at including John Joe in the round until Mike assured him that he was taking him on the *Mary* for the season.

That contract with Bill Hannen guaranteed a secure and constant market for the *Mary's* fish and gave her crew an incentive to go to sea every day. Rain or shine, wind or calm, the sturdy new boat left the cove at dawn and motored purposefully towards the trawling ground best suited to the day's weather. The Wild Bank gave its best results in a northerly wind and a flowing tide; in a southerly breeze the fish seemed to congregate in the Sound between the Shark and Black Head. The shelter of the Bay was reserved for heavy weather from the west.

In less than a month Mike got to know the rough grounds far from home: the cluster of rocks off the Fang, the lone spike in the Sound, the hulk of a forgotten wreck, and the patches of loose weed that clogged the trawl uselessly. John Joe became very expert at the engine. His questing mind hunted down the whys and wherefores of Donovan's rule-of-thumb ways of coaxing work out of the Kelvin. He got to know its "innards" as well as Mike knew the hidden floor of the sea. Ollsen supplied the Nordic force that drove the *Mary* out in all weathers. Whenever Mike or Maurisheen yielded to the easygoing Celtic philosophy of life and planned a day of rest other than Sunday, he routed them out of bed before cockcrow and kept the *Mary's* horn tearing the air until they came aboard. He made the *Mary* a byword among the fishermen of Manistir who laughed him to scorn with Gaelic wisdom. "*Is mó lá sa cill orainn*," they said whenever she came to the old quay with a good catch on one of their off days. "We'll be a long time dead."

As the fish had to be landed early to catch the train, the crew had long evenings on their hands when they got back to the cove. They dropped into a routine of separate jobs. Mike looked to the needs of the cattle and the land, Ollsen to the constructive work; Maurisheen cleaned and mended the nets and Donovan went from one to the other as extra handy man.

John Joe pursued his plan to marry Mai's money with unobtrusive persistence in which Maire connived with even greater unobtrusiveness. He was better than many women at housework and justified his frequent presence in the kitchen by relieving the girls of the heavy chores they did not like. Joany glared to warn him off her reservation the first time he approached the fireplace with helpfulness writ all over him. She said she would have no man poking into her griddles and bastables. But Maire and Mai were less exclusive. They liked his deft handling of fragile crockery and his craze for spotless cleanliness, especially Mai. She took pride in her American wardrobe and went to great pains to keep the gaudy dresses as immaculate as they were when her mother sent them to her. John Joe knew that, and used their common love of fine raiment as a bond of union between them.

Maire devised another link to bind them. She arranged that John Joe be given charge of the lobster pots, which were in danger of being overshadowed and forgotten in the more engrossing business of trawling. She went with him in the punt at first to show him where the pots were laid, but, as soon as he knew the locations, she quietly stood aside and let Mai take her place. Mai was nothing loth. To have a spruce, forthcoming young lad all to herself in the friendly dusk was her concept of terrestrial happiness, especially when she was finding Ollsen unresponsive after his one and only demonstration of manliness in the wheelhouse of the *Mary*. Of course, Maurisheen and Donovan did not count. The only transgressions to which they were prone were the unilateral pleasures of sloth and gluttony. The sixth and ninth commandments meant nothing in their animal lives and Mai meant less than a pint of Guinness fresh from the cask. Their indifference repelled her. So John Joe had a clear road and no competitors for Mai's favours.

One afternoon, at the finish of the big meal of the day, Ollsen made a call for all hands to help him in laying the foundation of a twelve-foot extension to the slip. It was too short as it was to accommodate the *Mary*; with the proposed extension it would berth her at half tide with a half load. He and Donovan had spent a week carting large flat stones with Mai's pony to the site, in readiness for the exceptionally low tides that were due for the next three days. When she heard this, Mai looked under her eyebrows at John Joe and raised them questioningly.

Ollsen's proposal would spoil their "lobstering" and she wanted to know what John Joe thought of it. He shook his head and, quietly pointing his knife towards the backdoor to tell· her to slip out ahead of him, he continued in the discussion of ways and means of laying firm foundations under water, until she had stolen away. When the men stood up from the table to give Maire a chance of clearing it, John Joe disappeared, as slick as a mouse that was there and is not, and sped down the off side of the path to the beach.

Mai had the punt afloat with its heel to the sand when he arrived, vaulted lightly into the stern sheets, and took his place at the afteroar in one concerted movement.

"We'd better be well out of hail when they get to the slip," he said over his shoulder to her. "So, put your back into it."

They had disappeared around the southern tip of the cove and into the Bay before any of the slip builders left the house. They eased up for the slogging pull around the island.

"Give me that oar of yours, Mai, and I'll paddle both of them. You know, you'll have to do the paddling when we get among the pots."

As they changed places, they pinched each other provocatively and got into an unnecessary tangle of arms and legs before they settled down facing each other.

"Did anyone ever tell you what a grand girl you are, Mai?" said John Joe, traversing her sensuous figure up and down with his eloquent eyes as he rowed.

"No, then," she drawled with a smirk which implied some previous experience of adulation. "What about you trying your hand at it? But, sure, what would make you or anyone else think I'm a grand girl —or half a grand girl?"

But she lolled back in the stern sheets and spread her arms wide along the upper strakes of the gunwale to let him see what a grand girl she was to any man's eye.

"Your match isn't in Manistir, Mai. No, nor in Cahirsally where all the fine ladies are; nor in the Cahirsally next to it, too, Mai girl. They're all mad jealous of you."

She basked in the radiant play of his eyes over her rich figure and stretched herself sinuously to display her curves.

"Why would they be jealous of me, John Joe? What have I to compare with them?"

"Your eyes, Mai, and your beautiful limbs. And look down on those darling collops; they're as smooth as two spring salmon fresh out of the water."

She purred with pleasure and raised the shapely salmonlike legs, side by side, for further praise. John Joe improved the smiling hour by breaking into the most famous of Gaelic love songs and timing it to the rhythm of his stroke.

> *"Tá do súile mar lonnrai na gréine*
> *Ag scaipe tré spéarha an ceo;*
> *Is deirge do grua ná na caorha*
> *Ar lasa measc craobha na gcnó."*

> "Your eyes like the sunrays a-streaming
> Through gossamer haze in the sky;
> Your cheeks like the berries a-gleaming
> Through creamy white blossoms on high."

She lilted the seductive air with him to express the poignant pleasure that filled her and to prolong the enjoyment of her golden hour. The song carried them around Rinnteas, the southern tip of the island, on which Maire had wrestled for Mike's life when he risked it for a box of eggshells, and northwards under the cliffs on the seaward side of the Shark.

They changed places again to leave John Joe free to handle the pots. The water was smooth and unruffled, except around the rocks projecting from the feet of the sheer cliffs. There the lazy swells swirled and sucked at the trailing seaweed in the indolent way of a giant at play whose gentlest touch is destructive. One flick of the tail of a swirl could fling the little punt against a reef edge and crack it like an eggshell.

It was Mai's job to paddle carefully up to the bunch of cork floats riding the swell just out of reach of the eddies and give John Joe a chance to hook them and haul up the wicker pot by the mooring line. It would be dangerous work for landsmen, but for John Joe and Mai it was routine and ordinary, they had done it so often. He usually worked over the stern, hauling the basketlike pot aboard, extracting the dark blue lobster with knowing fingers from the arched trap within, and dropping the pot overboard again, freshly baited with gobbets of dead fish.

Sometimes it was easier for him to work from the bow of the punt. He was in the bow when Mai swung the punt out from a recession in the cliffs under the Lookout to round a huge buttress of rock that tapered up to the dizzy top. As she rowed she watched the crows squabbling and jostling with untidy wings in the high crannies above her, and listened for John Joe to announce the position of the next bunch of floats. But he was not minding his job. Instead of peering ahead he was standing behind her, entranced by the lissome grace of her limbs in action. Seized by a sudden longing he caught her head in his palms as she swayed backwards and bent it towards his face to kiss her. She screamed in surprise and snatched at the hands under her chin, dropping the paddles from her own. Before either was aware of the disaster, the paddles slid outwards between the worn tholes and flopped overboard. They were helpless. Helpless and adrift in a dead boat within a rope's length of the waiting rocks.

"What'll we do? What'll we do?" Mai moaned in despair. "We're drifting in to the rocks. Oh, God! the rocks!"

John Joe made the quickest and the bravest decision of his life.

"Sit tight, Mai, and don't look behind you. I'm stripping."

Even as he spoke he had pulled off his seaboots and was drawing jersey and undershirt, as one piece, over his head. Standing up with nothing on but his pants he measured the chances of his reaching the nearest oar in one jump and shook his head at the desperate gamble. He could not swim. If he missed the oar, they were lost. In grim resolve he sprang, with hands outstretched, towards the floating oar. Though he landed on the water with a flat crash that shot his vitals with pain, he got one hand on the oar before he sank. His wits were working even under the water. While he struggled to the surface he drew the submerged oar towards him and got the loom under his armpits to support him. He came up facing the punt and started to thrash his way awkwardly across the few yards of water that separated him from it. The oar, lying full length across his course, impeded his progress. But it slewed sideways under the disordered flailing of his arms and brought the blade within reach of Mai's fingers. She grasped the tip and held it and called to John Joe to stop swimming lest he work it out of her hand. Soon she had the blade in both hands, dragging John Joe alongside to get a grip of the gunwale near the bows.

"Put that oar in the sculling hole astern, Mai, and scull her to the other oar. I'll climb in while you're at it."

He gasped for breath as he spoke and started to clamber in. But climbing into a boat from the water is one of the most difficult feats of swimming. It has to be learned by much practice in deep water and John Joe had never been beyond his depth before. He tried and tried again, pulling himself breast-high on the gunwale and slipping back again when the dead weight of his body came on his arms. In despair he called for help to Mai, who was intent on sculling and swayed the punt violently in the process.

"Come here and help me in, Mai. I'll never do it myself."

Mai shipped the oar and stooped over the side to get a hold of his arms, but the double weight almost capsized the frail craft and she had to jump back quickly to the centreboard to escape swamping.

"Work yourself back to the stern, John Joe. We'll have a better chance there." Her voice was shaken with fear. Still gripping the gunwale desperately, he moved hand over hand until he got behind the wide stern and made another attempt to climb aboard. The waterlogged pants would have defeated him even if he were not exhausted and inept at the trick of it.

"Give me your hands," said Mai, who now stood over him in the stern sheets.

Bracing her legs against the stern post to get a good purchase, and gripping John Joe's wrists in her hands, she threw all the weight of her body into a great heave and hauled him aboard. They lay on the floorboards as they fell and panted laboriously with open mouths, among the crawling lobsters. John Joe was the first to rise and sit on a thwart. He helped Mai up and held her hand.

"Only for you, girleen, I was gone." He fondled her calloused hand in his own as he spoke and looked at her with a new light in his sparkling eyes. For once, the radiance came from his heart and not from his scheming mind. He was in love with Mai Hogan with no thought of her worldly goods. He would love her from that moment if she were as destitute as the poorest beggar in Manistir and as fickle as the wind.

Mai read the truth in his eyes and for the first time knew that there was a love finer and more precious than the lust of the flesh. She knew at last how Mike and Maire loved each other and she knew that John Joe loved her in the same way, calmly and profoundly and for ever. As she looked at him she found a new interest stirring in herself, a desire to give to this transformed young man rather than to receive; to take him in her arms and mother him rather than to be taken in his and spurred to desire in the old way. She felt a new happiness and joined her hands in his in a quiet communion of feeling. Suddenly he remembered their plight and looked for the second oar.

"Why, Mai!" he exclaimed. "You didn't follow the other oar as I said. You sculled out too far, dear."

"You'll be glad I didn't," she replied with a note of submission in her voice. "Look in to the rocks and see where it is now. If I followed it, we'd be there too."

The oar had drifted into the swirling eddies while John Joe was struggling to return to the boat and had been taken up as a thing to play with. An incoming swell carried it high on its lip, held it poised precariously on a shelf of rock for a moment and retreated, gurgling at the fun. Down came the oar, slithering and bumping on the rocks, to be caught again and flung higher by the next frolicsome wave. By night it would be splintered and shredded to ribbons; the punt would have lived there a bare five minutes.

"By gorr, you were right, Mai, though it will be a tough job to scull all the way home from here. I suppose we'll have to say good-bye to the rest of the lobster pots and make for home. They'll be wondering what's keeping us late."

So they sculled their way home, taking spells at the oar, and reached the cove as dusk was closing in. They heard the voices of the men at the slip and the occasional ring of the sledge on a flagstone that needed shaping. Dumping their lobsters into the floating store box they waited until the darkness drove the men from the slip and then sculled slowly ashore.

Hand in hand, in a new relationship, they walked up the path and entered the kitchen where the household were sitting down to supper. Maire read their faces at a glance and rejoiced in the success of her plan.

"We thought ye were gone off to *Tir na nOgue* for yourselves," she shouted gaily. "Come and sit near me, Mai, till I see your face. Girls always bring a blush from the Island of Youth."

"Don't mind her, *a chree*," Joany intervened to set Mai at her ease. " 'Tisn't so long since she was there herself. Sit down near John Joe, child, just to show her you don't mind her humbugging."

The men listened to the shuttle of women's raillery, picking out the thread of innuendo that ran through it and going on with their eating in silence, until Mike noticed how wet John Joe's pants were.

"Hallo! *Tir na nOgue* must be flooded these days, John Joe, to say you had to wade through it. What about you, Mai? Did you wet your skirts or did John Joe carry you in his arms?"

. John Joe, who had hoped that the condition of his nether garment might pass unnoticed, was not altogether displeased by Mike's remark. It gave him an excuse for going out to change his pants.

"No," he said, "it wasn't in *Tir na nOgue* I got wet. I thought ye had finished the new head on the slip and I stepped out where it ought to be. Down I went up to my oxters."

"Don't believe him, Mike," Mai hastened to defend her unusually modest hero. "He's only trying to cover up how he saved the punt from being destroyed on the Lookout cliffs."

She told the whole story from the time she dropped the paddles until she dragged John Joe out of the very teeth of the cliff, and waxed warm in the telling. The silence, which followed the end of her dramatic version of the tale, was broken by a stupid question of Donovan's.

"How'n hell you come to lose the two oars, or what were you thinking of to do such a dam'fool thing?" he asked, his mind being too limited in experience of amative remissness to guess what Mai might have been doing. Maire saw the blush of remembrance spread over Mai's face and intervened to spare her further confusion.

"Tell him mind his own business, Mai, girl," she suggested. "He thinks everyone gets spells of woolgathering like himself," and then in a demonstration of housewifely fuss, she stood up from the table and shooed the men out of the kitchen. "Clear out of our way and give us women a chance of clearing up the mess ye have made. Out of my sight!"

She took Mai to her bosom when they had the place to themselves and led the enraptured girl to open her heart and tell how matters stood between her and John Joe. Mai's confession of love for John Joe, and her assurance that he was as deeply in love with her, filled Maire with contentment. She had carried out Father John's wish and had justified her own method of putting it into effect. But she did not forget how indiscriminate Mai had been in the pursuit of men. There was no certainty that she would not tire of her present attachment when the fresh bloom wore off it. That risk must be removed once and for all. She must be tied up immediately in the bonds of holy matrimony.

"Go out, dear, and bring John Joe in here to me. I want to wish him joy," she said.

When he came in, she seated Mai on one side of her and John Joe on the other, in the warm embrasure of the fireplace and dropped her voice to an intimate confidential undertone.

"Ye are a happy pair this blessed night," she began. "But ye aren't a bit happier than I am or than Father Miles will be when he hears it. Of course, Mai, he must be told first thing in the morning. Along with being your parish priest, he's your guardian. He has charge of you and your means and he will be wanting to have a chat with you, John Joe, about Mai's dowry and your own prospects."

"Now, what I suggest to the pair of ye, is this," she went on. "We'll go and see him tomorrow morning before he goes out on sick calls. We'll lay the matter before him and let him make all the arrangements. What do ye say to that?"

They both agreed that that was the best thing to do, but with a hesitance that Maire understood. They felt a natural timidity in facing their formidable pastor and telling him of their desire to become man and wife and live privily together even with the sanction of the sacrament.

Maire laughed at their callow fears, assured them that she would be with them at the interview to smooth over all obstacles, and ended the conference by bundling them out into the dark for a last exchange of pledges of love. She smiled complaisantly as she went to the bedroom to help Joany put Donal Michael to sleep.

CHAPTER 33 · *Matchmaking*

T HE *Mary* dropped Maire and the two lovers on the Old Quay and
went off to trawl the fair grounds under Black Head. She would pick
them up again when she had delivered the catch to Bill in time for the
evening train.

Maire decided that they would walk the two miles to the presbytery
and pass the hotel without making the usual friendly call until they
knew what arrangements Father John would make for the marriage.
They waved hands to Big Bill, who was sorting the morning mail in
the post office, but pretended they did not see Conny Shuckrue, who
was coming up the boreen for a morning pint before he went lobstering.
There was no sign of either of the priests at the church, which signified
that they were gone home for breakfast after saying Mass, and would
be still in the presbytery.

The girls stepped out in a cheery companionship that needed no
conversation and reached the presbytery gate in time to open it for
Father Boyle, who was coming out in the Hillman. Maire suppressed
an impulse to ask him, as he slowed for the narrow gateway, if the
parish priest were still at home. She did not want to risk his usurping
the marriage as he had usurped the christening of Donal Michael.
The irrepressible Thade Carey appeared in the kitchen doorway with
a coarse broom at the ready as they approached the front door and
cut across the rectangle of yard to intercept them.

"*De ur mbeaha-sa!* And isn't it early ye are ashore from the island,
God bless ye? I hope there's nothing wrong with my friend Mike

Mack. . . . But there couldn't be and you here— Bless my soul, if it isn't John Joe Barrett and Miss Mary Hogan! In their Sunday clothes too!"

"*Go mairir-se ivad a Thaig!*" Maire broke in on Thade's searching barrage. "I hope Father John hasn't gone on a sick call. But he couldn't and you here." She slanted a derisive eye at him as she mimicked his own phrase in reference to Mike.

The front door opened to cut off Thade's acidulous rejoinder and Father John appeared, breviary in hand but still unopened, ready for his after-breakfast walk up the garden. He stood on the top step and looked down on his visitors with a reserved, conditional welcome. He did not like intrusions on the only time he had free for the daily obligation of reading his breviary. With a shrug he pocketed the stout morocco-covered book and smiled at his visitors.

"Thanks, Thade," he said blandly, dismissing the old man. "I'll look after these good people now."

To cover his discomforture and discount the immediacy of his dismissal, Thade proceeded to brush the steps industriously, even as the visitors mounted them to follow the priest into the house. He succeeded in getting, at least, one thump of the broomhead on John Joe's passing feet. He desisted as soon as the door closed and wrinkled his whole face in a parting grin of disgust before he returned across the yard to the kitchen.

"Well, Maire," Father John said when they were all seated in his study, "what's the good news? You all look very cheerful this morning, God bless you."

"John Joe will tell you, Father John. I'm sure he's bursting to tell you." Maire nodded encouragement to the young man, whose habitual assurance was overcome by the embarrassment inseparable from the occasion.

"Mai and myself were thinking of getting married, Father." He stopped short, confused by his ineptness in blurting out such a portentous announcement without the customary preamble. He felt ashamed of himself and could not proceed. Father John understood and diverted attention from him by addressing Mai.

"And what does Miss Hogan say to that?"

"I suppose it would be wrong for me to belie him, Father," she replied smiling demurely through her curved eyelashes.

The priest turned to John Joe again.

"Tell me how you stand at home. Who owns the house and the land and what arrangements have your mother and sister in mind when you do get married?"

"The place is in my mother's name, but she always told me she'd hand it over to me if I marry a girl of her choosing. Of course, she'll live in the house with us. But my sister will marry out of the place as soon as I am in a way to pay her fortune. Her match is as good as fixed with Martin Cronin of the Coombe. All they are waiting for is the dowry so that Martin can give it to his own sister."

"Yes and *that* sister will hand it on to *her* husband's sister until the one dowry will have married off half the girls of the parish before it comes to rest," said Father John in jocular appreciation of the thrifty habit that enabled his impoverished parishioners to provide marriage portions for their daughters.

"But tell me how much your sister is expecting from you."

"Two hundred pounds, Father. That's what Martin Cronin's sister will need to marry into Foley's farm at Killeen. I'm not sure where the money will go after that."

"And have you, or your mother, any dry cash?"

"We have only what we'll need to work the land, Father, after I get married," he replied with some hesitance.

"How much, John? The freer you talk now, the better you will come off these negotiations. No reservations, please."

"I have £50 of my own. I'm not sure what my mother has in the stocking—maybe £100 more or less."

"And she'll leave that to her daughter, of course, when she dies," Father John observed dryly. "All the old women do that, bless 'em. That is their last slash at the daughters-in-law who usurp their authority. Very well, John. You had better go home now and bring your good mother to me. I shall wait here for her. She and you are entitled to know how Mai Hogan's affairs stand. I am her guardian and I hold certain monies in trust for her. I shall not divulge the exact amount to you or to her until you are married, but I can assure you that the amount is considerable."

Neither he nor Maire Mack betrayed by the slightest sign that they were aware that John Joe already knew how considerable Mai's dowry would be. Indeed, Mai Hogan was the only one in the room who did not know how much money she had and she thought the time inopportune for asking Father John any questions about it.

When John Joe went off for his mother, Father John showed the two girls around the garden and led them to the kitchen where he left Mai with Debby Sweeny. He wanted a private chat with Maire before Mrs. Barrett arrived.

"Of course, my young intriguer, you have everything cut and dry for those two innocents," he said when they were back in the study. "Would you let me know your plans, please."

"Ah, Father John, that's not quite fair to me. You know it was you and the district nurse, who first planted Mai on me. The whole plan was of your making, Father. I only did what you told me to do."

"And you went one better, Maire. My immediate concern for Mai Hogan was to remove her from harm's way and see that she got a good training. You have gone much farther; you have found her a husband and settled her in life. No, my child, don't take me as dissenting from what you have done. Indeed, I am very pleased, easier in my mind than I might have been if that wayward child remained on our—on my hands. What I want to know from you is how you would handle Mrs. Barrett if you were in my place. You see, child, I am giving you credit for more knowledge of old women than I have."

"Well, Father, as you put it that way to me, I'd say the most important thing to do is to make Mrs. Barrett agree to an immediate marriage. She will be holding out for a month or more to give her time to whitewash the house and put clothes making for herself, so that she can fling her flounces in the neighbours' faces. Of herself she will be thinking and not of her son, or Mai Hogan. You know, Father, delays are dangerous with a flightsome girl like Mai. If there is no

law of the Church against it, you will be surer in your mind if you tie
her down first thing in the morning."

The priest smiled indulgently at Maire's forthright methods of man-
agement and in his inner mind commended the wisdom of Mother
Church who, by ordaining celibacy on her clergy, saved them from the
importunity of domineering spouses.

"I know of no impediment, my child, and, as they are both parishioners of mine, no question of letters of freedom, as you call them, can
arise to cause delay. I could, in all the circumstances, marry them tomorrow morning, but it will start a flood of gossip, of whispered slander,
against Mai's good name, if the marriage is rushed. That would be
a bad start in married life for the poor girl, which I must forestall."

"May I make a suggestion, Father John?" Maire hazarded.

"*Ne quid nimis, Maria,*" he answered quickly with a quiet resumption of authority. "No, child. Do not overplay your hand. I sought your
counsel in regard to Mrs. Barrett's view of an immediate marriage,
but I'm sure I shall be quite competent to deal with anything else."

He leaned back in his chair to think out his problem without any
concern for the confusion his rebuke had brought upon Maire and,
after a few moments, cracked his thumb and finger at her to mark
the discovery of a solution.

"I have it. We'll make an important ceremony of it. I, as parish
priest, shall marry them, but by my side on the altar I shall have the
support of Father Boyle and Father Murray from Cahirsally. Such an
august array of authority will silence the tongue of scandal. Yes, I
think I shall marry the happy pair tomorrow morning at eight o'clock.
You had better go and find Mai in the kitchen and set about making
preparations at once."

The sound of voices at the front door broke in on them, Thade
Carey's in expostulation and a thinner, high-pitched one trying to
placate him. Father John winked at Maire and placed his forefinger on
his lips to enjoin silence and listen.

"Must I tell you again, ma'am that it would be as much as my job
is worth to go near Father John, with my finger in my mouth, not

knowing what business you have with him. You must tell me what brought you, before I can tell him you want to see him. Sure that stands to reason, woman."

"But, Thade Carey, *a chree*, it was the priest himself sent for me, and he told me to bring these papers with me," said the thin, plaintive voice.

"Papers?" Thade exclaimed. "Give them here to me till I see are they the right ones. 'Tis me he'd blame if you brought the wrong ones. Where are them dam' specs of mine? I can't see a splink without them." He paused in a vain search for the spectacles and then went on ingratiatingly. "Maybe you brought your own specs with you, Mrs. Barrett, and you'd give me the loan of them. You did? That's fine."

Father John thought it time to intervene. Going towards the front door he stood a moment in the corridor to give Maire time to pass through to the kitchen and then opened the door on Thade who was engaged in the tricky operation of balancing strange spectacles on the high plateau of his nose.

"Good morning, Mrs. Barrett," said Father John with a benevolent inflection of voice, designed to set the tone of the delicate negotiations he was to have with that old lady. "I see that you and your old friend, Thade, are getting on well with each other." Holding out his hand for the documents, which Thade was keeping out of sight on the off side of his rusty soutane, he continued, "Thanks, Thade. I don't know what I would do without you. You anticipate my every wish and forestall all my necessities. Come in, Mrs. Barrett."

Thade twisted his mobile features into a grotesque whorl of disgust at this further frustration of his hunger for parochial news. But, as he turned away from the closing door, he caught sight of John Joe's back disappearing in the direction of the kitchen. Returned hope smoothed his face and lit his eyes as he hobbled down the steps and shuffled across the quadrangle after his new quarry. Alas for his hope! The three young visitors were standing by the table, drinking a parting cup of strong tea that Debby Sweeny insisted they should take before they left her kitchen. Thade gave them a nondescript grin and went off about his business to the high spot in the garden from which he kept an eye on the comings and goings of all and sundry.

Mrs. Barrett was no match for Father John in the alien and overpowering precincts of his own study. She accepted all his proposals without discussion and issued forth from the front door, sure only of two things: that there was to be a marriage at eight o'clock in the morning and that she was to get £200 for relinquishing her title to the farm. She was not sure whether it was John Joe or her daughter Kate was to be married, or both, but her own position in her daughter-in-law's house was assured by Father John himself. She was recapitulating her confused memory of the interview when the others overtook her and Maire introduced Mai Hogan to her.

"Hogan?" she repeated doubtfully. "Sure, there are no Hogans in Manistir nor ever was in the memory of man."

"She's Mary Lee's granddaughter," Maire explained. "Mary Lee of Fermoyle that was, God rest her soul."

"Oh, now I have you," the old lady said with a rude note of familiarity in her voice. She was on her own ground again and prompt to assert her authority on this chit of a neighbour's child who was coming to supersede her. "You are the one your mother sent home out of harm's way from the States. Stand there in front of me till I see what my John Joe saw in you."

She would have stopped and subjected the embarrassed girl to the calculating scrutiny she gave to articles of merchandise had not Maire taken her by the arm and marched her down the road in a great gush of friendliness. After a sympathetic discussion of the rights of dowagers, she left the old lady at her own door fully convinced that her future in her old home was bright and assured.

Maire looked back along the road for Mai and John Joe who should have been following her. Seeing no sign of them and concluding that they had gone into seclusion as lovers do, she went on to the hotel to wait and arrange with Betty for the wedding breakfast in the morning. But they had not gone into seclusion. Mai's proper pride was outraged by Mrs. Barrett's disrespectful reference to her mother and her grandmother and, by inference, to herself. It pinned her to the ground. She stood for a while on the road, too stunned to speak, following the old woman with eyes that burned with resentment. Then she wheeled about and let loose her anger on John Joe's diminished head.

"So that's your mother—the great Mrs. Barrett, that's too grand for the Lees and the Hogans. 'Let me see what John Joe sees in you,'" she mimicked the hard, supercilious old voice and then broke back into her own surcharged contralto. "I'll let her see what's in me. It'll be something she didn't bargain for."

She turned on her heel and sped up the road to the presbytery with head high and arms swinging with purpose. John Joe sped after her and timed his progress to reach her side as she mounted the steps and knocked on the door. She was still indignant but had worked off much of her fury in the strenuous walking. John Joe took her free hand in his.

"Don't do anything rash, Mai. Old people are strange in their ways but they mean no harm." He wisely refrained from particularizing, lest the mere mention of his mother's name rekindle Mai's waning anger. "Hist!" he counselled when he heard Father John's step coming to the door. "Let me do the talking."

She ignored the suggestion and waited for the door to open.

Father John concealed his surprise and invited them into the study, not without a regretful look at the breviary which he had just started to read when Mai knocked on his door. John Joe sat down but Mai, still too tensed by her emotion to bend her limbs in a chair, stood erect and burst into speech.

"I will not live in one house with that wicked old woman," she exploded. "She's a cruel heartless thing; she's—she's—she's a spiteful jealous old witch. She's—"

Her voice rose in an excited crescendo that overran her descriptive power and choked off her speech. She could only quiver with suppressed feeling and stare in mute exasperation at the impassive face of her pastor.

"Sit down, child, and take things easy for a moment," he said with a quiet, paternal quality in his voice.

"I can't, Father. She treated me like the dirt of the road."

"Well, my dear child, if you persist in standing, I must stand up, too." He rose with great deliberation as he made the guileful statement and stressed the incongruity of the situation by getting behind his chair and talking across it to her. "We won't feel very comfortable like this, will we?"

Of course, she sat down and burst into tears. Father John gave her plenty of time and then spoke to John Joe.

"Perhaps it would be better if you went out and had a chat with Thade Carey, while Mai tells me her trouble. We won't keep you long, I'm sure."

When he was gone, Mai told of her unpleasant encounter with her future mother-in-law and revealed in the telling the age-old antipathy of the old and the young. She finished her spirited account of the incident on a determined note.

"I have no notion of putting my foot across the threshold of that house, as long as that bad-minded old madam is in it. And that goes for her daughter, too. 'Tis one of them, two of them."

"Aren't you forming a hasty judgment of two very worthy women, my child? They *are* good women, very good in fact, and I'm sure you'll come to like them."

"It isn't you, Father, but me, will have to live with them, and what chance would a girl like me have against the pair of them? If there is no other way out for me, I will settle the matter in my own way."

"What way, child?" the priest asked in a sincere desire to follow her line of thought to an amicable solution of the impasse to which she was tending. He knew that the inexperienced girl had been inspired by a pardonable anger to put her finger on the gravest defect in rural marriages, the lack of separate homes for young married couples. He had seen so much of the fine fire of consecrated love smothered and swamped in overcrowded houses, that he had started a crusade of house-building in Manistir and spent most of his free time importuning conservative parishioners and cautious government officials to embark on the crusade with a courage to match his own. He understood Mai's reluctance to submit her future to the doubtful good will of Mrs. Barrett and sympathized with her.

"By not marrying at all," she said with a curtness that emphasized her determination to take that extreme course.

"Ummm."

Father John was brought as near to perplexity as he had ever been. The girl had right on her side and would be justified in refusing to enter the married state on Mrs. Barrett's conditions, but if she were driven to break her engagement with John Joe she would become foot-loose again and free to give rein to her inherited propensity for love. The consequences for him, her parish priest and guardian, would be intolerable.

"There is no need for such drastic action, my dear child," he said with a confidence he did not feel. "There is a solution for every diffi-culty. God never closed a gate without opening a door, but we have to search for the open door. *Ni fiu duine gan seift*; a shiftless man re-mains in the mire."

He was talking in platitudes while his mind probed the tangled skein Mai had flung at him so recklessly, but a gleam in his eye showed that he was done with them. He had a plan.

"Of course, the solution of your problem is simple. You and your husband go on your honeymoon. You have plenty of money to take a good long one—a week or more. When you come back, I promise you, on my word as a priest of God, that the way will be free for you and your husband to live your own lives in your own home without interference from anyone. Does that satisfy you, my dear?"

"It does, Father," she replied, now more dutiful than when she be-gan the momentous interview. His even monotone had soothed her jangled nerves and brought her back to the easy untroubled humour that characterized her. She felt shame for the hardihood that be-trayed her into speaking so presumptuously to her spiritual director, who was also her worldly guardian. In an access of contrition she threw herself on her knees before him.

"Would you give me your blessing, Father?"

Deeply moved by her unreserved submission, Father John was proceeding to administer the formal blessing, when she got a second thought.

"May I call John Joe in, too, Father?" She flitted quickly out of the room at his nod of approval and returned, hand in hand, with her shamefaced captive to kneel with him for the priest's benison.

The rare, almost sacramental simplicity of their faith in him gave an unction, a freshness, to the familiar words of the sacerdotal blessing that had worn off with use.

"Benedictio Dei Omnipotentis, Patris et Filii et Spiritus Sancti, descendat super te et maneat semper. Pax Tecum."

He imposed his hands on each bowed head in turn and with the final handclasp drew them to their feet.

"God bless you both," he said from the top step at the door as they turned down the avenue to leave him. "Go into His church on your way and pray for His grace and guidance for yourselves and for me."

Maire and Betty Hannen had completed their arrangements for the wedding feast when John Joe handed Mai over to them for a final female palaver on the momentous matters of dress and procedure. Mai had told him of Father John's promise to have a clear house waiting for them when they returned from their honeymoon and he wished to get in touch with his sister Katie at once. He would be staying in the old home anyhow, that night; Mai would spend it on the Shark. So, off he went, after promising to be in time for the ceremony at the church.

MAIRE and Mai had to wait for some time at the quay for the *Mary* to come in with her catch and take them home. The crew were strangely quiet when she slowed in towards the steps. Even the carefree Maurisheen stood silent and glum by the near gunwale with a fender rope in hand. He had no cheery hail for the waiting girls, nor did Ollsen or Mike display any of the activity that attends the landing of fish. Indeed, there were no fish on board but a dozen or so of fluke and star-fish.

Postponing the inquiry until the men felt ready to speak without urging, Maire and Mai stepped aboard and awaited developments. Mike looked so gloomy that they bided their time for telling him the exciting news of the wedding and the sumptuous breakfast the morning would bring. But the silence persisted too long and when they were nearing the island Maire's concern overcame her forbearance.

"What's wrong, Mike?"

"There's plenty wrong—and damn wrong too," he replied curtly through clenched teeth and then subsided into silence again. Seeing that he was not yet inclined to unbosom himself, Maire called to Oll-sen, who sat apart working off his bad temper with marline spike and seizing.

"Come and talk to us, Knut. We're feeling out of it when no one condescends to notice us after our long day ashore. Come here and tell us what struck you all dumb."

Without taking his eyes off the intricate splice he was fashioning, he pointed the marline spike towards Mike.

"Mike'll tell it better than me. He has more practice at cursing the Sassenachs."

"*Lei Dia orra mar ropairi!*" Mike hissed and spat overside. "God melt their thieving bones! They never took anything but by highhand and robbery."

The men relapsed into black silence and got busy at tidying the boat up for mooring long before they turned into the cove. It must have been something very serious, Maire thought, that threw them out of their natural tolerant calm. She would let them settle down and ask no questions. The morning had been so full of incident ashore that the girls felt it as long as an ordinary day and were surprised to find Joany only starting to prepare the midday meal of bacon and greens when they reached the house. They were glad to take the job off her hands and let her sit and listen in complete absorption to the story of the mating of Mai and John Joe. For her, it was the latest episode in the age-old serial drama, of which woman never tires. Even when forced off the stage by the weight of years, she still lingers in the wings or dressing room to prompt or make up the younger actors. She leaves the theatre only with death.

The girls told the tale again to the men at dinner and lured them out of their dejection by the skilful arts of designing women. Before the meal was half finished they had them laughing at Thade Carey's maladroit attempts to satisfy his curiosity and condemning Mrs. Barrett's unfriendly reception of her future daughter-in-law. They were ripe for questioning.

"What about your report now, Knut?" said Maire when she had finished her narrative. "We told you what happened ashore; now you tell us what happened afloat. One good story deserves another."

"We weren't as lucky as ye were," he replied and looked at Mike for his cue. Reading a tacit acquiescence on the thin features, he spread his elbows wide on the table and began in a flat monotone that revealed a stress of feeling he rarely showed.

"We went straight for Black Head grounds after we put ye ashore on the Old Quay in the morning, and Maurisheen shot the trawl a mile on this side of the head to fish the first leg of the clear ground. The

Black Head itself, as you know, hid the second leg from us until we came abreast of the cliff and straightened our course two points to the nor'ard. It was then we got the first glimpse of the Englishman steaming dead ahead of us. He was trawling away as cheeky and independent as if he was out in blue water instead of being well inside the three-mile limit and breaking the law."

"A fat lot those robbers think of laws that aren't backed up by big guns," Mike observed with the angry snort he breathed on all things British. "But the only navy we have is the poor old *Murchu*, that couldn't raise a bow wave as big as Pats Kelly's moustache; and she has too much water to watch."

"Shame on you, Mike, to be damning the whole flock for one black sheep," Maire interposed. "Think of all the decent trawlermen you met in your time."

"This scoundrel wasn't one of them," said Maurisheen taking the tale out of Ollsen's mouth and making known, by a rasping cocksureness, that his opinion of the Sassenach tallied with Mike's. "He was a barefaced robber, that's what he was."

Ollsen silenced Maurisheen with a look and resumed the tale.

"There was no sense in fishing the ground he had scraped as clean as the palm of your hand, so we hauled our gear aboard and made after him full pelt. He hauled in his trawl, too, and made off at top speed for deep water before it was rightly aboard. But he is no racer and we drew up with him before he got outside the three-mile line. We wanted to get his name to report him but he had covered it with an old net, thrown over the stern, so that we couldn't read it. But he forgot to hide the registration number on the bows. We got that—M278. She's a Milford Haven boat and we can find out her name, if we want it. I'm not so sure we do. We'll settle with her skipper ourselves."

"Sure," said Mike. "He'll come around again, but we'll meet him and teach him a lesson. He badly wants a lesson, that fella, with his foghorn screech and his filthy tongue. 'Twas bad enough to ruin our fishing, but to finger his nose at us and pitch us to blazes was too bad."

"Yes," Ollsen added. "He'll come again and we'll be there to welcome him."

The men idled down to the slip and got started on the tricksome business of laying the top layer of flagstones with the sheerlegs Ollsen had rigged up. The women, as soon as they had the house to themselves, ransacked Mai's trunks for garments gay enough to express the joyous nuptial spirit. They got them in plenty, for Mai's mother had the courtesan's eye for brilliant hues and both Maire and Mai had the primitive love of their kind for strong colour. Mai finished up in a two-piece suit of rich carmine jersey cloth, with orange piping, and an impudent little butterfly red-straw hat sitting on top of her lustrous black hair.

Out of the plenitude of raiment, Mai set aside for Maire a rough-finished duck-egg-blue tweed streaked with cherry red, that fitted her robust figure as if it were made for her. They found, too, a high-draped turban hat to keep her rebellious amber hair smart and tidy. For their own and for Joany's pleasure they dressed themselves in full panoply and strutted with mincing steps about the kitchen. They were the two happiest girls in Manistir and she the saddest old woman; for they were bubbling with the youth for which she pined as they flaunted it in her face with the unthinking cruelty of the young.

Reluctantly they took off their gorgeous raiment and spread it in the sweetening air to kill the fumes of camphor while they prepared supper for the ship builders. Meals must be prepared for men and beasts even on the eve of high festivity. Women cannot escape the treadmill. They work it willingly for love and grudgingly for hire, but for love or hire they cannot escape the inevitable turning of its cycle of recurrent chores. Supper was too overshadowed by the events of the day to be the talk feast it usually was. The good people were weary for sleep and went to bed early.

When Maurisheen and Donovan were settled down in their bunks on the *Mary*, Ollsen went back to the cabin and turned on the radio at quarter volume. Sitting close to the speaker, he tuned in the lower register of the medium waveband just under 200 metres, and worked carefully down to 160. Within those limits were to be heard the radio messages sent out by steam trawlers to one another and to their headquarters in Britain. Ten o'clock in the morning and ten at night were the times set apart for this intercourse and Ollsen's watch showed ten o'clock coming up. With his ear pressed against the cloth of the speaker, he picked up a faint voice dead on 170 metres and increased the volume gradually until he could hear the message clearly. Trawler SA206 was calling SA371 who was not answering. Ollsen shook his head and moved slowly down the dial, picking up and rejecting message after message until he tuned in, at great audibility, the raucous voice he had heard shouting in derision at him and Mike from the bridge of M278 that very morning. He went rigid with suppressed excitement, like a setter that has scented its game.

"M278 calling M343," he heard repeated with monotonous regularity to end up in a sharp-cut "O-ver," and a short silence for listening. Again and again the hoarse repetitive call went out, with the insistence of a muezzin's summons to prayer, until at last the answer came, faint at first, but growing in volume, as Ollsen tuned it on the vernier.

"M343 calling M278, M278, M278. O-ver."

"M278 to M343. That you Dai, old blood'n guts? This is Treffor calling, off the Blaskets. Where the heck are you? O-ver."

"M343 to M278. Dai calling, south of Arran. Going north to Killery to fill up before going home. Had one good scrape inside Galway Bay, but the festerin' *Merchew* stuck her festerin' nose in the bay and I had to skip. How you doin'? O-ver."

The name *Merchew* puzzled Ollsen until he remembered the fisheries patrol boat *Murchu*, which Mike in his Gaelic tongue called the *Murahoo*. She was a thorn in the flesh of thieving trawlermen.

"M278 to M343. I was doin' fine last night in Manistir Bay till a bloody suckin' Paddy bounced me. He followed me out past the thirty-fathom line to get my name, cheeky blarsted sucker. The bay is lousy with fish and I'll have another go at it on my way home. O-ver."

"M343 to M278. Sound bloody fella, but watch out for the festerin' *Merchew*. I'll give you the tip if she passes me for the south. When will I be seeing you in Milford, at Mollie's, I mean? Haw! Haw! O-ver."

Ollsen held his breath for the answer that would deliver the lawless Treffor into his hands.

"M278 to M343. You're a dirty old man, Dai Jones, but you can tell Mollie *bach* I'll be seein' her a week come Saturday. And you keep your bloody festerin' paws off her till I come. So long, old tub o' guts. O-ver."

When the dialogue was finished, Ollsen sat on with furrowed brow, working out his problem.

"This is Wednesday," he calculated. "In ten days from now M278 will be back in Milford Haven. But it takes an old tramp like her thirty-six hours to get there from here. So, she will be stealing into the Bay in the dark of Thursday night. We have eight clear days to prepare a good welcome for her."

He turned off the set and went to his bunk.

CHAPTER 35 · *A Marriage and a Parable*

THE news had flashed through the parish with the surprising speed at which news travels in remote, thinly populated places that there was to be a remarkable marriage in the morning in the parish church. The unexpected mating of the least compatible pair in Manistir, without prior lovemaking or matchmaking, stirred parochial curiosity so violently that a crowd of grey-haired gossips and emulous maidens thronged the precincts of the church long before the appointed eight o'clock. Among these free sightseers, and distinguished from them by an air of importance, stood the invited guests. The Dan Macks, the Con Macks, the Shuckrues, the Fitzes, and the Kellys got invitations from the islanders. The Cronins, the Foleys, the Sheas, and the Sheehans got their's from John Joe. Big Bill, Betty, and Paddy Brown enjoyed ex officio rights to be present, Bill having given the wedding party two cars to drive them to the church, "buckshee and with my compliments," and Betty having supplied the flowers for the altar from the hotel garden.

The church was more than half full when Thade Carey, in a rusty soutane, issued from the side door leading from the sacristy to the altar and proceeded to light the candles. He moved about as stiffly as an automaton and stopped from time to time to look down the church at the waiting congregation like a shepherd scrutinizing his flock of ewes and wethers. He was looking for the bridal party who should have been in the place of honour in the front seats near the altar rail.

His eye caught a glimpse of their clamant colours, sunk out of sight in the drab greys and blacks of the middle rows, like columbines in the heather. Thade was accustomed to the occulting habits of his sheep on such occasions and revelled in the chance they gave him of exercising his limited authority within the sacred confines in the presence of a large assembly. Better still, this bridal party had laid themselves open to reprisal for ignoring him at the presbytery a few short hours ago, and now he had them at his mercy.

"What hide-and-seek are you playing down there, John Joe Barrett?" he said with an exaggerated, sacerdotal accent. "Do you think Father Miles will go hunting for you through the crowd. Come up here to the front row like a man and bring Miss Mary Hogan with you, so we can all see ye. Not that we haven't seen ye often enough, God knows. Hurry up and don't let the clergy see how ignorant ye are—"

Just then his angry little eyes lighted on the ragtag and bobtail of professional beggars and brazen husseys, who had shamelessly taken possession of the front seats. The wretches, displaying an ecstatic enjoyment of the fine start he himself was giving to the raree show, gaped in approval at him and shocked him into indignant silence. He glared at them and, with an imperious sweep of his hand, ordered them to leave the seats. But they only thrilled the more and sat tighter. At last he found words.

"Ye vagabones in the front seats, clear out. Clear out, I say." He opened the gate in the altar rail and came among them with flailing arms to expedite the exodus. He drove them down the centre aisle into the bridal party who were coming up and created a confusion that began to alarm him. Suppressed giggles and surreptitious pinches aggravated the disorder towards the limits of decorum, and far beyond the narrow licence that Thade conceded to the laity within his bailiwick. His anxious ears caught a low-pitched whining roar approaching the church. The priests were coming in the Hillman and would surprise him and his flock before they were reduced to the order that beseemed them and the occasion.

"Whisht, ye limbs of Satan," he urged in a hoarse windy croak. "Is that the way to behave in the House of God? Or are ye a pack of Comm'nists out of Russia, God help ye? Shame on you, Mike Mack, that don't keep your friends in control."

But Mike had already sized up the situation. Tipping a good-humoured wink at Mai and John Joe, he led his party from their seats into the side aisle and up towards the altar where they quickly distributed themselves along the two front seats, the groom's party on the Epistle side, as custom ordained, and the bride's on the Gospel side.

By the time Father Boyle opened the sacristy door to see if everything was in readiness for the joint ceremony of the marriage and the nuptial Mass, order was well restored. He saw the bridal pair kneeling on cushions at the altar rails, flanked on the right hand by Tommy Fitz, as best man, and on the left by Katie Barrett, as bridesmaid. Behind them, Maire, in the duck-egg-blue costume and saucy turban, sat between Mike and Big Bill. On the off side of the centre aisle Mrs. Barrett sat stark and unbending in her blanket of black shawl beside Martin Cronin. Her straight back and high head showed that she thought as little of Martin, her son-in-law-to-be, as of Mai, her daughter-in-law-in-the-making.

Nodding approval of the decorous setting, Father Boyle returned to the sacristy to report, and at the stroke of eight Father John came forth, followed by the assistant priests, and crossed the sanctuary to stand over the bridal pair.

"You may stand up," he said in a calm conversational tone to set John Joe and Mai at their ease. When they were on their feet, he turned a quizzical glance at the groom.

"You haven't forgotten to bring the ring, of course."

"No, Father," John Joe replied, and produced with no little complacency a neat cardboard case containing the ring, a gold sovereign, and a silver crown piece.

Big Bill had provided the sovereign with the assurance that "the pleasure was his." The nurse had given the crown piece to Mai to mark her satisfaction at the happy ending of her solicitude for that fickle maid's future, and John Joe had spent a full and enjoyable hour haggling with Gandy, the only jeweller in Cahirsally, for the ring. Father Murray took the precious symbols from the case and placed them on a salver upon the altar rail near Father John's hand.

Before the self-conscious couple were sure that the ceremony was properly started, it was all over and Father John was reading the concluding prayer.

"*Ut qui, Te auctore, junguntur, Te auxiliante serventur.* May they, who are joined by Thy authority, be preserved by Thy help."

He added a "God bless you both" from himself and went up to the altar to say the nuptial Mass.

Ollsen did not go ashore for the wedding. He would have felt like a fish out of water in a Catholic church and shrank from being made the cynosure of curious and hostile eyes by his ignorance of the Church service. Donovan and Maurisheen, having no such inhibitions and foreseeing a lavish dispensation of food and drink after the ceremony, sailed off with Mike and Maire in the *Mary.* But they went no further than Bill's. They found it hard enough to attend obligatory church services; voluntary attendances fell outside their practice.

The Norwegian spent the morning making preparations for the welcome he proposed to give M278 when she crept furtively inshore on Thursday night to plunder the forbidden fishing grounds. On a spare six-prong grapnel of Mike's, he bent a ten-fathom length of stout Manila rope, every foot of which he tested carefully for strength and flexibility. He sharpened the *Mary's* light ax to a razor edge on the grindstone and oiled the joints of a heavy two-handed cutting pliers. Smiling grimly in anticipation of the use he was going to make of those destructive weapons, he hid them in a clump of furze and sat on a rough stone to wait for Joany's call to dinner.

What a forlorn stony place the island was, without Mike and Maire, he thought. A splinter of rock, sparsely covered by heather and coarse grass, eternally buffeted by the sea and sluiced by the skies. Of itself it offered no inducement to a restless ambitious man to spend his life, or even a portion of it, on its unprofitable acres. But Mike and Maire transformed it by their very presence. Their great generous hearts put life into its cold carcass and warmed the very air about it. They were the island.

A thin reedy hail from the house cut in on his musing. Dinner was ready.

His solitary plate, though piled high with hot, appetizing fare, looked very lonely on the great table at which eight hungry, talkative people usually fed. It seemed to emphasize his own foreignness, to set him apart from the indigenous inhabitants. He had expected to see Joany's plate across the table from his own and to hear her chatty commentary on the day's happenings as she ate in her sparrowlike way. Instead, he saw her sitting by the cradle, austerely calm as she gave Donal Michael his midday allowance of diluted milk.

"Had you your own dinner yet, Joany?" he asked invitingly.

"Time enough for me when you and the child have ate," she replied without importing any colour into the phrase.

He started to eat, but he could not continue in the neutral atmosphere and laid down his knife and fork.

"You don't like me, Joany."

She took the bottle from the child's mouth and laid it on her lap but gave no other sign that she had heard him.

"Why don't you like me, Joany? What have I done to you?"

"You have done nothing to me, to myself, I mean, and I like you well. Why wouldn't I like you? You are a decent and a fine young man that any woman would be proud of. Your own mother prides out of you, I'm sure, wherever she is. But this island is no place for you and you know it. You came back here, but 'tis your heart drove you back and not your head. The heart is a poor guide for a wandering man when it leads him to another man's hearthstone. I like you all right but I don't like your intentions."

"Have I done anything or said anything since I came back that a decent man should not have done? You know I haven't and you know that I never will as long as I stay here, be the stay long or short." His words thrilled with feeling as if he were, for the first time, voicing aloud the considered rule of life he had laid down for himself after much silent consideration.

"I know no such thing," Joany retorted with a conviction as pronounced as his own. "I admit that you are careful in what you say and do, but any one can read your heart in your motions, and that same heart will be your undoing. You and Mike Mack are like two brothers. You love him and he loves you, but the beam of a woman's eye can curdle brotherly love and turn it to hate. It did it before and will again."

His incredulous smile goaded her to justify herself.

"Did you ever hear the *oidhe*, the—what shall I call it in English— the sorrowful fate of Kiar and Flann? You did not. Well, I'll tell it to you."

She sat up stiffly, laced her fingers on her lap and composed her features in the austere cast of tragedy as became a traditional storyteller.

"*The Sorrowful Fate of Kiar and Flann.* Long ago, long before the Dane, the Sassenach, or the Jew set foot on this distressful country, Eire was a beautiful land. The sun shone all day in a blue sky and the stars shone all night in a firmament of deep purple. Rains came at Beltane to freshen the plants of the earth and snows at Samain to cleanse the air and cool the resting soil. All creatures roamed free in their own domain, the birds in the air, the beasts in the plains, and the fish in quiet pools and running waters. Man forgot the Fall in the joys of this Eden of the West and roamed freest of all.

"Of all the men of Eire of those tranquil days none lived and laughed as carefree as the two young foster brothers Kiar and Flann. Kiar of the curling black hair and flashing teeth and Flann of the wheaten locks and the bright blue eyes were seldom out of earshot of each other. They chased the same deer, ate off the same platter, and slept in the same bothy. They trained together in the arts of war and fought side by side in creach and foray. They were closer of heart than brothers of one womb.

"One evening at the end of the harvest days of Lugnas, Kiar and Flann went aside from the reapers, whom they had helped to gather in the corn. They had guarded it faithfully during the long sultry days of Samrad against the birds of the air and the beasts of the plain and garnered it painfully with sickles of bronze. They were weary of the arts of peace and bethought themselves again of the pleasures of the chase. They laid their bronze glaives and long-handled spears beside them on the stubbles and thumbed the edge of them for gaps and dunts and were not pleased. The weapons were worn with use and unworthy of them, who were the foremost warriors of the clan.

" 'We will go to Darg, the coppersmith of Ross, and get us new glaives and lance blades,' said Kiar.

" 'Not so,' replied Flann. 'You will go to Darg for the blades and I shall scour the forest of Airne for choice woods for the hafts, for yearling ash and ancient holly without bend or blemish. These I shall have ready against your coming.'

"And Kiar went northwards over hill and dale, through dark woods and open plains, till he saw the blue smoke of the coppersmith's furnace rising over the tops of the trees on the island of Ross. He plunged into the water and swam across the narrow channel and made his way through the trees to the open glade that rang with the clanging of metal.

"Darg received him well. He took him to his dun and gave him the newest of his meats and the oldest of his drinks before he would hear the cause of the young man's coming. And he bade his daughter Saive to prepare a couch of the sweet-smelling branches of pine, that Kiar might rest upon it during his stay in the dun. For two days the coppersmith worked on the weapons, shaping the moulds out of the finest of fine sand with his clever fingers and pouring into them the molten blend of pure copper and precious tin. And while he worked, his beautiful daughter, Saive, ministered to the young man's needs and walked with him among the trees until she woke in his heart, and in her own, the strange longing that grows to a great love.

"Darg rejoiced that his daughter had won the heart of the young warrior who was to become chief of his nation and added to the gleaming glaives and spearheads, by way of marriage portion, a goodly store of cauldrons, milking cans, and cooking vessels, all beaten out of red copper and riveted by his own hands.

"When Kiar brought Saive home, Flann's heart turned against her, for he knew that she had come between them and put an end to their brotherhood. But her comeliness and gentleness grew on him as it had grown on Kiar and woke in his heart the strange longing that grows into a great love. He watched her comings and goings and tried to smother his hunger for her. He went away to live apart, lest his longing overcome his loyalty to Kiar, but his desire for her brought him back to where she was.

"One day he saw her coming through the forest as graceful and lightfooted as a faun that knows no fear, and a great madness possessed him. He called her name aloud and ran towards her to encompass her in his arms, but she eluded him and ran away, shrieking her terror to the trees. And Kiar, hearing her cries, hurried to protect her and came upon Flann as he placed his hands upon her. Their brotherly love curdled into hate under Saive's eyes. They drew from their scabbards the new glaives her father had fashioned for them and fell upon each other with death in their hands. They thrust and lunged without thought of defence until Flann drove his blade deep into Kiar's breast and pierced the heart that had beat only for him until the woman stole into it. Shouting a wild shout, he ran and clasped the prize of victory in his arms, but Saive drew the short dagger from his belt and drove it deep into his vitals."

Joany stopped and looked at Ollsen before she ended her tragic tale.

"Three long days of mourning clouded the land, one for singing the praises of the dead, one for singing laments for the dead, and the last for raising memorial cairns over the graves of the dead on twin hilltops. Saive sits to this day on Kiar's cairn, lamenting for her dark-haired man, and turns her back on the unhappy one, whose love destroyed them all."

The Norwegian shoved his full plate away and pushed his chair from the table as if to free himself from the constraint in which Joany's tale had bound him. The old woman had picked her allegory with crafty wisdom and told it with an art that pointed the moral for his sensitive ear. He wanted to get away from her shrewd accusing eyes and evade discussion of his problem until he had digested it for himself. Rising to his feet, he turned to leave the kitchen but the old woman called him back.

"Sit down and eat your dinner, *a chree*," she said with a maternal softness in her voice, that sounded unusually tender after the colourless monotone of the story. "Or wait. Let me warm it up for you and I'll have mine, too, to keep you in countenance."

He did sit down and, recovering his appetite in the friendly warmth of Joany's chit-chat, ate the good dinner she wished him to eat. But they avoided the old tale of Kiar and Flann and the new version in which he and Mike took the leading roles. When they were finished, he went around the table to her and, stooping low, placed an arm around her and kissed her on the cheek.

"You are a wonderful woman, Joany. Pity Flann had no woman like you to read him a parable and show him his course. Have no fear of me, Joany. I have but one job to do here. As soon as that is done, I shall do the right thing by Maire and Mike."

Tears filled her motherly eyes as they followed him down the path to the cove. She blessed herself when he went out of sight and set about washing up the few dinner things, deeply preoccupied with concern for his future.

It was broad day when the *Mary* brought the wedding guests home to the island. Mike steered her up to her moorings with more way on her than she needed and overran the buoy to Maire's discomfiture. She got no time to fish up the mooring rope with the boathook. She took the wheel from Mike on the second run and let him make fast. Mike had enjoyed the wedding feast and was more merry and bright than was his wont. Maire was intrigued by this new, elated, and talkative Thahailen and egged him on to reveal himself while his tongue was loose. Womanlike, she could condone convivial lapses in her man if they disclosed no meanness of spirit. Besides, she welcomed the opportunity of getting to know "Philip drunk" as well as "Philip sober." Mike gave her few such opportunities.

Maurisheen and Donovan had spent the day in the serious business of engorging fat meat until they belched with repletion and engulfing uncounted pints of foaming Guinness until they fell into the helpless stupor that was, for them, the high-water mark of human regalement. They knew that kindred souls would look after them in their happy coma and dump them, with roughhanded solicitude, into the hold of the *Mary* when she started for home. They themselves would have done the same by Tom or Dick or Harry in similar circumstances.

Maire gave a detailed account of the marriage, the Mass, and the wedding breakfast to Joany when they closed around the fire that night. She reproduced, verbatim, Father John's humorous speech from the head of the table and got Mike to sing Father Murray's comic song, *Cé Bean is fearr agam* and to imitate the cold-blooded bachelor whose worries it recounts. She told of Father John's skill in drawing Father Boyle out of his defensive silence and actually inducing him to propose the health of the bridal pair. "Alas," said Maire, "when the young priest got out of his shell, it took Father John all his time to get him back into it again."

"Oh, no, Joany," she hurried to assure Joany. "He took nothing stronger than tea. He's a strict teetotaller like all the young clergy. Do you know what's at the root of Father Boyle's abrupt manners? Shyness, Joany. He never mixed with people when he was growing up and he's afraid of people now. But he'll soften out in time."

She carried the tale to its grand finale—the triumphant progress of the wedding party in Bill's cars from Manistir to Cahirsally railway station, where the wedding guests cheered as the train steamed out, its engine whistling a continuous staccato in honour of the happy pair. Joany followed the story eagerly and kept taking Maire back to fill gaps she had leaped in the breathless rush of her narrative. At last it ended, questions ran dry, and yawns proclaimed the urgent need for sleep. As Ollsen, the only extern of the four, rose to go, Maire appealed to him.

"Why not sleep in Mai's room, Knut? It was yours, you know, before she came and it is much more comfortable than the bunk."

Joany cocked her ear for Ollsen's answer which would show whether he preferred to flee the danger of proximity to Maire or perish therein.

"Thanks, Maire, but I'd rather sleep aboard. I'm more used to the bunk rising and falling with the lift of the sea, than a bed that has no give in it. Anyhow, I must see how the pair of boyos are. They might walk overboard when they wake up, looking for a drink to soften their tongues. *Oiche maih yeeve.* Good night all."

CHAPTER 36 · *A Wristwatch*

ON Saturday night Ollsen picked up the M278 again on the radio. She was working southwards through the trawling grounds off the Shannon and expected to finish her run in the middle of the week if the fishing were good. He learned, too, that the foul foghorn voice belonged to Treffor Evans and that the ugly untidy trawler he skippered bore the incongruously affectionate name *Mifanwy*. Turning off the set when Evans growled "O-ver" for the last time, Ollsen lay on the flat of his back in his bunk with his eyes closed, planning a schedule of work for the five days ending on Thursday evening. Joany's allegory had forced him to the decision that he should flee the danger as soon as he had settled his account with Treffor Evans. To go sooner would leave Mike and the fishermen of Manistir at the mercy of the lawless steam trawlers. They would scrape the inshore fisheries bare if their incursions were not challenged. But go he must, if he would avoid the fate of Flann whom "a great madness possessed." Like Flann, he was prone to frenzies. Had he not struck his captain down in a fit of madness on the *Bernadotte* and shown violence to Maire, of all people, in his rage on the ridge?

There was much to do on the Shark. That copper lode on the sea cliff north of the Lookout clamoured to be worked. The site for the new dwelling near the cells, which Maire and he had selected on that wonderful day when he first saw her flush warmly under his eager gaze, was lock-spitted and cleared for action. But they were out of the question now. They were heavy jobs and would take a lot of men a long time to

332

do and only five days remained for him on the island. He would devote those five days to Maire's service and place at her hand certain devices which would ease the heavy labours of her life and help her to remember him.

He went ashore with the Mass party on Sunday and spent the morning in Big Bill's hardware store, picking out miscellaneous nails, bolts, bends, and brackets for the jobs he had in mind. When Mass was over and the people trooped back, he took Paddy Brown aside and asked him how early he could have the lorry on the Old Quay in the morning, not knowing that Sunday morning was Paddy's bilious morning.

"How early can I be there, is it?" Paddy asked rather tartly. "Let you name the earliest hour you can think of and I'll be there earlier than that. I'm none of your drowsy lie-a-beds, that have an alarmer to pull 'em out in the morning. No, sir. What I put before me at night is enough to wake me in the morning."

"What do you say to five o'clock, then?" said Ollsen quietly.

"I say nothing; 'tis for you to say it," Paddy retorted.

"Very well, Paddy. I'll be waiting for you on the pier at five o'clock."

"It wouldn't break a tooth on you to say, 'Please God,' even if you are a black Protestant. *Sé an duine a deireann, sé Dia a dheineann.* Man proposes but God, glory be to Him, disposes. And you won't be waiting for me; 'tis I will be waiting for you."

The *Mary* loomed large in the darkling murk on Monday morning when she slowed in to the quay on the stroke of five to find Paddy waiting in the cab of the lorry, as he had promised.

Mike and Ollsen squeezed themselves in beside him and off they went to Cahirsally. It was still dark when they parked the lorry outside Spitton's timber yard and Mike went to knock up the yardman; and it was still early enough for town breakfasts when the lorry stood, fully laden with a strange assortment of measured scantlings, synthetic slates, and glazed-enamel sanitary fitments. Ollsen exuded energy. He found the articles he needed before the yardman had grasped the names of them, and hustled Mike and Paddy to load them up with speed. He overbore the great Spitton himself, who wished to have his breakfast before he undertook the irksome task of pricing so many separate articles and making out the bill. "Where's the hurry, man alive?" he objected. "Sure there's time for everything." But Ollsen had his way and Spitton presented the bill grudgingly and accepted payment dubiously. Preparing bills was one of his leisurely pastimes, prices were so plastic and mutable in his capable hands. He hated being bustled in Ollsen's fashion.

When Mike took Paddy and the yardman with him to have a parting pint of Guinness in the good old neighbourly way, Ollsen crossed the street to the clockmaker's shop in which John Joe had higgled and chaffered for the wedding ring. It was a narrow-fronted poke of a shop with a smudged window and a spoon latch on the door that rang a bell to announce a customer. The Norwegian winced at the strident signal and stared about the stuffy little interior at the dozens of live clocks, large and small, that stitched the air with their asynchronic metallic tick-tack-tocking. The insistent din of dissociate sounds took him aback like a ship caught in stays, driving out of his mind the business that brought him into the remarkable shop. An inner door opened halfways and Gandy sidled unobtrusively in.

The clockmaker's startling resemblance to the famous Hindu ascetic accounted for the agnomen that had ousted for ever from common usage the Daniel Twomey under which he traded. Clasping his hands together, he bent his eyes on Ollsen's feet and asked in a faded voice what he could do for him.

"I wanted to buy a—to get something— Oh, I don't think I'll bother about it now." Ollsen was still under the spell of the clocks and unable to collect his thoughts.

"Perhaps you wish to make a present to your young lady," the wraith-like voice suggested with veiled craft.

"It will do next time," Ollsen temporized.

"I can show you a nice range of rings, brooches, necklaces, compacts, toilet sets." Gandy litanized his wares with a muted reverence that lifted them out of the common grade of cheap Brummagem. "How much do you wish to spend?"

"I was thinking of a gold wristwatch," said Ollsen, nibbling at the clockmaker's skilful lures. "A real good one."

"A wristwatch?" Gandy imported a respectful deprecation into the question. "Wristwatches are not the best love tokens. They are time-keepers first and only ornament as an afterthought. Girls are given to fiddling with watches. They go out of order and when they do, sir, they make poor ornaments. What about a nice gold bangle, now?"

The old man's insistence and the clacking of the clocks got on Ollsen's nerves, aggravating his natural resistance to opposition.

"No. I'll have a wristwatch or nothing," he said shortly.

"Very well, sir. You said you wanted a high-class one. Would you go to—£10? You will? Thank you, sir."

The little man went back through the inner door and returned with a glazed tray that contained a dozen glistening midget watches. He got Ollsen to indicate the watch he liked best, withdrew it carefully from its velvet nest, and showed the sailor a circular vacant space in the ornamentation on its back.

"That's for the initials—hers and yours. I can engrave them, tastefully entwined, without extra cost. I do it myself," he added, dropping his voice to a whisper of self approval.

The suggestion startled Ollsen. He had not thought of that symbolic union, sailor though he was, and the exciting notion thrilled him to his marrow. But he had to reject it and instruct Gandy to inscribe a lonely capital M in the vacant plot.

"Yes, sir," the clockmaker assured him after he had paid for the only demonstration he could ever give Maire of his hopeless love for her. "I shall send it this evening to you, care of Mr. Hannen's hotel. Good morning, sir, and thank you."

Paddy made good time on the way back to the Old Quay, lent a hand in loading the mixed freight on the *Mary* and waited on the pierhead to wave his cap in good will as she turned for home. He looked at his watch.

"My God, it is only nine o'clock! Them Norwaygians are hard drivers, poor craitures. But, sure, they can't help it. 'Tis the way God made them, glory be to His holy name."

Ollsen drove himself and his team of three mercilessly for the rest of that long day, and to such good effect that by nightfall Maire saw the

structure of the pantry and scullery Ollsen had planned for her, standing firm and strong outside the kitchen backdoor. On Tuesday a sink
and a copper were installed in the scullery and connected with the ridge
tank for running water. On Wednesday shelves, cupboards, and bins
were fitted in the pantry and a start made on the structure of an extension lavatory, the plumbing of which was completed by midday on
Thursday. At dinner Maire called a halt. Where was the good of killing
themselves, she asked, trying to squeeze a week's work into a day? Even
the Almighty Himself took a rest on the seventh day. Let them all take
the half day off. They *did*, and Maurisheen and Donovan, following
sound primitive practice, went out to their bunks in the *Mary* to soak
themselves in sleep. But Ollsen and Mike were too keyed up for a sudden cessation of activity. What they needed was a diversion and Ollsen
suggested that they and Maire climb to the Lookout and rest there.
They sat under the mass of Carrigard for a while, surveying the wide
expanse of the Bay and the patchwork pattern of fields around the
house, making lazy comments that demanded no answers. A slant ray
of sunlight struck the new back kitchen, picking it out from its neutral
setting of weather-bleached thatch. By a strange fortuity, the brilliant
ray grew longer, illumined the path to the cove, lit up the smooth white
cement of the new sliphead, and sped across the water of the little harbour to make the fresh blues and reds of the *Mary* sparkle in its radiance.

"Look at it, Knut," Maire exclaimed with a lively glint in her eyes.
"Like an angel's wing sweeping the dark shadows off the island to show
us what a bright happy place the island really is."

"Look again, girleen," said Mike. "Look at what it is shining on, the
house, the slip, and the boat. 'Tis them that make the island; without
them it would be a cold spot."

He turned to lean on his elbow and throw a kindly glance at Ollsen,
who was watching the brilliant stream of light move steadily on.

"I'm thinking, Knut, that angel of Maire's is a friend of yours, too.
See what he is polishing up. The back kitchen, the sliphead, and the
Mary. The work of your own hands."

He left it at that. His natural reticence prevented him from expressing in direct words the gratitude he felt to the big Norwegian. Maire uttered the unspoken word for him.

"How can we ever repay you, Knut, for what you have done for us in one short year? You lifted us out of the slough we were born in and showed us how we can help ourselves. It was a lucky day for Mike and me, the day you came to the island, and may God reward you, for we can't."

The sailor placed his hand on her arm to put an end to her embarrassing praises, but withdrew it instantly at the effect of the mere touch on his already overstrained feelings. He sought to cover his emotion with a show of levity.

"The pleasure is mine," he said in a rough imitation of Bill's hearty voice and beaming smile.

Reverting to his own deliberate way of talking, he pointed at the base of the shaft of sunlight that shone on the cove.

"You see only the gaudy things, Mike. Put on your spectacles and tell me what that little black thing south of the *Mary* is."

"That's the old two-oared spillering boat, of course," Mike replied rather ingenuously. "I admit she'd be the better of another dab of tar to freshen her up."

"Only for that little boat and two dear friends of mine there would be no *Mary* and no slip and no back kitchen for the sun to shine on. And I wouldn't be sitting here with the pair of you, but away to the south'ard under twenty fathoms of water."

As he spoke, the ope in the clouds, through which the lance of light had broken, closed up and cut it off, throwing the wide prospect of sea and land back into its neutral greys and browns and broken blues. They sat in silence, looking at the picture changed from brilliance to quietude, until Ollsen spoke again.

"This is a quiet peaceful place and I have been happier here than I ever thought I could be. I am sorry to be leaving it so soon. . . ."

"What's that you say?" Maire exclaimed. "Leaving us? What put that notion into your head? Of course, you're not leaving us."

Ollsen shook his head at her impetuous rejection of his announcement and went on with the quiet insistence one uses to overbear friendly opposition to an inevitable course of action.

"You know, Maire, I can't stay here for ever. I must go away sometime, and the longer I stay the harder it will be to leave. I am going on Saturday morning's train."

The suddenness of the declaration shook even Mike out of his reflective habit of mind into hasty disapproval.

"Nonsense, Knut. Sure, you wouldn't have time to settle anything between now and Saturday. If you have to leave us, give us time to get used to the notion."

Knut put his hand down the neck of his thick blue jersey and took out of an inner pocket the neat box case which Gandy had sent him, "care of Hannen's hotel." He snapped it open to display the gleaming wristwatch and gave it to Maire.

"For you," was all he could say.

She took it, still warm with the heat of his breast, more moved by the finality of the gift than by its beauty. Her eyes filled with tears that fell upon the watch face when she removed it from its snug velvet nest and held the wrist towards Ollsen. With a touch of her native spirit, she shook away the tears and forced her tongue to speak.

"Let you put it on, Knut."

Mike was caught in the surge of emotion, too, and fearing that he might break into tears and disgrace his manhood, he sprang to his feet. He flung an inarticulate something about "Cattle" over his shoulder and ran headlong down the hill, not towards the house, but to where the cows were grazing on the levels near the dunes. His sudden, precipitate flight startled the two he had left so unceremoniously behind and brought them back to their senses.

Ollsen made a move to rise but Maire held him back.

"He'll be all right. He's only running away from himself."

They watched the lithe blue figure leaping down the heathery slope till it eased to a sling trot in the brown turf flats into which the hill spreads its hem. The sailor was the first to speak.

"Maire, you are blest more than you know in having Mike for your man. He's the best of us all. Better than you, Maire, and I think you are the best *girl* in the world. I often wished he was like the rest of us, like Donovan or Conny Shuckrue or John Joe. Then I would not mind crossing him; aye, or robbing his nest."

His voice took a more vibrant note as he clasped the wrist on which he had fastened the watch.

"You must know I love you as truly as Mike does. It was to be with you again I came back to this Godforsaken rock, and if Mike was like other men I would take you away from him in spite of hell and high water. But I can't do it, God help me. It would be worse than to murder a child in its sleep."

He dropped her wrist and turned his eyes out to sea, but she took his hand in both of hers and made him look at her.

"Don't be disparaging yourself like that, Knut. Mike is all you say and more, but he is not a whit better than you. It is the goodness of your own heart that is saving you from ruining yourself and Mike and me. And now let me open my own heart to you, Knut. It will do no harm, now you are leaving us. I am not the good woman I thought I was before you came. Ever since that day at the cells I have thought of you in a way that no married woman should think of any man but the man that owns her. When you are gone, you will always be in my heart, next to Mike. And, Knut dear, Mike knows it. *I told him.*"

She released his hand and sat closer to him.

"And he will not grudge us a fond farewell. Kiss me, Knut."

The open air, the open confession, and Maire's evident trust in herself and in him cleansed Ollsen's mind of the passion that thrives only in secret places. He kissed her warmly on the lips and swung her to her feet with a flourish.

"Well, Mrs. Mack," he said, brushing the heather chips from her skirt, "the day is eating itself away and we have had our chat. May I see you home, madam?"

Maire looked down towards the grazing fields where Mike was moving among the cows and cupped her hands to send him a loud "O-he, Mike." Hearing his answering hail, she linked her arm in Knut's and they went down the hill to the house together, where Mike soon joined them, his own calm collected self again. They took their time eating the simple supper Joany had ready for them and lingered on at the table discussing the consequences of Ollsen's departure. He settled the fate of the *Mary* in one short phrase. "She's yours, Mike; yours and Maire's," and fixed it by getting a sheet of notepaper and making the transfer in writing. A curious sense of well-being filled them all, a happy fellowship that partings or misunderstandings could never sunder. When Ollsen at last rose to go, Mike walked with him to the slip and pushed him off in the punt with the old unhurried sweep of his arms.

CHAPTER 37 · *A Fight at Sea*

WHEN dusk fell slowly over the island, Ollsen paddled noiselessly ashore for the grapnel and the other equipment he had hidden in the furze bush and brought them as noiselessly back to the *Mary*. He slipped her moorings without a splash and put Maurisheen and Donovan into the punt to slew the *Mary's* head around and tow her out to the mouth of the cove before he started the engine. He did not want to attract Mike's attention to her manoeuvres with its roar. Maurisheen came aboard and swung it into life as soon as the *Mary* felt the ocean swell under her keel, setting it at three-quarter throttle.

Ollsen stood at the wheel, wondering had he chosen rightly in steering north towards Black Head rather than south to the Fang. Treffor Evans might make his parting raid over the ground that had proved so profitable before or he might try new ground. But whichever course he took, he had to come in from the nor'ard around Lobus Head that stood sentinel between Shannon and Manistir waters. Ollsen decided to lie in wait for him under its sheltering lee and let circumstances decide his subsequent actions.

It was very dark when the *Mary* got there and lost herself to sight in the gloom of the beetling cliffs. She showed no lights and Ollsen measured her distance from the rockface by the sound of the surge upon it. At ten o'clock he turned on the radio and listened for the grating voice of the Welshman. When he picked it up, its faintness alarmed him into thinking that the trawler was hundreds of miles away, until he remembered that he might be inside the skip distance of her radio wave length. The faint reception probably showed that she was very near at hand and he smiled grimly in satisfaction. He set Maurisheen and Donovan to keep a keen lookout on the patch of dark sky that showed off the steep jet-black mass of Lobus. Through that dim obscurity the M278 must pass, if she came at all.

It was a nerve-racking watch, maintained in a silence broken only by the suck and surge of the swell against the unseen cliffs. The watchers were a strange complement for those waters: A Norwegian, a Cape Clear man, and a roving Dingle trawlerman, keeping watch and ward for the sleeping natives of Manistir. At midnight Donovan made some strong black coffee and passed scalding mugfuls, heavily sweetened, up to Ollsen and Bowler "to clear the scum off their eyes" as he put it. At long last, Ollsen suddenly froze into the rigid set of a pointer scenting its game. He peered into the dark ahead.

"He's coming at last," he whispered. "See! That's the glow of smoke from his funnel."

A spot, darker than the surrounding air, seemed to detach itself from the solid black of Lobus. It moved slowly across the view. Over it the watchers could see the glimmer of furnace fires on the base of the billowing smoke, like a dim crimson halo, faintly discernible in the dark.

"That's the bloody robber, sure enough," said Maurisheen, "coming in as bould as brass, as if he owned the place. Will we go for him now or wait till he comes abreast of us?"

"We'll wait till he shoots his trawl and he won't do that for a while," said Ollsen. "It's my guess he'll steam in to the island and make his shot there and have one good drag out to the Wild Bank. We'll stalk him here in the shelter and catch him when he reaches the Bank."

"But he might trawl off to the south'ard," Donovan objected.

"We'll see that in time to go after him. He won't be making more than two knots with the weight of the trawl. We'll catch up with him, never fear," Ollsen assured him.

They kept the *Mary* moving in the shade of the cliffs, parallel to the trawler as she steamed boldly in. They were hidden under Black Head when the Welshman came about and dropped his huge trawl overboard, a bare half mile away. They heard the rough voices of the trawlermen giving and answering the routine orders of their work and then settling down to silence again when the squat old steamer threw its weight into the thick cable that stretched out from her stern.

Ollsen's mind was centred on that cable. Though he could not see it in the dark, he knew exactly how it looked, running from gunwale to trawl, with one third of its length above water and two thirds under. Ten fathoms astern of the trawler it dipped into the water and sloped so gradually downwards that it was but an oar's length deep at twenty fathoms' distance from the ship. It was at that distance he planned to make his attack.

Posting Maurisheen at the stern of the *Mary* with the grapnel balanced on the gunwale, ready to tip it overside at the word "Go," and Donovan at the engine which was just ticking over, Ollsen brought her bow to bear in the general direction of the raider and waited until he loomed dead ahead.

"Let her have it, Donovan, all you got," he yelled when the moment came and the need for silence was past.

Donovan opened the throttle flat out, sending the *Mary* roaring at full speed through the dark at her quarry. She ate up the distance before the Welshman was aware of her hostile intent and almost swamped the punt she was towing behind.

"Ease her to half. E-asy," Ollsen cried as he neared his victim and swung the *Mary* a point to port to bring her over the submerged part of the warp.

"Ready, Maurisheen," he called out in warning to the little Dingleman. "*Grapnel awa-ay!*"

"Grapnel away!" yelled Maurisheen in reply as he ran to the winch to control the grapnel rope.

The operation was perfectly timed. The *Mary* had barely passed over the sunken warp when the grapnel hooked it and slowed her down with the drag.

"Keep her going, Donovan. Keep the pull on it," cried Ollsen, steering the *Mary* gradually away from the trawler until the two boats faced in opposite directions and pulled dead against each other. The grapnel slid along the warp under water until it reached the trawl and clawed its flukes deep into it and held fast.

Evans at last woke up to the seriousness of the situation that had been forced upon him. He was trapped in prohibited waters with the choice of escape by sacrificing his valuable trawl, or running the risk of arrest and a severe penalty by fighting for it. He roared blasphemies through the dark and opened the fight.

"What the bleedin' festerin' hell you doin' with my gear, you festerin' blighter? Cast yourself loose or I'll tow you out to sea and swamp you. D'ye hear me?"

No answer came from the *Mary*, but her Kelvin throbbed powerfully and the pawls of her winch clicked merrily as they lifted the trawl clear of the bottom and forced it to the surface between the two boats. Once it was clear, it came up with a rush under the opposing compulsion of the two straining ropes and broke the surface much nearer the *Mary* than the *Mifanwy*. It was a strange tug of war in which the superior power of the steamtrawler was more than matched by the planned purpose of the motorboat. Evans was fighting an unknown adversary in the dark, while Ollsen knew his man and knew his own mind.

The Welshman climbed back to his bridge and rang angrily for full speed ahead, hoping to break the line that sought to steal his trawl. But Ollsen heard the clanging bell and read its message as soon as the trawler's engineer.

"Ease her down a bit," he said in Donovan's ear. "He wants to burst our grapnel rope by a sudden rush. We'll let him tow us for a while."

When the trawler threw all her power into the warp she met no opposition. The *Mary* trailed passively behind, but not accommodatingly. Ollsen put her wheel hard to port, throwing her aslant of the trawler's course and upsetting his steering. Evans held on doggedly for ten minutes and then rang the engine room for full speed astern in an attempt to force the *Mary* to run into the floating trawl and foul her propeller. But Ollsen forestalled him again.

"Pep her up, Donovan," he cried. "And you, Bowler; take up the slack of the grapnel on your winch. Lively!"

This action defeated Evans's manoeuvre and brought the trawl almost within reach of the *Mary*'s counter, while the trawler was still a hawse length off. But the darkness was dissolving and the dawn would break on the waters before Ollsen had completed his design, if he did not act swiftly. Telling Donovan to keep the grapnel rope taut at all costs, he hauled the punt under the stern quarter and jumped into her with catlike agility. Evans saw him in the growing light and, though he could not guess at Ollsen's intention, he decided to derange whatever it was by a sudden change of tactics. He rang the engine room again for full speed ahead and ordered the winch man to wind the warp in.

Donovan, having no Ollsen at hand to warn him, kept the Kelvin at full throttle and the opposing forces yanked the warp high out of the water, quivering with high tension and the weight of the suspended trawl.

Ollsen jumped at his chance. Standing up in the punt, he pushed her towards the half-submerged trawl, worked her around it, and grabbed the heavy towrope, now breast-high and stiff with tension. He balanced himself wide-legged in the swaying boat and drew his sailor's knife to cut the rope in two.

Evans roared in rage when he saw that his trawl was doomed. He leaped down to the deck and seized an ice ax which he wheeled in a great arc about his head and brought with all his might down on the towrope, sheering through it, deep into the elm gunwale.

"Take the bloody lot to blazes, you buckin', festerin' pirate," he shrieked and flung the ax wildly at the man in the punt.

The result was disastrous. Ollsen kept his eye on the flying ax to dodge it and did not see the deadly rope, whizzing and whirling like a giant whip towards him. It struck him cruelly in the nape of the neck with the blind devilry of inanimate things and cut him down in the very moment of his triumph. He lay where he fell and never stirred again.

The Welshman scurried away in the cold twilight, leaving the *Mary* to drift, while the two stunned fishermen brought the limp body aboard and laid it reverently on the foredeck. They cut the grapnel rope and let the calamitous trawl sink to the bottom without a thought for its value as salvage or as evidence. With a subconscious sense of propriety, they kept the *Mary* at half speed on the way home, and changed into their Sunday clothes before they went ashore to tell their tragic story to Mike and Maire.

CHAPTER 38 · *A Funeral at Sea*

O LLSEN was buried like a viking. His valiant defence of the inshore waters of Manistir raised him at once to a high place on the
calendar of martyrs to foreign aggression. The manner of his death in
the elation of victory started a wave of prideful sorrow that spread far
and wide along the coast.

The Macks had expected a modest company of friends to come
and watch with them at Ollsen's wake and accompany them to the
churchyard. They were overwhelmed by a swarming multitude that
came from every airt in black boats that crept like water beetles across
the Bay and outer waters. They kept coming all the morning until
the cove was full to confusion of moving craft and the shore astir with
moving people. Old Pats Kelly took on himself the marshalling of
the boats; Brehony, the schoolmaster, posted his men along the path
to the house to keep the crowd moving in decent order and Mike received them at the door. They entered the kitchen in batches of twenty,
knelt reverently at the foot of the improvised bier to say a short Gaelic
prayer, and then passed on through the backdoor to spread at ease
over the surrounding fields.

When the tide was at the full and every one had paid respect to the
dead, the *Mary* left her moorings to thread her way through the crowding boats and back slowly in to receive the flag-draped coffin—the only
splash of colour in the sombre scene. A large Irish tricolour swathed
the casket from head to foot and on its breast was spread a neat Norwegian flag, made at night by Betty Hannen to Jim Brehony's coloured

sketch. The blue cross and red field of Norway warmed the vernal hues of Ireland and struck a joint note of high courage in the face of death.

The *Mary* moved slowly out again with the lonely coffin on her foredeck and the island folk, that knew and loved Ollsen, standing silent abaft the engine. She stopped at the mouth of the cove while Pats Kelly scurried about in the punt and lined the motor boats up at equal distances behind her. To each he assigned three rowboats to be towed astern across the Sound, lest they fall out on the way and break the unity of the funeral. Then, with a wave of his hat, he gave the signal to start. When the last boat cleared the harbour's mouth, Joany and Donal Michael were left alone on the Shark. Fearful of staying in the house among the trappings of death, the old woman wrapped the child in her shawl and climbed with him to Carrigard. She wanted to keep contact with Maire and Mike as long as her eyes could see them and thus strengthen her spirit against the influence of the dead that seemed to people the air around her. The poor old shanachie was beset, in her loneliness, by the ghosts she perpetuated in her tales. She followed the progress of the long flotilla of motor boats moving in line ahead, each towing its train of rowboats behind. Even when it came end-on to her vision in the Sound and the units lost individuality, she still kept her eyes fixed on it, as on a talisman against the unseen spirits of the dead.

The Old Quay was thronged with sympathizers when the *Mary* came into the shoreward berth, and her old crew, headed by Mike, brought the coffin ashore. Although Manistir churchyard was a long mile to the west, the people insisted on taking their hero, by adoption, on their shoulders to a bed among their own. Relays of bearers fell in behind with military precision to carry Knut Ollsen on the last short leg of his earthly wanderings. Along the narrow Gaeltacht road he went at the head of a close-packed throng, halting frequently at short intervals to change bearers, until he reached the ancient gateway. There Mike and his crew took him on their shoulders for the last time and laid him down beside the open grave. When the interment was done and the kneeling multitude had said the last Gaelic prayers for his soul, a party of self-conscious young men came from the crowd and fired a very ragged volley over his grave.

While the echo of the volley was still wandering around in the hills, Paddy Mick, a slick, red-faced politician from Cahirsally, seeking to gather some of Ollsen's fame to himself, mounted the fresh grave with callous feet and cleared his throat to speak.

"A Cháirde Gael—" He started in his hard metallic voice, but he got no further. Hot indignation at the impending anticlimax spurred the schoolmaster into instant action. Darting from behind on the vulgarian, he seized an arm and gave it the jujitsu wrench that tamed Brohul Sweeny. He rushed the protesting orator out of the graveyard, bundled him into his car, and banged the door on him.

" 'Mig leat!" he cried. "Scram, you rat!"

With the amazing volatility of crowds, prayers and peace changed to curses and war. Brehony's cry was taken up by the outraged throng. They sprang to their feet and surged out of the churchyard to seize the culprit, and, finding him gone, pursued his fleeing car with jeers and catcalls till he was lost to sight.

None were left by Ollsen's grave but Maire and Mike, kneeling together hand in hand, too full of feeling for prayer. They let their tears flow out for the friend they would know no more, until the peace of the place brought them to a quiet acceptance of the sadness of death. But they left a part of their being with Ollsen when they turned away to go home.

Sunday brought a fleece of white fog that smothered the island and marooned the islanders. Neither Maurisheen nor Donovan came back from the funeral. They, too, were heroes of the sea fight and could not resist the generous fees that were poured out at each recital of their oft-told tale. They stayed ashore with their popularity.

Mike and Maire gave up the idea of going to Mass on the mainland and got back into their working togs. The very change soothed their overwrought feelings and lifted the load off their hearts. Maire moved about the kitchen, restoring the easy comfort that was thought too informal for a wake. She put the prim cloth-backed chairs, the holy pictures, and the little red lamp of the Sacred Heart back into the privacy of the bedrooms and brought the sensible straw chairs and wooden stools in from the outhouses to which they were banished.

Mike cleared from the outer premises the scrappy tids and bits that crowds leave to mark their passage and moved out of Maire's sight the tools that would remind her of Ollsen. With a kindred thought for Maire's feelings, Joany laid Ollsen's clothes aside in a place apart, until she could finally dispose of them in the manner approved by ancient custom. "*Magna est mos et praevalebit*" being Joany's guiding principle, she was determined to find a worthy young man to wear the dead man's clothes at Mass on three consecutive Sundays and pray for his soul. Thereafter the fine London suit would be his very own.

While they were working, the fog lifted and the sun shone down on a Sabbath calm of smooth sea and silent fields.

"Let ye call it a day and go out in the air," said Joany after dinner with ulterior solicitude. She had a few discreet things to do to lay the ghosts that hung about the house and she wanted Maire out of the way while she did them. As if it were an afterthought, she added:

"Ye might as well take the child with ye. The poor pet is smothered for lack of fresh air."

Mike led the way to the Lookout and let Maire carry Donal Michael to the top without a thought of sharing her load. Being a pure Gael, he avoided intimacies with infants. They sat on the cairn with the sun to their backs and looked out to the horizon where a patch of ruffled water marked the Wild Bank.

"Out there we found him and 'tis there we lost him," said Maire voicing their common thought. "Do you know, Mike, I feel that Knut came to us the way missioners come to benighted lands, to open our eyes and teach us the way to live. Before he came we were in the dark about many things. We were too easily pleased. But he showed us what to want and how to get it."

She slid into a silence in which their thoughts ran side by side in perfect communion.

"Poor Knut would never have made a happy man," Mike observed quietly. "He couldn't leave things as he found them. He had to be improving them. God made our little island what it is, but Knut started where God left off, sure he could make a better job of it. That's the way he was built, I suppose. He couldn't help it."

"And he did improve the place, Mike," she replied with a trace of assertiveness. "The sign of his hands will remain on the island when his name is forgotten, even by us. No, that's wrong. You and me will never forget him as long as we live, God rest his brave and loving soul."

"Amen," said Mike with feeling. "He was our friend and he did what he did out of love for us. But listen here to me, Maire, girl. Knut had the seed of unhappiness in his mind, like all his kind. They must be making things—wells, roads, machines, ships, guns, and aeroplanes. But the most thing they make is *trouble*. They make trouble for themselves and trouble for their neighbours."

Mike was on the only subject which could loose the tight rein he kept on his tongue.

"Danes, Norwegians, and Sassanachs are chips of the same block, as different from us as chalk and cheese. They can't leave things as God made them like we can. All three of them are as ready to 'improve' a nation that doesn't see eye to eye with them as they are to improve an island. What does that bring but trouble? Wasn't there a namesake of Knut's long ago—a King Canute—that couldn't stay at home and mind his own business?"

"Surely, Mike, you wouldn't compare our Knut with that murdering Dane and you're not thinking of undoing the good work Knut did for us out of the goodness of his heart."

"Far from it, girleen. 'Twas for love Knut worked all his time here and love never breeds trouble. I was only pitying the restless men like him who haven't time to be happy in their youth, like you and me."

She rumpled his black curls affectionately with her fingers.

"Dear old Thahailen! You have the heart of the red robineen that can sing on a winter bush and share his song with the world. Do you remember the day you brought me here in an old two-oar boat to a small thatched house and a well under water? That was the happy day for me and I thank God for it every day that follows it."

"It was, Maire, and for me too. It was grand to be alone with our own two selves. A lot of people crowded in on us since then—the Frenchmen and Knut and Sean and Mai Hogan and the rest—but they went as they came, and here are we alone with our own two selves again, thanks be to God."

"Alone, do you say? Heigh, you! Donal Michael! Speak up to your dad and claim your rights."

END